☠ ☠ ☠

Treasure awaits in the Azure Sea. . .

"Heave!" roared Hornbill.

Eight arms hauled on the thick ropes. Wooden rollers groaned in greased blocks until the gun carriage banged against the gunwhale.

As he stepped away, weight fell on Calab's shoulders and dragged him to the deck. Thrashing, he realized that loops of rigging sliced from high on the mast had fallen onto him. He wriggled his way out of the tangled mass, all the while watching Hornbill and Shank lever the gun carriage sideways to bring it in line with the Commissioner's ship.

Again Hornbill set the glowing linstock on the gun's touchhole, and it crashed backward in a burst of flame and concussion that forced Calab's eyes shut. As he opened them, still lying on the deck, the gunwhale exploded inward. Jagged splinters of hull as big as Calab's forearm and sharp as cutlasses whipped and spiraled over his head. Shank fell to the deck screaming in front of Calab, where the boy saw that the toes and front half of Shank's right foot were gone, and a piece of splintered oak was speared through his calf.

Smoke drifted across the deck, stinging Calab's eyes and parching his throat. His ears rang so painfully that, though he saw Shank was screaming, he could barely hear it.

Someone jerked Calab to his feet. It was Hornbill, now motioning for Calab to grab Shank by the arm and drag him away from the gun.

"Get 'im to land'ard, lad!" the gunner shouted. "Get 'im to Arl!"

—From "The Haunted Isle," by Steve Winter

But so does sudden death!

Other Blue Kingdoms Books:

Blue Kingdoms: Buxom Buccaneers
Blue Kingdoms: Shades & Specters
Blue Kingdoms: Zombies, Werewolves,
& Unicorns

Available from www.walkaboutpublishing.com.

Pirates of the Blue Kingdoms

Stephen D. Sullivan, Jean Rabe & Friends

Walkabout Publishing • 2008

www.bluekingdoms.com

Walkabout Publishing
S.D.Studios
P.O.Box 151
Kansasville, WI 53139
www.walkaboutpublishing.com

First Walkabout Publishing edition.

ISBN: 978-0-9802086-4-1

To my in-laws: Burton Scott, recently departed and greatly missed, and Evelyn Scott, happily still with us--thank you for many years of love and support.

—Steve Sullivan

☠   ☠   ☠

To Ron and Jack: who would have made most excellent pirates.

—Jean Rabe

CONTENTS

INTRODUCTION

Many years ago Wizards of the Coast sponsored a contest to create a new world for the D&D game. The top prize was a hefty amount of cash, and so thousands entered.

Including Steve and me.

After the contest was over (and neither of us won), we compared notes.

And discovered that, separately, we had created something similar—an ocean world filled with pirates and fantastical creatures and islands.

- Islands that appeared and disappeared, seemingly at random
- Islands made of ships lashed together
- Islands where no living creature could set foot
- Islands where adventure beckoned

We loved our creations too much to let them fade, and so we established the Blue Kingdoms, a place where we and other authors could play. The good folks at Popcorn Press gave wind to our sails and agreed to publish our first venture.

Sit back in your favorite rocker, grab a mug of ale, put on an eye-patch, and come aboard.

—Jean Rabe, March 2007

            ☠   ☠   ☠

What Jean wrote is absolutely true. Our game-world ideas were so similar that, if we hadn't been old friends, we might have suspected each other of stealing. It was almost uncanny. So we decided to team up and keep the Blue Kingdoms going.

Bit by bit, we cobbled together a bible for the milieu (a bible that now tips in at well over 20,000 words). I began writing stories in the setting—including my upcoming novel, *A Reliable Dragon*—and Jean began running game adventures and thinking up stories as well.

Over the years, the two of us tried to get various publishers interested in doing a Blue Kingdoms anthology. Then, in January of 2007, Jean and I were sitting in a pancake house, having breakfast, and lamenting that—despite the popularity of the Johnny Depp film series—none of the big publishers seemed interested in taking a chance on *Pirates of the Blue Kingdoms*.

"We should just do it ourselves," I suggested.

Jean agreed. And edgy, hungry, up-and-coming Popcorn Press became the perfect venue for the project. (After that printing sold out, we turned to Walkabout Publishing for a second edition—as well as for our future Blue Kingdoms releases.)

All we needed was a crew of writers.

One e-mailed submission call later, we had more great stories from more great writers than we ever could have expected. And we pulled it all together in time to capitalize on the latest pirate movie, too. See what you can do if you don't take "No," for an answer?

Happily, most of that crew stayed with us for *Blue Kingdoms: Shades & Specters* and *Blue Kingdoms: Buxom Buccaneers*—both now available from Walkabout Publishing and at better book outlets everywhere.

So, like Jean said, grab some grog and prepare yourselves for high adventure! We're setting sail for the Blue Kingdoms, and every last one of you scurvy sea dogs is invited along!

—Steve Sullivan, April 2007 & June 2008

Visit
www.bluekingdoms.com
www.walkaboutpublishing.com

LOCAL LEGEND

by Lester Smith

Would you believe that barren chunk of stone,
That lonely island, long ago was home
To a solitary oak, ancient and gray
As the shadow of creation's birthing day.

Then some minor manor master in these parts
Got it in his head that he had a pirate's heart,
So he built a sloop, and he ordered that the oak
Be cut down and stripped of limbs to mast his boat.

But when they stood the oak upon the keel,
She rooted there, sprouting vines with thorns like steel,
And swept men from the decks in showers of blood
While strangling their poor master where he stood.

Then she unfurled leafy sheets and sailed away.
She prowls the seas for blood yet, some men say.

THE ACCIDENTAL PIRATES
by Marc Tassin

Dysart Draymore strode through the rain-soaked alleys of Cape Thorn as his youthful protégé struggled to keep up.

"I still don't understand sir," the boy said, out of breath from trying to match his master's long stride. "You *won* a *ship*?"

"That's correct, Sparrow," Dysart replied, his rich baritone voice filling the space between the buildings. "Not bad for an evening of dinner and cards, don't you think?"

The night was thick and muggy, and it clung to their skin like wet silk. Around them, the sounds of the city filled the air, a mix of raucous singing, throaty laughter, and creaking wagon wheels. Under it all whispered the ever present murmur of the sea.

A drunken sailor staggered out of a doorway into the alley and collapsed at Dysart's feet. Without missing a step, Dysart stepped over the inebriated seaman and continued on. Sparrow skirted around the sailor, wrinkling his nose at the heavy stink of rum that surrounded the man.

"Well, yes, I imagine it was an excellent night of dinner and cards sir," Sparrow answered, "but what did you wager? To my reckoning, we've just ten coppers left to us."

"My villa in Marguerite of course," Dysart replied. "Its spacious halls and extensive holdings were more than a fair bet against Count Marin's ship. As for our financial situation, that is no longer an issue."

He patted his coat, and coins clanked. Sparrow, having fallen behind again, raced to keep up. As he reached Dysart's side, the words of his master finally hit him.

"You . . . you don't own a villa in Marguerite, sir."

Glancing over, Dysart gave Sparrow a devilish grin and winked at him conspiratorially.

"Well then, I'd say it's fortunate I won, isn't it?"

Sparrow stopped and blinked in amazement. When he finally recovered he had to run to catch up once more.

"Master," he called. "If I might be so bold, this isn't some back country nobleman. He's the count of Cape Thorn, sovereign Lord of the Twelve Isles. If you'd lost and he'd discovered—"

"Why Sparrow, do you think I'd have made the wager if I thought I'd lose?"

They paused where the alley opened onto a narrow side street, waited as a wagon loaded with huge casks of rum trundled by, then continued across to the alley on the other side.

Before responding, Sparrow glanced about to ensure that they were alone and then moved close to his master's side.

"But if he had discovered you were *cheating*. . . !" the boy whispered.

Dysart stopped and looked down at Sparrow, flashing a disappointed frown.

"Sparrow," he scolded. "You know I hate that word. I didn't cheat. I simply adjusted the odds slightly in my favor."

"I imagine the count would use the former definition."

"It isn't my fault that the count's young maid took a liking to me. And if she wished to assist me in knowing which cards the count held via a system of clever hand signals, of her own devising I might add, who was I to deny her? The fact that this happened to work to my advantage is just a fortunate coincidence."

"But sir, what if he finds out?"

"Not *if* he finds out, Sparrow. *When* he finds out. The Count is an intelligent man. When the drink wears off, he's sure to put the pieces together. That is precisely why finding a crew is of the utmost importance!"

Dysart must have recognized the worried look on Sparrow's face, for he tousled the boy's dusty blonde hair.

"Don't worry, Sparrow. I've never failed you, have I?"

"You mean other than the incident with the Merchant Guild in Forimir?"

"Right," Dysart agreed. "Other than that."

"Or the time I had to spring you from the dungeons of Edren Soul after the, erm, misunderstanding regarding Lady Marianne?"

"Fine Sparrow, you've made your point."

"Or the—"

"That's quite enough, lad. If we're going to pull this off we need positive attitudes. Anyhow, even if things don't always go as planned, they've always worked out in the end, haven't they?"

Dysart cracked a mischievous grin, the one that always meant their excitement was just beginning. Sparrow couldn't help but smile. In the two years since his thirteenth birthday, the day Dysart took him under his wing after catching Sparrow picking his pocket, Dysart had always come through in the end, no matter how absurd the scheme.

"Very well, sir," Sparrow conceded. "So where is it that we're going?"

"Here," Dysart said with a dramatic sweep of his arm. They stood before a filthy tavern with cracked windows, crooked walls, and a thatch roof so thin that light shone through from within. Over the door, hanging from a single rusty chain, was a sign painted with an obscene depiction of a scantily clad elven lady straddling a keg.

"The Pinched Keg," Dysart continued. "A tavern frequented by the finest sailors in all of Cape Thorn, or so I've been told."

"The *finest* sailors, sir?"

"Well, not the finest perhaps but the most available, which considering our situation is what we need."

"But sir, wouldn't the ship's current crew be better suited to man her?"

"As it turns out, Sparrow, the *Golden Maiden* didn't come with a crew. I might have complained about that had I not considered it prudent to make a swift exit after winning our little wager."

Reaching into his coat Dysart produced a folded square of dark blue felt. With a snap of his wrist the cloth unfurled into the unmistakable crown and folds of a three-cornered cap.

"What's that sir?" Sparrow asked.

"My captain's hat. Unlike the crew, it *did* come with the ship," Dysart said. He fitted it onto his head, placed his hands on his hips, and puffed out his chest. "How do I look?"

"Um, like a captain?" Sparrow ventured.

"Excellent," Dysart said. With a vigorous shove, he threw open the door to the tavern and slipped inside, leaving Sparrow—once again—scrambling to keep up.

☠   ☠   ☠

The Pinched Keg was, remarkably, darker, danker, and more odiferous than Cape Thorn itself. It was packed from wall-to-wall with glaring, yellow-toothed, beady-eyed, scoundrels of the worst sort.

"Sir, perhaps we should try somewhere else?" Sparrow whispered.

"No time for that, lad. Just follow my lead."

Dysart pushed his way through the motley mob, and Sparrow stayed close behind. Even wearing their court finery, they received no more than a few unpleasant grunts from those they passed. These were men who had learned long ago that minding one's own business bore a direct relationship to life expectancy.

Reaching the center of the tavern, Dysart leaned over the nearest table. Three bitter old deckhands sat hunched over mugs of ale. They looked up at Dysart with something significantly less than welcome.

"Gentlemen, may I have this table?"

The eldest of the three sailors began to object, but before the words could leave his mouth Dysart tossed three gold coins onto the table. The men scooped them up before the coins stopped spinning and, with ales in hands, they stood and faded into the crowd.

After checking the table for stability, Dysart jumped atop it.

"Your attention please!" he called. "I am looking to hire a crew for my ship!"

Silence fell over the room. Dozens of deep-set eyes glared at Dysart, and a few men muttered curses.

"Perhaps I was mistaken. I'd been lead to believe that this fine establishment served a clientele particularly well-suited to my needs. I guess I'll take my coin elsewhere."

Dysart hopped down, jingling his coin purse for effect, and started for the door. A brick of a man with an ugly scar running down one cheek called out from the bar.

"This is the right place," the man growled, "but this crew is already signed to a captain."

The sailors murmured in agreement, but Sparrow noted an undertone of resentment in their voices. Dysart must have noticed as well, for he seized on that fact and approached the man who had spoken.

"Very well then," Dysart said. "Where is this captain of yours? Perhaps he and I could make an arrangement that would serve both of our needs."

"*She*," a strong feminine voice called out, "is right here."

Sparrow and Dysart turned to find a tall, well-proportioned woman with fiery red hair and dark green eyes standing in the doorway to the tavern.

"And my crew," she continued, "would do well to think twice before entering into negotiations with another captain."

The sailors physically drew back from her gaze as she cast a long look around the room. Sparrow recognized that this wasn't the type of woman Dysart typically dealt with. This woman, with her long, red hair pulled back and tied with a simple leather thong, was no court butterfly.

She wore dark brown leather leggings laced up the sides, high black boots with folded cuffs, and a white blousy shirt open just enough at the neck to give a tempting glimpse of what lay beneath. She had on dark green gloves, and one hand rested on the hilt of a long sword, curved in the style favored by sailors of Acacia. The other hand, clenched in a fist, rested firmly on her shapely hip.

"Look at her, Sparrow," Dysart whispered. "Look at that face. Hair like fire. Skin kissed by the sun, but smooth as silk. Those lips, frowning, yes, but perfectly shaped. And the eyes. Wrath and Mercy, Hanher eyes! So green, like the depths of the sea, almost hypnotizing in the way they draw one in and—"

"Sir? SIR!" hissed Sparrow, pulling urgently on the sleeve of Dysart's coat as the woman approached.

"Oh, right, thank you, Sparrow," he whispered.

Straightening his captain's hat, Dysart spoke.

"These men are not at fault, madam."

"Captain," she corrected him.

"Captain. This was purely my doing. I am in need of a crew willing to depart at first light and was told that I would find the men, and women apparently, that I needed here. Clearly I was mistaken. I shall depart at once."

When Dysart moved to step around her, she placed her open hand firmly on his chest.

"I didn't say they weren't available. I just said they aren't the ones who should be negotiating." She smiled. "Come, we'll talk over ale," she said, not bothering to look back over her shoulder.

Dysart looked down at Sparrow.

"You see, Sparrow. Things are working out quite well already."

And with that he followed her, leaving Sparrow to puzzle over just what part of their current circumstances were working out at all.

☠ ☠ ☠

15

It turned out that the captain, Fiona was her name, lacked a ship due to something she described as "a filing error" that led to some difficult questions about the ownership of her vessel. Dysart simply nodded knowingly, as if this were all perfectly normal.

Not surprisingly, she asked for proof of Dysart's ownership, something Sparrow was curious about as well. Dysart was pleasant about it and presented her with the letters of register.

"The *Golden Siren*? Never heard of her," she said, handing the papers back.

"A fine vessel from the shipyards of New Aronnay. An excellent ship, I assure you."

"We'll see. Let's get on with it then. What are you offering?"

At this point things got foggy for Sparrow as the talk became dry and he began to nod off. He didn't know how much time passed, but a gentle jostle from Dysart woke him. Sparrow jumped to his feet.

"Ready, Master," he called out.

"He's a spry one, isn't he?" Fiona said with a smirk.

"You, my young apprentice, are going back to our room at the Inn. I'll walk you there. I, on the other hand, still have a few arrangements to make before we leave in the morning. Provisions and that sort of thing. With any luck, I may even manage an hour or two of sleep myself!"

The two of them pushed through the noisy crowd with Fiona following. Dysart stopped and turned back to the room.

"Barkeep!" he shouted. "See to it that my crew is well watered! I like my men in good spirits before a journey!"

He pulled a coin pouch out of his coat and tossed it across the room into the waiting hands of the bartender. The men cheered and spontaneously broke into a round of "The Cap'n is a Friend of Mine."

Dysart grinned, but Fiona, seemingly unimpressed by Dysart's generosity, leaned in close.

"Oh, and *Captain*," she whispered.

"Yes?" Dysart replied.

Reaching up she turned his cap around to face the other way. "Your hat is on backward."

Dysart simply smiled, gave her a wink, and then turned and stepped out the door; Sparrow raced to keep up.

☠   ☠   ☠

The sun was just creeping above the distant horizon when Dysart and Sparrow arrived at the docks. Dysart looked resplendent in a full captain's uniform, which he'd somehow acquired during the night, complete with epaulettes and gold braids. Sparrow felt shabby by comparison, wearing the blue and white striped cabin boy's outfit Dysart brought him.

Dysart called over the last of the men he'd hired to stock the ship and prepare it for departure. They all looked bleary eyed and exhausted, but the pouch of copper coins he slipped into each of their hands as they passed seemed to invigorate them. This gave Sparrow a chance to examine the ship.

It looked impressive to say the least. With three masts it was the largest in the harbor, and the count had dyed the sails a brilliant blue. The rails and hull were adorned with carvings of sea serpents, merfolk, and other aquatic denizens, all of which had been exquisitely painted and highlighted with gold leaf.

After seeing the last man off, Dysart came over to Sparrow's side.

"By Hanitaro's hammer," Sparrow said. "The count can't have been happy to lose this!"

"I would say not, Sparrow," he replied. "Which is why it's fortunate our crew has arrived on time."

Coming up the pier, they spotted the crowd from the tavern. The crew looked like they'd just left their chairs at the Pinched Keg and come straight over. All except Fiona, that is. She wore the same outfit as the night before, but it had clearly been cleaned and pressed. Her hair glistened in the sun, contrasting markedly with the steely resolve in her eyes. The mob approached Dysart and Sparrow and came to a rough stop.

"Crew reporting as ordered, Captain," she stated crisply.

"And a fine crew it is," commented Dysart without a hint of sarcasm.

"Permission to board sir?"

"Permission granted, First Mate Fiona," Dysart replied.

Sparrow noticed a slight stiffening of her shoulders and a tightening of the lines around her eyes and mouth as Dysart used the title. Giving up the captain's post had clearly irked her but, to her credit, this was the only sign she showed. She barked a series of terse orders to the crew and they leaped into action. Within moments men swarmed over the ship, untying the heavy lines that held *Golden Siren* to the dock, and climbing the rigging.

"Correct me if I'm wrong, Captain Draymore, but this looks like Count Marin's ship, the *Golden Maiden*. I thought you said your ship was the *Golden Siren*," Fiona said, giving Dysart the first look of respect she'd offered since they'd met.

"*Was* the count's ship," Dysart corrected. "Until last night that is, at which point ownership was transferred to me, along with the right to name her."

"Naturally," she answered. "And I imagine this early departure is a reflection of your desire to get an early start on a task, rather than a need to get out of town quickly."

Dysart grinned wickedly, evoking the slightest smile from Fiona as well.

"Let's just say," Dysart said, "that I'd like to leave port before the count reconsiders our transaction."

The crew worked with incredible speed. In fact, for all their disheveled appearance, they worked more efficiently and with greater skill than any crew Sparrow had seen. He was no expert in such things, but like all denizens of the Blue Kingdoms he'd spent a goodly amount of time on and around ships.

17

He knew when a crew understood their job and when they were a newly trained batch of recruits. These men were old hands indeed.

The ship was soon underway, cutting through the waves, the wind filling her sails. The crewman at the wheel cried out, "What course, Captain?"

"Due North, lad, keep her true," Dysart commanded.

"And then sir?" Fiona asked, coming down the stairs from the aftcastle.

"I'll let you know this afternoon. I have a few more calculations to make first."

"As you wish," she answered, her eyes narrow and probing.

"Come, Sparrow!" Dysart called.

Sparrow followed him down the stairs into the lavishly appointed captain's quarters.

"Where exactly are we going sir?"

Closing the door, Dysart gave Sparrow a crooked smile.

"I haven't the slightest idea."

☠ ☠ ☠

Dysart followed their conversation with a nap. Although Sparrow still felt tired from the night before, he was far too nervous to sleep. Even though things always worked out in the end with Dysart, that moment before the plan took shape invariably left Sparrow feeling unstable and exposed. After about an hour, a heavy knock sounded on the door.

"Go see who it is, Sparrow," Dysart called from his bunk.

"Yes, sir," Sparrow answered. He'd thought Dysart asleep, but the quick way the captain had responded to the knock suggested otherwise.

Sparrow opened the door. Standing in front of him was the ugly man with the scar on his cheek and the bulldog body.

"Barnaby Winright, requesting to see the cap'n," he growled.

"I'm sorry, but he's—" Sparrow began, but Dysart cut him off before he could continue.

"Come in, Barnaby. My door is always open."

Sparrow stepped back, and Barnaby hunched in through the low entry. The sailor had his coat pulled shut, as if hiding something. Sparrow let his hand slip to the dagger on his belt in the slow and casual way Dysart had taught him. If the sailor had some misdeed in mind, Sparrow would be ready.

Dysart was seated comfortably behind the massive oak table that dominated the center of the room, looking as though he'd been there all along. Behind him, the sea rolled and tossed beyond the yellowed glass of the windows that looked out over the ship's stern. As Barnaby approached, Dysart pushed his chair back and stood.

"What is it, Barnaby? Trouble with the mizzen mast? I saw you working at it earlier."

Sparrow was always impressed by Dysart's ability to spot tiny details. Sparrow hadn't noticed which mast the scar-faced sailor had been working on. Most of the time, from Sparrow's perspective anyhow, the crew blended into an unshaven, sweaty mass of sun-leathered skin and stained clothing.

"No trouble, sir, but I 'ave somethin' 'ere for ya. Somethin' me an' the crew put together."

"Well, that certainly wasn't necessary, but thank you. Let's have a look."

Sparrow's grip tightened on the dagger as the man pulled a bundle from his shirt.

"A jack for the main mast, sir. It's good luck to make a new one whenever a cap'n and crew come together. We 'ad to work a bit faster than usual, so we 'ope you approve."

Barnaby unfolded a large black flag on the table and smoothed out the wrinkles with a surprisingly gentle touch. Satisfied, he stepped back and allowed Dysart to take it in. On the black field stood the stark white form of a skeleton. The legs were raised and bent as if it were dancing, and beneath it laid a second skeleton sprawled out with a sword lodged firmly in its ribs.

Barnaby watched expectantly as Dysart examined the flag. Sparrow bit his lip to avoid gasping at the sight. Finally, Dysart gave a curt nod and offered Barnaby a broad grin.

"This will do just fine, Barnaby! I approve, and thank you and your mates for the effort. Assemble the crew. I'll come out to have a word with them momentarily."

"Thank you, sir," Barnaby answered, grinning and showing off a mouthful of crooked yellow teeth. "I'll let them know, sir."

"One other thing, Barnaby. How do you like my ship?" he asked.

"If you don't mind me saying, sir, she 'andles like a crate with sails," he replied. "She plows the waves like nothing we've crewed before, though. I pity the cap'n who lets his ship drift in front of this monster."

"Excellent! Thank you, Barnaby. You may go."

Nodding once, Barnaby stepped out of the room, shutting the door behind him.

Sparrow could take no more.

"Sir! These men aren't sailors. They're *pirates!*"

Dysart picked up the flag and held it out to admire it. "I like this flag, Sparrow. Fun wrapped in a sense of danger," he said. He pointed to the skeleton on the ground. "I especially like what they've done with the sword here, don't you? Rustic simplicity and yet powerfully symbolic."

Sparrow gaped.

"So what is it that has you so upset, my young apprentice?" Dysart asked.

"Our crew, sir. They're . . . they're *pirates* sir. What are we going to do?"

"Why Sparrow, I'm surprised with you," Dysart said. "Haven't you always wanted to be a pirate? I know I have."

Dysart lovingly folded the flag and stepped out from behind the table. Sparrow could find nothing to say.

"The way I see it, we've been handed a golden opportunity," he continued. Wrapping his arm around Sparrow's shoulder, he guided him to the door. "Come, Sparrow! A life of adventure on the high seas awaits!"

☠ ☠ ☠

When they reached the deck, Barnaby and Fiona had assembled the crew. Fiona stood on the aftcastle, arms folded, boots planted firmly on the swaying deck, and the wind dancing through her hair. Dysart climbed up to stand beside her, and Sparrow made sure to stay close behind.

"Thank you, First Mate," Dysart said to her. She gave a curt nod and continued to watch him carefully. Dysart stepped up to the railing overlooking the main deck and examined the crew.

"Gentlemen, goodmen, and kind hearted souls . . ."

Dysart paused. There was dead silence, and Sparrow winced at the lack of response.

". . . if there are any such men on this ship today, they'd best be off, as we've no use for them!" Dysart shouted with a laugh.

The crew broke into a roar of cheers and guffaws. Dysart flashed them a broad smile, letting the cheering go on for a moment, then held up his hands for silence; the crew quickly complied.

"Men like us aren't content to sit back and wait around for fortune. We grab life firmly by the throat and demand that it give us what we want!"

Another roar of agreement.

"But I say life's been holding out on us! I say we've never squeezed tight enough!"

More cheers.

"Well, I'm done settling for the discarded leavings of society. I'm done with table scraps. I say we deserve more!"

A roar of agreement, clapping, and hoots broke out. Sparrow looked over at Fiona and noticed that the good mood of the crew had failed to move her. Arms tightly crossed, she continued to eye Dysart.

"So tell me this, lads. What is the one prize that every pirate desires, that singular bounty of which all buccaneers dream, that greatest of treasures that stands like a shining beacon to all those who want fame, wealth, and eternal glory?"

The crew roared as one, their voices carrying out over the sea.

"Blackstone Isle!" They cried.

"That's right!" Dysart shouted, not missing a beat. "Blackstone Isle! Too long has it sat unmolested. I say it's time that changed. Now is the time to pluck that gem from the crown of the Northern Verge, and I say we're the ones to do it!"

The men screamed, they crowed, they pounded their feet on the deck.

"We've got the finest crew!" Dysart yelled.

"AYE!"

"The best ship!"

"AYE!"

"And the spirit to grab fate by the shoulders and show her who is her master!"

"AYYYEEEE!"

"So, steersman, set a course for Blackstone Isle, and let us secure our place as the *greatest pirates the Blue Kingdoms have ever known!*"

Dysart stepped back smiling, enveloped in the wild cheers of the crew. Over the din, the crew chiefs barked orders, and the men scrambled into position. Within moments, the ship came about to an easterly heading. Sailing into the rising sun, the men broke into an old chantey about mermaids, treasure, and the glory of a death at sea.

☠   ☠   ☠

With the sounds of the pirate song fading behind them, Sparrow followed Dysart back down to the captain's quarters. Sparrow's head was spinning with questions, but one in particular nagged him. He didn't dare ask it while the crew was within earshot, but in the privacy of the cabin he could resist no longer.

"What is Blackstone Isle sir?"

Dysart stepped over to the bookcase. Among Dysart's midnight purchases were numerous tomes of nautical lore.

"That is precisely what I plan to find out," he said, pulling a heavy leather-bound book with gold-tipped corners from the shelf.

"You mean you don't know? But how did you—?"

Dysart cut him off and took a professorial stance.

"Lesson, Sparrow: the best way to get people on your side is to tell them what they want to hear, and the best way to find out what they want to hear is to have them tell you."

As with most of Dysart's lessons, Sparrow found this one simple on first hearing, yet thoroughly confusing when analyzed. Meanwhile, Dysart moved to the table and set down the book. He flipped through the pages for a moment.

"Ah ha!" he announced. "Blackstone Isle! According to this, it was ceded to Alasandro Veras by the Lord of Nevar years ago. Veras fortified the island and turned it into his personal treasury. It has remained so until this day. Well now, that *is* interesting. Veras is the wealthiest lord in the Jewel Isles. No wonder the men were so keen to make a try for it."

The door to the cabin flew open, and Fiona stalked into the room.

"We need to talk, *Captain,*" she growled.

"Why, First Mate Fiona," Dysart said, a smile on his face and a twinkle in his eye. "Do come in. No need to knock."

Sparrow noticed that Dysart was slowly closing the book. Taking the cue, Sparrow gathered up the book, as well as a couple of mugs from the table, in his best imitation of a cabin boy tidying up. Taking his load, he scurried off toward the bunks.

Fiona stomped across the cabin and came around behind the table to stand directly in front of Dysart.

"Blackstone Isle?" she said. "You're either insane or an idiot, and I'm beginning to believe the latter."

"Oh, I can assure you that it isn't either of those," he responded, still smiling. "Although I will admit, others have suggested the same. But couldn't there be a third possibility?"

"What, that you've discovered some way to raid the most well-fortified island on this side of the central isles? That you've somehow come up with a way to do something that even the finest pirates of the Northern Spur have failed to accomplish?"

"Is that so impossible to believe? I would think that this ship alone is evidence enough of my abilities."

"And that," Fiona said, "is the only reason I'm willing to follow this lunatic course . . . for now."

Dysart moved in closer.

"The *only* reason?" he asked.

Their faces were so close that they nearly touched, eyes locked, cheeks flushed.

Sparrow quickly busied himself straightening the books on the shelf, stealing glances over his shoulder but blushing at the suddenly intimate situation.

"Let me make one thing clear," Fiona said. "I have one concern and one concern only."

"I'm listening," Dysart purred.

Dysart leaned in, his lips nearing hers. She raised her chin so that her lips brushed against his.

Suddenly Dysart's eyes widened and he let out a soft "Urk!" Too late, Sparrow spotted the glint of steel behind Dysart. Fiona had produced a dagger, seemingly out of thin air, and had it held firmly against Dysart's back, the tip barely cutting through the fine blue wool of his captain's coat. Sparrow reached for his own blade, but Dysart noticed and shooed him back with one hand.

"My crew," Fiona continued. "That is my *only* concern. They're good and loyal men, all of them, and I won't have their lives thrown away on a madman's folly. If I decide that you're endangering my crew without good reason, I *will* see to it that your captaining days come to an end. Do I make myself clear?"

"Perfectly," Dysart answered. For a moment they held the position, pressed together, lips nearly touching, dagger in Dysart's back, until finally Dysart broke the silence.

"Is it safe to assume that you'll be dining with the crew tonight rather than here in the captain's quarters as is customary?"

Fiona glared, drew back, then removed the blade and slid it into her belt. With a sharp turn she marched out of the room, slamming the door behind her.

☠ ☠ ☠

Aside from that particular encounter, Sparrow found the remainder of their journey comfortable enough. The crew was in good spirits, with the favored topic of conversation being Blackstone Isle. More than a few arguments erupted over the island's defenses, or what tricks Captain Dysart might have to bypass them. Dysart, of course, had no plan at all.

He did, however, give Sparrow orders to stay close to the men and to remember everything overheard. Each night the two of them reviewed this information, and, in time, they learned a fair amount about the island.

Blackstone Isle was a natural crescent of rocky cliffs, the remnants of a long-dormant volcano. A portion of the eastern edge had collapsed entirely, creating a narrow inlet to a protected cove. A small part of the west cliffs had collapsed as well, but not to sea level.

Apparently, one of the War Captains of Hellios had constructed a keep in the western gap and mounted a pair of massive iron doors in the eastern gap. The result was a military outpost of unprecedented security.

It eventually fell into disuse and was claimed by Alasandro Veras, who converted it to his personal treasury. On any given day the island was patrolled by at least four Hunters, three of which were at sea at all times. These swift, black-hulled brigantines were armed with a full compliment of cannons and manned by veteran sailors. Some of the pirates literally salivated when talking about these vessels, suggesting that they were fine ships indeed.

The keep itself was guarded by a standing force of thirty men who patrolled a wall built around the top of the cliff. Guards also manned a winch house on the cliff near the doors. There, a mechanism allowed a single man to open or close the gates.

The defenses did seem formidable. For days Dysart thought about the problem—drawing maps, making notes, and otherwise pondering the challenge. It dismayed Sparrow, however, that for all Dysart's effort, it seemed the captain still had no clear plan for attacking the island.

At last they reached Blackstone Isle. It was the ninth day of their voyage, a moonless night, black as pitch, and the *Siren* was running dark except for the dim glow of a partially shuttered lantern at the aftcastle. They approached from the west and had a strong wind at their backs. A whispered call came down from the masthead that the island was in sight.

"Heave to!" Fiona called, from her position at the aftcastle's rail.

"Cancel that order," hissed Dysart. "Maintain speed, in fact, erm, make her go as fast as she'll go."

"You mean bring her to flank, Captain?" Fiona growled.

"Right. That," Dysart replied dismissively.

"Aye, sir," Barnaby whispered back from the main deck.

Dysart and Fiona stood side by side at the front rail of the aftcastle and Sparrow stood just behind them. Fiona had been badgering Dysart all night for details on the plan. Every time he put her off, her mood worsened. Sparrow could tell she was nearing her limit.

"Any chance of you letting me in on the plan soon, *Captain?*" she hissed.

For a moment Dysart just stood there, unmoving, but suddenly he turned to Fiona. Sparrow could just make out a mischievous grin on Dysart's face. Whether the crew knew it or not, things were about to get interesting.

"Yes, I think now is a good time," he answered. "Barnaby, pull all the crew up to the stair here at the maindeck—except those needed to maintain speed. Have the men prepare to board."

"What?" Fiona said. "Board? There is nothing here to board! That's it. You had your chance."

"You've followed me this far. Aren't you at least curious?"

Fiona grimaced.

"Fine," she said. "But make it quick."

"Excellent," Dysart beamed. "Here it is. Are you ready?"

Sparrow cringed. Dysart's smile told him everything he needed to know. Dysart had come up with his plan, and whatever it was, it was something big, even by Dysart's standards. Fiona was glaring hard enough to carve granite. Sparrow tapped his buttons for luck.

After a suitably dramatic pause, Dysart finally spoke.

"We're going to *ram* the island."

Sparrow thought Fiona would burst.

"Well, not the island per se. The keep, actually. Think about it. This is what, a four hundred ton ship? At full speed with the wind behind her she'll put a hole in the keep the size of a small sloop. They expect people to climb the walls or attack the gates. But ramming the keep? They'll never see it coming."

To Sparrow's surprise, Fiona looked as if she were slowly buying into Dysart's plan.

"You assume we'll get past the Hunters."

"Which, in this dark, with us running black, I'm sure we will. They won't know we're coming until our figurehead is in bed next to them."

Fiona rubbed her chin.

"We'd strike the heart of the keep," she said. "They'd have no ready defenses for that."

"Exactly! We head straight for the vault and strip it clean before they know what's happening."

"Excuse me, sir," Sparrow chimed in. "Didn't we just sink our ship by ramming the island? How will we get away?"

Fiona looked at Dysart who was grinning like a madman. A light of realization washed over her face.

"Of course," she said. "The Hunters. Rumors say they always have one at dock."

"Right!" Dysart exclaimed. "We escape by stealing one of *their* ships."

"That's beautiful," Fiona said, smiling now as well.

"Isn't it? It's poetry."

"But what about *this* ship?" Sparrow asked. "I thought you said it was a good ship? Why would we abandon it?"

"Good for blasting things to pieces," Fiona rebuked. "And while that has its merits, *Siren* stands out like a sore thumb, handles like a floating brick, and some day the count *will* come looking for her."

"Precisely," Dysart agreed. "But a Hunter . . . now there's a ship for pirating."

For a long moment Fiona stared at Dysart, a half smile on her face, eyes narrowed.

"It's the first one," she said at last.

"Sorry?" Dysart said. "What?"

"The first one," she said. "You're not an idiot. You're insane."

Dysart began to object, but she cut him off.

"But in a good way. This is, perhaps, one of the most insane plans I've ever heard. And maybe I've gone a bit over the edge myself, but I think it can work. In fact it might be the only way someone could take the island."

"So you agree?"

"Yes, I agree, but under one condition."

"Of course, what is it?"

"You make me the captain."

"Agreed!" he replied, thrusting his hand out to her.

Fiona grasped it and shook vigorously, then pulled Dysart to her and planted a rough kiss on his lips.

"That was to seal the deal," she said with a grin. "Now let's do some pirating!"

☠ ☠ ☠

The *Golden Siren* plowed full on into the seaward wall of the keep. The ship shuddered as her beams groaned and cracked. The jib boom hit the wall and shattered, and the bowsprit splintered halfway down its length before breaking through in a shower of stone. Following it came the figurehead, like a gilt juggernaut.

Huge portions of the wall fell away, some crashing to the deck, others tumbling into waves. Light from inside the keep shown through the holes, silhouetting the panicked forms of soldiers trying to react to the explosive intrusion.

Beneath them, *Siren's* crew heard the whoosh and gurgle of water pouring into her hull. It was a terrifying sound for any sailor, even one who'd known it was coming. Dysart leaped to his feet and drew his blade to rally them.

"What are you waiting for, lads! Onward to glory!"

He dashed up the slanting deck shouting a battle cry. Sparrow, Fiona, and the crew leaped to follow. The footing proved difficult, and, as they clambered through the gaping hole in the keep's wall, one of the crewmen fell over the edge and into the embrace of sea and broken stone. The others did not falter. If pirates can smell anything over the odor of their own

25

unwashed bodies, it's the scent of treasure and glory, and on this night the air was thick with it!

As the crew burst through the gap, they found Dysart engaging three soldiers in a furious melee. Blades glittered and the sound of clashing steel filled the room. The soldiers put up a good fight, but proved no match for Dysart. He ducked and dashed between their strikes, returning their assaults blow for blow.

As the screaming crew poured into the room, the soldiers abandoned the fight and fled down the hall.

"About time you showed up!" Dysart laughed. "I was beginning to think I would get all the glory for myself."

"Not a chance," returned Fiona.

They fought their way through the keep, and it became increasingly clear that they'd caught the defenders completely unawares. Bleary eyed, half-armored men stumbled from bunk rooms, but proved no match for the crew of the *Siren*. Those who did not immediately surrender found themselves intimately acquainted with two and a half feet of pirate steel.

The flow of the battle took Dysart's pirates down a spiral stair, and they soon stood before a huge pair of iron doors mounted with iron rings. Dysart grabbed a ring and gave it an experimental pull. The door moved.

"Heh!" he laughed. "Not even locked."

Fiona grabbed the other and they pulled the doors open wide. Beyond lay a large chamber filled floor to ceiling with crates, caskets, and chests spilling over with gold and jewels.

"By the horn of Naruth," whispered Fiona.

"Cap'n, I think we're rich," added Barnaby.

"Come on, then," Dysart commanded. "The gold won't do us any good if we don't get it out of here first. Let's go!"

The men cheered and followed him in. They filled pockets, pants, hats, and pouches with as many coins and jewels as they could carry, then seized chests and began hauling them from the room. Like rats descending on a fresh slop pile, they swarmed over the treasure until nothing remained but a few loose coins scattered on the floor.

"All right, men!" Dysart yelled. "This was the easy part. Now let's find a ship and be off!"

Moving as quickly as they could, laden with their booty, they ran back up the winding staircase. Bells were tolling throughout the keep now, and in the distance a sea horn sounded.

"They're calling back the Hunters," Fiona yelled. "We haven't much time."

They reached the main hall and ran through the tapestry-enshrouded room, loose coins and gems jingling onto the floor behind them. Bursting through the massive doors at the end of the hall they found themselves facing the cliff-walled cove at the center of the island.

A single, black-hulled Hunter was moored at the pier. It had recently arrived and the crew was just tying her down. Beyond the ship, the doors to the cove stood open wide.

"There's our ride, boys," Dysart called.

The pirates dropped the treasure and charged. The startled sailors scrambled off the ship, pulling swords and sliding down from the ropes. The two forces met and flowed into one another with bloody cries and the ringing of steel.

Sparrow stayed close to Dysart as they fought their way through the mob and toward the ship. Suddenly, Sparrow spotted the ship's captain on the bridge, holding a lantern and pouring something over the deck.

"Sir!" Sparrow cried. "The captain's trying to scuttle her!"

Dysart looked and frowned.

"He's too far for us to reach, but Fiona is closer. Fiona!" Dysart shouted.

"I see him!" she called. Grabbing a loose halyard she ran three steps, pushed off the dock, and swung out over the water and onto the ship. She landed along the side of the aftcastle and had to climb the rest of the way.

The captain, seeing her coming, smashed the container he held. Glistening oil poured out of it, coating the black planks. The captain raised the lantern over his head.

"She'll never reach him in time!" cried Sparrow.

Dysart swung his blade around and caught the edge of a sailor's sword, knocking it aside as it nearly skewered Sparrow.

"Lesson, Sparrow," Dysart called, parrying and thrusting against the sailor as he spoke. "Retaining focus on the task at hand is imperative when working in high-stress situations."

The sailor thrust, but Dysart swirled his blade, catching his opponent's sword and sending it spinning out of the man's hand. With a kick, Dysart sent the sailor tumbling off the pier.

"Right, sir. Sorry, sir!" Sparrow answered.

Try as he might, Sparrow could not resist watching Fiona's progress. As soon as her hands grasped the rail, she performed a graceful maneuver that sent her up and onto the deck. Oil or no, she landed as sure-footedly as a cat, and in a blink she held her dagger at the ready.

But when a burly sailor charged him, Sparrow was forced to turn his attention to the main battle. Calling forth all his courage and training, Sparrow resisted his body's desire to flee. He let the sailor close, and at the last moment, jumped to one side. The sailor plowed headlong into one of the dock pilings, knocking himself silly.

Sparrow looked back to Fiona and found her and the Hunter's captain trading jibes. They circled like duelists, the captain holding the lantern aloft and Fiona fingering her dagger. Sparrow could not hear what they said, but the captain was shouting something, his face red and the hand holding the lantern shaking.

Another quick exchange of words and the captain grimaced, and then heaved his lantern at the deck. Fiona leaped and loosed her dagger in a single, smooth motion. She hit the deck on her side, slid across the oil-soaked wood, and, with arm extended, caught the lantern a finger's width from the planks.

The captain stood, wide-eyed and confused, a scarlet flower blooming where Fiona's dagger sprouted from his chest. He opened his mouth as if to speak, stepped, stumbled, and then reeled back over the rail.

A moment later, the last defending sailor fell and Dysart's pirate crew jumped onto the ship. They pulled their wounded, of which there were blessed few, along with them. Soon, they had the Hunter ready to sail and began pushing the ship away from the dock using long poles.

A low, creaking groan filled the cove.

"The gates!" one of the crewmen shouted. "They're closing!"

Everyone looked. True enough, the massive doors were swinging slowly shut.

"Damn it," Fiona cursed. "Get this bucket moving!"

Dysart ran up beside her, eyeing the doors.

"We'll never make it. Look—they've got three men on the winch," Dysart said, pointing up to the winch house on the edge of the cliff. "The doors will close before we ever reach them."

"Fine," Fiona said. "We'll bring her back around, go up and secure the winch, jam it, and then return to the ship."

"The other Hunters will be back by then, and they've got us outnumbered. We won't stand a chance."

The pirates were still pushing away from the dock, the gap growing ever wider. Dysart looked at the doors, then at the dock, and then over to Sparrow.

"Right sir, I'm ready!" Sparrow shouted.

"Fiona, see that he's well cared for," Dysart said, then leaped across the gap to the dock.

Sparrow made ready to follow him, but Fiona shouted "Barnaby!"

The big scar-faced sailor grabbed Sparrow around the chest and hauled him back from the rail.

"NO!" Sparrow cried. "I've got to go with him!"

"It's too late, lad," Barnaby growled, as the gap continued to widen. "And your captain gave you an order. You'd best follow it."

Slowly gaining speed, the ship floated out into the cove.

☠   ☠   ☠

"Hye! Hye! Hye!"

The rhythmic cry rang out across the ship as the men poled the Hunter onward. All the while, the doors drew closer together.

"We'll never make it, Captain," Barnaby told Fiona.

Sparrow agreed, but didn't care at this point. He stared at the winch house, wondering where—inside that warrior-filled mass of stone—Dysart might be. A slight gust of wind whispered across the boy's face, drying his eyes and forcing him to blink.

Fiona turned to the crew and shouted, "To the sails! We've got a wind!"

The men cheered, pulled the poles on board, and scurried up the rigging. With a rustle, the sails dropped. At first they hung limp, but then the breeze came again, and the canvas caught it like fish in a net. With a snap, the sails puffed out; the men let out another cheer.

The ship moved faster now, but the doors kept closing. A tense silence fell over the men as the gap continued to tighten. Another foot and the ship wouldn't fit.

The screech of metal pushing against metal sounded from high above, and the doors shuddered to a stop.

"Up there! On the cliff! It's the Captain!" cried the crewman in the masthead.

The crew craned their gaze upward, and there—fighting along the cliff's edge in the torchlight—stood Dysart and another man. Glittering blades swung and clashed. Dysart ducked and bobbed, but the other man matched his moves.

The two edged backward, with Dysart now defending. Soon Dysart backed out along the top of one of the massive iron doors.

"Take the wheel!" Fiona shouted.

Sparrow looked around and realized that he was the only one there. The ship began to drift to port, and the wheel spun freely. Sparrow leaped over and grabbed on. It took all his strength, but he managed to steady their course.

Fiona jumped from the aftcastle, ran across the deck, and grabbed the main-mast's port shroud. With an ease that made Sparrow wonder if she'd been born on a ship, she quickly swung and climbed to the top of the mast.

Meanwhile, Dysart was still moving backward, blocking his foe's cuts and countering with a few of his own. Sparrow gasped as Dysart stepped back and nearly careened off the end of the door.

His foe cackled and prepared to run the pirate through.

"Dysart! Jump!" Fiona cried.

She hung from the very top of the main mast, the tip of which stood nearly as tall as the doors. Holding on with only her legs, she stretched her hands toward Dysart. Dysart laughed, saluted his adversary, and then leaped.

In mid-air, his hands met Fiona's. She hauled back, pulling Dysart up onto the mast with her as the ship swept out the gate and into the open sea. Down on the deck, Sparrow and the crew let out a tremendous cheer. Up above, Dysart and Fiona, entwined with the mast and each other, locked lips in a fervent kiss.

☠   ☠   ☠

Three weeks later in Port Reeyar, Sparrow, Dysart, and Fiona stepped off the Hunter's gangplank and onto the docks. Sparrow and Dysart both carried large satchels filled to the brim with their shares of the treasure.

"I can't convince you to stay on?" Fiona asked Dysart.

Dysart flashed her a wry smile.

"Ah, would that I could, my good lady—I mean *Captain*, but I fear the life of a buccaneer isn't for me. This little adventure has more than sated my desire to play the part of a pirate."

Fiona stepped closer, slipped her arm about his hips, and yanked him close.

"And there's nothing I can do to convince you?"

Sparrow blushed and looked the other way. Dysart, meanwhile, gently disentangled himself.

"You do tempt, but even if I felt the call of the sea, I still have my young charge to think about. His training is far from complete, and once I've made a vow, I keep it."

Fiona heaved a sigh that betrayed more feminine feeling than she'd shown previously.

"Well then, Captain," she said, a sad smile on her face. "I bid you 'Good journey.' May the wind be at your back."

"And at yours, my lady."

She turned and climbed back onto the ship. Dysart and Sparrow watched the crew cast off. As the ship slipped from the dock, Fiona called out:

"If you change your mind, let me know. That offer of First Mate still stands."

With a salute, she turned and took the wheel. The ship—newly named *Dysart's Folly*—edged slowly out into the harbor.

"What now sir?" Sparrow asked.

Dysart brushed a bit of dust from his now-tattered captain's jacket.

"I could use a change of clothes," he said to Sparrow. "And after that? Well, I've heard that the Duke of Port Reeyar is known for his noble hospitality. Perhaps you and I should drop by and find out if the rumors are true."

As the morning sun crept over the horizon, Dysart strode off down the shadowed streets, with Sparrow—as always—racing to keep up.

TREASURE
by Jean Rabe

They're lying when they tell you that it's not about the treasure.

And that's what they will tell you, those gentlemen of fortune.

They'll tell you that it's about the freedom of the sweet trade, and that heady rush that overtakes them as they're boarding a swift blackbirder with a belly full of slaves or facing down a merchantman with enough ballistae and spell-cannons to blow a ship to slivers. They'll claim that it's all about the lure of the wind that whips their matted locks around their sun-leathered faces, and the waves that rise and fall to rock them to sleep at night.

Or they'll swear that it's a penchant for a big mug of caulker to end a long drinking session, and a passion for the sweaty squeezes of plump, busty women in their swinging hammocks at night.

Aye, they'll tell you piracy is about all of those things.

But they're lying.

It's all about the treasure.

I know this because I'm blessedly one of them. My name is Green William, and I'm a mate on the *Mary Louise*, a schooner currently plying the waters off the southernmost of the Monster Isles. I'm the lookout way up in my nest, have been since the day I was conscripted into Ironjaw Nathan's nefarious crew eight years ago. There's no other post for me, not one that I'd accept without a serious drubbing or a threat to be keelhauled or to walk the plank . . . Ol' Ironjaw truly does use the plank from time to time on misbehaving mates or prisoners who have outlived their usefulness.

I like it up here. The salty air smells better from my lofty perch, away from the stench of those in the crew who've been far too long without a dip in the ocean. The work is achingly simple, watching out for ships—be they galleons from Azure Sea islands that might be hauling valuable cargo that will soon be ours, or Northern Verge brigantines trawling for our kind. The latter we avoid by running fast in the shallows and ducking into hidden bays where the ships with deeper drafts cannot follow. Ironjaw's a sly one, quick and clever at the wheel, and able to run blockades better than just about anyone in the Wild Seas.

It was Ol' Ironjaw who taught me that it's all about the treasure. Ironjaw's a Derenki, native to one of the islands to the far, far south, and so his ruddy skin is thick and inures him to the cold winds that whip across the bow at night. He's tall and reed-thin, perhaps all his kind are, with coarse red hair and midnight blue eyes. When Ironjaw swallowed a bit too much rum a few months past, I heard him sing a sorrowful chantey about his city being destroyed by an evil dragon decades ago, and that the survivors took to the sea and learned to harvest the great fish and gray seals of the cold waters.

Ironjaw never knew his father, but from time to time he'll talk about his mother, especially when he's drinking. Never speaks her name, though some of us suspect it was Mary Louise; Ironjaw has no one mistress he cares enough about to so honor by calling a ship after her.

He's a fair captain, not known for cruelty unless he thinks one of his men is doing wrong by him. And that's what he's thinking now—I can surely tell by his swagger, his blousy red shirt making swishing sounds, and his leather heels clacking against the deck. I'm leaning over the edge of my nest, and through gaps in the rigging I can see him clearly.

Pacing.

Raging.

Pointing his leathery finger at Rusty Bamford, Leo the Red, Dalka and Palmer, and Donner the dwarf—who I think has no business being on a ship, too stubby. I lean farther to get a better view.

☠ ☠ ☠

"Disappeared from my cabin, the baubles have!" Ironjaw thrust out his cleft chin, the gesture being the thing that earned him the nickname. He stabbed his finger at Rusty's chest, making him wince. "And you were in there last—in my cabin."

"No, sir, I wasn't."

"Brought charts to my cabin, you did."

Rusty held firm when the finger stabbed him again, but he cast his eyes down to avoid Ironjaw's venomous glare. "Yes, sir, I did that, brought the charts. Laid them out on your table, I did. You asked for them, and . . ."

"In there you were, last, and took . . ."

"No, sir." Rusty's voice was louder and clear. "I didn't. I didn't take anything, sir. I wouldn't. Someone else must've done it."

Because there was no quaver in Rusty's words, Ironjaw's eyes softened, and the deep furrows melted from his brow. But then the moment passed and the Captain's eyes were daggers again, aimed straight at Rusty's heart.

"Where are they . . . the brooch and the string of pearls? That long string of silvery pearls that should be hanging around a fair woman's neck? I did not find them in your bed or bag. I searched, I did. Turn your pockets! Turn them now!"

Rusty shook his head, beads of sweat flying off his fleshy face. But he complied, turning the pockets of his gray pants and shirt inside out, three pieces of gold thunking onto the deck and gleaming in the sun.

"Where did you hide them? The brooch and the pearls, and that pretty gold pin, so delicate and glittering that it must have belonged to a fine, fine lady?" Ironjaw ran his fingers along the thick silver chain around Rusty's neck.

"I said I didn't take them. I swear, Captain. I would not steal from you."

One more finger stab, this so hard Rusty rocked back on his heels and nearly lost his balance.

"I can't have it, my men stealing from me." Ironjaw started pacing again, the heels of his high leather boots clacking louder across the deck. "Oh, you've been careful about it, I'll give you that." He stopped and stomped, thrust his arms in front of him and laced his fingers, cracking them as he shook his head. He took a deep breath, and then another one before releasing both in a great *whoosh*. "Never more than a few shiny pieces at a time have vanished. Ha! You've probably been stealing more than a little bit, but you were so careful I hardly noticed. Probably been stealing from me since the day we left the Core and sailed through the Ogron Abyss to find better quarry."

He resumed his pacing, back and forth in front of Rusty, Leo, Dalka, Palmer, and Donner the dwarf. Leo was sweating profusely; he favored light-colored clothes fashioned by the H'leng-ru clans in the south part of the Core, and the damp stains around his neck and under his arms stood out. Dalka and Palmer were flashier dressers, but the sweat showed on them, too, though not to the same degree. Donner the dwarf always dressed in black, so his fear only showed in his quivering, bulbous lip.

Ironjaw tapped his foot. "Sometimes, Rusty, I'd think to myself that something had gone missing from my share of the booty. But I figured it was my imagination, a small pretty piece missing now and again, an emerald ring in the shape of a clover, a silver cloak clasp in the form of a wolf's head with glittery sapphire eyes. I remembered a pair of dangly ruby earrings I'd set on my table last year, intending to gift them to one of the . . . ladies . . . at Port Scallese. Figured I'd misplaced them, the earrings. Didn't want to believe the truth—that my own men, my sea brothers, were stealing from me."

This time Donner shook his head. A thickset dwarf with a clean-shaven head slick with sweat, the vehement shake nearly loosed his eyepatch. "Captain Ironjaw . . . Captain Nathan . . . sir . . . none of us would steal from you." He thumped his chest with his fist. "I . . . sir . . . would never do such a thing."

"Gold, too, you most likely took." Ironjaw stopped pacing again and tipped his face back, the slight wind catching his red hair and sending it fluttering to look like a disturbed ghest's web. The sun flashed in his eyes and set them to shining like wet black pearls. "Took things precious to me to satisfy your greed. Pirating from a pirate. I'd leave you in the Belspa Keys if we were close enough." His face was red, from anger, not from the sun. Ironjaw's skin was so dark from his years under the sun that it never showed a burn. "My share of gold that I never bothered to count after it had been divided—pilfered from me. Why should I count it? Why should I think one of my crew would steal from me?"

Dalka cleared his throat. "You're a good captain, sir." He spoke with a musical voice, rolling the Rs. "I've never crossed you. I never would." Dalka was the oldest mate, signing on with Ironjaw more than ten years past when the pirate captured this schooner from a commander plying the waters north of the Core. Ironjaw's old ship had been a sloop, smaller and in worse repair. He willed that to his first mate and took this schooner and half his original crew, keeping just enough of the surviving sailors to fill it out. "I've no reason to pinch, sir. My share has always been more than enough."

Ironjaw stood in front of Dalka, shoulders square, in a pose a military man might hold. He gestured with his head, indicating that Dalka should join the rest of the crew, which had assembled amidships to watch the trial.

"Neither would I, sir. I . . ." Leo had shifted over into the space vacated by Dalka.

Ironjaw's narrowed eyes silenced him.

In that instant Rusty relaxed, seeing that the captain's anger was now focused on someone else. He'd been holding his stomach in, and it poked out now over the buckle of his thick leather belt. His fingers fluttered over the pommel of a knife at his side. Every man in Ironjaw's crew wore a weapon of some sort—a knife, belaying pin, or a cutlass.

Leo shifted back and forth on the balls of his feet. "I'm a thief, surely as I stand here before you. We're all thieves. But I didn't steal from you."

Then Ironjaw gestured that Leo could join the others, leaving Donner the dwarf and Palmer and Rusty to face his wrath.

☠ ☠ ☠

I watched all of this intently from my high, high post, grateful for the view and more grateful that Ironjaw's midnight blue eyes had never been thusly aimed at me. I knew to stay on the good side of my captain. I'd seen what this otherwise fair and reasonable man could do when so stressed.

None of the men below spoke for several uneasy moments. . . not Palmer, nor Donner the dwarf, nor Rusty. Neither was there a whisper among the men and women looking on. It was as if they all held their breaths, waiting for the verdict, watching their mates sweat some more.

Ironjaw wasn't speaking either. He was letting the silence settle thick as the silt off a muddy island. I could hear the sails flapping, though not loudly, and from somewhere in the distance I heard the cry of a few gulls . . . rats with wings Dalka called the birds. But I liked the sound of their song and concentrated on it to take my mind off the trial below. We weren't too far off Port Scallese, and so the seabirds were likely scavenging along the docks there. I thought the air carried the stink of dead fish, but the wind wasn't coming from the direction of the port, and so I knew the smell to be my imagination. My stomach chose that moment to rumble, and I was glad I was too far from the action for it to be heard. It rumbled once more and I tried to mentally quiet it. So hungry!

Would dinner be late tonight because of what was transpiring below? I prayed not. I'd been at this post through the darkest part of night and all through this morning, and I'd not bothered to come down for a tidbit to hold me over. The cook would probably fix some straight rush, meat shoved over the fire with no preparation. Not that fare for me. I didn't care to eat flesh.

At length, Ironjaw's gestures pulled my attention back to the three men lined up before him. He was standing in front of Rusty again.

"There'd be a witness to your perfidy, Rusty. Someone else was in my cabin last night when you brought in the charts. Green William was there, resting before taking to his lookout. I'm certain he would have seen you." Ironjaw stared up at me now, squinting through the sun and through the rigging and gaps in the sails, locking that hard gaze on me, expression softening just a bit when I nodded. "Green William!"

"Aye, Captain!" I hollered. "Aye, Captain!"

He raised a leathery hand and waved to me, raised the other hand to cup above his dead lights—his pirate eyes—to see better. "I've need of you down here, Green William. Don't be slow. I've a matter to discuss with you."

Perhaps he didn't know I'd been paying close attention to what was playing out on the deck. He likely thought I was intent upon my task of scanning the waters for signs of other ships. There was one in particular we were looking for, one with the tall, tall masts of the ogres from the Cursed Seas.

"I'm holding court, Green William, and I'm calling you to be a witness. Hurry now!"

Ah! He surely didn't know that I'd been listening in and was lax in my duty as lookout.

"I say, I've need of you down here! I'll not call you again!"

"Aye, Captain!" I leaned over the edge of my nest even farther, spread my wings and rode the breeze down to Ironjaw Nathan's shoulder. I was careful not to dig my claws into his vest, as it looked reasonably new. He usually wore a grogram shirt that easily suffered my snags. He reached his fingers to the back of my neck and gave me a good scratch. I fluffed my feathers and closed my eyes appreciatively and clicked my beak twice.

"Green William." Ironjaw returned to his military posture and once more stabbed a finger at Rusty's chest.

I watched the mate suck in his gut and—if it was humanly possible—sweat a little harder. I stared at the thick silver chain around Rusty's neck. It glittered in the bright sun.

"Green William, you were in my cabin early last night, weren't you? On your perch?"

"Aye, Captain," I agreed, turning my attention away from the jewelry—a difficult task, as practically everyone in Ironjaw's crew wore bits of their treasure, and I liked the way it all shined.

"There in my cabin on your perch when my . . . trusted . . . boatswain Rusty Bamford brought charts to my table?"

"Aye, Captain." I saw a fleck of spittle form at the corner of Rusty's lip, and I caught a whiff of his breath. Some of his teeth were rotting, and there was the scent of grog and something worse. I worked to keep from gagging. Wouldn't do to empty the meager contents of my stomach on the Captain's near-new vest.

"He spread the charts out, as I'd requested?"

"Aye, Captain." I watched Rusty's eyes turn to needle-fine slits and lock onto me. I don't think Rusty ever liked me, certainly had never taken to the idea of Ironjaw treating a parrot as an equal to a sailor—as an equal to boatswain Rusty Bamford.

"That bird don't say nothing else but 'Aye Captain,'" Rusty risked in his defense. "He's going to agree with everything you say, Captain."

"Aye, Captain," I repeated for effect.

Ironjaw's hand came up to stroke at his chin. I noticed that there was a faint shadow of stubble on that chin, more evidence that my Captain was upset. He likes to be clean-shaven, not even a mustache mars his weathered face. The stroking gesture hinted that he was considering Rusty's words.

"That bird . . . that blasted green buzzard . . . you can't rely on it to witness against me. Blow me tight! I didn't steal from you, I say. You must believe me."

Ironjaw turned to glance at Donner the dwarf and Palmer. Then he pivoted and stepped away from the trio, walked to the rail and put his hands on the wood. I had to clamp my claws tighter to hang on. Together, we stared down at the water. The sun was high and dappled it, making it glitter like gold.

"I want to believe you, Rusty," Ironjaw whispered too softly for all but me to hear. "I want to believe that my men would not steal from me."

My Captain took a deep breath and I copied him, holding the blessed salt-tinged air in my lungs for as long as I could. I'd always breathed the sea air, first from the shore of Tuluna, where I was hatched and later caught and caged and sold to an old man with a wooden leg. I breathed it better from a cage on the deck of a ship that Ironjaw boarded eight years past. He slew the man with the wooden leg and treated me as the real treasure of the take that day—claiming me and releasing me from the cage, tossing the cage over the side to give me my freedom, teaching me the sweet trade of piracy and setting me up as the *Mary Louise's* sole lookout.

In return I've given him my loyalty and all of my respect. I've scanned the horizon until my eyes couldn't stay open, finding ships to pursue and ones to run from, delighting in each victory and each narrow escape. I intend to swallow the anchor with Ironjaw, retiring together to some port that welcomes old pirates.

"It's not that missing a few baubles is hurting me." Ironjaw continued to whisper, his words lost in the lapping of the water against the hull.

His voice was tinged with pain, and I rested against his neck in solace. I knew he was well off; it was tradition that the captain take a double share of any haul before dividing the rest evenly among his men. Well . . . almost evenly. The *Mary Louise* had a fine Il-Siha healer in her complement of crew, and she always received a share and a half.

"I've plenty of coin in my chest, Green William." He fluttered his hands, the sun reflecting off the rubies and emeralds and sapphires anchored in the thick gold rings on his fingers. "Jewels, plenty of those. More than I need." He paused. "But not more than I want."

Ironjaw taught me that a pirate never has enough treasure.

He shook his head, and I dug my claws in just a little more so I wouldn't fall off. Then he eased back from the rail, turned smartly on his heels, and clacked his way back to the suspect trio. I thought he might go easy on the men, especially since he had so much gold and jewels in the sea chests in his cabin, more gold and jewels buried near a little cove on the smallest of the Monster Isles. He soon would be gaining more—we'd caught word that an ogre square-rigger would be coming up from north of the Ogron Abyss, and taking on supplies before heading toward Mar Sangua for trading. We've just enough ballistae to make certain that square-rigger doesn't even catch sight of Port Scallese.

But when Ironjaw cracked his fingers again, I knew he wouldn't let the matter of his missing baubles rest, and there'd be no "going easy." I understood; the Captain couldn't look soft in front of the rest of the crew, couldn't let them think it was all right to steal from him.

A punishment was in order.

"Green William."

A harsh one, I suspected.

"Green William!"

I ruffled my feathers and stood tall, opened my beak and looked menacing.

"Aye, Captain?"

"Green William, did you see Rusty, my boatswain, steal a ruby brooch from my table?"

"Aye, Captain." I tried to make my voice sound sad, but I have little luck showing any inflection—only volume. "Aye, Captain!" I said louder.

"And a string of pearls long enough for three ladies?"

"Aye, Captain!" I bobbed my head for emphasis.

Rusty opened his mouth to protest, but no words came out . . . only a trickle of blood spilled over his lower lip. Captain Ironjaw, ever quick, had thrust a knife through Rusty's heart.

Ironjaw nodded to Donner the dwarf and Palmer. "Weigh him down and throw him over." A pause, and he turned to face the assembly. "Full sails," he barked. "We've an ogre square-rigger to find." To me: "Green William, up in the nest with you. Keep your eyes wide for our prize."

"Aye, Captain." I spread my wings and launched from his shoulder, flapped hard, and angled myself between the lines and toward my post. Within a few heartbeats, I was perched on the edge of the nest and staring out across the water.

The sun had set the waves all to glimmering, like pieces of gold magically floating for as far as I could see. I felt mildly sad for Rusty, but there was nothing else I could have done except call him guilty. If Ironjaw knew Rusty was innocent, he'd be looking elsewhere for the thief.

"Poor Rusty." I briefly bowed my head in his honor. "He was a right fine mate."

Then I breathed deep of the salty air and craned my neck for the best possible view. I love the sea when it glitters.

Glitters like the treasure lining the bottom of my nest. The ruby brooch and that string of pearls? And that pretty gold pin, so delicate and glittering that it must have belonged to a fine, fine lady? They are lying on top of my haul, shining in the sun, glimmering along with an emerald ring in the shape of a clover, a silver wolf's head with sapphires for eyes, and a pair of ruby earrings my captain had intended for some . . . lady. My favorite piece is a thick gold bracelet with purple stones shaped like teardrops—that was the heaviest bauble I've managed to fly with.

It's quite an accumulation I have, each piece carefully and quietly taken from Ironjaw's cabin during the past eight years, hidden way up in this nest when no one was looking. Admired every day when the sun strikes it and makes it glitter, every night that the moon is bright enough to make it all practically glow. Oh, there are pieces of gold, too, and chunks of turquoise and many things I haven't names for . . . some of them taken from drunken mates. And I'll be adding more to it . . . adding something else that glitters brightly . . . after we take on the square-rigger. Ogres always have a lot of loot.

Only this time I'll be a little more careful.

I told you it's all about the treasure.

THE PIRATE WITCH
by Paul Genesse

Maeve pushed the dead man off the floating walkway with the heel of her boot. He slid from her rapier and splashed into fish-gut-smelling water where a swarm of hungry offal sharks tore into his flesh. Locking her eyes onto the next pirate in line, Maeve pointed her bloodied sword at his tattooed chest.

The pirate held up his notched cutlass as the eight hard-looking men behind him tensed for a fight. "Cap'n Coyle warned us that you were prickly."

"Coyle?" Maeve's angry visage faded. She flashed a questioning glance over her shoulder at Baxter. The tall man's pockmarked and sword-scarred face scrunched up in confusion. She turned back to the pirates blocking their way, knowing firsthand about Coyle's cruel tactics and the black-hearted men who followed him. "Never heard of him." Maeve stepped toward the tattooed man, who bumped into one of his mates.

"You're just as Cap'n Coyle said," the pirate challenged, "curly black hair down to your arse, hazel eyes and a fiery temper. You're Maeve Tierney, wife of the dead Cap'n Bull Tierney, and you're coming with us."

"Got the wrong woman, you do." Maeve wiped the blood off her sword with a frilly white handkerchief. She shook her head at the stain then pretended to curse under her breath—instead speaking the secret words of power her mother had taught her. Maeve used the raw power in the fresh blood to cast her spell and felt the magic rising in her throat. "I'm Lace Connelly and my business is running punch houses for freebooters like you lot."

The pirates blinked with surprise as Maeve's words hung in the air, blocking out the splashing of the sharks feeding in the water. The blood on the handkerchief disappeared, utterly consumed by the mind-controlling spell that had been powered by the dead man's blood. Maeve held her breath, knowing that if her magic failed, Bax would die protecting her and she would end up a prisoner on Coyle's ship.

"There's a punch house in Bilgewater?" Several of the pirates asked, their surprise turning to excited grins.

"Two wrecks that way with the red flag by the gangplank." Maeve gestured over her shoulder, hoping all of them had been fooled. Just to be sure, she stuck out one of her curvaceous hips, outlined perfectly by her tight black trousers, and suggestively sheathed her sword—twice. "Tell my man that Lace sent you. But you better get going, 'cause the crew from *Crosswind* are coming this morning and there ain't enough girls to go 'round."

Baxter and Maeve graciously stepped aside as the excited men hurried past. Only a few of them gawked at the low-cut of her white blouse. One man looked at her as if he had forgotten what he was going to say, then shook his head and followed his mates.

After they'd gone, Maeve let out a sigh of relief and Bax grinned, showing all three of his front teeth. "You're such a witch."

Maeve slapped the ugly sailor across his stubbly cheek. "*Pirate* witch. Now come on before the spell wears off, or more of them buccaneers will come looking for us."

"Lead on. I'll watch your back."

"More likely my *backside*." Maeve winked at her most loyal and best friend, wondering if Bax knew how much she cared for him. It was no secret that he loved her. Still, Maeve wasn't ready to share herself like she had with Bull. It had nothing to do with Bax being so ugly. She liked the scars on his face and that one of his eyes was blue and one brown. He always treated her with respect and made her laugh when it seemed she'd never be happy again. Someday, if they could find an island where no one knew who they were, maybe she and Bax could become more than friends. For now, they had to escape from the second pirate captain who had come after her since her husband's death. Then they could think about digging up Bull's treasure, which would buy them a new life together, one that didn't involve piracy.

Maeve stayed alert as they hustled along the maze of floating plankways toward the outer edges of Bilgewater. As they headed toward the quays where the ships were docked, the early morning heat and humidity took its toll. She wiped sweat from her brow and shifted her heavy cloth bag from shoulder to shoulder. Maeve almost wished she'd packed more than just gold; but wherever they landed next, she could buy whatever they needed.

"I'll carry it," Bax offered, adjusting his two heavy bags of coin.

"No, Bax, you're too heavy already."

"I'm skin and bones!" He patted his flat stomach. "All I've had to eat for a week is rats and boiled seaweed."

"Keep your voice down." Maeve rolled her eyes and noticed the dozens of holes that rats had gnawed in the hull of a Kernish merchant cog. All around them tightly packed ships from every kingdom and several primitive barges covered with sailcloth tents threatened to sink to the bottom of the deep lagoon. Scores of captured vessels had been floated into the reef-protected waters inside the tiny atoll in the Northern Verge. The ships had been lashed together to form a floating island where rats now outnumbered the starving pirates of Bilgewater.

Maeve and Bax trundled along the rotten and ill-traveled plankways, trying to avoid being seen. Baxter's big feet cracked several timbers, though he always caught himself before falling into the polluted water. The quiet was a blessing, but Maeve wondered why there were so few sailors about. There hadn't been any barrels of rum brought in for weeks, and fever couldn't have killed all of the old sea dogs in one night. Could it? Not even one toothless freebooter had begged them for food or grog since they'd left their hideout after receiving the warning that Captain Coyle had arrived and was looking for her.

Maeve almost smiled when she saw the first collapsed sailor of the morning. Then she blanched at the purple lesions on his face that leaked a purulent liquid. She stepped carefully over him, trying to ignore the cloud of swarming flies.

Baxter furrowed his weathered brow, the expression making him look much older than his one score and seventeen years. He wrinkled his nose. "We should have gone long before now."

"I know, Bax, I know." Maeve wondered if she'd live much beyond her one score and nine summers, considering they'd been found after only a month in hiding. At least they'd gotten word before Coyle's crew arrived at their bunks. It would be a stiff wind in their face as they tried to get free of the accursed dung heap now.

Maeve led Bax around a half-burned elvish cog. She didn't remember it from the week before. Another prize. Another wart against the sagging jowls of Bilgewater.

A gang of men appeared on the forecastle of the elvish ship. Maeve squinted into the sun as a man with a crimson tricorn hat stared down at them.

"Maeve Tierney, what an unexpected pleasure." Captain Coyle tipped his hat and smiled. "Climb up here and I be pouring you some rum." A rope ladder dropped beside her.

Maeve smiled back, hiding her fear at being caught unaware. "Not just now, Cap'n, there's a good wind for hoisting a sail."

Coyle nodded. "That there is, Maeve. And once you join my crew, *Vulture* will fly even faster. No prize from the Azure Sea to the Northern Far Reaches will be too swift for us."

Maeve stepped sideways. "I'm finished with that kind of sailing, Cap'n."

"You can't ever leave the sweet trade," Coyle grinned, "'specially after you went and married yourself to a great Cap'n like Bull Tierney."

Maeve scowled, squeezing her sword hilt. "Since you think so highly of him, Cap'n Coyle, maybe you should have married that dim-witted lout with ballast in his head. I've had enough of Cap'ns like you and Bull-damned-Tierney."

Coyle shrugged his shoulders. "You be having yer own cabin and a full share of the loot after you sign articles with me, Maeve. I'll keep you safe from the Angallians who want your pretty little head on a spike next to Bull's back in Port Angal. Shame how he was killed—betrayed by one of his own crew."

Maeve raised a dark eyebrow, wondering if he knew her part in Bull's death. She guessed he did and went on the attack. "Rum-addled cabin boys lie better than you, Coyle. I know what you want, and unlike you, I ain't afraid of the Angallians."

Captain Coyle took off his hat. "Bereaved as you are with the loss of your fine husband, I be willing to overlook your womanish ways. Now come up here and have a drink with a thirsty old sailor."

Maeve looked at Baxter, hoping he wouldn't be too angry with what she was about to say next. Bax let out a big sigh when he saw her determined expression. Maeve took another step sideways. "Next time I'm in port, we might have that drink, Cap'n."

"You'll be reconsidering before too long." Coyle turned to his men. "Take her alive, you filthy dogs!"

Ropes dropped over the side and sailors began clambering down. Bax and Maeve took off running as men landed hard on the plankway behind them, causing it to shudder and list to port. Maeve's sea legs kept her steady, but Bax stumbled, his burden of gold unbalancing him. Bax's foot found a rotten timber and he crashed through two boards in the middle of the plankway. Both his legs splashed into the water.

"Bax!" Maeve shouted as Bax tried to drag himself out. Her heart jumped into her throat as she lunged toward her friend. Maeve leaped over the broken plankway with a drawn sword and desperately parried a cutlass that would have opened Baxter's skull. She cut some space between herself and the crew of *Vulture* with her flashing steel.

Out of the corner of her eye, Maeve saw the dorsal fin of an offal shark speeding toward Bax. He lifted one knee onto the plankway trying to drag himself out of the water without dropping the gold.

Maeve stabbed a pirate in the leg with her rapier and punctured another man in the groin. Drops of blood dripped into the inky water. A shark swam under the walkway and Bax screamed as he struggled to pull out his other leg. "Choke on it!" Bax yelled as he yanked out his now-bootless extremity.

Maeve used the basket-hilt of her rapier to turn aside a determined attack from a tall, freckle-faced Derenki man with red hair. The force of his blow left her teetering on the edge of the hole Bax had made. She nearly fell into the water where offal sharks circled. The Derenki raised his thick cutlass over his head for a two-handed blow.

Bax threw a silver-handled dagger, hitting the Derenki in the chest— handle first. The weapon bounced harmlessly onto the walkway. The pirate touched his chest, found nothing protruding from his ribs, and, with a harsh laugh, raised his sword again.

Taking advantage of the distraction, Maeve steadied herself and hopped across the gap before the blow fell. Bax slashed the air over the breach in the plankway, keeping the big red-haired pirate at bay. The Derenki sneered at Bax and picked up the expensive dagger and slid it into his belt.

Bax nudged Maeve to get going as he kept his eyes on the pirate's cold blue stare. Maeve knew they couldn't get away from the unburdened pirates. Holding her panic at bay, she spoke the words of power. Maeve backed up while dragging the tip of her bloody sword in an arcane pattern along the wooden planks for three long strides.

"Bax, run!" Maeve yelled as she imagined the boards rotting and breaking. Bax shuffled away, and the red-haired man leaped over the hole with three others right behind. The planking shattered and the pirates crashed through the magically weakened walkway. The water frothed white, then red as the sharks tore into their screaming breakfast.

Maeve and Bax sprinted toward the quays as the *Vulture's* crew shouted to each other about finding another way to give chase.

"Handle first?" Maeve laughed as she wiped the few remaining drops of blood from her sword. "Why did you throw that one?"

"You know my best throwing blade was in my damn boot!" Bax pulled off his other boot and threw it at the pirates.

Maeve cut her laugh short as they ran onto the solid wooden quay. *Crosswind's* birth lay empty. She scanned the entire length of the dock. A handful of dejected looking sailors milled around, but all the ships were gone. Save one, *Vulture*, with the carving of a massive scavenger bird perched on its prow.

"Where *is* everyone?" Maeve asked a one-armed and sun-shriveled sailor.

"Word came with *Vulture* last night. A fleet of Angallian frigates is coming this way. They're going to kill every buccaneer in the Razor Islands. All the able-bodied seamen escaped this morning."

"Sea-dragon's balls!" Baxter spat. "They believed Cap'n Coyle?!"

Maeve's heart sunk as she realized *Vulture's* Captain was a better liar than she thought. Now there was no way to get away from Bilgewater.

"*Vulture* will take you on," the sailor told Bax. "But I don't be knowing 'bout a lady friend. There's the question of sailor's luck after all."

Maeve scowled. "Sailor's luck be damned. Cap'n Budge and *Crosswind* will pay for leaving us here. We had an agreement."

Baxter started to say something, but Maeve cut him off. "Stowe it, Bax. I thought we could trust him."

"But he's a pirate!" Baxter rolled his eyes and Maeve realized how stupid she had been.

"Old Chippy said a sloop came in yesterday for repairs," the one-armed sailor offered.

Maeve scanned the quay. Aside from a few dinghies, there was nothing to steal. They headed for Old Chippy's shack on a shadowy plankway that paralleled the docks.

The shouting of an angry crowd in front of the berth near Old Chippy's shop drew Maeve's attention. The combined smell of more than two dozen sailors who hadn't bathed or washed their clothes in years mingled with the scent of burning tar. Maeve tried not to breathe through her nose as she noticed the top of a mast bobbing up and down. She couldn't see much of the sloop through the furious crowd. Bax asked a scrawny sailor, "What's happening here?"

"The Cap'n of yonder sloop won't take us old sea dogs, and we ain't even asking for pay. Off this wreck is all we want."

Maeve noticed very few in the crowd who were fit to sail, all being too old, too weak, or missing too many limbs. If she couldn't out sail and out fight these worn-out mongrels, she wasn't fit to hold a blade and taste the salt on the wind.

Booted feet thundered on the plankway behind them. Maeve and Bax pushed into the crowd as a gang of men closed in. Another party marched toward them from the quay near *Vulture's* birth. Bax and Maeve suffered through the stench, with Bax leading until they arrived at the front. Maeve's jaw dropped when she saw the condition of the small forty-foot sloop. Wet tar leaked through holes on the starboard side and scores of barnacles clung to the hull. The gunwales were broken in several places as if grapnel hooks had torn them away.

Blotches that could only be from blood stained the entire deck and marred the once-white roof of the crew cabin at the aft of the ship. Arrowheads lodged in the wood poked out of the vessel as if it had been attacked by a regiment of archers.

Two gray-haired sailors manned the pumps on the deck, working them hard.

"She's sucking water in port." Baxter shook his head in disbelief. "I seen baskets more seaworthy than that."

Maeve read the ship's name painted on the side: *Lady Gail.* "Not much of a lady," she spat. The ship's mad captain was trying to get underway, but *Lady Gail* would be a hundred fathoms down before sunset without a shipwright and a miracle.

Besides the two old sailors manning the pumps, the only other crewman was a long-limbed hooded man nearly mummified in dirty bandages. He stood near the helm aiming a ballista on a swivel at the agitated sailors on the quay. A crossbow rested at his feet and a cutlass complimented the daggers hanging on his belt. Soiled linen bandages partially covered the oozing sores on his arms. The man's cheeks and nose were black and deformed, as if his face had become the root of a gnarled and charred tree.

"Dark leprosy." Baxter shuddered as he stared at the diseased man. "Maeve, if we get on that ship we'll catch it for sure. Little pieces of us will turn black and fall off."

"Iron poisoning or dark leprosy," Maeve said, "one kills slower than the other."

Bax groaned. "Let me do the talking then." He stepped forward and shouted above the others unhappy about being refused work. "Cap'n! Able-bodied seaman Baxter asking to join the crew."

The man's harsh gaze fell upon Bax. "I ain't offering pay, only passage south to the Core."

"I be paying my way with work and gold, Cap'n." Bax tossed him a small pouch of coins and Maeve instantly hated the idea of going south. If they were ever going to find peace it would be away from the Core Islands.

"I'll have some answers before I let you aboard."

"Yes, Cap'n." Bax nodded.

"Will you follow my orders?"

"Yes, Cap'n. I will." Bax's tone even convinced Maeve, though he did tend to follow orders when on ships.

"Have you killed a lot of men?"

"Yes, Cap'n. I have. Though some of them tried to kill me first."

The black-faced man studied Bax for a moment longer, then yelled, "Come aboard!"

Harsh shouts and curses erupted from the crowd. A sea dog past his prime leaped toward the boat, intent on either proving his skill as a sailor or his talent as a pirate. The captain shot him through the chest in mid-jump. The skewered man crashed into the gunwale and plunged into the sea. The sharks appeared, and some of the crowd backed away from the edge once the feeding frenzy began.

The captain picked up a crossbow and ordered one of the sailors onboard to reload the ballista. Baxter tossed his bags aboard and leaped onto the *Lady Gail's* bloodstained deck. "Cap'n, sir. I hate to cause trouble, but I can't leave behind my mate." He pointed at Maeve.

"Baxter, you be the last sailor I need for this boat."

"I know she's a woman sir, but a fine sailor she is. Her eyes see farther than most, and she's a good cook besides." Bax offered another bag of coins.

The crowd surged to life, hollering and screaming that any of them were ten times as good at sailing as any woman. The sailors jostled and pushed Maeve. She teetered on the edge of the dock, glancing at the sharks in the water and trying not to fall.

"Cap'n," Bax shouted, "ain't none of them got the talent she has. And she won't cause no trouble neither."

"Hoist the mainsail, we're shoving off," the captain ordered as he stood by the wheel. "Baxter, cut the mooring rope. We ain't waiting for those Bilgewater rats to untie us. Now follow my orders! No one disobeys Cap'n Finneous Crab while they're on my ship."

"Aye, sir!" The two old sailors began hoisting the sail into the rigging as Baxter stood by the mooring rope staring at Maeve on the dock.

"Cap'n, sir!" Baxter shouted, holding a third bag of coins. "I can't leave without her. Shall I be getting off the ship, sir?"

"Belay that! Help raise the sail or I'll put a bolt up your arse!" Captain Crab aimed the ballista at Baxter.

Maeve considered jumping aboard and putting her sword through the leper's neck. She hesitated since the chance of the captain shooting her or Bax before she killed him was pretty good.

One strong arm covered in coarse red hair wrapped around Maeve's neck while the other groped at her breasts. Fear turned to rage. Maeve bit the man's wrist and tasted dirty seawater. She gouged at his eyes, then slammed the sharp heel of her boot against his shinbone. The pirate stumbled back in pain. Maeve spun around to face the red-haired Derenki man. Three others pushed their way forward, trying to corner her at the edge of the dock. She crouched beside *Lady Gail's* mooring rope as the water below the dock roiled as offal sharks consumed every scrap of flesh from the dead sailor.

Maeve unwound the line from the mooring cleat. As they reached for her, Maeve closed her other hand around her handkerchief still spotted in pirate's blood. Hoping there was enough blood to cast the spell, Maeve sprang backwards off the quay. She flipped in the air, floating like a leaf on the wind. Maeve landed softly on the deck of *Lady Gail* with perfect balance. The crowd gasped in shock as she slipped the now spotless handkerchief in her pocket and faced the captain. "Permission to join the crew, Cap'n Crab, sir?"

The dark-faced leper aimed the ballista at Maeve. His knuckles turned white as he squeezed the weapon's stock. His voice exploded with fury, "Tie off that line, woman!"

Pirates from *Vulture* stood on the edge of the dock preparing to board, but captain Crab turned the ballista at them. Bax snatched up a loaded crossbow hidden by the port gunwale, and the red-haired pirate gritted his teeth in frustration.

The mainsail caught wind and *Lady Gail* pulled away from the dock. Captain Crab stepped to the wheel and turned the ship into the breeze. The stink of Bilgewater faded and fresh sea air filled Maeve's nostrils as the sloop cut through the waves. She looked back and wondered how long it would take Coyle to get *Vulture* underway.

Maeve coughed as the odor of rotting flesh hit her like a cat-o-nine-tails. Captain Crab towered over her as she choked on the smell. His already-twisted face snarled into a knot of rage. "Don't be expecting any special treatment aboard my ship, woman. You be working the pumps just as often as them others."

"Aye, Cap'n." Maeve nodded, looking away from his grotesque face.

"Now, get on those halyards and raise the jib." Crab put his hands on his hips as the wind blew harder and a bank of gray clouds appeared in the distance. Maeve helped the two old sailors with the lines. Both of them had weathered skin from a lifetime at sea. Their calloused hands tugged on the lines as if they wore leather gloves, while Maeve felt the ropes' bite.

The sailor beside her reeked of sour sweat and rotten fish. She suspected he might have fleas, though she wondered how the bugs could stand the potent aroma. He turned to her. "Name's Lemmy Fowler," he said loudly, offering a toothless smile, "but call me Lem."

The other sailor finished with the jib. Lem motioned to him, "That salty sea dog is Codfrey Saltpans. We both just came aboard in Bilgewater, though me and Cod been on ships together more years than I can count."

"That means more years than his fingers and toes all summed together," Cod said, "but we ain't never been crewmates of a woman the likes of you."

"What kind of woman is that?" Maeve raised an eyebrow at Cod, who had to be sixty years old.

"Ain't never seen no woman do what you did back at the dock," Cod said.

"Surprised you saw it at all, you blind fool," Lem shouted, as he scratched the flogging scars on his back.

"Quit yer bellowing, Lem." Cod gave the old sailor a dismissive wave and turned back to Maeve with a hard stare. "How'd you fly like that?"

"Right. Fess it up!" Lem's voice was just as loud as before.

"With witchcraft." Captain Crab stood with arms crossed and glared at Maeve. "Don't try denying it, woman."

"Stop calling me, *woman.*" She glared back. "My name is Lace Connelly."

Crab shook his head. "Don't be telling false tales on my ship, or I'll put you in a sack of sailcloth with a ballast stone and pitch you over the side."

Maeve reached for her sword, remembering when the priests tied rocks to her mother's legs and dropped her into the sea as punishment for practicing witchcraft.

"Now, who are you?" Crab's gaze narrowed.

Maeve wanted to cut off his diseased nose with her rapier. She thought about lying again, but something in the intense way he looked at her made Maeve suspect that Captain Crab had some magical power of his own. "I'm Maeve Tierney, once the wife of Cap'n Bull Tierney."

"That's why Cap'n Coyle came to Bilgewater." Cod's mouth hung open. "He thinks you know where the queen's ransom is buried."

"What he say?" Lem asked, eyes wide. "Loot?"

Maeve pressed her lips together.

Lem slapped his knee. "The king wants his queen and treasure back, don't he?"

"He got his queen back, Lemmy." Cod tried to cuff Lem on the head, but the old man ducked and raised a fist.

"Best keep your tongues still," Bax advised Lem and Cod.

Cod ignored him. "The king got her back all right, with Bull's bastard in her belly. The way I heard it, the queen didn't want to go back to her limp fish of a husband after Bull gave her his—"

Lem stopped laughing when Maeve's sword touched the skin under Cod's left eye.

Cod's hand moved away from his cutlass, then Maeve shoved him back. Cod spat. "Her damn fool of a husband is the reason the Angallian king's fleet has been burning pirate hideouts in the Razor Islands. The king wants his gold back and revenge for what cow-brained Cap'n Tierney did to the queen."

Maeve's blood rushed to her head and shame colored her skin. Did every sailor in the Blue Kingdoms know what her husband did with the Angallian queen?

Cod pointed at Maeve. "I heard tell that she be the only one who knows where Cap'n Tierney buried the queen's ransom."

"I don't care one wick about what she knows," Captain Crab spat. "I don't like none of it, but crew is crew. Witch or not. Now put them swords away and work those pumps. We best be dry as tinder before it rains."

Captain Crab was at the wheel when the first drops fell onto the ship. The wind picked up and the sloop bounced across the sea. Maeve wiped the salt from her lips as she worked a pump. Her mood turned as dark as the sky.

It seemed like a lot longer than eleven years past when handsome Bull Tierney stormed into White Abbey and "rescued" her. The priests who had murdered her mother had left her to rot with the Merciful Sisters of the Virgin Goddess Evaleen. The Sisters had taken her in and tried to redeem her, but some girls weren't cut out for a life of prayers, chastity and forgiveness.

The memory of Bull "saving" her from her prison and her virginity all in the same night made Maeve wonder what had gone so wrong after they'd been married. Did the love potion she had given him wear off? She vowed silently to never trust a pirate again—except Bax. And if they ever found a place to settle down, she promised herself she wouldn't use any witchery on him. Especially not love potions.

In the distance behind them she caught a glimpse of a billowing topsail and recognized *Vulture*. Maeve pointed abaft as she matched Baxter's pace on the other pump.

"Coyle's on us already." Bax grimaced at Maeve. "Should have left you in Bilgewater."

"Ships off the port bow!" Lem yelled.

Riding the waves on the horizon a fleet of tall clipper ships and frigates flying full sails and golden flags came into view.

"Angallian warships." Lem frowned and hid behind the gunwale. "They're headed right for us!"

Captain Crab turned hard to starboard and barked orders to adjust the sails. *Lady Gail* lost some of her speed, and the mast creaked in protest of the new direction as Lem and Cod swung the boom. *Vulture* immediately altered her course to match theirs. The little sloop wallowed in the waves, too beaten to make a good run. On her best days, she could have stormed to the horizon, but not today.

"More ships dead ahead!" Lem screamed.

Rain and clouds obscured the horizon, but Maeve saw a flotilla of war galleys and a smattering of what appeared to be pirate ships.

Cod let out a joyful cheer. "The Razor Islanders have finally decided to stand up to the Angallian king!"

"No, look. Those are jenrat galleys," Lem said. "The jenrats have joined us."

"Not bloody likely." Captain Crab turned away from the collision course with the new ships. "Razor Islanders don't never ally with jenrats."

"What'll we do, Cap'n?" Lem frantically glanced from fleet to fleet.

"We'll run the gauntlet between them," Crab announced. "If we don't, we end up like the pirates who used to crew those ships."

"What do you mean, sir?" Lem asked.

"It was jenrats who attacked my boat and killed my crew. They were on a schooner called *Ghost* when they attacked."

"That's a buccaneer ship," Baxter said.

"It's a jenrat ship now." Crab turned the wheel, setting a course that led in between the approaching fleets.

"What happened to *Ghost's* crew?" Lem asked.

"Jenrats took on fresh supplies, most likely," Crab said. "They don't care what they eat, as long as its meat—and that it's still alive when they start biting."

Maeve wished she would have accepted Captain Coyle's offer just then as the two armadas of ships squeezed them and *Vulture* closed in.

Rain pelted *Lady Gail* while the distance between the Angallian and jenrat fleets narrowed. *Vulture* gained on them as the rain stopped. The air became even more humid, and the wind eased up. Mist rose from the sea and a bank of fog rolled in.

The Angallian fleet turned to port so the wind was behind them, taking the same course as *Lady Gail*. The gun-ports of all the warships opened and fireball cannons poked through the gunwales. The jenrat war galleys rowed forward as drums beat faster, apparently unconcerned that the Angallians had brought their guns to bear first.

Baxter eyed the Angallian guns from the helm. "We're in the line of fire."

"So is *Vulture,*" Maeve said. She glanced aft, then at the galleys rowing toward them. The decks and rigging swarmed with scores of wiry, khaki-skinned jenrats. The prows of the war ships had been painted with fierce black eyes and toothy maws, which gaped above the bronze rams at the waterline.

"We could surrender to the Angallian ships." Lem glanced fearfully at the jenrat galleys. "I be too old to row."

"Keep a steady course for the fog," Captain Crab said as the first volley of fireballs launched from the Angallian cannon. The burning orbs passed over the aft of *Lady Gail* and the foredeck of *Vulture,* leaving a sulfurous odor in the air. The fireballs hissed as some hit the water short of the jenrat fleet, but a few exploded on the decks. Smoke and fire erupted as the matted hair of the jenrats caught fire.

Volley after volley of fireballs arched toward the jenrats, but the vicious creatures spawned by goblin sorcerers never wavered or changed course. They returned fire from their forward guns, and Maeve estimated the Angallians were outnumbered three to one.

The first burning jenrat war galley rammed an Angallian frigate just as *Lady Gail* entered the fog bank. White mist cloaked the ship, and Maeve lost sight of *Vulture* and the battle. The sound of rams splintering hulls, men screaming, jenrats squealing, and fireballs exploding drifted over the sea. War cries and the clash of weapons became ghostly echoes as the fog thickened. The wind ebbed and *Lady Gail* drifted in the current for some time, sails slack. The raging battle faded in the distance as Maeve worked her pump with an arm turning into lead.

"Cap'n, me and Cod can go below and tar up the hull." Lem stood by the crew cabin door.

Crab stalked toward him and reached for his shoulder. Lem moved aside, afraid of the captain's touch. "No one goes below deck, savvy?"

"Yes, C-Cap'n," Lem stammered.

"Now take another turn on that pump," Crab ordered, as he wiped a black liquid that dripped from his necrotic nose. He gave the whole crew a warning glare before he disappeared below deck.

Maeve stood by Bax at the helm and whispered, "What's he hiding down there?"

"The ship is sucking more water than he wants us to know about," Bax said.

Maeve shrugged as the sounds of the battle became even more faint. Captain Crab came on deck with an open cask of biscuits and a pail of water. He dropped them by Baxter and took over the helm. Lem, Cod, Maeve, and Bax took their meal on the foredeck, as far away from Crab as they could.

Lem rapped his rock-hard sea biscuit against the gunwale and shook out the weevils before dunking it in the briny water pail. As he tried to gum the biscuit, blood stained his lips. "Not even a taste of grog to wash this down." Lem groaned in unison with Cod.

Maeve crunched her moldy biscuit and kept an eye on Captain Crab. Fog wafted over the ship and she could barely see the aft. *Lady Gail* drifted on the current, no telling where they were heading.

Something banged into the hull, and Maeve sprang to her feet. Another thump and a bang on the prow caused them all to stare over the side. In the water below, floating debris bumped against the ship. Casks, planks, barrels, and other bits from sunken ships bobbed in the sea. Cod used a gaff hook to pull up a barrel marked with the letter A. Lem helped him pull it aboard. They twisted the tap and poured out a drop of clear liquid.

"Angallian rum!" Cod announced as he sampled from the barrel. "Our luck has changed, Lemmy!" They both laughed and clapped each other on the back.

"It ain't lucky to have drifted back here," Bax whispered to Maeve as the faint smell of burned sailcloth tainted the air.

"Look." Lem hooked three more barrels of rum and one cask of soggy biscuits.

Cod dumped the water from the pail and started to fill it with rum. Captain Crab kicked over the pail of alcohol. "Get back on the pumps," he ordered Lem and Cod, and then stood supervising them. "Woman, you and Bax stow those barrels in the hold. No one drinks any rum while on watch, and we're all on watch until I say we ain't."

"Aye, sir." Lem and Cod sulked back to the pumps licking their fingers.

Bax and Maeve lowered the barrels into the shallow hold. The captain moved away and scanned the fog bank. Maeve seized the chance and inspected a stack of small casks. She found one with a black skull painted on it and pulled out the cork plugging the tap hole. The cork smelled of bitter almonds, and she immediately turned away and took a cleansing breath. Her mother had taught her about poisons, and *kyanos* was one of the worst. Maeve wondered if Crab knew that he had *kyanos* onboard, or if some merchant had paid him to deliver it to a master of assassins in the Core.

Poisons were rich cargo, if you could stomach the penalty for getting caught—drinking your own haul and dying with the twitching spasms.

Wondering about Crab, Maeve climbed up the ladder and noticed a large patch of fresh tar on the hull. It appeared to have been applied in the past hour. She realized that Crab would not have had time to do it. Maeve heard the sound of a pump being worked in a room beyond the hold. "Bax, someone's down here."

Baxter stepped toward the sounds.

"Get back up here," Captain Crab ordered from the edge of the hatch.

Maeve and Bax climbed out. Crab locked the hatch as more debris banged into the hull and scratched along the waterline. Maeve marched toward the prow as a pallid hand with long fingernails came over the side. Yellow eyes with red points of hate in them stared at her as the creature's head appeared over the gunwale. The jenrat had a dagger in its pointed teeth, and its wet, black hair splayed over batty ears.

"Repel boarders!" Maeve shouted as three more jenrats came over the side. They charged forward screaming as Bax drew his cutlass. She stabbed the first one in the eye and Bax cut two down with vicious chops. The fourth one waited on the bowsprit, daring them to come forward. Maeve heard more scratching on the sides of the ship and stumbled backward as at least a dozen five-foot tall jenrats poked their heads over both gunwales.

Bax pulled Maeve aft as the dripping jenrats crawled onto the ship with wicked smiles on their half-goblin half-human faces. Captain Crab stood with a cutlass at the crew cabin door with Lem and Cod.

"More of the little blighters are 'round the ship," Cod said as they put their backs to the wall of the crew cabin.

"There's too many," Lem said, changing his grip on his dagger.

"We'll cut them all down, as poorly armed as they are." Captain Crab pulled a dagger. "No one will ever take my ship."

The first wave of jenrats screamed forward with belaying pins, knives, and makeshift clubs salvaged from the debris in the water. Maeve and Bax dispatched the creatures with practiced blows, while Lem and Cod fought side by side, hacking away at any that got too close. The old men were suddenly panting, their strength fading.

Captain Finneous Crab threw back his hood and glared at the first jenrat who approached him, startling the creature so much that it froze as he cut it down. The horde of jenrats swelled in front of them. Maeve heard something scuttling behind her. She turned to see five jenrats perched on the roof like animated gargoyles.

"Behind us!" Maeve shouted as one landed on Lem's back. Cod stabbed it as the jenrat raked its claws on Lem's shoulders. More appeared on the roof, and others swarmed into the rigging, ready to pounce on them from all sides. The horde swelled, like a tidal wave about to dash them against the rocks.

Bax slashed wildly in front of them to keep the jenrats at bay, but the creatures pressed forward with sharp claws and hungry mouths.

"Inside!" Captain Crab ordered as he pulled Lem and Cod to him. Maeve darted toward the door. A jenrat on the roof grabbed her by the hair as she entered. Maeve yelped, and Baxter cut off the jenrat's arm. Dark blood spurted onto Maeve's hair.

Three jenrats tackled Bax as he turned to help Maeve. They clawed at his already scarred face, trying to find his throat. Captain Crab bellowed, "Get off my ship!" He slashed at the beasties piling atop Baxter. The volume of his voice and the steel of his blade made the surviving jenrats fall back. Maeve dragged Bax down the stairs. Crab bolted the door as the jenrats threw themselves against it, pounding and clawing as they howled for blood. They would not give up, and Maeve decided that before she would let the jenrats skin her alive and eat her flesh, she would fall on her sword.

Crab ushered them down the steps below deck as he guarded the door. Maeve whirled as movement behind a curtain drew her attention. She slashed open the sheet and beheld three teenage girls huddling together. All three wore the white robes of novice Sisters, putting them between sixteen and eighteen years old. Around their necks the tear-shaped symbol of the Merciful Goddess, Evaleen proclaimed their faith.

"Get away from them, *witch!*" Captain Crab ordered.

Maeve's eyes met the terrified stares of the young girls. Memories of when Bull and his crew rampaged through White Abbey flooded her mind. She remembered the novices and Sisters huddling together like these three were now. Guilt about what had happened to the kind women and young girls of White Abbey flared up in Maeve's chest. She raised her sword at Crab, fury spewing from her mouth. "So this is what you're hiding, Cap'n. Your own little collection of abducted girls for you to infect with your disease. You'll pay for this." Maeve decided to put a hex on Crab that would damn his soul to an eternity of pain.

"You don't know what you're talking about, witch," Crab spat as the jenrats smashed into the door with something solid. "I'm escorting them north to Seaton Abbey."

The girls' fear-filled eyes turned to Crab, silently pleading for protection. Despite all Maeve knew of the heartless ways of the sea, Crab's story seemed true.

"Pardon me, Cap'n," Cod said, "but you said we was going south to the Core Islands."

"Do you think I'd announce to all those sea dogs in Bilgewater my true heading?" Crab's stubby nose wrinkled.

The cabin door burst open. Jenrats poured down the stairs. Crab cut them down one after another, making a barricade of corpses. No normal seafarer could handle a blade that well. Maeve guessed he was a Defender of Evaleen, an instrument of wrath to protect the Merciful Sisters.

"You're a Defender, aren't you, Crab?" Maeve asked as she skewered a jenrat.

"Someone has to be." Crab flashed a hideous smile, then lodged his sword in a jenrat's eye-socket. As he pulled the blade free, a jenrat pounced with a cat's speed. Crab fell back, and the girls screamed.

A desperate wish to keep the young women alive spurred Maeve into furious action. Never would she stand by and watch those who had dedicated their lives to the Merciful Goddess be harmed. The Sisters of White Abbey embraced Maeve, though they had known her mother was a witch. They'd been kind, despite Maeve's little skill at worship or piety.

Maeve stabbed the next jenrat to come over the pile as Bax cut the throat of the little monster clawing at Crab. Maeve slew another with a single stab through the ear. She glanced at the blood on her sword and felt the wetness in her hair. As more attacked, Maeve spoke the words of the ancient witches—using the blood on the floor and on her person to power the magic. The jenrat blood in her hair hissed and evaporated like steam as terrible strength filled her. She pushed the jenrats back, stabbing with her dagger in the close quarters of the stairwell.

Maeve's hair rose from her scalp. She felt as though she was charged with unholy lightning from the Gods of Wrath. Maeve knew at that moment that the "mercy" she would bring would be swift and violent. The jenrats paused their attack, driven beyond the doorway by her ferocious defense.

Metal bit into wood of the gunwales. The *thunk* of arrows hitting flesh and the screams of injured and dying jenrats set Maeve's heart racing even faster.

"The Angallians!" Lem shouted as the sound of more arrows and splashing noises reverberated outside. *Lady Gail's* starboard gunwale bumped into a ship that had pulled alongside her. A booted boarding party landed on the deck, and the clash of weapons and war cries echoed in the fog.

"What are they shouting?" Lem asked, favoring his bleeding shoulder.

"*Vulture,*" Maeve said, wiping the jenrat blood from her face, "it's Cap'n Coyle and his crew." Maeve stared at the three frightened young women. A cold realization settled over her as she pondered their fate at the hands of the notorious pirates. They wouldn't be as lucky as she had been when handsome Bull Tierney spirited her onto to his ship and made her a woman.

"I can't let them be taken." Crab turned to the terrified novices. "Pray girls, and turn away," Crab said in a gentle voice. "Ask the Goddess to forgive what I'm about to do." He moved toward them with a dagger, and put his hand on the first girl's shoulder. "Sarah, Goddess be with you." Crab moved to cut her throat.

"No!" Maeve grabbed his wrist. "There's another way." She looked into his teary eyes, full of pain and remorse. "In the hold, there's a cask of *kyanos* poison. You don't have to do this yourself. Only a sip will take their lives."

The fighting on the deck stopped and a great cry of "*Vulture!*" went up from the victorious crew.

Maeve told Crab and the girls the doses of poison needed, and then sent them down the tiny hallway to the hold where they would face their end.

"Maeve Tierney." Captain Coyle stood at the top of the stairs, "What a pleasure it is to find you in all this fog."

☠ ☠ ☠

Aboard *Vulture*, Maeve sat in Captain Coyle's cabin on the edge of his bed with her boots off. He smiled as his crew started a raucous celebration on deck, yelling, drinking, and dancing at their good fortune.

"I didn't think you'd be so . . . accommodating, Maeve Tierney." Coyle's gaze lingered on her chest.

"Don't call me *Tierney* anymore." Maeve sauntered forward and slipped her blouse off her shoulders. "How does Maeve Coyle sound to you?"

"So, are we to get to know each other better?" Coyle asked.

Maeve nodded. "It's time for that drink." She ran a finger down the middle of her chest as she sashayed toward him.

"I'd rather not be tasting this old rum." Coyle put down his cup and wiped his lips.

"Maybe you'd like to taste it here?" Maeve poured the rest of Coyle's drink on her cleavage. He buried his face between her breasts. After a moment he pulled away, his tongue protruding from his mouth. In shock, Coyle fell to his knees.

"Hear that?" Maeve asked. The sounds of the party on deck had gone silent. Coyle clutched his throat, unable to catch his breath. Maeve whispered over him. "The queen's ransom is in a cave on Stove Pipe Island. Not that you'll ever see it." She wiped the rum off her skin as he fell to the floor.

"*Witch*, what have you . . . ." Coyle's body spasmed as he had a seizure and gasped his last breath, dying with the shock of her betrayal frozen on his face.

Maeve went on deck and inspected the bodies of *Vulture's* crew. Some men were slumped near the barrels of rum taken from *Lady Gail*, apparently trying to get one last drink before they died. She found the red-haired Derenki and kicked him in the side—just to be sure—before she reached for Baxter's silver-handled dagger. The Derenki's eyes opened and he grabbed her ankle. Maeve's pulled the blade from his belt and stabbed him in the heart.

After freeing Bax, Lem, and Cod from the *Vulture's* brig, they all climbed down a rope ladder to *Lady Gail*. The girls were still hiding in the half-flooded bilge holding vials of poison in case they were discovered.

"Did they like the rum?" Crab asked as he climbed out of the wet crawlspace.

Maeve shrugged. "I'm afraid they drank too much."

Crab moved to hug the three girls and Maeve said, "Stop. You'll infect them."

Finneous Crab let out a hearty laugh and ran his hands over his face. A golden light flared from his palms and the leprous skin was gone, replaced by tan wrinkles any man who had spent his life on the sea would be proud to have.

"He's a wizard!" Lem said.

"Not exactly," Crab smiled and hugged the girls.

Maeve laughed. "Just a trick to scare off the pirates?"

"A Cap'n worth his salt has to have his tricks." Crab winked.

Bax cleared his throat. "Now let's top off our supplies from *Vulture's* stores and get underway. We don't want to wait around for more jenrats or the Angallians to come aboard."

"What's our course?" Cod asked.

"North," Crab said, "to Seaton Island where I can drop off Faith, Winnie, and Sarah. I've made a solemn vow to bring them to safety."

"North, you say." Maeve's eyes sparkled. "There's an island up north where I'd like to stop."

"Which one?" Crab asked.

"Stove Pipe." Maeve said nonchalantly.

Lem and Cod jumped. Dread masked their faces.

"Those waters are full of pirates and worse," Crab said. "I'd have to be a fool to sail my ship there."

"You'd be a fool not to," Maeve said, "because there's a queen's ransom waiting for us. Equal shares for everyone. Then we can go to Seaton Abbey together. The Merciful Sisters who raised me said the marriage chapel there was a sight to see." Maeve smiled at Bax, who seemed rather stunned. "I've always wanted to live in one of those white houses above the cliffs."

"Told you she knew where the queen's ransom was." Lem slapped Cod on the shoulder.

"Maeve, why tell me, a Cap'n you barely know?" Crab asked.

"Because I know I can trust you." Maeve smiled confidently.

Crab raised a bushy eyebrow. "Why is that?"

Maeve glanced at the novice priestesses. "Because you're not a pirate."

"Don't be so sure about that." Crab grinned as he walked away.

Bax stared at Maeve in disbelief. *"Equal shares?"*

"Well, not *quite* equal," she whispered.

THE COINS OF DARKUN
by Robert E Vardeman

"Captain! What are you doing?" Wollof, first mate of the *Sea Blade*, dashed to the prow of the barque and nervously watched Anba Eklimondus swing an axe. "That's the figurehead you're cutting off." The Al-Kabarian snuffled a little but did not move to stop his commander as Eklimondus lifted the axe and brought it down with a vicious cut that sent wood splinters flying.

"I know what I'm doing," Eklimondus said. He braced his feet against the heaving deck, and his broad shoulders tensed for another swing against the figurehead. A tear came to his eyes as he continued to chop. The Mero inside the carving moaned wordlessly as he kept up the attack. Finally, the securing wood parted and the figurehead holding the water elemental that had guided the *Sea Blade* faithfully and well for more than three years fell into the sea.

"The elemental," Wollof complained, "it has all our blessing stones." He went to the rail and watched as the barque quickly left the figurehead behind in the rough sea. "We will be doomed, Captain, without the protection of the blessing stones."

"I did not want to do it," Eklimondus said sadly. "Trust me, good friend, that it was necessary." He looked into his mate's soft, brown, doglike eyes and saw conflict there. The captain knew the risks he took. There had been a bond more than magical between the Mero with its blessing stones and the crew. The Mero had steered their ship through dangerous waters and was able to return the *Sea Blade* to their home port on the floating island of Suspendere, no matter where they traveled. The only other reliable method of regaining port on the ever-moving island was the chart marked with the eccentric route taken by the floating island. On any given day of any month Captain Eklimondus could pilot to the island using arcane calculations and the map.

But not now, not with the Mero gone and his secret chart burned. He had replaced the destroyed chart with a new one showing mismarked islands and dubious directions on the skewed compass rose.

"We must rely on you, then, if we are to see our families again," Wollof said. "My wife has just whelped."

"I didn't know," Eklimondus said. "You should have told me. As much as I rely on you, Wollof, you could have missed this journey."

"Like the others?" Wollof looked around. A dozen barefoot humans and a pair of elves struggled with the barque's rigging. More than half the crew had been left behind at Suspendere, including Megan Farsight, a warrior-Siren able to reconnoiter better than any human or elf and outfight any five. "Is this not a pirating journey?"

"It is," Eklimondus said, heaving a deep sigh. Already he missed the presence of the Mero and felt strangely adrift. If his scheme did not work, there was no way the *Sea Blade* and what remained of its crew could ever return to Suspendere.

"Why cripple ourselves? I am loyal, Captain, you know that I would give my life for you, but in any fight we will be at a disadvantage with so few to swing swords and use grappling hooks. Even fat, wallowing merchant ships carry warriors to protect them."

"I know," the captain said. "We will find more gold than you can imagine, Wollof. Soon. It will be soon. I feel it in my gut."

Wollof clamped his snout shut and shook a shaggy head. "I would feel better with Megan here."

"I would, also," Eklimondus said, "but she is still on the floating island. Let's return with our booty and stories to make her feathers rise in admiration and envy."

"Ship!" came the cry from the crow's nest. "Port side, a league distant!"

"Heel over and make for it," Eklimondus ordered without hesitation.

"Shouldn't we watch how she runs, Captain?" Wollof spoke only sensible Freemarinering.

Eklimondus dared not travel such a cautious course. His brother, Lord Palus, ruler of Suspendere, had begged him to accept this mission on the high seas. Eklimondus would never turn down a few months of sailing, hunting for fat merchant ships and decent adventure away from the staid corridors of power on the floating island, but his brother had couched the mission in the direst of terms. If Eklimondus did not bring back the proper cargo, Suspendere would no longer be known as the floating island but the submerged one, abandoned by the gods and of no interest to any but Vortex Gladiators.

"Life or death of our island and everyone on it," Palus had said, and Eklimondus believed him. His brother was a good man, honest as any and more deserving of his throne than most this side of the Coraltooth Archipelago. Angering the god that moved your island across the waves transcended foolishness and attained the rank of suicidal idiocy. Palus had no choice; neither did Eklimondus.

"Prepare for battle," Eklimondus told his mate. "We will overtake the other ship before sunset."

"Anba, my friend," said Wollof, moving closer so his snout was almost touching his captain's ear, to speak without the crew overhearing. "Think, man! At sunset the winds slacken. Becalmed next to an unknown ship! It could mean our death."

"I did not ask for your opinion," snapped Eklimondus. "You have your orders. Obey me!"

He felt a pang of regret for the harshness of his tone. The Al-Kabarian slunk off. If he'd had a physical tail, it would have been tucked between his legs. Eklimondus quickly pushed the rebuke from his mind. It was possible none of them would be alive by sunrise. He alone of those aboard the *Sea*

Blade knew what they sailed so speedily toward. Although Megan Farsight was safe and he wished her free of danger, he also wished she were here beside him to lend both her fighting skill and the sheer power of her presence.

"Boarding parties, prepare!" he bellowed. The crew grabbed their weapons, short, wickedly sharp swords and daggers nearly as long but heavier of blade to use in parrying. Two elves prepared grappling hooks while others in the rigging worked the lines to give the barque full speed.

"Looks like a big one, Captain!" The lookout above laughed gleefully. "I can almost see the gold in those bulging holds!"

"Gold," Eklimondus called out so his crew could hear him. "We'll all have their gold soon." His heart felt heavy at the fight to come, but he did not lie. They would reap plunder unknown to any other freebooter.

He put a spyglass to his eye and watched as the other ship, a slower, heavier merchanteer, tried to tack and find a way to escape the faster square-sailed barque. The *Sea Blade*'s triangular spanker snapped in the breeze as it billowed out, giving the barque added speed and maneuverability. Eklimondus knew neither was needed. This merchant would be overtaken soon.

"Keep your wits about you," Eklimondus ordered. "This fight will—"

The lookout cut him off with an excited cry. "Gold! They got heaps of gold on the deck! It's spilling from chests. I see hundreds of coins!"

Eklimondus knew anything more he might say would fall on deaf ears. The crew was not overly greedy as pirate crews went, but the promise of so much gold coin would focus them to the exclusion of all else.

"Captain," said Wollof, coming up beside him. The Al-Kabarian held a thick-bladed cutlass in one hand and a gaff in the other. His favorite fighting tactic was to use the hook to pull his opponent closer, then slash with the cutlass. When he got into a proper fighting rhythm, he could kill three or four foes a minute—and had. "Got me a question before the fracas."

"What?" Eklimondus found himself hypnotized by the rapidly approaching merchant ship. No longer content to evade, the ship sailed directly for them. It was the one out of hundreds that Eklimondus sought.

"Why did you chop off the figurehead binding the Mero? It might have steered us better." Wollof pointed to the possible collision of the ships. If either ship made the slightest mistake in navigation, they would collide with disastrous result. Possibly this was what the other captain wanted, but Eklimondus doubted it.

"I had my reason. Now ready yourself." He reached over and cinched up a segment of armor on Wollof's arm, then slapped him on a sloping shoulder.

"They're firing on us!" The warning from aloft came not an instant too soon. Eklimondus and Wollof knelt behind the thick railing as arrows thudded into the wood. A few sailed a handsbreadth above their heads, but they did not immediately poke up their heads to see how near they had come to the merchanteer. This was not their first battle. Long seconds later came a second flight of deadly missiles intended to kill the curious or the battle virgin.

"We're closing," Eklimondus said, holding his sword up and watching the other ship reflected in his gleaming blade. "Grapples, ready!"

"Grapples, aye, Captain!"

As the ships ground together side to side, timbers creaking under the immense strain of impact, grappling hooks sailed out and caught the merchant ship. The barque continued on, but the ropes were thick and the grapples secure. For an instant it was as if the *Sea Blade* stopped and then moved backward. If the merchanteer had been fully laden, this might have happened. Eklimondus had seen how high the other ship rode in the water and knew the *Sea Blade* was drawing the other after it—something that did not bode well for a huge cargo to be pirated.

"Gold! On the decks! Gold coins scattered everywhere!"

There was no holding back Eklimondus' boarding party now. The ships hove back together, and they jumped before a second impact could carry them apart again. Aloft, the crew in the barque's rigging worked to furl the sails and keep the ships bound securely together.

Anba Eklimondus had trained his pirates well and knew there was no further need of him calling out orders. He lifted his blade once more, saw his way clear, and vaulted over both ships' railings to land on the deck of the merchanteer. Beside him came Wollof, half turned so they protected one another's backs.

The rush of warriors almost overwhelmed the pirate captain. He had not expected a fight, but it came. How it came! Wave after wave of frantically fighting seamen threw themselves against his men. Wildly flailing seamen holding a sword or dagger for the first time against well-trained pirates—it was a slaughter.

Deck slippery with blood, Eklimondus fought his way to the hatches, then stopped. His lookout had been right. A huge chest of gold coins stood open at the edge of the hatch. The light from the setting sun reflected like blood from the coins.

"The coins of Darkun," he said.

"What's that, Captain?" called Wollof.

"Be careful of the coins," was all he replied. Eklimondus' hand shook as the last of the merchanteer's crew died, leaving only the ship's captain alive.

"Do you surrender, sir?" Eklimondus shouted to the portly, stoop-shouldered man.

"Aye, my vessel is yours, as is my cargo."

A cheer went up from the *Sea Blade's* boarding party.

"What are your orders, Captain?" Wollof asked.

Eklimondus stared at the other ship's captain and turned cold inside. Although he had never set eyes on this man before, he knew him. He knew him too well.

"Yield," Eklimondus said, knowing it would not be.

"Captain, he has surrendered." Wollof looked at him as if he had gone insane.

"You do not escape so easily." The merchant captain's face showed a flash of fear, then a curious contentment settled on it. He whipped out a small dagger and plunged it into his own breast.

"He feared us so? The fool," said Wollof. "If he had known who captured his vessel, he would have been overjoyed at the treatment we would have given him."

"The rest of his crew also committed suicide," Eklimondus said, "though they did it on the tips of our swords."

"They *were* terrible fighters."

Captain and mate faced each other as solid and unmoving as statues. Then Eklimondus gave the fateful order. "Wollof, have the men divvy the gold. Each man gets a share."

"But, Anba, we never—"

"Do it. Now." Eklimondus' eyes never left the merchant captain's unmoving corpse on the blood-soaked deck.

"He must have thought we were Purple Tern pirates," Wollof said, staring curiously at his commander.

"No, he didn't think that. He only wanted us to have the gold." Eklimondus reached into the chest and touched one of the coins. It was as if a powerful jolt of lightning seared into his body. He spun about and stumbled a few steps before regaining his balance. Eklimondus held out his sword and looked at his reflection in the bloodied blade. Nothing had changed. Wollof stood a few paces away, clutching a coin. The Al-Kabarian appeared no different. Nor did any of the crew aboard the merchanteer.

"Get the chest onto the *Sea Blade*," he ordered. "Let the rest of the crew have their share right away."

Eklimondus turned to examine the hold for additional booty but found himself unable to move in any direction but off the merchant ship. Pausing at the railing, he fought his own muscles to turn away. Instead of obeying his command, his muscles acted with a mind of their own and he easily cleared the distance between the two ships.

"What do we do with our prize, Captain?" Wollof had already returned to the deck of the *Sea Blade*.

"Let it drift," Eklimondus said. "There's nothing aboard worthy of our time."

"Each of the crew's got at least one coin," Wollof said, looking puzzled. "Does this matter?"

"Set sail for home port," Eklimondus shouted. He bit his own tongue to quell that order but could not.

"How do we do that, Captain? The figurehead's been destroyed," Wollof said.

"The chart's in my cabin. Fetch it. We can sight in on the pointer stars and be underway immediately."

60

Wollof obeyed, not once questioning why they were returning to Suspendere after only one engagement, and one yielding only a single chest of gold coins. The *Sea Blade* stayed out for months and might plunder a half-dozen vessels before filling its hold with only the finest in booty. To return to Suspendere with nothing more than a paltry few coins would make them the laughingstock of all other Freemariners.

Try as he might, Eklimondus could not counter the order. He flipped the coin taken from the chest, watched it spin about prettily and then settle back in his callused palm. He tucked it away when Wollof came back on deck with the chart.

"This smells different, Captain." The Al-Kabarian's keen nose worked rapidly over the new chart until Eklimondus grabbed it away.

"You're no navigator," Eklimondus snapped. "Only I am able to steer the ship."

"Megan is back at port," the first mate said slowly, as if realizing the extent of the *Sea Blade's* dependence on its captain. "She could have navigated us. Or the—"

"To your station, sir!" Eklimondus felt nothing as long as he worked to return to the floating island. Any deviation from that goal froze his muscles.

"Clouds are parting. Should I take a sighting on the Armored Rat?" Wollof craned his neck around and peered nearsightedly up his snout at the constellation of eight bright green stars and the solitary golden one that was the Rat's slowly winking eye. With the ringed moon yet to rise and blot out weaker stars, the time was perfect for celestial navigation.

"I'll do it. You know how difficult it is to get a bearing on Suspendere. We head not for where it is but where it will be, Darkun willing." Eklimondus felt as if a sun had blossomed within him as he spoke. He opened his hand and stared at the coin he still held.

Darkun's coin, he thought, then bit his lip. Eklimondus waited a few seconds, then found it impossible not to pick up the astrolabe Wollof had brought with the chart and take the sighting.

A smile settled on his lips, a cruel one. He and his crew might have their bodies controlled by ensorcellment, but his thoughts remained his own.

Or did they?

Eklimondus finished the sighting, made the arcane geometrical calculations on the edge of the chart, then turned it this way and that and finally decided on a heading. He called to the helmsman and sent the *Sea Blade* speeding along on an unusually powerful night wind.

Wollof paced restlessly. "How long before we reach port, Captain?"

"Something biting you?"

The Al-Kabarian looked at him sharply and snapped his powerful jaws. Saliva spewed out, and the soft brown eyes turned into killer's orbs.

"I want to reach Suspendere as quickly as possible. So does the crew."

"The gold's burning a hole in their pockets, eh?" Eklimondus held out the coin he clutched in his hand. He had tried to toss it overboard more than once only to have his muscles turn to water each time.

"How long?"

Eklimondus pushed his finger down on the chart. "We are only a few dozen leagues from the floating island. We rendezvous with it just after sunrise. Tell the lookout to keep an eye peeled. If we miss it, a new rendezvous will require an additional month of sailing. The island is speeding up for the next couple weeks."

Wollof yelped his pleasure and went to inform the crew. Eklimondus sagged a little, then straightened. He needed sleep, but his body refused to relax. When he tried to eat, he found it impossible. All he could do was hang onto the chart and make sightings on new pointer stars to plot the shortest course to Suspendere. Somewhere during the night, when he was certain they were not deviating from course, he sank down to the deck and slept, his dreams—nightmares—haunted by utter hatred.

Suspendere will be destroyed. This echoed through his head, and he awoke with a start. Salt spray broke over the bow and rained down on him. Eklimondus forced himself to his feet and caught his breath when he peered through the curtain of spray to see an inviting cove a short distance off.

"Island ahoy!" came the cry from the crow's nest. Eklimondus worried that he would have to discipline the lookout. The warning should have been given long since.

"Is it Suspendere?" Wollof crowded close beside him. "I do not recognize the terrain."

"It's the hind side of the floating island," Eklimondus said. "My brother Palus and I used to come here as children and swim in the cove. It is protected from all but the worst storm."

"We approached from the back? I didn't think that was possible. Always we have come upon the island and the main harbor. I expected to see the palace high on the mountain and—"

"Old friend, we are home. This is Suspendere," Eklimondus said hastily. "See how the stone of the land barely touches the water? What other island could it be?"

Wollof dropped to all fours and peered along parallel with the water. When he jumped back to his feet, he said, "You are right. The island floats in the air. There is none other than Suspendere that does this."

Destroy the island!

The thought exploded within Eklimondus' head and staggered him. He pressed his hands into his temples to quell the pain. Wollof never noticed his captain's reaction.

"Furl sails on all but the aftermost mast. Let the fore-and-aft sails carry us home."

Eklimondus turned his hand over and opened curled fingers. The coin he held began to glow. It became so hot it burned his flesh, but he could not throw it away. His muscles refused to obey even when he cried out his intention of dropping the coruscating coin overboard. Beside him Wollof held out his coin. It blazed hotter than the sun, but the Al-Kabarian did not drop it, either. Fear clutched at Eklimondus' gut as he turned and saw every member of his crew similarly holding their fiery coins.

The main sails were furled, leaving only the smaller one for maneuvering. The *Sea Blade* slowed as it entered the cove and the anchor dropped. He felt a curious blend of triumph and horror.

Wollof threw back his head and let out a howl like one of his distant ancestors. Eklimondus stepped to him and clapped his hand holding the coin down over Wollof's. When the coins touched, both crewmates stiffened as rictus seized their muscles. Eklimondus thought he saw a faint outline of a man, dressed in black armor, moving with precise steps. But it faded quickly. As the paralysis died, he saw that his entire crew had assembled on the main deck. All held out a hand, a gold coin in it. As more and more touched hands, a scintillant column of pure golden light solidified above them.

Go, join them, Eklimondus heard distantly in his head, as if overhearing a whisper from a league away. Without breaking contact with Wollof and his coin, Eklimondus led the way down the steps from the upper deck and joined the crew. As their hands touched and the coins clanked together metallically, the dancing golden cloud changed suddenly to the purest black.

"At last!" Bursting from the column stood a Midknight, clad in armor darker than a starless night and brandishing a longsword that trailed tiny black teardrops as he swung it through the air.

"The coins of Darkun," Eklimondus gasped out. "You stole them!"

"I stole the most precious treasure a god can possess," the Midknight crowed. "From under his seaweed-clogged nose I stole the coins. Now I will exact my revenge on him."

"On Darkun? What business do you have with a god?" Eklimondus tried to pull his hand away but the coins welded him to the rest of his crew. Tendons standing in bold relief on his arm, blood vessels at the bursting point in his neck, Eklimondus finally relented. Better to save his power.

"The triton-god destroyed my entire family. We had just seized a floating city of forty ships built by the Megashark Clan—"

"They were Darkun's disciples!" Eklimondus blurted.

"The triton-god rose from the sea and used his trident to kill my brothers relentlessly. Only I and a handful of others escaped his wrath. We vowed to destroy all that Darkun held dear."

"Suspendere," Eklimondus whispered. "Darkun favors the floating island and moves it about for those who worship him. You will destroy it. But how?"

"How?" The Midknight laughed without humor. "I stole his treasure and I will use it to destroy his most precious island and with it, all his followers. When I cast the coins onto the land of Suspendere, Darkun's power will be sapped. He will either have to drop the island from his back or perish under its weight. Either will satisfy me."

"Kill his disciples or kill a god."

"He will regret ever having touched a Midknight sorcerer."

"How will the gold coins rob him of godly power?" Eklimondus asked. He twisted and turned, trying to win free of the powerful bond with Wollof and the rest of his crew. If he freed himself, he was only a sword thrust away from the Midknight. In spite of the knight's shining black armor, Eklimondus knew he could kill if he worked his sword tip under the arm and into the torso.

"I learned the spells controlling the coins. That is how I came to seize the merchanteer. The coins allow a bit of my soul to enter and dominate anyone touching the gold. If I scatter the coins across Suspendere, I can draw a bit of the god's soul into each coin. With all of the gold coins dispersed, Darkun will be torn apart."

"What if this isn't Suspendere?"

"Don't try to gull me, Captain. I forced you to return to your home port. I made your first mate fetch the chart. I forced the crew to sail. I forced *you* to return to your precious floating island."

"The Mero," Wollof gasped out. "It could have taken us to Suspendere, but you destroyed it!" The first mate stared wide-eyed at Eklimondus.

Eklimondus looked at the Al-Kabarian and nodded. Wollof began to understand. Megan Farsight could have navigated the *Sea Blade* back to Suspendere, also. And the chart had seemed . . . wrong. Because it *was*. Eklimondus had personally burned the original and replaced it with the chart leading to this island.

"But it floats!" Wollof jerked savagely, trying to free himself. The power of Darkun's coins held him as surely as if he had been put into manacles. "I saw that it glided just above the water!"

"What are you saying?" The Midknight grabbed Wollof by the throat and squeezed. "This *is* Suspendere, isn't it?"

"Yes . . . No . . . I don't know!" The Al-Kabarian began to sag as the Midknight squeezed the life from him.

Eklimondus awkwardly drew his sword left-handed and slashed. He could not perform the needed thrust to penetrate the Midknight's vile heart, but the slash against an armored wrist forced the knight to release Wollof. The first mate gasped for air.

"This *is* Suspendere?" The Midknight reached over, batted Eklimondus' sword from his hand and grabbed him by the throat. "I need to know. Did you bring me back to your home port?"

Eklimondus gagged as mailed fingers clamped down on his windpipe.

"Tell me!" raged the Midknight.

The pressure on his throat suddenly vanished. Eklimondus fell back and sat heavily on the deck. He saw that all his crew had been simultaneously released from the binding power of the coins. The Midknight fought to keep his balance as the deck heaved, and the *Sea Blade* began to spin around.

Eklimondus saw his sword sliding away. He dived, belly down, and wrapped his hand around the familiar sharkskin-covered hilt. Slamming hard into the railing, the captain got to his feet—and looked down over the side into a vortex that had to extend to the bottom of the world. The *Sea Blade* was sucked down into the swirling funnel and spun about faster and faster until it was all he could do to hang onto the railing with both hands. Behind him he heard the frightened cries of his crew as they were thrown about and pinned against the railings, too.

Most of all he heard the anguished screech of the Midknight.

The warrior would need more than reincarnation to escape this trap. Eklimondus heard Darkun's roar and then saw the triton-god rise above the railing. Behind the seaweed-trailing fish-tailed god whirled a solid wall of ugly green water pulling the barque down with inexorable power.

Eklimondus tried to close his eyes against the awful visage of his island's god but could not. Darkun roared in anger and stabbed out with his trident.

The black-armored Midknight swung his sword double-handed and parried the thrust. Darkun spun the trident about as if the ponderous weapon were nothing more than a dried stick. The second thrust sent the center point of the trident through the Midknight's body.

Eklimondus swallowed hard when he realized the penetration did not kill—it only impaled. The Midknight was still alive and kicking feebly as Darkun lifted him from the deck and tossed him into the center of the vortex. Still, Eklimondus wanted to avert his eyes from Darkun's horrific visage but could not.

He stared directly into the god's sea-green eyes.

And he knew. He *knew*.

Eklimondus sprawled on the deck in the hot sun, slowly regaining his senses. All about him moaned and sobbed his crew. Men who had seen death and laughed at it now cried openly, without guilt. He crawled on hands and knees to Wollof. The first mate lay twisted at a crazy angle. Eklimondus touched him, and the Al-Kabarian jerked straight and tried to scuttle away like a crab. Seeing his captain, Wollof fell to the deck.

"I saw Darkun," he said in a choked voice.

"I did more than see a god," Eklimondus said. He sat cross-legged on the deck, his legs still not strong enough to let him stand. "I spoke with him."

"Spoke? What happened? Did Darkun tell you what—?"

"He did," Eklimondus said. His mind had been permanently etched with the god's description of what would be done to the Midknight—and what would be done to the captain and crew of the *Sea Blade*.

Eklimondus opened his hand. The coin of Darkun was embedded in his flesh. As he stared wide-eyed at it, he heard gasps from the crew. Their coins were similarly driven with cruel force into their hands.

"It is Darkun's gift for delivering to him the thief of his treasure."

"How do we get rid of the coin?" Wollof shook his hand and then drew a dagger, ready to cut it free. Eklimondus stopped him.

"It's Darkun's gift we all carry, not his curse. None of us can ever drown as long as the coins remain in our palms."

"I can't even swim," one crewman said. "You think that—aieee!"

Two of the crew picked up their mate and tossed him overboard. In spite of wobbly knees, Eklimondus pulled himself to standing and looked over the side. The crewman who could not swim walked on the waves, wobbling about as the ocean heaved and surged under him.

"It's like walkin' on sand!"

"Get him aboard," Eklimondus ordered. "It's time to return to Suspendere."

"How do we do that, Captain?" asked Wollof. "You burned the chart. Finding the floating island is nigh on impossible without it."

Eklimondus took his first mate's arm and drew him to the bow.

"The figurehead's back!" cried Wollof. "The Mero has been restored!"

"Aye," said Eklimondus. "Darkun is a merciful god—to those who honor him." He turned and bellowed orders for the crew to get into the rigging and set the sails.

Anba Eklimondus held out his right hand and let the sunlight reflect off the coin embedded there. He and his crew could never drown—and the Midknight would spend an eternity doing nothing but that. Darkun was as cruel as he was merciful.

"We've got good wind and full sail, Captain," Wollof reported.

"Then let's follow the Mero for home!" The sooner the *Sea Blade* returned to Suspendere, the sooner he could assure his brother that their patron god was pleased.

THE DREAD PIRATE FUZZYTAIL
by J. Robert King

Ask what ship is most feared on the Azure Sea, and any man with a brain in his pan will say *Reaper*. She is a ghost ship, crewed by unseen hands and rapacious for gold.

A mere glimpse of her black sails brings an "All hands!" and drives the rudder to the boom and sends men scrambling up the ratlines to gather the wind and flee. Some few ships escape, but if *Reaper* sets her blood-red bow to them, the end is doom.

Seamen can only watch in horror as the empty ship closes and rams and staves; can only grasp at hunks of their ruined vessel as the unseen ghosts sweep aboard with a keening wail that maddens the ears of the living; can only gibber and gape as every last bit of gold skitters up from holds and across the deck and into *Reaper*; can only go down with their sinking ship or ride the tide in hopes of rescue or lose their grips and drift down to the fathomless dark.

Reaper is the scourge of the sea, and I was sent to stop her.

I am Captain Wade Sutherland of the *Avenging Angel*, hired by merchants and kings to save their precious ships. But I am more than a mercenary. I'm a priest and a sworn foe of the occult powers—and I am the son of Captain Theodore Sutherland, whose ship was sunk with all hands . . . by *Reaper*.

Today, I will destroy the ghost ship.

"Black sails!" comes the cry from the crow's nest. "Black sails!"

"All hands!" I reply, ringing the bell at the helm.

Crew pour up from the hatches and gaze out at a white-blue sky and a black-blue sea. I meanwhile lift the captain's glass to my eye and peer a quarter off starboard.

The ghost ship lurks on the horizon: black sails in brigantine rig, stepped masts, lines in a tangle . . . I see a glint of glass near *Reaper*'s helm and have the uncanny sensation that it is the ghost captain's glass.

I cannot see him, but he sees me.

"Mr. Compton, bring us about. Thirty degrees starboard! Men, trim us into a beat to bear on her!"

The helmsman drags on the wheel, and the mates drag on the lines, but the eyes of the men gape with dread. When I hired them, I explained they would be hunting ghosts. But now that *Reaper* hangs on the horizon, my crew fumbles about as if they were dead already.

"Captain Sutherland!" cries the man at the tops. "She's turning on us. She'll take us head-on."

"No!" I say savagely. "We'll take *her* head-on."

Compton at the helm holds the heading, but his eyes flit from our bow to our foes. "The guns, Captain. We've got but one that can sweep fore. *Reaper's* got six."

I nod, staring through the glass at that hateful ship. Its black bow spanks the white billows, and already the cannon bays open and the muzzles point our way. "One good shot is all we'll need. One good shot. . . ."

"But they'll have six good ones before we close, and six more before we land a ball."

I lift the holy symbol of Ghede: a compass rose bound by a chain. "Ghede will lock the gates between the living and the dead. The ghosts will be warded from our ship, and they will not be able to drag us to death." Even as I say it, there is doubt in me. My father wore just such an emblem on his throat when the ghost ship took him. Ghede didn't save Theodore, so why would he save me? Still, I hoist the symbol high and cry, "Release the banners!"

Men amble out along the yards and loose the lashes and let fall great banners that bear the symbol of Ghede. The emblems stripe every sail. *Avenging Angel* takes on the raiment of a priest.

"*Reaper's* running fast, Captain," Compton tells me. "She's eating up the sea. We should turn leeward to catch more wind." His hand shifts on the helm, but I drag the wheel back.

"She wants to drive us into a run so she can ram alongside," I snarl. "Stay the course and meet her head-on!"

With sheets cleated and rudder chains champing against the swells, we hold a hard line on *Reaper* and swoop toward her as any *Avenging Angel* should. While Compton braces his arm on the wheel, I brace my soul on the immortal champions:

I call to Ghede, the Harbormaster, that he might bind the harbor between life and death.

I call to Osir, the Keeper of Souls, that he might draw the dead down into the Underworld.

I call to Shi, the Dancer between Life and Death, to give me a glimpse of my dead father.

All the while that I summon the guardian spirits, the killing ghosts rush toward us. *Reaper* draws near. A wave breaks across her red ram and makes it drip as if with blood. From a cannon on one side of the prow, gray smoke blooms into the air. The shot shrieks toward us.

" 'Ware the main!" cries the man in the crow's nest, and a moment later a cannonball strikes the sail and punches through the holy symbol of Ghede.

Ghede, where are you?

Reaper's cannons unleash more shrieking iron. One ball shatters the starboard rail. Another strikes the tops, and the man who gave the warning plunges to the deck with a crunch.

So much for immortal champions. . . .

"Fire!" I cry to the fore gunner.

He sets the charge to the fuse, and the cannon blasts and yanks back in its chains. The ball roars out over the churning deep but then falls, impotent missile, a hundred yards before the red ram of *Reaper*.

She is closing fast.

Her bow cannons speak again: three starboard and three port, and all six belching iron above the waves. Cannonballs smash into our prow. They penetrate the foc's'le and boom in it and roll like thunder. Splinters and shredded tatters of hammock fly up from the hatch.

"We're breached!" shouts the fore gunner. He leans at the port rail and stares down. "The sea's coming in!"

Compton spins the helm, and wind spills from our sails, and *Avenging Angel* heels toward starboard.

"Away!" I shout, knocking Compton to the deck and cranking the helm back to bear on our foe.

He cowers below me and stares up in shock. "The bow's shattered! We're taking on sea! You can't hold us in this list, or you'll drive us to the bottom."

"I'll drive us to *Reaper*," I snarl even as the wind bellies our sails again.

The ghost ship bounds toward us now, so near I can see the rats scuttling up her lines. The moment our prow aligns again with hers, I cry: "Fire!"

Our own gun blasts, and the ball sails out as before. This time, though, I can tell it is not an iron ball, but crystal. The glass globe arcs over the rail of *Reaper* and crashes down amidships. A perfect shot—and the crystal shatters and sprays out its payload of holy water.

This is blessed by Ghede from the sacred spring. This is water to drive the souls of the undead back to their briny graves.

My men cheer to see the killing stroke so delivered. Their cries of joy are overtopped only by an angry keening—ghosts in torment. I stare avidly at *Reaper*. Any moment, the spirits of the dead will peel away from her and she will fall off course, and my employers will have all the gold in her hold.

And I will have two ships instead of one.

But the ghosts do not leave the ship, and *Reaper* does not fall off course. She is almost upon us. Her black sails blot out the sky, and her cannons blaze again. Six iron missiles crash through our bow and rip out the foc's'le bulwark and rebound amidships. A wave follows the iron and pours brine across our decks.

"Ghede, protect us!" I cry.

Reaper dives before us, surging into a trough. Her blood-red ram disappears below our bowsprit, and her deck displays a swarm of scabby rats. Then she mounts up the wave beneath us, and with a profound boom, drives her ram through the breast of our bow.

The deck leaps and steals my feet from me, and I fall to my knees—I and my crew on our knees before the wicked spirits.

Still *Reaper* rises. Timbers boom and planks snap, and out of the fo'c's'le deck erupts that blood-red ram.

"We've been staved!" shouts Compton as he scuttles away from me. "We're wide open to the sea."

The crew run for the landing boats. I watch them go—abandoning ship, but I must go down with it.

The captain must.

Avenging Angel is hardly a ship anymore; she's merely a wreck that hasn't yet sunk.

The crew jostle past me, their fingers rammed in their ears. Already I hear the keening wail begin. It rises, maddening, a shrieking sound as of a hundred whistles sounding at once. But I do not deserve to plug my ears.

I deserve to go mad.

I have failed my crew, my employers, myself. I have failed my father. Ghede did not chain the gates between life and death, and the dead are coming through to take me with them.

As men jump down into the landing boats or into the sea, the keen redoubles and shatters the lanterns all along the rail. The ghosts sweep unseen aboard, bringing with them a hundred scuttling rats.

At last, I clutch my hands to my ears, but it is too late for me. Already, I am going mad.

The rats seem to be wearing clothes. They seem to be running on two legs and swinging little cutlasses and drinking grog from little tankards. They swagger, these mice, and they sing a shrill and horrible song:

The ghosts of the Azure Sea
Have got their claws into me!
We slit a man's throat and chitter and gloat.
We gather our gold and fill up our hold,
The ghosts of the Azure Sea!

With a great crack, *Reaper*'s ram rips through the remains of our bow and vaults free. *Avenging Angel* rolls to the fore, and the sea bubbles up through her hatches, and she starts to sink.

I cling to the helm as we go down, rats all around me. And then I know I am truly mad, for one of those rats shakes the water from his fur and suddenly seems a squirrel and says to me, "Wade?"

I lose hold of the helm and lose hold of consciousness.

For a time, I know nothing. All is black.

But then a light dawns in the center of the darkness—a bright, beaming light that grows gradually to fill the whole world. I blink and see that the light is a sky filled with rolling white clouds.

I must be in the heavenly realm of the gods. The champions must be here, waiting for me: Ghede, the Harbormaster, who opened the gates to draw me from life to death; Osir, the Keeper of Souls, who will write my name in his book; and Shi, the Dancer between Life and Death, who will show me my father at last.

"Father. Father!" I cry.

"Hewantstoseehisfather!" someone says, very rapidly, in a shrill, small voice.

I startle and sit up. The heavenly clouds turn out to be only regular clouds in a regular sky. And I turn out to be very much alive—and captive. Shackles chain my hands and feet to the base of a mainmast: the mainmast of the ghost ship, *Reaper.*

"No!" I cry.

"NevermindwhatIsaid. Hedoesn'twanttoseehisfather."

The rats of the ship surround me, and they are indeed standing on their hind legs, and they do indeed wear little greatcoats and carry little swords— and they are, indeed . . .

Squirrels.

"It's madness," I murmur to myself. This is the very phantasm reported by any survivor of an attack by *Reaper*—that the ghost ship is actually a squirrel ship! "Madness."

"Madness, indeed, todriveashipintotheveryteethof*Reaper.*" The speaker is a squirrel with an eye-patch, a fierce grin centering on a pair of busted teeth, a stout body buttoned into a tiny greatcoat, and a bushy tail that twitches angrily behind him.

I blink and say, "What?"

"Itismadnesstodriveashipintotheveryteethof*Reaper!*"

His shrill voice is like a needle piercing my ear and brain and other ear to transfix my head. "Slow down. I can't understand you."

"Speedup. Ican'tunderstandyou."

I grip my hair in my fingers. "WHAT ARE YOU SAYING?"

"What'reyousaying?"

We both sigh explosively and shout, "You're insane!"

A terrible silence follows these words, and then a terrible gasp comes from the hundred squirrel mouths that surround me. These tiny pirates are offended. They draw their little swords and growl little growls at me.

Their leader stands to full height—perhaps nine and a half inches—and fills his lungs with a cupful of air and begins a ferocious oration. "Wearenotinsane. Wearesmall, yes. Wearefuzzy, yes. Wearesquirrels, yes, butwearenotinsane. Itisnotacrimetobeasquirrel!"

"No," I agree, somewhat following his rapid-fire words." It is not a crime to be a squirrel. But it *is* a crime to be a pirate."

The miniscule marauders laugh heartily at that, pleased with their infamy.

I add significantly, "And, it is an even *greater* crime to be a pirate *squirrel.*"

A roar of puny fury answers my words, and many of the squirrels step toward me with swords raised, ready to kill me with a thousand cuts. Still, the one-eyed pirate captain spreads his arms to hold off the rodent horde and begins his speech again.

I listen closely, as every madman eventually does to his madness, and find that I can understand him.

"What difference is there between us, Captain Wade Sutherland? I am small and you are big—but the whole world fears me, and no one fears you. You are free of fur while I am covered—and yet you are in chains, and I am free. You are a freemariner and a priest sent to destroy a ghost ship, and I am a pirate squirrel and the terror of the high seas. You have everything in your favor, but you have failed. I have nothing to commend me, but I have succeeded." Now, he steps very close to my face. "I am the Dread Pirate Fuzzytail! Do not address me as a squirrel again, or your throat will spill across my deck."

Whenever a madman listens closely to his madness, he hears speeches such as these. He also finds himself asking absurd questions.

"You mean to tell me that the ghost ship *Reaper* is actually crewed by . . . squirrels?"

"Look around you," says the Dread Pirate Fuzzytail.

I do, and see gray squirrels and fox squirrels and not a few chipmunks, all of them fixing me with an angry stare that tells of their oppression by large, bald-skinned folk like me. Still, I have doubts. "You mean to say that a thousand ships and a million bars of gold have been stolen not by ghosts but by . . . squirrels?"

In answer, the Dread Pirate Fuzzytail strides through the rodent crowd, sinks his sharp nails into the mizzen hatch, and hurls it back.

Below lies a miracle.

I stare into a hold filled from front to back and side to side with a treasure that would make a dragon blush.

Now, only one question remains: "How?"

Fuzzytail ambles toward me, using his cutlass as a cane. "Squirrels are better pirates than men. We climb at four times the speed, pull lines with all the strength, and gather gold like acorns. But humans cannot admit that we overmatch them. They invent tales of ghosts to explain how they are bested by rodents.

"We are the victims of those tales, but we cannot end them. So we use them to terrify humans, to destroy their ships and take their wealth—and anyone who honestly reports that squirrels have done all this is deemed mad."

It all makes sense. Squirrel terrorism. Humans think they are up against ghosts, and so they fight using the power of gods. But in fact our foes are flesh and blood, are creatures misunderstood and demonized. Gods are powerless against fellow mortals, and so the squirrels use human ignorance to take our gold and sink our ships.

Still, Captain Fuzzytail has not answered part of my question. "How did you . . . how did squirrels get a ship? How did you become such . . . infamous pirates?"

Fuzzytail nods and smiles his broken-toothed smile. He carries a large key to me, sets it to my shackles, and twists. The irons fall to the deck. "Follow me." Winking, Captain Fuzzytail leaps down through the hatch, atop the pile of gold and silver, and gestures for me to follow.

I do, though it is not a leap for me but a simple step. The next part of our journey, though, is easier for Fuzzytail than for me. The squirrel pirate scuttles away across coins and crowns and strings of pearls, his furry ears only brushing the beams of the mizzen deck. I must crawl. The treasure trove bites into my hands and knees, and the rafters scratch my back.

We crawl down past the reach of light, past countless piles of looted gold and into the deep darkness. When at last Captain Fuzzytail halts, we are in a small chamber half-filled with loot and filled the rest of the way with stale air.

A light flares in the paw of the squirrel pirate, and he lifts a jackstraw to a lantern mounted on the wall. The lantern ignites and sends its golden beams down across an amazing sight.

A huge chest stands before us. Iron braces stripe its lid, and atop the lid looms a golden statue of a squirrel rampant—reared up with forepaws splayed and mouth gaping in warning.

Captain Fuzzytail smiles and gestures broadly. "This was our first true treasure. Before this booty, we were pirates in name only. Before this treasure, we were not squirrels, but men.

"Yellowbeard had been our captain, and a good one, with a large trove. But when the freemariners found the trove, Yellowbeard risked all to save it. In the fray, he took a bullet in the face and fell to the deck."

The Dread Pirate Fuzzytail draws a deep breath. "Pirate ships are democracies . . . and democracies are pirate ships. We'd lost our captain, and so we voted to elect a new one . . ."

☠ ☠ ☠

Longnose Pete, a man whose nostrils could hide a pair of chipmunks, stood on the poop deck and shouted down to his human comrades—the crew of *Reaper*. "All who want Freddy Zale as captain, cry aye!"

"Aye!" shouted the pirates all around me on the deck.

The vote was unanimous. Captain Zale, was I, then? I'd been Yellowbeard's first mate, but now it was my turn at the helm.

Pete waved me up beside him, "Come on, Captain, and tell us where we're bound!"

I passed among the men and mounted the stair. "Where we're bound is privileged information, suitable only to my first mate—" I clapped Pete on the shoulder, and then pointed to Sloan One-Eye down below "—and to my navigator. You two, come with me!"

As we headed to the captain's quarters, the rest of the crew howled with disappointment.

Pete puffed out his chest and said, "Avast, you dogs! You'll get your share of the loot—but not of the location!"

I, Pete, and Sloan entered the captain's cabin and locked the door behind us and turned our backs to the faces that leered in the glass and unrolled a map of the South Azure Sea.

"Here's the place: Isla Luna." I pointed to the map.

Pete rubbed his hand on his bristly jaw. "But, Cap'n Zale," he tapped the empty spot, "there's no island there."

I smiled. "Not now, there isn't. Isla Luna is a disappearing island. It's there only one night of the year—the night of the autumnal equinox."

"One night a year . . ." Pete said in wonder.

"Which makes it a perfect trove island. It's not on any map, and only a handful of seafarers have even heard of it. I'm the only one left who can find it."

"A trove island, aye?" Pete said. "Whose trove?"

I lowered my voice to a whisper: "The Golden Hoard of Redwhiskers!"

"No!" both men gasped. Redwhiskers had been the terror of the high seas a full century before, and every pirate's heart lusted for his fabled hoard.

"It's been a hundred years since Redwhiskers sailed," Sloan pointed out. "Are you sure the gold's not been pillaged already?"

"Yellowbeard believed it was still there. He said men had tried to take the treasure, but none had succeeded. The island's hidden, as you know, but it's also cursed. Any man who sets foot on the island must not only find the treasure, but also take it before sunrise—or be turned to stone."

Pete snuffled at this, and he dragged the kerchief from his brow, mopped out each nostril of his long nose, and put the kerchief back. "What makes you think we can find it?"

"Yellowbeard had a map to the Golden Hoard, but he hid it away from everyone—even me. After he died, though, I found it—tucked away safe beside his very heart." I reached into my pocket and drew the thing out: a small square of pale leather about the size of a man's hand, with blue lines forming a crescent-shaped island. Occasional tufts sprouted from the island, looking like palm trees, though they were in fact Yellowbeard's chest hair.

"A tattoo over his heart." Pete grinned. "Yellowbeard surely must've believed in this treasure."

Sloan took the little leather map from my hand and fitted it to the empty spot on the large map. Then he walked his fingers from our current location to the spot where Isla Luna should be. "If we sail hard, we can reach these coordinates in three weeks' time."

I nod: "On the day of the autumnal equinox."

We sailed hard, and three weeks later to the day, we arrived at a spot of empty sea. The sun was just setting, and the night of the equinox was about to begin.

"Drop anchor!" I cried.

The crew let fly the capstan, and the chain paid out to its full depth—thirty fathoms—and yanked taut. The anchor had not touched bottom. We drifted half a league before it caught and held. Then Pete ordered a crew of twelve strong men to lower the landing boat and get within.

"Landing? Landing where?" the men grumbled. "The captain's led us to nowhere!"

"Shut your gobs and train your eyes on the sunset," Pete advised.

As the great red orb sank down like a bleeding heart, the twelve men climbed down the ladder into the landing boat and waited for me to join them—while they murmured of mutiny. But the moment the sun slipped below the rim of the world, a cry went up from the crow's nest: "Land ho!"

Bewildered, the men spun about to see a small, rocky island directly astern. *Reaper* floated in her crescent-shaped bay. The men gawked for a moment before someone shouted, "The ship's drifting!"

"The bottom's come up!" I replied. "Bring in the anchor chain!"

The men at the capstan cranked until they felt the weight of the anchor—a mere three fathoms down.

"We've not a moment to spare," I said, swinging my leg over the rail and descending the ladder to the landing boat. Pete and Sloan followed after, and the twelve strong men already in the boat set oars to the waves and drove us toward the island.

And what a forbidding island it was. The rocks of Isla Luna showed no signs of life—not tree nor shrub nor coney. But all across those gray stones stood plenty of signs of death: white statues that once had been men. They all had been caught by the dawn—all without the fabled loot. As we drew nearer, we could see legs frozen midstride, arms flung wide in running, desperate faces locked on the water that they would never reach.

"We're risking everything, Captain," said Sloan under his breath.

"We're pirates," I replied, and then commanded, "Put ashore there!"

Our boat ran aground on the gravelly rocks, and as night deepened, we lit and lifted lanterns. I used mine to shine on the leather map in my hand. I led my men ashore. They were, of course, terrified to walk among those statues—graves and gravestones in one, but I cared not. I wished only for the Golden Hoard.

In time, the map led us into a box canyon that ended in a great wall of stone. The wall was too steep to climb, the defile too narrow to allow any other passage. Clearly we could not go forward.

"There's nothing here!" a crewman grumbled.

I ignored him, raised my lantern to study the gray wall, and saw a tiny white pebble wedged in a crack of it. "Here's something: a finger bone."

"A finger bone?"

I nodded. "And the only way a finger bone would be wedged in a crack like that is if the stone had slammed shut on it."

Fetching a stick, I wedged it into the crack and pried. More men added their sticks and strength, and in time the stone rolled back. The finger bone—and the skeleton it belonged to—tumbled out at our feet.

Beyond was a cave mouth sealed in cobwebs.

"The cave of treasure," I said in vindication. "Hack those webs away, and in we go!"

With cutlasses swinging and lanterns lifted high, we wended our way into the cave. Along the route, we found more skeletons, their hand bones clenched in fists.

Longnose Pete eyed them warily. "We'll have to avoid the mistakes they made."

At last, we came to an inner chamber with a strange chest—broad and tall and topped with a golden statue of a fierce squirrel. On the wall above the statue, a strange inscription was carved into the rock:

"Take but a single acorn from my horde, and ye will die this day."

I flashed a smile at that fierce-looking squirrel, winked at him, and lifted the lid. The chest was filled with gold in the shape of acorns. Delighted, I reached toward the pile, but a shout stayed my hand.

"Look!" cried Sloan, crouching beside a skeleton in one corner. He pried open the skeleton's hand and plucked up a golden acorn. "It's got a nugget, see?" Sloan lifted the golden acorn above his grinning face.

Next moment, though, Sloan's mouth sagged open in shock, and then his flesh turned gray and fell to ash and sloughed away. In an instant, my navigator was reduced to a heap of bones, the golden acorn clutched in his skeletal hand.

I drew my fingers back from the cursed treasure and let the lid drop closed. "No one touch the acorns!"

"We have to get out of here!" someone shouted.

"Belay that!" I said. "Any man who leaves without the treasure will be turned to stone. Come along now. Every man grab a corner of this chest."

They gathered round and set their fingers and heaved, but the chest would not move. Twelve strong men couldn't move it!

I called them off and growled and nodded, staring at that rampant squirrel. "If we take your acorns, we turn to ash. If we fail to take them, we turn to stone." I felt as if that damned squirrel were winking at me.

Only then did I notice the cobwebs on the wall behind him. Part of the inscription had been obscured. I blew, and spider silk and ash fell away from a new group of words below the first:

"'Take all, and ye will have the blessing of the folk that gathered this gold.'"

That was the secret. Some men had tried to take but a few acorns, and they had fallen to ash. Others had tried to take the whole chest, but they couldn't budge it because some of the acorns had already been removed. "To escape with our lives, we have to take the whole hoard."

I walked to the skeleton of my navigator, reached down to grip his arm bone and twisted it free. Then I turned and bashed the grisly prize on the edge of the treasure chest. The acorn fell from Sloan's hand and back into the hoard.

"Spread out, boys! Search through the cave and find the skeletons and bring their bones here so that every last acorn can be accounted. Then we'll be able to lift this chest and escape with our lives—and the Golden Hoard of Redwhiskers!"

☠   ☠   ☠

"You took it all," I say.

"We took it all," confirms Fuzzytail, holding out his squirrel hand to indicate the treasure in the chest. "We took it from Isla Luna and rowed it back to our ship before the sun rose. As dawn broke, the island vanished from sight, and the seabed pulled away from our anchor, and we were adrift again. But we were rich, and we were pirates!"

I smile ruefully. To think I'd asked for Ghede and Osir and Shi to save me from the likes of squirrels! "When did you stop being men?"

"When we awoke the next morning, the Golden Hoard of Redwhiskers had worked a strange magic upon us. That was the true meaning of the second part of the inscription: 'Take all, and ye will have the blessing of the folk that gathered this gold.'"

"Blessing?"

"Yes, for Redwhiskers himself had been a squirrel pirate. That's him atop the chest. When he died, his crew coated him in gold and set him to guard his hoard forever."

I laugh. "Why didn't you just take the treasure back and reclaim your humanity?"

"Isla Luna would not return for another year. We were stuck in squirrel form until then. And so the Dread Pirate Freddy Zale became the Dread Pirate Fuzzytail.

"That year taught us Redwhiskers' secret: that squirrels make excellent pirates. We could outsail any ship, and every crew of men thought we were ghosts. We pillaged what we wished, and in a scant year, our empty hold has been filled with loot."

My good humor fades. "But you didn't steal just gold. You took lives— the lives of the seamen you sank. The life of my father!"

Fuzzytail fixes me with a solemn expression. "Yes. We took his life. Not that we killed him, but that we let him stay with us, and the treasure took hold of him: Your father is a squirrel pirate."

I hear furtive footsteps on the gold behind me, and turn to see a most familiar squirrel. He has great round eyes nestled in wrinkled brows, a grinning mouth ringed in silver whiskers, a scrawny neck and scrawnier shoulders and a withered body.

"Dad!"

The old squirrel smiles and hobbles onto my hand. I lift him, and he reaches out his squirrel hands to embrace my neck. "Son!"

I never hoped to see him again, to feel his embrace. But his little claws are sharp. I pull him back. "You're a squirrel."

"I'm happy," he says with a shrug. "And you will be, too."

"What?" I ask.

The Dread Pirate Fuzzytail steps up between us. "By tomorrow morning, you'll be a squirrel like us."

"What if I don't want to be a squirrel?"

Fuzzytail nods. "There's one final line in the blessing—inscribed right here within the chest: 'Bring me back my own, and ye'll become ye're own.'

If any squirrel takes an acorn from the horde and returns it to the cave, he will regain his humanity and can leave the island safely. Some of my men are doing just that tomorrow night—when the autumnal equinox brings Isla Luna back."

The sun is setting above us, and the gold-filled hold turns gray with twilight. I grasp my father's tiny hand and say, "Let's see what comes tomorrow."

☠ ☠ ☠

The morning brings wonders!

"I'm a squirrel!"

Look how fast I climb! My claws sink into the ratlines and my legs shoot me up to the flags on the main faster than I could have fallen down as a man. And see how I can leap out on the wind and slow myself with the rush of air under my fur and can catch hold of this sail or that and scamper down the lines and be on deck again with no questions asked?

The morning seems to last forever. With three hundred heartbeats a minute, everything around me seems five times as slow—but only because I'm five times as fast.

And look at Dad! I thought he was dead, but no! Look at how he scampers beside me up the spanker and along the line to the mizzen and main and fore and spinnaker and down to the bowsprit where we both lounge and feel the spray of the billows on our fur as *Reeper* surges along.

By the way—that's the real spelling. R-E-E-P-E-R, like the sound we make—Reep! Reep! I'd always thought it was spelled like the Grim Reaper, but I guess that's because I was human, and humans see only what they expect to see, right down to the spelling.

Oh, it's grand to be a squirrel at sea, to be a squirrel pirate!

But ahead lurks decision. The sun has quitted the world, and Isla Luna has just appeared from the sea floor and enwrapped us in her arms. Some of us will drop to the sea in landing craft and will row to the island with golden acorns in our grips and will put the things back where they had once been and will walk away as human beings. Others will stay on the ship and remain rodents.

"What do you want, Dad?" I ask as the two of us perch together on the prow rail, looking at the beautiful, statue-studded island before us.

"For a whole year, I've wanted this," he says, and my heart sinks, because I think he talks about becoming human again. "For a whole year, I've wanted to sit here on the prow rail beside you."

My little squirrel eyes grow wide with tears, and I have to look away and dash them surreptitiously and pretend I am only cleaning my whiskers. And so Dad and I sit quietly while the landing boat fills with nineteen squirrels who row ashore, each carrying an acorn in his hand and a hope in his heart of being human again.

They row ashore and climb from the boat and disappear into the crescent land of Isla Luna, and I can only feel sorry for them. They will go from being the terrors of the high seas to being simply people.

The night wears on. The dawn approaches. The landing boat shoves out from shore, and the nineteen who went return. In the shadows and the sadness of this moment, I do not realize until the boat bumps alongside *Reeper* that it holds only squirrels, and that they hold golden acorns as they scamper up the ladder and down into the hold and put back the nuggets.

I look to my father and smile, and he returns the look. And Fuzzytail himself mirrors the expression on his busted teeth. He says simply, "All claws on deck! Action stations, you rats! Let's find us another ship of men and show them what it means to be real pirates!"

CYREN'S EYES
by Kathleen Watness

In the darkest corner of the seediest tavern in the Razor Islands, he found them. At least, Cyren hoped that this man and woman were the right ones; sometimes it was difficult to sort out the strands of possibilities that wound through the present into the future.

His left hand closed over the plump leather pouch that hung from his belt. The fingers of his right brushed across a dark blue pearl, the size of his thumb joint, that hung around his neck on a fine strand of braided silver. He twisted left and stepped, light as sea spray, over a sailor snoring just past the tavern's entrance. Another step and an empty rum bottle sailed through the space where his head had been a heartbeat before. The bottle thudded off the bare chest of a burly, black-haired man missing half an ear.

Drawing a long, thin dagger, Black Hair charged at the bottle tosser. Folk scattered.

Cyren scrambled to a table shoved against a plastered wall. He clutched the end of the table, while the world around him tilted and blurred, shrouding him in a white fog. When his sight cleared, he saw Black Hair staring down the length of a crossbow. The woman tending the bar aimed at Black Hair's heart.

"Put it up, Dorn," the barkeep said to him.

Dorn's lip curled, and he waved his dagger at a tall, sinewy man with lank brown hair holding a glittering, leaf-bladed dagger in each hand—the man who'd thrown the bottle. The barkeep's dark eyes never left Dorn's face.

"You too, Oman," she hissed. "In fact, since you broke peace, I think it's best you leave."

"He came after me."

"You threw the bottle, Oman."

"Wasn't aimin' for him," Oman muttered.

Cyren frowned. He'd been the target? He wasn't sure how to read the dark thoughts that flickered through Oman's black eyes.

"I don't care who you were aiming for, Oman. Just get out."

Between one eye blink and the next Oman sheathed his fancy daggers. He strode from the room, never looking to either side. A half dozen men and women followed in his wake. Dorn scowled at his back, and only slipped his own dagger back into its sheath when Oman and his crew had cleared the tavern.

The barkeep lowered her crossbow and loosed a breath.

Around Cyren, folk resumed interrupted conversations. There was the rattle of dice cups and the dull thunk of mugs being set down.

Cyren released the table and flushed when he noticed the barkeep grinning at him. The grin widened and she waved him over. He shook his head and stepped back, turning toward the door. Best to leave and let things settle before he approached the couple in the corner.

Dorn glided up and gripped Cyren's arm above the elbow. He smiled, gently turned Cyren around, and pointed at the frothy mug the barkeep had just set out.

"No, thank you. I appreciate the offer, but—" Cyren started.

Still smiling, Dorn tugged at his arm. Cyren hung back, but only for a moment. He'd rouse more attention by refusing. He risked a quick glance at the two he'd found. Their heads bent close in whispered conversation made it easy to compare their features. Both shared curly brown hair, the man's long enough to tie back. Though the woman's was cropped short, it suited her. The similar angle of their jaws and the fine straight noses just a breath apart meant only one thing—siblings.

Dorn slapped Cyren on the back and mimed drinking.

The barkeep pushed the mug closer.

"Name's An," she said, then drew another mug and set it by Dorn.

Cyren hesitated, then shrugged. The barkeep wasn't one of his, so to her his true name was only a name.

"Cyren."

She chuckled. She laughed easily, this woman with light brown hair streaked with gray and fine lines defining the corners of her eyes. Cyren decided he liked her; though he wasn't sure if he liked the drink. It fizzled unpleasantly on his tongue and tasted like something used to strip barnacles. But he smiled politely and nodded at An's inquiring look. He understood that much of mortal courtesy, at least.

An leaned forward and flicked a finger at Cyren's throat.

"Word of advice, friend. Best keep that big pearl of your'n hidden. Oman's killed for far less." She glanced behind him. "Still, no sense in temptin'. . . is there?"

Cyren loosened the clasp and let the pearl slip down till it was hidden beneath his shirt.

Dorn raised his mug to An and drained half in a single gulp. An nodded and wiped a rag across the bar.

"A pretty bauble," she commented. "Mind my askin' where you . . . found it?"

Found? Her words implied that he was a thief. Cyren's hand closed around his mug. He planned to use one group of pirates to retrieve what another had stolen, so perhaps that indeed made him a thief.

He stared into the brown ale in his mug. The foam reminded him of the sea.

His grip tightened and he drained the mug in one long pull. Dorn slapped him on the back, his grin reaching into his dark eyes.

"The pearl was a gift," Cyren finally said, an edge in his voice.

"Meant no offense," An said, then refilled his mug. Someone called to her from the other end of the bar, and she left Cyren and Dorn to their drinks.

81

Dorn was still grinning at him.

"It was a gift," Cyren repeated.

Dorn shrugged and mimed drinking again. Feeling queasy, Cyren shook his head and pushed the mug toward the black-haired pirate. The man raised his mug to Cyren then drained it.

Cyren grimaced as his queasiness increased and his head started throbbing. The air felt rank and close. Ah, he shouldn't have downed that vile brew so quickly. As Dorn focused on the second mug, Cyren slipped away, moving lightly despite the growing sickness in his gut. Concentrating on finding his way through the maze of tables to the door, he never noticed Dorn making his way to the curly haired pirate siblings in the corner.

Halfway down a long, narrow dead-end alley between the tavern and a warehouse, Cyren spent the next few minutes heaving up the ale. The night wind shifted, and the clean, salt scent of the ocean washed over him.

Cyren leaned back against the warehouse and tilted his head so he could see the stars. In his blood, the sea was singing, urging him back. He should follow it. He dearly wanted to. He wanted to plunge into its welcoming depths and ride the currents to find those who had stolen his eyes and his people. Ever since the long string of islands he guarded had been pulled into this world, he'd been searching for them. He wanted to call the winds and the dark gray storm clouds, command the seas to rise against them and smash their ships to the bottom of the deepest trench of this world's oceans. Not for vengeance, but for justice. For the emeralds and his home.

Moonlight silvered the alley walls and cast shadows as deep and dark as the depths of the sea. Voices drifted down to him. He stared at the moon's rings that edged into the narrow slice of sky above him.

This was not his world.

He wore flesh now, and while he sensed that his power was no less, without the mediation of his "eyes"—as he thought of the matched emeralds that let him focus his power—he could do little more than light a candle. Flesh let him shift shape, though, and he was still able to trace the strands that led to different possibilities.

Cyren slipped farther into the alley, instinct rather than sight guiding him around piles of refuse. The cool stone wall of the tavern felt good against his flesh as he leaned back and closed his eyes. As softly as the breath of dawn stirring over the waters, his awareness slipped into the time streams, searching for the single green strand that led to his eyes. He found it anchored where he had left it and breathed a sigh of relief. The position of his eyes hadn't changed.

His awareness snapped back just in time to feel the solid thud of a fist against his jaw. Cyren staggered, surprised but not stunned. His attacker grunted in surprise as Cyren skipped back from the second blow meant to lay him out.

"Hold, Mako." Oman's voice said behind the attacking pirate.

Cyren shifted to the balls of his feet, the hair at his nape prickling from magic as Oman slid up to stand beside the scruffy man named Mako. Behind them, three swords glinted in the moonlight that filled the alley. Five ruffians all told.

"So, fish bait, you not be as fragile as you look. Might be you're worth more then a few silver to the slavers, after all," Oman said.

"Slavers?"

Oman laughed and drew his fancy daggers. The prickle of magic intensified, centering on the daggers, and Cyren did not like the feel of it. But the pirates were too close together for him to slip between them and get away, and he was too far from the water to shift forms. He stepped back and his heel hit the wall.

"Not too bright, is he, boys? Swimming into a net," Oman said with a nasty chuckle.

Cyren's gut twisted, and he wondered briefly if this was what fear felt like.

"Are there more of those pearls in that purse of your'n, boy?" Oman said.

Cyren's eyes narrowed and anger surged through him. He shoved away from the wall and whirled, his kick aimed for Oman's crotch, his left elbow for Mako's jaw. Oman collapsed with a strangled cry, one of his daggers scraping sparks from the warehouse wall. Mako's head slammed against the wall and he slid, unconscious, to the ground.

"Gut him, boys," Oman gasped, trying to rise. The three remaining ruffians rushed to oblige.

Cyren danced back from a cutlass swing, but the bulky thug pressed forward, reversed his swing, and sliced through cloth and skin, leaving a strand of fire burning across Cyren's belly. Only a surface wound, but it bled freely, soaking into his shirt.

Cyren hugged the wall, one hand clamped over his wound.

"Hold, boys," Oman said and staggered to his feet. His crew closed ranks behind him. "I'm going to enjoy this," he said and raised his daggers.

"Is this a private party? Or can anyone join?" came a man's voice from farther up the alley.

At a nod from Oman, one of his men edged his sword tip under Cyren's chin. Oman glanced over his shoulder, and then turned, slowly.

Halfway down the long alley, the siblings from the dark corner stood at ease. An oval stone set in the end of the woman's short staff shed light, pushing away the shadows. The man leaned against the wall, his thumbs hooked in his wide black belt, his light blue eyes shining in the stone's glow. Behind them, Dorn, grim-faced now, crouched with a long dagger in each hand.

"This be no quarrel of your'n, Murchadh," Oman said.

Cyren realized Murchadh was the man with the light blue eyes.

"No. But I'm thinkin' you've not got a quarrel, either. Leave the stranger be."

Oman scowled. "What I got or don't got ain't no business of your'n, mage spawn."

Murchadh straightened, the lazy smile on his face vanished as his hands drifted to his weapons, left on the hilt of a slender sword, the right to a long dagger. His eyes went dark as storm clouds as he drew them. The woman stepped back and raised her staff, both hands gripping the middle.

Oman's daggers began to glow. "Hold off or I gut him now, witch."

At the same time, the strands surged up and teased Cyren with possibilities, none of them good.

"I said, hold off, the both of you!"

She lowered her staff and Cyren felt the strands recede, gently for once. Oman's daggers kept glowing.

"Smart woman. Smarter than you," Oman said, pointing a dagger at Murchadh's weapons. Murchadh returned them to their sheaths.

Without direct contact, Cyren couldn't read the enchantments on Oman's daggers. But it had to be strong if the pirate called Murchadh was willing to back down so easily. The pain in Cyren's belly started to fade as the edges of his wound began knitting together.

"Let me claim my prize," Oman said. "All I want is them baubles."

Cyren's hand crept up to grasp the pearl. Lose it and he would lose his control over the strands of possibilities. Besides, it was a gift. Grimacing, he pulled off the pouch that hung from his belt and loosened the strings that closed the opening.

Oman turned back to him. "Them baubles . . ."

A flick of Cyren's wrist sent a dozen pearls the size of the one around his neck sailing through the air. Deep silver, bone white, and shadow black, they glowed in the moonlight, bounced off walls, and came to ground with the sound of rain on the sea.

Oman cursed as his men scrambled for the pearls.

Cyren dived past Oman in a tight roll that took him only a few yards beyond the thugs. His wound split open, and he staggered into the tavern wall as he gained his feet, blood streaking down his belly. Cyren caught the glow of Oman's daggers coming up behind him. He twisted away and cried out as one of the blades plunged into his right shoulder. In the intimate contact of flesh and blade, Cyren read the nature of the magic set into the steel. The magic made its wielder faster and stronger when it tasted blood.

Cyren barely wrenched away before the blade could take more than a tiny sip of his life. But the blade had never tasted flesh like his before.

Oman staggered, his right blade glowing bright green between the dark streaks of Cyren's blood.

"Let's get you out of here!" Murchadh charged up, grabbed a fistful of Cyren's shirt and shoved him up the alley. Close behind him, Dorn intercepted a cutlass swing aimed for Murchadh's neck.

Cyren stumbled back several paces, then collapsed on his backside at the woman's feet. His shoulder still burned from where the dagger had struck.

The woman started chanting, holding her staff with both hands, her voice strong and sure. But the magic she called felt wrong to Cyren. It curved and twisted, escaping the shape she was attempting to give it.

"Accept my help," Cyren said. He grabbed her belt and twisted hard, pulling her toward him. Off balance, it was easy to bring her to the ground. As his hands closed over hers on the staff, he heard Oman shout in triumph.

Two of the thugs had Murchadh trapped. The third battled Dorn, who didn't see Oman moving toward him with the swiftness of a surging wave.

Cursing, the woman tried to wrench her staff out of Cyren's grasp.

"I said, accept my help." He threw his weight against her, shoving her flat. Rather than pulling against her grip, he moved with her, twisting the staff so it pointed to the back of the alley. In the instant he read her magic, he also realized he could use her staff to re-shape it. With no time for the elegant subtlety he preferred, he snatched up what she had called and redirected it.

A thick green shaft of light shot out the end of her staff and split into four slender lances aimed at Oman and his crew. The clothes of the two attacking Murchadh erupted into green flame. Screaming, they dropped their weapons and beat at their tunics. Dorn's opponent was slammed against the wall, the magic burning out his heart. Only stunned, Oman stumbled, the green glow in his dagger fading.

Cyren took back what Oman's blade had stolen . . . and a tiny bit more. Oman screamed and fell to his knees. The daggers tumbled to the ground, his left hand a withered claw. Cyren knew a moment of grim satisfaction before he drifted into darkness.

☠ ☠ ☠

There was the smell of salt and tar, the rhythmic sound of water slapping against wood, and the sense of close walls. Cyren's shirt was gone, and his shoulder no longer burned. And while his belly felt tender, the fiery pain had vanished.

With his eyes still closed, Cyren laid his right hand against a ship's hull. Through the wood, he heard the sea singing and the desperate concerns of men racing across the dark blue water. The ship ran as close to the wind as her captain dared take her, but as far as Cyren was concerned, it wasn't fast enough.

He sent his senses through the ship and found Murchadh at her stern, his legs spread for balance. The pirate's left hand curled around a line, and strands of hair whipped around his face as he studied two ships halfway to the horizon behind them. His sister stood beside him, her hand on his shoulder, her staff secured across her back. A grim-faced woman minded the wheel while at least a dozen men and women scurried about tending sails and lines.

And Dorn . . . well, Dorn was with Cyren in the tiny cabin.

Cyren opened his eyes. Dorn smiled and held out a horn cup. Water, stale, tasting slightly of tar, but still better than ale, slipped down Cyren's throat.

Cyren slid off the narrow bunk and returned the cup. "Thank you."

Dorn nodded and set the cup on a small table bolted to the deck. Then he pointed at Cyren's belly and shoulder, and made wrapping motions with his hands.

"Your work?" Cyren asked.

Dorn nodded and held up one finger, then extended three more.

"I'm sorry. I don't understand."

"He means he's got three more jobs on this ship besides keeping her crew in one piece," Murchadh said. He left the door opened as he entered.

Dorn's hands moved in patterns Cyren couldn't read.

"No, the sharks are still trailing us, Dorn. Get up on deck and take another sun reading. See if you can find a course that will shake them off our tail."

Dorn nodded and then slipped away.

Murchadh's blue eyes took on the sheen of steel and he waved at the pearl around Cyren's neck.

"You should have given Oman that bauble, boy. No treasure is worth a man's life."

"This one is."

Murchadh scowled. "Gods, boy, you're green as sea glass. Wanderin' into An's tavern carrying enough treasure to buy the *Promise* five times over. Even Oman isn't that stupid."

The muscular pirate settled on the bunk, leaned back, and rested a heel on the edge of the bed before continuing. "Oman starts a fight with you, drags it outside, and then. . . ." He shrugged. "You're minus a few pearls. Unfortunately—or fortunately—dependin' on how you want to look at it, Dorn's got a short temper when he starts drinkin'. He usually settles down after the fifth or sixth ale." Murchadh paused. "He's also got a weakness for strays."

Before Cyren could decide whether he should be insulted or amused, the sister slipped into the cabin.

"This is Moirainne," Murchadh said.

"I have to sleep in that bunk, bro," she said, jabbing a finger at his boot. Murchadh gave an exaggerated sigh, but removed his foot.

"And I was just getting comfortable, sis."

Moirainne smiled sourly. "Don't get too settled. Oman's still closing in on our wake."

"We've outrun him before."

She shook her head. "It doesn't look like we will this time."

"I may be able to help," Cyren volunteered.

"Like you did in the alley?" Moirainne's voice was tight with anger. "I had control of the magic before you interfered. It's your fault Oman's called vengeance on us."

"The magic was twisted. It—"

"It was a light spell, to blind them. I can control those."

"The magic was twisted," Cyren repeated, his hand slicing through the air between them. "You would have incinerated yourself and your companions, as well as Oman and the others."

"I know my limits."

"Let it go, Moir," Murchadh said quietly, leaning forward.

Moirainne rounded on him, her fists rising.

"Please, let it go," Murchadh repeated. His eyes gripped hers for a long moment. Then, like a sail emptied of wind, she sagged against the bulkhead, her fists down at her sides.

"It's still his fault," she said in a monotone, her gaze rooted on the deck. Then she shoved away from the door, sparing a final glare for Cyren before she stalked out.

"She's spent half a day filling my ears with suggestions on how you can repay us," Murchadh said after his sister disappeared from the passageway to the upper deck. "Keelhauling was mentioned several times, but that wouldn't leave you in any condition to pay up. Besides, I can think of a better use for you."

"And what is that?" Cyren kept a tight reign on his anger. Even now, when he was in flesh, the seas tended to stir up when he lost his temper.

"I'm thinking someone who can take control of another's magic, change it, split it four ways all in the space of a few breaths must know something about the arts. Maybe enough to help Moirainne find her control."

Cyren knew a bargain when he heard one. It wasn't the one he'd expected to make: an offer of treasure in return for retrieving his eyes. Or perhaps it was. Not all treasure was silver and pearls now, was it? First, though, there were a few things he needed to settle.

"You accept my perceptions of the spell over your sister's. Why?"

The pirate captain shrugged.

"She doesn't sound as though she'll be willing to accept my . . . help."

"She's got a long temper, but she'll cool. Eventually." Murchadh flowed to his feet and smiled. "It's her pride that's smarting. But she's no fool. Her good sense wins out . . . usually."

"Usually?"

"Aye. Well, do we have a bargain?"

At the base of Cyren's soul, the threads chimed and quivered, the sign of a bargain offered in good faith. Besides, his sense of justice demanded that he protect those who had tried to protect him. And there was still the matter of his eyes. The threads tightened and tugged him toward Murchadh, who waited patiently, thumbs hooked in his belt.

"I will agree on one condition," Cyren said.

"I'm thinkin' you're not in much of a position to make conditions."

"This one is needful, if I'm to help your sister."

"Why am I thinkin' that I'm not going to like where this is going?" the pirate muttered.

"The focus for my magic was stolen by sea raiders who came in ships with black sails. They—"

"Black sails?" Murchadh bounced to his feet and began pacing the length of the tiny cabin. "Ah, Gods of Wrath and Mercy! Black sails. Of course, it had to be black sails." He stopped pacing and laughed, a strained, mirthless sound. Then he sank into the chair opposite Cyren. "There's only one group I know in this part of the World-Sea that uses black sails: Storm Riders."

Cyren couldn't read the emotions that flickered in Murchadh's eyes as the pirate's hand shifted to his dagger.

"Boy, I'm thinkin' you're most fortunate to still be alive if you ran afoul of Storm Raiders." Murchadh drew his dagger and held it flat across his belly. "Why are you still living, boy? And still holding treasure?" His eyes flicked to the pearl around Cyren's neck.

Cyren unclenched his hands and laid them flat on the table. The strands stayed still. Time stretched between them. A man of infinite patience was Murchadh, Cyren decided.

"I ought to put you on a boat, boy, with three days of food and water and let the gods judge you."

"You believe in the gods?"

Murchadh shrugged. "A man's got to believe in something."

It was Cyren's experience that the deepest expressions of faith were often the simplest. Murchadh shifted his dagger just high enough. Cyren lunged across the table, his left hand closing over the pirate's wrist, squeezing hard and forcing the hand open. Cyren caught the dagger in his right hand, then leapt back, toppling the chair behind him. Murchadh surged to his feet, drawing his sword. But before the pirate could do more than raise his blade, Cyren plunged the dagger into his own heart.

Cyren's hand still on the hilt, he fell to his knees gasping. A Storm Rider had taught him that plain steel couldn't kill him, but—Sand and storm!—it hurt!

Murchadh's sword clattered to the deck and he dropped to his knees in surprise.

"I lived through my meeting with the Storm Riders because they'd left me for dead," Cyren said. He pulled out the blade; his heart's blood dripped off the dagger onto the deck between them. "They left me for dead," he repeated. "Watch."

Murchadh's eyes slid down to Cyren's chest, then widened as the wound began to close, the slit edges sealing together till not even a trace of a scar remained. "How, boy?" The word was barely more than a hoarse whisper.

Cyren rose awkwardly. Still gripping the bloody dagger, he leaned against the table, wincing as the pain receded in diminishing waves.

"How, Murchadh? I'm a god."

☠   ☠   ☠

Murchadh returned about ten minutes later, a fine blue shirt in one hand and a large brass pitcher in the other. Dorn followed almost on his heels, carrying a tray with a small bowl and a stack of folded cloths. The mute pirate set the tray on the table, then bowed deeply to Cyren, now sitting in one of two chairs. Murchadh set the pitcher beside the tray.

"I told him what happened," Murchadh said. "But I told no one else."

Dorn poured some water into the bowl and then began gently washing the blood off Cyren's chest.

Murchadh sat, holding the shirt in both hands. "Don't take this wrong, but you don't act much like a god."

"And how are they supposed to act?"

The pirate shrugged. "Oh, I don't know. More lofty I suppose, but then, I've never met one before."

Dorn dropped the wet rag on the tray. His hands moved, and he looked like a parent scolding a child. Murchadh chuckled and rose to give Cyren an elegant bow.

"He said I should show more respect."

Cyren touched Dorn's arm to get his attention.

"It's all right."

Dorn glanced at both of them. He dried Cyren's chest. Then he gathered up the bloody rags and bowl and left.

"Can I ask you something?" Murchadh said. "Why didn't you kill Oman and the others?"

"Why didn't *you?*" Cyren returned.

"I don't kill a man unless there's no other way."

"Neither do I."

The pirate regarded him thoughtfully. Murchadh nodded, as if he'd decided something. He handed the shirt to Cyren.

"Dorn's found us a bit more speed, but they're still climbing up our tail."

Cyren recognized a prayer when he heard one. He slipped the shirt on before answering it.

"I'll do what I can to shield you. But without my focus stones I'll need your sister's help."

"She'll give it."

Cyren followed him up on deck. His blood hummed at the light touch of sea spray on his cheek as he emerged from the hatch. The seas were ridged with white-flecked waves, and the ship sang under the press of wind against her sails.

Cyren moved lightly across the shifting deck, following Murchadh to the stern where Moirainne kept watch. Her hands tightened on her staff when she spotted Cyren.

"Have you come to help?" She glared at him.

"Moirainne, you—" Murchadh began.

"Stow it, bro. I—"

"Can you cast a spell for calling fog?" Cyren asked with quiet authority.

"In the middle of the day?" Moirainne frowned and shook her head. "Yes, but it won't do us much good. Can't cover the whole ocean. And the mages on Oman's ships will burn it off as soon as it forms."

"It's worth a try, Moir," Murchadh said.

Moirainne turned to stare at the ships behind them. "You should have killed Oman, not left him in that alley screaming vengeance on us." She sighed softly. "All right, what have we got to lose?"

☠ ☠ ☠

This time the green light that shot out the end of Moirainne's staff spread out in a wide arc, hitting the water a hundred yards off the stern of the *Promise*. For a moment, the sea glowed green. Then white mist boiled up in a thick column twice the height of the main mast. It spread out in a wide, thick band to port and starboard, at least a mile long on each side.

"How thick is it?" Murchadh asked.

"Half a mile," said Cyren.

"Won't take them long to sail through or around," Moirainne muttered.

Cyren pointed to the fog bank quickly falling behind them. "Watch."

The fog bank's course continued straight, then shifted hard to port. Murchadh laughed.

"They can't sail out of it," Cyren said. "Not until well past sundown."

Murchadh bounded down the ladder to the main deck, bellowing orders.

☠ ☠ ☠

After Dorn prepared an excellent dinner in Murchadh's cabin, Cyren told them of the shifting of his world, and how that shift had stripped his islands of most of their defensive magic and many mages of their power. He did not tell them of the madness that too many of those mages had fallen into after the shift. Or of how he had washed up on the beach outside a small town, naked and shivering, still in shock from being thrust into the world of flesh, clutching a matched pair of emeralds—his focus stones. He said nothing of the chief priestess who'd nursed him and had gently pried the stones out of his grasp to store them, safely she thought, in the temple.

He did describe the coming of the Storm Rider ships and what they had stolen. Cyren mourned again the loss of so many who died before they could reach the waters safely and shift shape to escape into the open ocean.

"My people know what it is to be hunted," Cyren continued. "But at least those who hunted us before spared the children. These Storm Riders . . . they killed everyone who came within reach of their swords."

"I'm sorry," Moirainne said, her eyes soft in the lantern glow.

Murchadh pushed his empty plate to one side and leaned on the table, rolling his cup between his hands. He glanced at Cyren. "Riders always auction off their hauls."

Moirainne slapped her cup down. "Hey bro, we agreed at An's to wait a year before looking for marks there again."

"I promised I'd help him get his focus stones back."

"Oh, gods," Moirainne said, shaking her head. "All right, but I'm not sure we've got enough coin to buy a matched set of emeralds." Her eyes snapped to Cyren. "Emeralds! You couldn't just use a wand or staff like any other mage, could you?"

Cyren shook his head. "The magic called both those times was yours. I only shifted the direction of it. And a staff can't handle the amount and kind of power I need to re-establish the wards on my islands." His voice went soft and dark. "I will not see my people ravaged again."

"Look, Moir, a pair of matched emeralds the size of gull eggs is going to generate a lot of interest. No one is going to look twice if we show up at two auctions in a row," Murchadh said before she could find another objection. "Besides, it's been three months since the last auction. So they've probably already given that bilge rat, Two-Finger Pate, the time and location."

"I know exactly where my emeralds are," Cyren said. "They lie about three days due west of here on a small island." He touched the pearl at his throat. "I can feel them."

Murchadh went over to his desk and studied the chart spread on top of it. Picking up a pair of dividers, he adjusted the space between the points and then sank one end into the map mark that was their present position. Three times he flipped the instrument along an imaginary line. He smiled when he saw where the point landed.

"You'll never believe this," he said, glancing at them.

"Believe what?" Moirainne said.

"The name of the island is Stone's Throw."

☠ ☠ ☠

The mid-watch of the night found Cyren at the stern with Murchadh. The god had stayed out of the conversation between the siblings while they discussed strategy. The seas were clear behind them, the wind steady. The woman at the helm sang softly as she steered the ship to the port at White Thorn Cove where Two-Finger Pate was lodged.

The god closed his eyes, the strands connecting him to his islands lay quiet and reassuring at the bottom of his soul. The green one that led to his eyes extended far, waving like a long strand of kelp. He touched it gently to read the position. The emeralds had moved, but no more than the distance from one small room to another.

"We should make port in two days," Murchadh said. He pulled a small silk pouch out of his inner vest pocket, sighed, and handed it to Cyren. "I managed to grab some of your pearls before we scuttled out of that alley. Moirainne would tie me to the rudder if she knew I was giving these back."

91

Cyren opened the pouch and three pearls spilled into his hand. All black. The color of confirmation, of certainty. Cyren slipped them back into the pouch. "Will these be enough to buy back my focus stones?"

"Hard to say," Murchadh replied. "Depends on who's bidding. Even if we can't buy them, we'll know who did. And this crew has been itchin' for a good raid."

Cyren grimaced. Murchadh, gazing out over the moon-dappled water, didn't seem to notice.

"This Two-Finger Pate . . . is his information reliable?"

Murchadh nodded. "But the Storm Riders use him too."

Cyren slipped the pouch into his pocket. "Why an auction?"

"Why not? Riders prefer coin, and there's more coin to be had selling it if there's no cut to a fence." The pirate captain studied the stars for a long moment. "I'll take you back to your islands when we recover your mage stones. But there's something you should know." He paused and let the silence settle thick before speaking again. "Your islands may not be there when we return."

Startled, Cyren pushed away from the railing and faced him directly. "What do you mean?"

"Lands can disappear as suddenly as they arrive in the Azure Sea."

Cyren's gut twisted. The strands at the bottom of his soul that connected him to his islands had been there for as long as he could remember. But he had no way of knowing if the flesh he wore now was strong enough to keep him connected if his islands vanished.

"If they disappear, will they return, Captain?"

"There's no way to predict."

Cyren's hands clenched. "And if I'm not there when they vanish?"

"You'll be trapped here. Just like Dorn was."

☠ ☠ ☠

Stones Throw was larger than Cyren expected. A deep, wide harbor on the north side of the rocky island easily held the two dozen large ships and the double handful of luxury yachts anchored there. Like the *Promise*, bright red auction banners fluttered from the top of the mainmast of each ship.

Cyren glared at the six large ships with black sails that guarded the entrance to the harbor. Tension still thrummed in his muscles when they dropped anchor in the southeast side of the bay. It didn't help that Moirainne paced like a nervous seabird in the stern where she'd kept vigil ever since they'd left White Thorn Cove more than a week ago.

His hand closed over the pearl at his throat, but the strands stay stubbornly buried, as they had for the past three days.

Moirainne slipped up to where Cyren waited with Murchadh near the helm, her face grim.

"He's here," she said. "That sea crow's slipped in ahead of us somehow. His ships are anchored near the main camp."

They turned to scan where she was pointing. Cyren recognized Oman's ships. Beyond them on the beach, black tents sprawled on both sides of a narrow trail that wound up the side of a hill to the mouth of a large cave. At least a dozen guards kept watch at the entrance.

"He won't risk an open attack," Murchadh said to Cyren. "Riders make noise about keepin' peace. And mostly, they mean it."

"I'm more worried about when we leave," Moiraine said.

☠ ☠ ☠

The auction was to begin an hour after sunset. An hour before, Murchadh ordered his ship's boat lowered. Moirainne settled in beside her brother in the stern, her staff resting in the crook of her shoulder. Murchadh looked more at ease than she, but he kept his hands curled around his weapons. The crew seemed content to stay on the ship, and none had asked about shore leave when Murchadh left his standing orders for the watch.

Dorn tried to wave Cyren away as the god settled beside him and took up an oar. Cyren shook his head. Like the sea surging and receding with every wave that swept the beach, he needed the rhythm of movement. His hands tightened on the oars as he moved in perfect rhythm with Dorn.

After they pulled the boat up onto the rocky beach and tied it to a stake, Moirainne held Cyren back a moment, placing a hand on his arm.

"Do you plan on seeking more than just the return of your focus stones?" she asked softly.

"I don't believe in vengeance."

"Some would name it justice." Her hand tightened on his arm. "Look, I don't care if you want to slaughter the lot of them. Just . . . not here. We're a small ship. And my brother—"

Without thinking, he laid his finger on her lips. For a moment, the god was distracted by their softness.

"I seek only my mage stones," he assured her.

She searched his face. They turned and followed Dorn and Murchadh up the lantern-lined path to the cave.

It was cool inside, a vast hollow of stone that held the booty of a hundred looted ships. Clusters of glowstones in wire baskets atop sleek pillars provided ample light. Black-shirted Riders bearing long slender swords kept watch over neatly stacked crates and boxes. Silk-clad buyers, both men and women, milled through the cave, talking softly, sipping wine or rum, careful to keep at least three strides from those long swords.

In the center of the cave stretched a wide raised platform surrounded on three sides by slim, lighted pillars and muscular armed guards. On the left side half a dozen large chests shared space with a table piled with bowls of glimmering jewels and ornate boxes of gold, silver, ivory, and carved red lacquer. Just to the right of the platform's center was a slender-legged table of black wood holding four small, carved gold boxes.

"Looks like they're goin' to be selling the baubles first," Murchadh murmured.

Cyren reached inward for the green strand. The light around him shifted and took on the shades of sunlight spilling through clear seas. The stones sang in his soul, and he stepped forward.

Suddenly, he was jerked back by three pairs of hands clamped on his arms. Half a dozen guards threatened him with raised swords. He stood scarcely a single step from the platform.

"Ah, a little too much rum," Murchadh said, smiling and pulling the god back. The only guard wearing a red sash gave them a hard look, and then ordered the others back on the platform.

Cyren shook his head and mentally released the strand. The stones' song faded.

"Are you mad?" Moirainne whispered.

"No," Cyren said softly, relaxing in their grip. "They were calling."

Silence washed through the vast chamber. They turned and saw a man in shimmering black robes striding down the center. He carried no staff or wand, but Cyren sensed dark power throbbing in the air around him. Cyren stepped back from the wizard's path—not from fear, like most in the cave, or caution like his companions, but from loathing. Cyren recognized the magic; it had broken the seals in his temple and burned his chosen servants to ash. That power brushed cold and dank as the wizard moved past Cyren toward the platform.

Cyren turned to find Murchadh, grim and silent, studying a Rider with a gold sash. The Rider fingered a black silk pouch, then smiled, and tucked it into his sash.

"We've just been marked," Murchadh said softly.

"Oman." Moirainne said.

Thirty feet to their left, Cyren spotted Oman. The mage-light from a nearby pillar highlighted the oily sheen of his lank hair.

Cyren pivoted to study the wizard who now stood poised on the platform, arms raised. Cyren knew, with a god's certainty, that Oman and the wizard were kin.

The wizard's deep, clear voice announced the start of the auction, promising items of rare and exquisite beauty. With a practiced flourish, he scooped one of the carved golden boxes off the small table and opened it to reveal, nestled against dark blue silk and held in by bands of magic, a pair of matched emeralds. The crowd pressed forward. Fingers closed around fat purses.

This close, even without touching the strand, Cyren heard the stones singing; it blurred his senses. His companions pressed closer to him, and while he heard their voices, they blended with the murmur of the crowd.

His hands closed into fists.

To be so close.

He shook his head, fighting the pull. Moirainne tugged at his elbow and he followed, not knowing where she led. They managed only a few steps before the world shifted. This time the strands connecting Cyren's soul to his islands did not shorten and thicken. They stretched thin and taut, and snapped one by one. He screamed, a long, wild, piercing sound.

When the last strand severed, his senses cleared to show the space around him where the crowd had drawn back. His eyes sought Murchadh's

"They're gone!" Cyren said in a hoarse voice. "My islands. They're—" His throat closed. The pain of loss roiled inside him. He sensed Oman and his crew slipping through the crowd toward them, saw the guards closing in, steel swords gleaming, felt the gathering of dark magic.

"Oh, gods," Moirainne said, clutching her staff and looking beyond him.

A prayer. Cyren snatched at it for strength. He whirled on the guard behind him and grabbed the blade of the man's sword. The steel bit deep as Cyren wrenched it out of the guard's hand and shoved the man into his companions. The enemy pirates tumbled to the ground and Cyren flowed through them as easily as water flowed between the rocky spires that bordered his islands.

As he reached the platform, he flipped the sword hilt into his hand.

The wizard was skilled, a single gesture away from completing some spell. Cyren darted forward, his free hand reaching for the emeralds in the wizard's grasp, his sword aimed for the man's throat. The wizard skipped back, completing the spell as Cyren's hand closed over the emeralds.

Joy and anguish in equal measure flowed through Cyren with the return of his power. Ah, but different, different, different was his power, and no time to master the shape of it. He threw it, unformed, at the wizard.

The black robed man crumpled to the ground, clutching his head and moaning. The wizard's dark magic scattered into a hundred pieces, striking at random. It burned out an eye here, singed another's hair, and melted the coins in a woman's purse without even warming the fine leather.

Cyren whirled and saw the guards closing in on Murchadh and his sister. Dorn had their backs. Cyren dropped the sword and shifted one of the emeralds to his other hand. Warmed in the god's blood, they melted and flowed up his arms in long slender strands like sea grass reaching through the tide.

No time, no time, he thought, his soul torn and bleeding from the pain of loss. He opened his mouth and called the winds.

☠   ☠   ☠

They found him floating in the bay, his arms wrapped from wrist to shoulder with slender green strands that glittered like jewels in the late afternoon sun. It was Dorn who pulled him from the water, wrapped him in a soft blanket, and held a cup of sweet wine to his lips.

Cyren opened his eyes and saw Murchadh kneeling beside him, Moirainne crouched behind, and the crew stood scattered beyond them. There was awe in their faces.

Cyren pulled out of Dorn's embrace and staggered to the railing. He remembered calling the winds, but recalled nothing of what followed.

Of all the ships, only the *Promise* remained intact, though she now floated in the exact center of the harbor. Of the Storm Rider ships and Oman's, not a scrap of sail or hull remained. The other vessels lay scattered across the beach and hillside—one even lodged in the cave mouth—their sails shredded, masts broken. Some survivors picked through the wreckage of broken crates and boxes.

"Well, one thing's for certain," Murchadh said, "I don't think we'll have to worry about anyone tailing us." He turned to his sister. "Have the crew get ready to sail. I'm thinking it's best to leave these waters before anyone recovers their bad sense and decides to claim payment."

She nodded and hurried to instruct the crew.

Cyren leaned against the railing, Dorn's hand steadying him. Gone. They were all gone. His islands. His people. Nothing left to protect, to cherish.

He stared at his palms, at the slices of green that marked where the sword had cut. He had his power back, but to what end?

Dorn's hands moved, supple and graceful.

"He's asking you to stay with us," Murchadh said softly.

Cyren looked back at the shore, at flocks of people scavanging the wreckage of stolen treasures. Murchadh was right. When the survivors repaired their ships, the thoughts of some would turn to hunting. Cyren folded his fingers, hiding the green scars.

"And you. What do you wish?" he asked Murchadh.

"I'd not be adverse to the company."

Despite his pain, Cyren smiled. The pirate had an odd way of showing respect. No matter; it made the respect no less sincere.

Cyren turned away from the wreckage of the island and put his face to the open sea. Then he opened his mouth and called the winds to fill their sails.

BATTLE WITH THE GRAY GHOST
by James M. Ward

His Majesty's Articles of War: Article Forty-one

The captain of a vessel in his Majesty's navy shall read his orders from the Admiralty at the beginning of every cruise and again upon leaving a port for sea duty. It is the captain's duty to interpret those orders from the Admiralty and carry them out to the letter of the intent of said orders.

☠ ☠ ☠

Six days out of Et Bay, on its maiden voyage, the DragonFrigate *Intrepid* cruised in advance of the treasure fleet. The hull, equipment, and crew were much like frigates made for hundreds of years. On the other hand, the male sea dragon used as the keel of the frigate made the vessel interesting at the very least. With its long serpentine-head scenting in the sea, suddenly the dragon became afraid.

Tutoring the midshipmen on the quarterdeck was a brand new captain—Halcyon Blithe. Clutched in his hand, the orders he must follow, gave him a moment of concern.

~

The *Intrepid* will lead the treasure fleet due south of Arcania to the Crystal City of the Mountain Dwarves. Keeping a distance of eleven to seventeen miles to the front of the fleet, you will serve as the first warning of trouble. Upon finding the enemy, you will initially engage to determine how strong the forces are, and then you will retreat to the main fleet with your scouting information. – Arcanian Admiralty

~

For the last hour of the morning, twenty-four-year-old Captain Halcyon Blithe always tutored his midshipmen in the ways of the Arcanian DragonFrigate. They sat on stools on the quarterdeck, slates and chalk in their hands. During the hour, they located their position on maps, calculated their speed, and recited his Majesty's Articles of War. This duty took place every day, at eleven bells—even though the ominous fog, suddenly appearing in the path of the DragonFrigate where no fog had been just heartbeats before, might cut this day's lesson short.

"Mr. Tobin, how many blast-tubes are there on our DragonFrigate?" Captain Halcyon asked as he watched the dark front of intense mist flow over the ocean waves toward his ship.

"Sir, the *Intrepid* has sixteen carronades of thirty-two pounds each, located on the quarterdeck," answered Alex. "The DragonFrigate also has thirty blast-tubes of twenty-four pounds each on the main blast-tube deck.

Three long blast-tubes are bow-chasers on the forecastle, and four long stern-chasers are to the back of the quarterdeck."

"Ms. Bray, what is the beam and length of our vessel?" Halcyon asked as he noted the breeze slacking off, first the jib-sails and then the fore sails of his ship. There was a good chance that soon only the motive power of the sea dragon itself would be moving the ship forward in the ocean.

"Captain, the *Intrepid* is two hundred and fifty feet long, not counting our sea dragon keel. The beam of the ship is forty-nine feet, without the width of the sea dragon," Janean Bray answered.

"Third Midshipdwarf Arn-un, how tall is our foremast and how thick is our hull planking?" Halcyon asked, suddenly gaining a premonition that his ship was in terrible danger from something in that dark mist.

"Captain, the mainmast of the DragonFrigate is one hundred and eighty-seven feet high," Arn-un answered. "Our ship doesn't have hull planking as other ships. The living dragon skin is tougher than the twenty inches of oak planking and copper that covers normal ships. Once every two years the shedding skin of the DragonFrigate is stretched and treated to become a larger hull as the dragon—"

The dwarf would have gone on describing the DragonFrigate, but Halcyon raised a hand to stop him.

Halcyon looked up into the fog bank he was about to sail his DragonFrigate into. The mist looked unusually dark, considering the midday sun. "Lieutenant Gray, rig for heavy seas. Safety lines fore and aft and the storm lanterns lit. Don't batten down the hatches just yet."

"Aye, aye, Captain," said the Lieutenant. He went to the ship's bell and rang out the signal to set the ship for heavy weather. The bell served many purposes besides telling the time at the top of every hour. The Lieutenant grabbed the clapper and rang it as fast as he could for twenty rings. Crew started boiling out of the hold. Topsmen rolled up all the topsails and the topgallants.

"Lieutenant, don't let them lash down the blast-tubes," Halcyon ordered.

"Aye, aye, Captain," replied Lieutenant Mikal Gray.

The middies all moved restlessly on their stools. Each wanted to leap up and move to their weather stations, but they couldn't budge until the captain released them.

"*The water tastes dead,*" the sea dragon that was the keel of the ship mentally told its Captain. The dragon's simple mind was able to contact Halcyon and Lieutenant Major Altoon Defore of the Marines. The Arcanian Admiralty always ordered at least two different officers with the ability to mindspeak on every Dragonship of the line.

One of the reasons to assign a captain to a DragonFrigate was his innate ability to communicate telepathically with the sea dragon. Halcyon Blithe could mentally talk with any type of dragon. As the seventh son of a seventh son, he was also a rope speaker, able to tell when a rope was weakened to its core. He came into his wizard abilities late in his teen years, but was making up for it now. The officials of the Admiralty all considered him an up-and-coming captain in the fleets.

"How can water be dead?" Captain Blithe thought back to the dragon, realizing the dragon sensed the same thing that Halcyon felt nervous about as well.

"A strangeness is leaking into the water from the mists. There is a dust here that's killing the fish and kelp. That dust wasn't there just heartbeats before," the dragon thought.

That's all Halcyon needed.

"Senior Chief Fallow, sound beat to quarters!" bellowed Blithe. "Place double shot in all the blast-tubes, Sergeant Darkwater!"

"Aye, aye, Captain," Fallow and Darkwater shouted back.

Double shot was only for close-quarters battle. It was wasted if the enemy stood off at long range and traded blast-tube shots with the DragonFrigate.

Somehow, Halcyon doubted his ship would be fighting at long ranges in the middle of the dense fog.

Every man, woman, and boy on the ship ran to their battle stations. For the first ten days in the sea life of the *Intrepid*, the Captain had drilled his crew at dawn and dusk regarding where their battle stations were and what they were supposed to do when at those stations.

"Lieutenant Gray, raise the signal flags. Tell the fleet we've sighted the enemy, and we're engaging same," ordered Blithe.

No one said anything about the order, even though hundreds of them knew no enemy had been sighted yet.

Men raised the boarding nets all around the rails of the ship. These nets would help to keep boarding parties from instantly gaining the sides of the *Intrepid*. The nets also had the ability to prevent masts and sails from falling on the crew during a battle.

Other crewmen splashed the staysails, foresails, mainsail, and mizzen sails with buckets of water. Hot shot from the enemy would not set these sails burning. Those same leather buckets were filled again and placed by the blast-tubes with long swabbing sticks plunged in them, ready to be used for the hot tubes.

Crew spread sand over all of the upper decks so sparks wouldn't burn the decking. The sand would also soak up the blood of wounded crew, so that the deck would not become slippery.

Other crewmen tied the bound hammocks from below decks up in the masts so they would act as nets to catch falling masts that were shot away by enemy blast-tube fire.

Darkwater, the half troll-marine sergeant, made sure all the blast tubes were double-shotted. She supervised the loading of the blast gel jars and the linked chain shot that went into the barrels of the main deck blast-tubes.

The carronades on the quarterdeck received larger loads of blast gel jars, and their short barrels were loaded with large bags of round shot. These carronades were new to the Arcanian frigates. The deadly short-barreled weapons were only meant for close quarter work, not more than one hundred yards from the enemy vessels. The enemy Maleen ships of the same size or larger hadn't started using carronades yet.

Senior Chief Petty Officer Ashe Fallow was in charge of the main blast-tube deck. It was his responsibility to make sure there were two jars of blast gel cases by every blast-tube. The young boys and girls that were tube monkeys would sit on both unused cases until one was needed. Then they would jump up and go down to the hold of the ship to bring up another case. Each hardwood case held a jar filled with volatile green blast gel surrounded by sand. There were different colored jars, with each color used for a different range on the blast-tube. The jar was inserted into the blast-tube first. Sail wadding and then the shot was forced down into the blast-tube by the back end of the swabbing stick. When the weapon was ready to be fired, a white-hot spike was driven into the touchhole. It broke the clay jar and ignited the gel, firing the blast-tube. Double-shotted tubes received a special load of two heavy bars linked with four chain sections. While the shot was not made for long distance firing, the bars and links would do much more damage to sails, masts, and ship hulls.

The marines lined themselves up at the center of the blast-tube deck. They stood at attention with blast-pikes at the ready. They were there to attack any enemies trying to board. They were also there to stop crewmembers from running from their stations during a battle.

The Middies Janean Bray, Jasper Arn-un, and Ulum Gorm took their battle stations in the tops of each of the masts. They commanded the crossbow crews that would fire their heavy bolts at the enemy on the decks of their ships. For some reason, Captain Blithe had ordered the special silver crossbow bolts used today. Such bolts were commonly used only against magical foes.

The luckiest of the midshipmen were Detorro and Asp. Today it was their turn to command blast-tube crews. Detorro directed the long tubes on the stern of the quarterdeck. The fourteen-year-old puffed up with pride as he gave the orders to load the tubes with the heavy sixty-pound shot. These were special arrow shaped loads also new to navy use. Blithe had insisted that all of his blast-tube round shot be replaced with these new pointed shots. The pointed shot had only seen use in the last five years in the armories of Arcania. They gave extra range. Most of the older captains didn't like using them, but Halcyon had been lucky with their use in the past.

"*Arrgh!*" roared out the challenge of the sea dragon as it blew a plume of seawater into the gray dinginess of the fog. The head of the sea dragon rose out of the water searching first for enemy dragons. Not finding any, it looked for Maleen ships. At the edge of its senses, the sea dragon felt a monstrous foe, coming fast. The dragon communicated this to its Captain.

Halcyon noted the direction of the water jet. Sea dragons could sense things that the ship's crew couldn't. "Hard to starboard! Prepare to fire the port tubes!"

The DragonFrigate thrust itself into the fog. Instantly its sails fell limp on their sticks. The sea dragon's giant flippers stroked the water, and the ship turned, despite the lack of wind.

The water-filled mists settled on each of the crew like a blanket, slowing them and drenching them to the skin almost instantly.

The mist to the port side of the DragonFrigate parted, and not one hundred yards away the prow of the first-rater broke through like a dark stain. The ship was murky gray and all of its sails were taters on the sticks. Wind did not move the ship forward.

The monster-sized vessel had three decks of cannon ports, none of them open. In silver letters along the side of the prow, Blithe read *Gray Ghost*. All the Arcanian crew, looking on what they knew in their souls would be a deadly enemy, felt the evil presence before them. The hull of the enemy ship seemed to be comprised entirely of bones.

Suddenly, what could only be the captain of the ship appeared on the forecastle railing. A tattered black uniform covered the skeletal ogre form. Its position on the railing allowed the *Intrepid's* crew to tell the ghastly thing stood at least fifteen feet tall. Sporting a skeleton's head, the undead creature raised its bony hand and began screaming. Tendrils of green gas vomited from its bony jaws and extended out toward the DragonFrigate.

Halcyon and the rest of his crew stood at their weapons, shocked by the visage of their new foe. Their astonishment continued as more skeleton crew appeared on the ship's forecastle, raising their bony talons and shrieking. The green mist increased a hundredfold as masses of ogre skeletons stood on the railing of the ghost ship and worked their deadly magic.

As Halcyon filled his lungs to order the firing of his weapons, the green tendrils licked out and touched *Intrepid's* crewmembers. Instantly most of his crew sank to the deck unconscious. Green mist continued to erupt from the jaws of the skeletal horrors on the *Gray Ghost*, flowing out in a great wave.

Two silver crossbow bolts flashed down from the tops of the DragonFrigate. One struck the large captain of skeletons in its skull and the other took the creature in its shoulder. More silver crossbow bolts slammed into the monster's body, momentarily thrusting it back to the foremast. The metal of the bolts sizzled as boiling silver vapors rose from the creature's body.

☠   ☠   ☠

Skeletal Captain Etan dar-Black looked up into the tops of the DragonFrigate and shook his massive bony fist at the two enemy crewmembers shooting crossbow bolts at him.

Most of the enemy crossbowmen hung by their safety lines, paralyzed by the green magic of the undead crew. The *Gray Ghost's* captain didn't understand why some were still able to move about on the enemy ship. Dar-Black still planned on boarding the vessel and eating its crew for his afternoon meal, but there would be fighting first.

☠   ☠   ☠

Seeing that the monster could be hurt, Halcyon sprang into action. The green mists now covered every area of his ship from stem to stern and from the tops to the deepest parts of the hull. Halcyon didn't know why he remained unaffected by the magic of the ghost ship attackers, but he leapt to take advantage of it.

Between each pair of carronades on the quarterdeck of the sea dragon, a brazier of coals held slim metal spikes. The spikes punched into the touchholes of each blast-tube to crack the jar of blast gel and explode the weapon. Halcyon picked up a pair of pincers and slammed a hot spike into the first carronade opening.

BOOM!

The weapon belched thousands of miniballs into the prow of the enemy vessel. Seven more times, without looking once at the enemy, Halcyon exploded the weapons along the port side as he jumped over the bodies of the unconscious crew. Smoke thicker than the fog all around him covered the blast-tube deck.

"They better not be dead," Halcyon raged at the enemy, not fifty yards away. The thought of his crew dying by magical means before his eyes was too much for the young captain to bear.

High in the tops of the two masts, Janean and Jasper looked down on the enemy deck and saw the bony forecastle destroyed by the carronades. The thousands of mini-balls had plowed through the railing and into the many skeletal bodies packed on the *Ghost's* forecastle, working their paralyzing magic. Bones littered the deck. The huge skeleton captain rose again as new arm and shoulder bones regenerated. But none of the other downed skeletons stirred. Surveying the decks of the enemy, hundreds of skeletons still worked their battle stations.

The crossbow snipers kept firing, looking for officers to slay. Impossible to tell one skeleton from another, except for the big one with glowing eyes, Jasper and Janean picked up the armed weapons of their unconscious crewmates on the tops shooting platforms and let fly at the four skeletons steering the enemy craft.

Successful strikes caused the *Ghost's* wheelmen to fall as the silver bolts inflicted massive damage to the magic that held the skeletons together.

On the quarterdeck of the DragonFrigate, Blithe spun the helm hard to turn the ship around. He intended to fire his starboard carronades at the enemy.

Around him, his crew started reviving. Midshipman Detorro shook his head and groggily rose. Looking out of his tube port, he saw the enemy coming into range of his first tube. At point blank range, he unleashed his four sixty-pound long tube shots, one at a time.

KA-BOOM!

The first shot blasted into the bow of the *Ghost*, ripping through the lower portside deck and tearing up gun platforms and skeleton crew alike.

Cannons crashed through the lower deck crushing skeletal crews trying to load them.

KA-BOOM!

The second shot went almost exactly into the same hole as the first. The sixty-pound mass of iron sheared through the foremast and smashed through more portside gun platforms. Tons of cannons went flying in all directions, crushing undead crew and waiting ghouls and zombies that were preparing to board the living ship. The tall foremast tipped over the side of the ghost ship.

KA-BOOM!

KA-BOOM!

Detorro fired his two other long guns, and their sixty-pounds of death ripped through the bony guts of the starboard side of the enemy.

Pulped by flying cannons ripped free from the emplacements, masses of *Gray Ghost* boarding parties fell to the deck in pieces. Zombies and ghouls gasped as flying cannon tubes smashed them to pulp.

☠ ☠ ☠

For the first time in the nine hundred and eighty-seven years since he'd made his deal with the devil, undead hellspawned Captain Etan dar-Black felt surprised. Manning the helm of the *Gray Ghost* because his thrice-damned enemy had turned all his helms-skeletons to dust with silver crossbow shots, the ogre skeleton realized he was out matched.

"Who keeps silver crossbow bolts handy?" Captain dar-Black couldn't help asking.

The undead ogre thought back to a few months ago. During the raid of a holy temple on an isle in the Northern Fringe, Captain dar-Black found a group of wizards where he expected to find only monks. Among their booty was a strange blue circlet. The captain discerned that the magical device had the ability to open a portal to another world. The chance to raid fresh waters couldn't be resisted. As soon as the *Gray Ghost* gained the open sea, Captain dar-Black activated the portal and sailed through a huge blue magical ring.

Coming out the other side, dar-Black spotted the strange frigate with a dragon for its keel. The undead leader didn't think much of the enemy vessel. After all, the *Gray Ghost* was a first-rater and twice the size of the little dragon. Upon seeing the ship in the fog, the undead captain ordered the beat to quarters and attacked.

Normally, the *Gray Ghost* would come upon a vessel without even opening the ship's gun ports. Dar-Black would start the paralyzing magic, his crew would join in, and after a few seconds, the crew of the enemy vessel would be petrified on their deck. The boarding parties would flow over the railing of the *Gray Ghost* and feast that night on the life force of the captured enemy crew. But not this time. . . .

Another silver crossbow bolt struck the undead captain's chest. Fire burned through his bony body as the silver started to sizzle and melt. The weapon strikes hurt like hell, but Captain dar-Black ignored the pain and steered his ship back toward the portal to escape this terrible dimension.

"What were those mortar things on the quarterdeck of the DragonFrigate?" Captain dar-Black asked. He had never seen such weapons, and what they did to his ship was amazing. When he got back to his home in the Blue Kingdoms, he intended to make a set of his own short-stubby-cannons for the quarterdeck. For now, the undead leader just wanted to get away from this world—and from the very annoying silver crossbow bolts that kept slapping into his body.

☠ ☠ ☠

Captain Blithe was of two minds as he watched the ghost ship retreat into a glowing ring of blue fog. He summoned his officers up to the quarterdeck to discuss his concerns, all the while turning the *Intrepid* to give chase.

"We have no idea if that is the sole enemy vessel in this fog," he said. "I suspect it's the only one. Our orders say engage the enemy and then report back. I want to hear your thoughts on this. Lieutenant Gray, you start."

"They are a first-rater, we're a fifth-rater. I would advise we retreat to the fleet," he said.

"Lieutenant Major Altoon, what do you think?"

"We surprised them with the carronades you were able to fire. They won't let us get that close again without using their blast-tubes. I say we report back to the fleet and hope they believe us."

Blithe paced on the quarterdeck. He didn't like what he was hearing. "Chief Fallow, your opinion please?"

"Begging your pardon, but I have to agree with these other officers. We need to warn the fleet about the green mist and what it does. If there are more of the enemy out there, we need to tell the fleet to keep at long range for as long as they can." Fallow bowed his head, knowing his captain wouldn't like what he said.

"Excellent advise from all of you, as usual. Fire off the double shot to clear the tubes. Keep the weapons run out, in case they are needed. Mr. Gray, make sail for the fleet. Take us starboard of that blue ring as close as you can. I want to study it."

No one but Chief Fallow could hear the disappointment in the Lankshire captain's voice. Captain Blithe went to the prow of the DragonFrigate. He moved along the ratlines to the very last flying jib.

The ship glided past the blue ring, as the magical transportation portal slowly started to vanish in the mist. Blithe stretched out and touched the fringe of the opening. Closing his eyes, he felt the blue threads of enchantment. His inner senses instantly grasped the air magic that went into making the portal. He could taste the creation process of the spell. He smelled the supernatural effort that went into opening the dimensional rift. In seconds, he knew how to cast the spell and knew it would take him to a new world. Maybe he wouldn't use the spell soon, but someday he and the captain of the *Gray Ghost* would have a reckoning.

"Paralyzing my crew indeed," Captain Halcyon Blithe said to himself. "There isn't a King's article against it, but dash-it-all there should be."

The young captain went to his cabin to write out a report that even *he* would find hard to believe.

THE SEARCH
by Lester Smith

Anything of any value
Seemed far from the isle I knew
As a boy, callow and simple,
Yet possessed of dreams too ample
To dwell within that small purview.

Following the cries of sea mews,
I joined a pirate's retinue,
Seeking, among the wide world's baubles,
Anything of any value.

I traveled to strange ports wherethrough
People of skin of every hue
Bustled, bartered, squabbled, wrestled,
Perished for gold. At last I winkled:
Only is there in life's own virtue
Anything of any value.

JUST MY LUCK
by Brandie Tarvin

The aftermath of a bad storm is like the end of a large party. The host is left alone in the dark to clean up the wreckage left by his guests.

That's how I felt now. All alone, save for my mostly human "family," with a very large mess to tackle and no good idea of where to start.

Good help is so hard to find, I thought as I surveyed the damage to my home.

Said home is a large, modified sambuq ironically called the *Hidden Treasure*. When we first met, she was a coastal fishing vessel. Shaped like a miniature caravel, she has a pointed prow, two lateen-rigged masts, five arbalests—weapons similar to giant crossbows—and a squared-stern with a raised platform instead of an aft-castle. And while the *Treasure* might not be the fastest ship in the World-Sea, we've been through too much together, she and I, for me to ever turn my back on her. She's the only ship I'd ever met with her own distinct personality, and she has saved my life many times over.

I surveyed her from the captain's platform, looking to see if she'd given up on me. Gratefully, I found that she hadn't, though her injuries were bad.

A broken boom, a rip in the mainsail the length of a man's arm, shattered supports on the bow-mounted arbalest, and a cracked rudder handle were immediately visible. She shuddered beneath me, creaking in agony as she pitched and yawed unsteadily upon the open ocean. We survived the sudden storm, which I suspected was magical, but that was our only piece of good fortune.

The still-clouded sky prevented me from getting a fix on our position, and the waves cracking against the *Treasure's* hull belied the fact that there was no wind to fill our sails. We had no food in the hold, only a few casks of water, and my foolish crew had long since given up fishing for their dinner to search for salvage after one of their number had caught a literal "goldfish"— a fish-shaped ornament carved of gold.

Now the misfits who served me as crew—Tick, Nara, Chiki, Tolly, Varna, Buzzer, Ol' Meg, and Spider—rowed the ship along a wake of shattered debris, searching for a fortune none of us could eat.

Able, my first mate, stood on the deck below me. Today he wore his pink dress with the orange lace trim, a rather festive ensemble better befitting . . . well, a woman. But I refused, once again, to question his fashion sense. I needed at least one competent sailor in my crew, and I worried he might leave if I did ask about the clothing. Currently, Able watched our stern while I searched the horizon with my view-scope.

"Pem!" I shouted. "Where is New Tortuga?"

My rangy navigator stood at the *Treasure's* prow. Pulling out the little waterproof picture book he always carried, he flipped through the miniatures to find the portrait of the island. His eyes narrowed on the picture as if he were trying to memorize it, then he lifted his head and pointed at a sharp angle between the *Treasure's* stern and the starboard rail amidships.

"Thataway, Cap'n Sheldon, Sir."

I sighed again. There had been a time when I had a proper navigator, one who could read maps, use a sextant and knew cardinal directions. Then my luck changed. In the toss of a whale's tail, I forfeited my status as privateer when I accidentally attacked the wrong ship. With my letter of marque revoked and my possessions seized by the crown, I had nothing but the *Treasure* and was forced to turn to true piracy for a living.

Unfortunately, at the same time, I also developed a reputation for being the unluckiest pirate on the World-Sea. I could work myself to exhaustion, and everything would still fall apart in my hands—unlike before. Now no decent sailor would sign with me; they claimed I was cursed. And the only people who would crew on my ship were misfits no other captain would touch.

Don't get me wrong. They aren't bad people, my crew. They're just horrid sailors.

"How far away?" I asked Pem, foreboding in my heart. The silence of our surroundings bothered me. If land were near, sea gull cries would be echoing across the sky.

Pem shrugged, confirming my fears. "Don' know 'xactly. Just know it's a long ways thataway."

"Ahoy, Captain!" My yeoman Tick, a man who couldn't remember things from day-to-day, cried out: "Look slight ahead to starboard! A sack upon the waves!"

I swung my view-scope in the direction Tick indicated. Sure enough, something looking like a brown sack wrapped partially around a shattered mast bobbed in the distance. I allowed myself to feel some excitement. Retrieving flotsam wasn't the same as lying in wait for some unlucky merchant ship, but it was certainly safer.

A sack was good. A sack was simple. It might have something valuable in it, or it might have nothing at all. Surely it wouldn't be bad luck just to look inside it.

"Thataway, ho!" I shouted, quoting Pem, unable to keep the glee from my voice. I didn't bother with degrees, port, and starboard. Most of the crew didn't understand nautical terms.

My "pirates" responded to my obvious cheer, putting their full strength behind their efforts. I kept my eye upon the scope and swore when I realized the sack was a person.

"Man overboard! Varna, Buzzer, haul him in. Spider, fetch your kit. I see blood."

The oars were shipped and the crew jumped into action. The two women who moved to obey my first order were the oddest pair. Varna was the only gnome I'd ever met who wanted to be a pirate, and Buzzer was an Umiri half-elf—the Umiri being a sea-faring race—who got sea-sick every time we entered and left port.

Spider, the spindly tailor who couldn't make a decently fitting outfit if his life depended on it, scuttled off his bench, all elbows and knees, and crawled down into the hold's dark entrance without even using the ladder.

First Mate Able gathered his skirts with one hand and leaped up to the platform, taking my view-scope to watch, while I jumped down to oversee the rescue efforts.

Was the man alive or dead?

The *Treasure's* side-to-side pitching slowed, calming to a soft sway as Buzzer and Varna hauled the man over the rails. The instant he was aboard, *Treasure* started rocking again. My ship wanted to get moving, as did I.

The man wore pants and a strange sort of wrapped tunic made of poor fabric with a sash twisted around his middle. His feet were bare, his hands were rough—and scarred from some sort of heavy labor—and they tightly gripped a long, waterproofed cylindrical case.

Varna pumped the water out of his lungs while Buzzer pried at his pale gray fingers, attempting to release the case. But the man's hold remained firm. By the time Spider returned topside with his sewing kit, the man was half-conscious and vomiting up water.

Spider gave Varna a light shove, and she obediently moved aside. Watery trickles of blood ran down the man's face from a deep gouge in his forehead. Spider frowned as he examined the injury.

"He'll need stitching, Cap'n, but I think he'll live. No tellin' yet if the storm beat his brains out, not till he's full awake."

"Do what you can, Spider," I replied, my attention focused on the case.

Were there jewels inside? It would certainly explain why the man held on to it so tightly.

"And Buzzer, stop trying to open his hand."

The half-elf glared up at me. "There might be somethin' in there," she retorted.

I gritted my teeth, trying desperately to keep my calm. "There's a cap at the top, Buzzer. Look at that seal. It might be some sort of magical protection."

Abashed, Buzzer ducked her head in a nod.

"Don't smell like magic to me, Cap'n," Varna piped up.

That comment threw me. I had no idea gnomes had that particular ability, to sniff out magic. Curious, I asked, "And what exactly does magic smell like?"

Varna put her hands behind her back and stood up to her full three-foot height, assuming her lecture mode. (She liked to pontificate about things.)

"Well, sometimes it smells like incense. Other times it smells like entrails. And then, there's the beef smell."

She had me until she mentioned the beef. Now I was really confused. "What does the smell of beef have to do with magic?"

She grinned, showing a mouth full of well-kept teeth. "Why that's simple, Cap'n. The smell of beef makes me hungry, which is magic enough for me!"

I bit back a groan, pinching the top of my nose with the tips of my fingers while everyone else snickered. For a moment I'd fallen for the joke, believing I had a found a crewman with actual magic powers. Gods of Wrath and Mercy, what should I do with these people?

"Crack the seal, Buzzer," I said, "and try not to break the poor man's hand."

"Aye, Cap'n," she replied.

While both she and Spider worked, the rest of the deckhands took up their fishing nets and returned to their salvage attempts. Tick, still clutching his fish made of gold, sat up beside Able. I paid them little attention, keeping my focus on the moaning, sallow-skinned man and off of my embarrassment.

Who are you, freemariner? And what did you do to earn the unwelcome attention of Kana of the Waves? I asked silently.

"Ship ho!" Able called out, just loudly enough for me to hear. I spun on my heels and caught the scope he tossed to me. He pointed silently, his clean-shaven face grim.

I could see it on the horizon, a speck of red sail against the gray-green clouds. It moved quickly, as if it had the wind behind it.

No wonder Able was worried. This was proof, as if I needed any more, that the storm that had caught us in its vicious grip had no natural origins. The *Treasure* groaned a warning, dipping her bow in protest.

The ship headed straight for us. It had no other possible destination; we were the only other ship in the area, and I could see no land around. *Another one of Kana's jokes*, I presumed with a sardonic grimace. The goddess had a strange sense of humor—of which I was usually the hapless target. The *Hidden Treasure* was going to be attacked by pirates.

A rustle of parchment caught my attention. "Cap'n," Buzzer said, handing over a scroll with gilded handles, "I can't read this."

I returned the scope to Able. He nodded, raising it back to his eye without comment. He would sound a warning before the ship got into attack range.

"Is this all that was in the case?" I asked. Buzzer nodded. When I looked at the scroll, I understood her confusion. There was no picture and no writing—at least not any sort of writing I'd ever seen. It was a collection of painted sticks and dots, angled and straight, curved and splashed. Some of the sticks and dots touched, while others stood alone. The paper looked like it had been painted on by a child.

Buzzer looked at me expectantly. "Is it magic, Cap'n?"

"I don't know, Buzzer. Put it back in the scroll case. We'll ask our new friend once he regains consciousness. Nara, Chiki, drop the rowing benches. Everyone else, grab your tools and prepare for a boarding."

Tools, not weapons. Very few of us had actual weapons. Able had his cutlass, Varna had made little bombs—which would be used in the midship's arbalests. Buzzer had her fishing spear, and I had my longsword. The others tended to use whatever came to hand. Tolly had a slingshot, but he could only hit things he wasn't aiming at.

My crew froze where they stood, startled by the order, then rushed to obey. I groaned as they dropped their nets, not thinking to stow them correctly in the rush to prepare for ship's defense. It wasn't their fault; they were green, and it was my duty to train them better. Before I could correct the error, the man we rescued staggered to his feet, holding the empty case tight, and stumbled toward me. As he neared, he fell to his knees, prostrating himself. Foreign words tumbled out of his mouth.

I looked at Able who shrugged in confusion. The man at my feet continued to babble in his unintelligible tongue, risking a cautious glance up at me when I didn't respond. His expression contained excitement, but also a hint of dread. He was scared of me, but thrilled to see me. The longer I waited, the more worried he became. Finally he stopped speaking, still lying prostrate at my feet with his face tilted to the side to watch me.

I knew fear, having experienced it enough times myself, and I felt guilty for unintentionally inflicting it upon this poor soul. I bent down and lifted him to his feet.

"Relax," I said slowly and loudly, hoping he understood Tegla, the trade-tongue everyone else in the World-Sea knew. "You're safe now. The storm's over and no one here means you harm. I'm Captain Sheldon, and this is my ship."

The man seemed to understand. His fear-filled expression changed back to an excited one. "Captain-hata," he said, bowing deeply. "You I am being."

I blinked. Not the answer I was expecting. "You're me?"

"Nie," the man thumped his chest with one hand. "You I am being."

"Your name is 'you?'"

"That's right," Chiki chimed in.

"What's right?" Nara declared, playing up Chiki's banter with a grin on her face.

"You's right," Chiki responded, his face alight with glee. Clearly the two were enjoying themselves.

"Enough!" I snapped at them, already tired of the jest. I turned back to the man we had rescued and asked again, "Your name is 'you'?"

The man shook his head and tried again, this time he pronounced the word with a hard "h" sound in front of it. "Hiu. Hiu I am being."

"Hiu?"

He nodded in pleasure as I said the word.

"Wind to your sails, Hiu. What were you doing in the storm?"

Hiu frowned. I repeated the words more slowly and he grinned.

"Core I am seeking, to be trading for *nakken*." He pointed to my sword, and then his face fell. "Boat has been sinking from bad storm. Lost are very rare items I am to be using for trade."

His Tegla was heavily accented and, at times, consisted of words I barely knew. I struggled to understand him, repeating aloud what I thought I heard, to see if I was correct. "You were sailing to the Core to trade for weapons? Swords? Don't your people have these things?"

111

"Nie, nie," he shook his head in frustration. "*Nakken*." Pointing to my sword again, he looked around the deck as if searching for something else. "*Nakken* is to be making of things."

"Metal," Tick ventured a guess. "He's looking to trade for metal."

"Met-al," Hiu agreed eagerly. "Met-al I be trading for. Having you such? Knowing you where this to being found?"

His question left me short of breath. I had never heard of an island with a metal shortage, but if there was one, my crew and I could make a fortune trading with them. We could leave off piracy and be honest, even wealthy, merchants. Blessed Kana of the Waves could have answered my prayers for once—assuming Hiu wasn't from one of those disappearing islands I'd heard stories about.

So I asked my next question carefully. "Hiu, where are you from?"

He answered the question promptly, as if completely unaware of the importance of his answer. "Tenka-Rii."

I've never been prone to seasickness, but now I knew how it felt. Dizziness assaulted me, my breathing became labored, and my stomach flipped over several times before I finally formed a coherent thought.

Tenka-Rii.

Impossible. Tenka-Rii was a legend, a fable shared amongst adventurers. It was said that Kogane, a wise and powerful dragon, left the Core more than five hundred years ago with a group of humans to create a grand civilization—Tenka-Rii—where magical artifacts were as common as fish in the World-Sea. Finding Tenka-Rii was every sorcerer's fantasy, every would-be pirate's dream. And here I stood, talking to a man claiming to be from this island nation no one had ever found.

Able appeared suddenly beside me, Tick and Ol' Meg, the ugly crone who served as my Wind Whisperer, at his shoulders. Obviously they'd also heard Hiu's statement. Able's face was white with shock, the same color I felt mine must be. "Gods of Wrath and Mercy," my first mate breathed.

A sentiment I agreed with completely.

"Sheldy, my love," Ol' Meg suddenly croaked. "Young Meg hears wind a-comin' our way."

The *Treasure* trembled in response, her slack sails flapping briefly as if they begged to be filled.

Able and I swung around as one, my scabbard nearly getting tangled in his skirts. He flushed briefly, though I wasn't sure if it was because he was caught ignoring his duty or because he'd come close to tripping me. I waved off the apology before he could make it.

"Spider, how long before you finish mending the mainsail's tear?"

"At least a quarter glass, Captain. I'll get right on it."

"Hurry," I muttered, watching the red-sailed ship approach. I didn't need the scope to see it now, though I couldn't see its crew. Out of the corner of my eye, I saw Spider scramble up the rigging to finish his chore.

"Soldiers," Able muttered, his eye to the scope. "Richly dressed. A few archers. All land lubbers by the look of them. Shields, pikes, heavy armor of

112

some sort. Throw 'em overboard and they'll sink faster than a ship scuttled by a whirlpool."

I heard, rather than saw, Hiu dive under the platform. Buzzer laughed aloud at his fear. Varna scrambled past me, her arms full of fist-sized pottery balls. Chiki helped her place the little bombs next to each of the arbalests while the rest of the crew scattered along the length of the ship. They looked nervous. I could hardly blame them.

I could see the enemy deck clearly now. The sailors were easy to tell from the landlubbers by the way each dressed and moved. On both sides of the ship, a double-row of soldiers stood at stiff attention, their shiny armor decorated with a dizzying blast of colors. At the center, atop the forecastle, stood an arrogant man in the same style tunic as Hiu wore, but made of gold cloth.

Beside the man stood two others dressed mostly in black trousers, loose shirts and facial masks that enveloped everything on their heads except two pairs of narrowed eyes. Hilts protruded above their shoulders, evidence of swords strapped to their backs, and on their feet were dainty golden sandals. Such strange footwear compared to the rest of their clothing made me think "magic," though I didn't know for sure.

Lastly, sitting on the deck in less ostentatious clothing, was an artist. This man had a paintbrush in his right hand and was using it on a roll of parchment held in his left. His manner reminded me of a scribe or court historian, but I had never seen anyone write with a brush before.

The ship turned its port side to ours and slowed. The wind snapped loudly against their sails, yet didn't touch ours. The *Treasure* tried to heave away, pitching violently for a moment.

"Easy, Girl," I muttered. She subsided with a muffled creak, clearly unhappy.

The strange rectangular ship with squared sails heaved to beside us. Suspicious, I wondered about the strangers' motives. If her captain didn't mean to attack us, what did he want?

A hollow thud sounded as something hitting the deck behind me, and wiry hands grasped my ankles. I looked over my shoulder and found Hiu prostrate again, his face hidden and the scroll case rolling around beside him.

"Beggings I am, Captain-hata. To be protecting I, such a small, insignificant creature, would granting Captain-hata's soul many riches in afterlife. Forever indebted to Captain-hata I am being for such magnanimous gesture and am never leaving your side!"

He sounded absolutely terrified. Was the approaching ship also from Tenka-Rii? "Hiu . . ."

"Beggings I am, Captain-hata! Worthless me will be doing anything. I am giving life to Captain-hata! Greatest treasure in World-Sea are to be giving if safety being granted!"

I suppressed a groan, trying to squelch the pity I felt for the man. I had enough misfits in my crew. I certainly was not going to help every last charity case I came across! At least, that's what I tried telling myself. The sinking feeling in my gut told me otherwise. *Sweet Kana, why me?*

Able tapped my shoulder and I turned back toward what I now thought of as the Tenkanese ship. The man in golden clothes spoke loudly, his words in the same language as the one Hiu first spoke. I waited patiently until the man was done, then replied, "Do you speak Tegla?"

The man exchanged looks with the "artist" and then with the sailor I assumed to be the captain. The trio exchanged a flurry of words, and the captain bowed deeply.

"I am being Yukio, Captain. This," he gestured toward the wealthy man, "am being Siuku-hata, personage of high importance. Siuku-hata be offering greetings to your captain and wishing to be speakings of great urgency."

"I am being Sheldon," I started to reply, then cursed myself for falling into that odd, broken version of Tegla the Tenkanese seemed to speak. "I am Sheldon, captain of the *Hidden Treasure*. How may I assist you?"

Yukio turned, conversing quickly with this Siuku-hata and the artist. A tense moment passed, my crew shifting nervously while we waited. A flying fish arched out of the water between the two ships, cutting back under the waves with a musical splash. Thunder rumbled in the distance, an ominous reminder of the recent storm. I took a deep breath of warm salt air, willing myself to relax. Finally, Yukio turned back to speak again. He gestured at his deck.

"Honorable Sheldon-hen are graciously invited to be enjoying Siuku-hata's pleasurable company for tea. Yes?"

He wanted me aboard his ship?

Able hissed unhappily in my ear, and Hiu's grip around my ankles tightened. I didn't need either of them to tell me this was a bad idea.

"No, thank you. I speak just fine to Siuku-hata from here."

The two black-clad men on the other ship shifted their weight ever so slightly, and the *Treasure* shuddered briefly in concern. "Storm and Surge," I cursed under my breath. Here it came, more of that bad luck only *I* seemed able to conjure. Kana help me, if those two weren't preparing for an attack, I'd eat both of my masts, sails and all.

Siuku stepped forward, his head lifted imperiously. His stiff shoulders and rigid manner spoke of aristocratic self-importance. I suppressed my initial spurt of distaste. I dared not risk my crew or the *Treasure* in a battle if it could be avoided. So I held to a calm expression and waited for him to speak.

He motioned to a few sailors who lugged a large trunk to the forecastle. With a slight bow of his head, he opened the lid to reveal a breathtaking mound of gold coins and jewels. I hadn't seen that much wealth in one place in a long time.

I swallowed my surprise. He smiled. "Sheldon-hen, you are being respectable man, like me. We are to be speaking as equals. Here be a small gesture of appreciating your company. Gift of friends. You come to be getting?"

Obviously they wanted me on their ship. Why? I doubted their "friendly" intentions and didn't want to leave my crew. Able's a good first mate, but hardly captain material; he hates making the hard decisions all captains have to deal with. If something happened to me aboard the Tenkanese ship, my crew might never get home.

"I am a poor fisherman and have nothing to give in return, Siuku-hata," I said loudly and slowly, hoping my ruse would work. *Gods, I hope Tick hid that fish of his.*

I winced when Yukio's gaze fell meaningfully upon my five arbalests. His Tegla might be archaic, but the man was no fool. What fisherman used such weapons? Still, he didn't call me out over the lie. He just nodded and whispered something to the artist who frantically whipped his brush against his parchment.

Siuku ignored the two and raised his chin, folding his arms behind his back. With his next words, he seemed to be changing his tactics.

"Criminal I be seeking, one responsibility for destroying great family heirloom and stealing of much treasure. We be tracking him here. On your ship he am being. This," he gestured grandly at the gold, "are yours exchanging for what mine is."

I swallowed in surprise. That was a lot of coin. Still, I wondered how he could be so sure of himself.

"I have no criminals aboard my ship."

"We are having tracker magic," Siuku retorted. "Criminal is being here. Knowing such for true, I am."

Well, that explained why his captain had headed straight for the *Treasure*. Spider and Tick would probably hate me, but I needed to test a theory.

"You want us to return the treasure he stole, the bits we've salvaged? Sure. But we only have a few bolts of silk and a golden fish."

Siuku frowned. "Silk and fish you are to be allowing to keep. Thief it is I am wanting. Hiu is being evil, vicious man. Will be death to you and your crew. Give him over, you be getting money, justice is being mine."

I hesitated. The quivering, sobbing man behind me hardly seemed dangerous. A thief, maybe. There were many reasons a man would steal, after all. Just look at me for proof.

Siuku must have misread my hesitation because he gestured again and another trunk was loaded on the forecastle, this one filled with silver ingots.

"Him also be taking ancestral history. This is exchanging for scroll he carries."

My pulse thudded in my ears, beating in time to the waves hitting our hull. That was a lot of coin to pay for a thief, even in the Core. I personally knew of fiercely hated pirates whose bounties were less than what Siuku offered for the man behind me. Parchment crackled as Buzzer clutched the scroll tightly to her chest. So, this is the price of friendship with the Tenkanese lord, Hiu and his unreadable scroll. Why would anyone spend that much for a stupid piece of parchment with sticks drawn on it?

"Beggings I am, Captain-hata," Hiu whimpered in fear behind me. A glance over my shoulder showed him still prostrate and shivering in fear.

"Hiu?" I asked, softly so Yukio wouldn't hear. "Are these things true? Did you steal from this man?"

"Hai. But Captain-hata must understand, I trying to be saving my people. We need *nakken*. Trading with Core am being necessary. But Great Curtain was prevents trading. I be breaking Curtain to find tradings and saving my people. Beggings I am! I be offering anything for Captain-hata's protecting!"

I hate groveling. I hate doing it, and I hate it when other people do it in front of me. And if I didn't feel guilty enough about wanting to take Siuku up on his offer with Hiu shivering at my feet, one quick glance at my crew—all of whom ended up on this ship during similar circumstances—twisted the knife in my gut.

"No," I hissed softly.

Hiu looked up, his face frozen in terror. Buzzer frowned and Able opened his mouth, only to shut it as I raised my hand to forestall his words.

"No," I repeated loudly enough for Siuku, Yukio, and his entire ship to hear. "I'm sorry, I cannot take your offer. I claim salvage rights. Hiu and all he has belongs to me now."

The Tenkanese were not pleased. Their eyes narrowed and lips pursed as if they had swallowed something sour. The artist said something in Tenkanese, and Siuku nodded sharply. At the hand signal given by the artist, so subtle I barely realized what it was, the black-clad warriors moved. They vaulted off the forecastle, over the side of the red-sailed ship, and ran across the water.

"How in the Holy Deep. . . ?" Able swore, dropping my view-scope as the two men leaped across the surface of the waves, barely getting their feet wet.

I was so enraptured with the impossible sight that I barely heard the whack of my expensive scope hitting the deck.

"Kiitaru!" Hiu wailed in terror, releasing my ankles and scuttling under the platform at my back. "Kiitaru warriors will be killing of us all!"

And just that quickly, these two mysterious warriors leaped to the gunnels of my ship, one drawing his sword and moving against the other members of my crew.

Chiki screeched as he dropped his oar, his "weapon" of choice, and stumbled away from this man who seemed to fly.

Able drew his cutlass with one hand, gathering his flounced skirts in the other, and ducked behind me to defend the crew. This left the second black-clad warrior to me, Buzzer, and the prostrate Hiu.

"Buzzer, with Hiu!" I shouted, ducking the approaching blade. A snippet of my blonde-brown hair fell to the deck. I ducked back from my attacker's assault. Vanity be damned. I fancied survival over stupid notions of bravery.

In the time it took to draw my sword, the Kiitaru warrior loosed several more swings at me, the first whispering so close to my skin, I felt the breeze of its passing. The second cut opened up my shirtsleeve, while a third sliced clean through the rock-wood corner of the platform. I hacked at my swift-footed opponent, my heart skipping a beat in fear.

Rock-wood couldn't be cut once it had cured. Burned with fire or shredded by underwater reefs, yes, but swords weren't supposed to harm it. Yet, a chunk of the platform fell from the blow of the Kiitaru's sword as if the wood were soft cheese shaved off by a hot knife.

As I fought for my life and the lives of those who depended on me, I suddenly remembered the *other* legend of Tenka-Rii: the one about mystical weapons, capable of cutting through any substance, and nearly indestructible armor.

Something warm dripped down my arm. Blood probably. I hadn't even felt the enemy blade touch my skin. I tried countering the Kiitaru's next swing and fell to my knees. The force of his blow shattered my sword, the shock jolting down my arms.

Someone screamed in the distance, but I didn't dare look around. My assailant's weapon sliced straight down at my head. Dropping my broken sword, I fumbled for my dagger, scrambling back. But I caught my free hand in one of the nets strewn across the *Treasure's* wet deck.

"Damn my luck!" Sliding my dagger out of its sheath, I struggled to cut myself free, even as death himself swung around and bore down on me. He stepped onto the net that had me trapped, his sword slicing toward my skull. I pulled my ensnared hand in front of my face, to protect myself, and felt a heavy tug on the other end of the net. The eyes of the warrior widened in shock and he slipped suddenly forward, landing heavily on my dagger.

When I could breathe again, I noticed the other end of the net wrapped around the man's feet. He was dead; his life's blood dripped across my hand. Pushing with my knees, I levered his corpse off of my dagger. I cut my hand free of the net, grabbed the odd one-sided blade my enemy no longer needed, and pushed to my feet.

One Kiitaru dead. Where's the other?

Hiu huddled beneath the platform, scroll and scroll case lying forgotten beside him. Buzzer, her fishing spear in hand, stood guard at the platform. I turned to the *Treasure's* bow to see how the rest of my crew fared.

Bits of several oars, also made of rock-wood, littered the deck. Like me, my sailors had found the oars were little match against the enemy's magical swords. Now the rest of the crew huddled along the rails, Spider had crawled down the rigging to tend their injuries, while Able fought to protect them.

If the situation hadn't been so dire, I might have laughed. Able was everything a swashbuckling pirate should be—handsome, daring, clever. But with his lace-covered skirts kilted up above his muscled legs and his beaded bodice heaving over his flat and hairy décolletage, he looked more like a traveling player than a freemariner. Still, he held his own until the remaining Kiitaru sliced at the broken boom, bringing it down on top of my first mate.

117

At that moment, the *Treasure* lurched, pulling her bow several inches out of the water and slamming it down again. When the boom dropped on Able, down came the attached sheets and sail. One of the lines whipped through the air and wrapped itself around the enemy warrior's neck. With as little warning as we had received when the enemy attacked us, the *Hidden Treasure* yanked the second Kiitaru high, smashing his head against a yardarm. The man's skull cracked with a sickening crunch. His body went limp from the unexpected hanging, and his sword bounced off the wadded sail and into the ocean.

With both the enemy warriors dead, Nara, Tolly, and Pem raced to assist Able, while I turned my attention back to the Tenkanese ship. I felt dizzy from lack of blood, but I refused to drop my guard. We could still be in danger.

Siuku and his men looked pale. The soldiers no longer stood at attention. The sailors openly gaped. The artist frowned, examining me for a moment, then said something to Siuku in tones that reminded me of an insistent bill collector.

Siuku shrieked, and his calm demeanor vanished. He flung out his arm toward the soldiers and sailors, shouting orders.

I didn't have to command my crew to do anything. They all recognized what the enemy's gesture meant. By the time the Tenkanese fire arrows streaked toward us, Tolly, Tick, Varna, and Chiki were already launching the pottery bombs in exchange.

The air around the Tenkanese ship filled with thick, pale clouds of lime dust, metal shards, and ground pepper. Cries of agony echoed from beyond the haze.

Buzzer hauled Hiu out from under the platform. "Water!" she yelled at him.

I smelled smoke, realizing my ship was on fire.

I blistered the sky with my oaths. Always when I thought my luck had turned, Kana would smite me down again. What did She have against me? It wasn't like I forgot to sacrifice to Her on feast and holy days.

Sheathing my new blade in the dead Kiitaru's scabbard, I joined Buzzer, Hiu, and Able in a bucket line. We concentrated our efforts on the stern mast and the lower sail. The platform was also burning, but I hardly cared. I could always get another built. The mast and sail were much more important.

Varna and the others launched the last of her nasty lime bombs. Ol' Meg stood at the starboard rail, her eyes closed and her gnarled hand clutching her crystal whisperer's pendant. She muttered to herself, swaying back and forth, trying to fill our remaining sails with wind.

Just as we put out the platform fire, something buzzed past my face. Rain was in the air. As I glanced up, the topsail ballooned out.

"Make fast the sheets!" I cried. "Meg's got us a breeze!"

The buckets were dropped in the hold and all hands jumped to action. As I mentioned before, they didn't know a whole lot about sailing, but they knew enough to pull tight the controlling ropes when I yelled out "make fast."

At the same time, the Tenkanese ship roiled with activity. My voice must have carried across the water, revealing our location, despite the haze of our bombs. Another spurt of fire arrows arced in our direction, scorching a trail through the sky. A few poorly aimed pikes flew out of the lime cloud, bouncing off our rail guards. But Meg proved our savior.

For the first time since I had known the old hag, she conjured up a wind, stealing it right out of the Tenkanese's sails. The *Treasure* didn't have half the sail she needed for top speed, but she lunged eagerly forward anyway. I let her pick her path. So long as we headed away from our attackers, any direction worked.

I fished about the cluttered deck for my view-scope, groaning when I found it with a broken lens. Without my scope, I could not keep a close eye on the Tenkanese ship. Instead, I watched its red sails fade behind with my naked eyes.

When I judged us far enough away not to be heard by Yukio or his freemariners, I got Hiu's attention. "Your turn."

Hiu paled and dropped to the deck, bowing and scrapping. "Anything for Captain-hata. You be saving life of such an insignificant one like I am being."

"Sweet Nyarra's tits, man! Get on your feet!" I couldn't contain my temper any longer. Blood loss and hunger will do that to a man.

Hiu scrambled to his feet, nodding so hard I thought his head would fall off. "Hai, Captain-hata. I am being slave to your wishings."

"I don't want a slave. I just want to know who you are and what is so important about that cursed scroll."

Hiu lifted his eyes and smiled, showing a mouthful of yellowing teeth. "Fisher I am being. Father and grandfather also being fishers. I am coming from long line of fishers."

"And the scroll?"

I didn't think a man could grin as widely as this man did. His lips expanded so far apart, he could have swallowed a porpoise whole.

"Ah. Scroll is containing great, great treasure."

Buzzer and I exchanged confused glances. How in Kana's name could sticks and dots be treasure?

"Scroll is holdings secret to making of swords."

Able laughed. "Our people already know how to make swords."

"Nie, nie." Hiu shook his head violently, then ran over to the Kiitaru warrior I had accidentally killed. He pointed to the hilt of the man's sword as if he dared not touch the weapon itself. "Secret of *this* sword."

I must have forgotten how to breathe, because the next thing I knew Buzzer and Able were hauling me upright where I had collapsed on the deck. The knowledge of making the magic swords was contained in that scroll? Small wonder Hiu had clasped it tight when his ship went down. And now that I thought about it, Siuku hadn't been offering me nearly enough for it.

119

"Where is it?" I rasped, excitement pounding in my chest. I was rich. Beyond my wildest dreams rich. My luck had changed, bless Kana and Her stormy temper, I was on my way back to legitimacy again.

Buzzer and Able released me once I was able to stand and we all ran toward the remnants of the platform. Ignoring the still-hot charcoal, we threw the debris away in a desperate attempt to find my salvation. The scroll casing lay there, on the unburned end of the under-platform, one side charred.

But all we could find of the scroll was a half-melted golden end-piece and a few fragments of burnt parchment.

Not enough remained to reconstruct the thing. Excitement ebbed away to be replaced by the dull sensation of failure that had become so familiar to me.

"Hiu," I asked, more of a matter of course than because I expected the answer I wanted, "could you write out what was on that scroll?"

He shook his head dolefully. "Readings? Nie. I am knowing what scroll say not. Just knowing it be holding great secret of making swords."

Fantastic. Just plain fantastic. A damaged ship, an injured crew, the key to redemption snatched out of my hands, and all I get out of this adventure is a fisherman.

Fisherman? I thought. *Wait, now. There's an idea. But first, we need to get farther away from the Tenkanese.*

"Pem!" I shouted out. "Point out New Tortuga. Tolly, stow the damaged rudder and see if an oar will work for steering. Head thataway and follow Pem's finger."

"Aye, Cap'n," the brutish-looking and simpleminded deckhand replied.

My misfit crew swung back into action, doing their best to repair my ship. I turned my attention back to Hiu.

"You owe me, remember?"

"Hai, Captain-hata. Great debt of life and honor I am owing."

"Good," I replied. "You're officially the ship's cook. When we get far enough away from your countrymen, we'll slow down so you can do some fishing. I'm starving."

The Tenkanese man practically glowed with joy. I shook my head and walked to the stern of the *Hidden Treasure*. Good help is so hard to find. But sometimes, it sneaks up on you when you aren't looking.

JUDGMENT
by Lorelei Shannon

The isle of New Tortuga had never seen anything quite like the crew of the pirate ship *Judgment*. Excited talk began when she cruised into port—a long, sleek vessel with strange pictograms carved down her flanks. Her flag, featuring a dog skull with crook and flail crossed beneath, had never been seen in this part of the Blue Kingdoms before. And when the crew rowed ashore, walked through the center of town liked they owned it, and settled down in the roughest tavern on the isle, jaws dropped and tongues wagged. Island folk flocked to the tavern, peeking in the windows, those that dared walking in for a drink and a closer look.

From behind the long, carved ironwood bar, Jenny goggled at the strangers.

They were Al-Kabar, or at least they seemed to be. Their ears were large and pointed, pierced with multiple golden rings. Their snouts were long and elegant. Every last one was female. They wore large, elaborate beaded neckpieces, bronze-colored breastplates, and narrow skirts split on each side to the waist, like Bethian dancers. But there was no mistaking them for dancers. The swords, daggers and pistols that hung from their belts marked them as pirates. Their fur ranged in color from jet black to light brown, and each woman's skin matched her fur exactly. Tall and strong, Jenny thought they were the most amazing creatures she'd ever seen.

"Back to the kitchen with 'e," the cook said, ruffling Jenny's hair. "There's a pile o' dirty pots taller 'n you what needs scrubbing'."

"Aye-aye, Jimbo," the little girl replied, tearing her gaze reluctantly from the strangers. *If only*, she thought. *If only I were strong like them.*

☠ ☠ ☠

Most of the *Judgment's* crew sat at a single table, laughing, talking in their strange accents, and drinking more rum than seemed possible. Mosi, the lanky first mate, sat at the edge of the group and gnawed on a beef bone as she scanned the tavern for trouble. It was not in her nature to trust strangers.

A few crew members had ventured beyond their circle to socialize with the locals. Akila, the bosun, sat with a motley group of buccaneers and scallywags, swapping sea stories. Her nut-brown arms were ropy with muscle that rippled as she gestured, describing sea monsters and savage battles.

Dendera, the gunner, was wrapped in the arms of a young, yellow-maned human male, nuzzling and laughing with him.

Captain Renenet shook her ebony head, and her muzzle wrinkled with distaste. To say that her younger sister Dendera's erotic tastes were eclectic would be an understatement. But how could she stand to get so close to that flat-faced, hairless monkey? Renenet snorted. Finishing the last of her ale, she stood and stretched her long, sinewy legs. Males of several species turned to look. Renenet didn't care in the least. She strolled to the bar, raising a hand to get the attention of the owner.

"Barkeep," she called, "I would have a word with you."

Blind Jeff was a hardened old pirate, now retired from the sea. He was not truly blind, but squinted through thick, round lenses at the dog-headed Amazon before him. "How can I help ye, lass?"

"Captain. Captain Renenet."

Blind Jeff grimaced, showing all four of his teeth. "A thousand pardons, Cap'n. Can I get ye another drink? Some food, per'aps? The stew is quite nice tonight."

"Thank you, no," said Renenet. "I seek a map."

Blind Jeff let out a cough of laughter. "Don't they all, Cap'n? And what treasure does this map lead to?"

"No treasure, but our lost home. The isle of Luxor."

The barkeep scowled, thinking. "The name sounds f'miliar."

Renenet's ears pricked up, making the gold hoops jingle. "Have you heard of it? It is a small but beautiful place. A great pyramid rises from the center of the isle, so large and so white that it can be seen for miles away."

"Oh, aye!" Blind Jeff nodded. "I have heard tell of it, madam. In fact, Cap'n John Sweeney was in here only last month, bragging that 'e had a map to just such a place. 'E said it was an island rich with gold. 'E and his men planned to travel there and plunder all they could."

Renenet gave a humorless grin, showing many sharp, white teeth. "If they reached Luxor, then their souls have surely been judged by our lord Anubis, and their foolish bodies lie at the bottom of the sea."

"But they didn't."

Renenet turned her head to see who spoke. The cook, a tall, red-faced fellow, had wandered out from the kitchen.

"What are ye blatherin' about, Jimbo?" Blind Jeff asked the man.

"Ain't ye heard about it? John Sweeney an' 'is whole crew was slaughtered, on the edges of the Cursed Seas. 'Twas Cap'n Billy Bones what did it. If anyone's got your map, it's 'im. If ye dare, look for 'is flag—it's three skeletons, dancin' side by side."

A few men nearby gasped; a few made warding gestures.

"I see," said Renenet. "This Billy Bones, he is a man?"

"Well, not 'zackly," said Blind Jeff. "Nobody's sure jus' what 'e is. 'Im and 'is whole crew are somethin' far worse than human. There's different stories, but some says 'e's like Red Jack Sirus."

Renenet cocked her head. "Sirus? He is a—a dog-man?"

Jimbo and Blind Jeff laughed nervously. "Naw," said Jimbo. "More like a dead man. A dead man what walks about killin' ever'thing 'e looks at."

Renenet did not so much as blink her moon-gold eyes. "Yes. The undead. We have dealt with such creatures before. Have you any idea where this Billy Bones might be sailing?"

"Well, o' course 'e could be anywhere, but 'e's been known to sail between the Cursed Seas and the Sea of Mists, preyin' on them unfortunate enough to cross 'is path."

"Thank you." Quick as a striking snake, Renenet flipped each man a silver piece. "Now I believe I will have another ale."

☠ ☠ ☠

Thomas, the yellow-haired human, whispered into Dendera's large, lovely ear. "You are amazing. I've never met a woman like you."

She giggled. "Of course you haven't. I don't think we're even from your world, golden-fur. We left our home to go pirating long ago, and when we returned . . . when we returned our isle was no longer there. And we were here."

Thomas nuzzled the soft, warm fur of her neck. "Things like that happen in the Blue Kingdoms."

She ran her tan fingers through his hair, licked his cheek. "We used to live for battle. Now all my sister the captain wants is to find our way back home. She thinks there exists a map that pinpoints the location of Luxor in this world." Dendera sighed. "I think she leads us on a fool's errand."

"I hope you're not leaving immediately." Thomas squeezed her tightly, and she squeezed him back, nearly breaking his ribs. He laughed. "Are all the women of your isle so fierce?"

"Just so, golden-fur. Our men are scholars, builders, keepers of the city. Most are content to stay on land and study the spiritual writings. They debate endlessly on the teachings of our lord Anubis." She grinned, nibbling at his shoulder with her sharp teeth. "We women—we are content to just send souls to Anubis. As many as we possibly can."

Thomas chuckled, low in his throat. "Tell me. Do you have a tail?"

"Come find out," she growled.

☠ ☠ ☠

The crew of the *Judgment* ate, drank and laughed late into the night. At last they retired to rooms rented on the upper floor of the tavern.

Renenet covered her head with a pillow, trying not to hear the horrible sounds coming from Dendera's room. She pounded her fist on the wall. "Go to sleep, you harlot! You'd lie with a jenrat if it winked at you!" Through the wall came laughter, and Dendera let out an impudent howl. Renenet couldn't help but grin. She grabbed a second pillow and burrowed under the covers.

☠ ☠ ☠

The *Judgment* prepared to sail early the next morning. First mate Mosi called out the captain's orders as supplies were loaded onto the ship.

Although Dendera had been up most of the night (and kept Renenet up with her), the gunner was bright-eyed and humming as she loaded barrels of powder into the hold.

"You know," grumbled Renenet, "if, a few months from now, my decks are crawling with half-human monster pups, I'll feed them to the sharks."

"Okay!" called Dendera.

"Or maybe I'll just eat them myself! With curry and onions!" the captain bellowed.

"Sounds fair." Dendera poked her head up from the hold and gave her sister a sassy wink. Renenet growled at her, trying not to laugh.

"Captain?" Renenet turned to see Akila, the bosun, and a small, skinny, none-too-clean human of indeterminate sex.

"What," said Renenet, "is *that?*"

"This is Jenny. She was the kitchen-maid at the tavern. She would join our crew as cabin girl."

Renenet scowled. It was a pitiful thing, scrawny and underfed, with mouse-brown hair cropped short and pale green eyes. The child's pallid face was lined with several bone-white scars. One of her ears was thickened and lumpy. "How old are you, girl?"

"Thirteen." Jenny raised her pointed chin. "But I'm strong for my age."

"You look like an uncooked chicken. The sea is no place for an undersized pup like you." Renenet started to turn away.

"Please," said Jenny, in a voice the captain could barely hear. "My pa beats on me all the time. I can't really stand it no more."

Renenet sighed, laid her ears back. "All right," she grumbled. "But we'll only take you as far as the next port."

Jenny's face lit up in a huge smile. "Thank you, Captain! You won't regret it! I'll work hard for ye!"

"Good. Start by taking a bath."

☠ ☠ ☠

By noon they were at full sail. The wind whipped by Renenet's face and ears and her nostrils flared, taking in the delicious odors of the sea. Blessed Ra, but she loved pirating. Part of her wanted to forget Luxor, to spend the rest of her days plundering the Blue Kingdoms. But her home called to her, leaving an ache in her heart that was with her day and night. She'd had a man there, a fine, handsome archivist named Geb. He'd wanted to marry her. Renenet had promised she would be his bride, when she returned from one last voyage. How long ago had that been? Months? Years? Time seemed different here, somehow flexible and slippery. In dark moments, Renenet wondered if centuries had passed, Luxor fallen, Geb merely dust and bones.

She had to get home. She had to find out.

"Captain!" Young Sabah called from the crow's nest. "A sail! Due east! I'd bet my ears she's a merchant!"

Renenet was suddenly surrounded by excited pirates grinning wickedly, nostrils flaring as if they already smelled blood.

"Captain! Can we get 'em?"

"Let's take 'er down!"

"Don't let 'er get away!"

Renenet had halfway decided to just pursue this Billy Bones as hard and fast as she could, to not dally with treasure until the map was in her hands. But looking at the sharp teeth and shining eyes of her crew, their tongues lolling with the lust for battle . . .

"Oh, why the hell not."

The cheer was deafening.

☠ ☠ ☠

The *Judgment* closed in on the merchant fast, deadly as a shark in the water. Sabah gleefully hoisted their colors. The merchant made a slow, desperate attempt to turn. "Dendera!" the Captain shouted. "Put one over the bow!"

Moments later, the *Judgment's* bow chaser roared. The crew barked and howled as the ball whistled over the merchant's nose.

An answering crack echoed through the air, and a cannonball tore through the *Judgment's* mainsail.

"Captain," yelled Dendera, laughing just a bit madly, "they're actually firing on us. What are we going to do about that?"

"Let her feel the full weight of our metal." Renenet's grin was savage.

"Broadside!" bellowed Mosi.

Keket, the helmswoman, cranked the wheel. Her shoulders bulged with effort as the *Judgment* swung around, bringing her starboard guns to bear. Dendera ran down the deck, shouting encouragement to her eager gun crew. Moments later, the *Judgment's* seven starboard cannons blasted, tearing into the side of the merchant, sending splintered wood flying into the air. The merchant rocked in the water like a toy.

"Prepare to board!" shouted the captain. "Watch the rail guns!" Mosi drew one of her many pistols and blasted a hole in the chest of a sailor as he tried to turn a swivel gun on the boarding party. He was smoking as he collapsed to the deck.

The pirates yipped and howled, swords and pistols drawn as they prepared to swarm the merchant. From the corner of her eye, Renenet saw Jenny, the human pup, standing with her feet planted and a sword in her hand.

"Get below decks, girl!" Renenet shouted at her. "You'll get yourself killed!" Jenny hesitated, eyes growing flinty. "Now!" the captain snarled, showing every tooth in her head. Jenny scurried away.

The pirates swung across to the deck of the merchant, with Renenet in the lead. Their vicious growling alone drove some of the sailors to drop their weapons and run belowdecks.

The fight was short and brutal. The few sailors who dared defend their ship died quickly, without mercy, and without excess cruelty. Killing was a thing of necessity to the Luxor pirates, and although some surely enjoyed it, torture and mutilation were not acceptable. Such things were offensive to Anubis.

Beheading was the specialty of the pirates—their height and strength and the massive weight of their cutlasses made it easy. After five sailors had been parted from their heads, the rest surrendered. Half the crew kept them at bay while the rest looted the hold.

It was not a spectacular haul—the merchant had been carrying mostly silks, which were certainly valuable but not as pleasing as gold. Dendera was delighted to find a small casket of jewelry. She rammed a gold and pearl earring through her already thoroughly perforated ear, grinning like a loon. "How do I look?" she asked Renenet.

"Like a harlot with a pearl in her ear. Let's go."

Dendera laughed, tucking the chest under her arm and grabbing a bolt of rich purple silk. They relieved the merchant ship of its gunpowder and grog. Sabah had the mainsail stitched up in moments, and the *Judgment* caught the wind.

A while later, as the pirates wallowed in the silks, rolled in perfume, and divided up the jewels, Jenny sidled up to Renenet. "Captain?" she said. "Ma'am?"

"What is it, child? Has some bauble caught your eye?" Renenet was mildly aghast to find herself smiling at the girl.

"No ma'am. I just wanted to know. . ." The girl bit her lip

"Know what, lass?"

"I wanted to know why you didn't kill them all. Sink their ship to the bottom of the sea. Burn them alive. All the things they say pirates do."

Renenet nodded. "I cannot speak for other pirates. But we of Luxor do not believe in excess bloodshed. Those who died in battle with us were marked by Anubis. It was their time to go. But to slaughter the survivors— that would be wrong. Our Lord disapproves of wanton waste. He and he alone chooses when to take a soul."

"That's one way to look at it." Dendera slapped Jenny on the back, almost knocking the girl to her knees. The gunner had a second pearl earring in her ear, and a new ruby as well. "Here's another. If we leave that fat merchant ship afloat, it'll eventually go home, and get repaired. Then somebody will stuff it with goodies for us again. See?"

The girl nodded, smiling.

Renenet bounced a silver coin off of Dendera's head. "Your spirituality is overwhelming."

"I'm spiritual! I am! When I rolled with golden-fur last night, I saw God. Several times."

"EW!" bellowed the pirates. Jenny collapsed into giggles.

☠ ☠ ☠

The excitement of plundering the merchant ship calmed, and as the *Judgment* entered the Sea of Mists, the waters calmed as well. The sailing was smooth, but the mists were eerie and claustrophobic. More often than not, visibility beyond the rails of the ship was next to nothing. From time to time great, slow beasts rocked the ship with their passing, but they were concealed beneath a swirling curtain of fog.

Days passed, and the crew of the *Judgment* might have grown bored and restless if it weren't for the little human, Jenny. Dendera spent many hours with the lass, teaching her to play guitar, and once let her touch off a cannon, much to Renenet's vexation.

Akila taught Jenny swordplay. The girl could barely hold up the huge cutlasses used by the crew, so the bosun found her a long knife from the treasure stores and began training her in attack and defense. Akila even taught Jenny the Luxor pirates' decapitation stroke, which the girl swung with great determination and force, slaying many a melon. The crew laughed that the little girl's blow would land no higher than a man's elbow. Although she reddened at the teasing, Jenny practiced all the harder.

Even First Mate Mosi eventually warmed to the girl (and it was common knowledge on the ship that Mosi disliked most everyone). She taught Jenny to load and fire a pistol, and Jenny had a good eye.

Now dressed in pants that Sabah had sewed for her and an oversized silk shirt, her knife and pistol in her belt, everyone declared Jenny looked the proper pirate.

Although Renenet watched Jenny's progress with an amused and even proud eye, the Captain was preoccupied, spending her time in her cabin studying charts with Talibah, the navigator.

Renenet's dreams were filled with nothing but mist.

☠ ☠ ☠

A couple of weeks into the voyage, the *Judgment* encountered another pirate ship. (They might have missed each other entirely, if the crews had not heard each other's voices through the mists.) They were of the Purple Tern Brigands, judging from their flag and their garb. The ships pulled alongside each other for cautious talk.

Yes, the Tern crew had heard tell of Billy Bones's ship, the *Plague*, in these very waters. If one were foolish enough to sail due south, one would most likely run directly into him. Jake McGraw, the captain of the Tern ship, warned strongly against this.

"Billy don't care who he attacks," he said gravely, stroking the long braids of his beard. "He'd just as soon sink a fellow pirate as he would a merchant. And Billy don't leave no survivors."

Renenet thanked him for the information. Supplies were traded, hands were shaken. Renenet very nearly had to drag Dendera away from a strapping, black-haired, blue-eyed young Tern.

"I didn't want to keep him," the gunner complained. "I just wanted to borrow him for awhile."

☠ ☠ ☠

The *Judgment* swung hard south and filled her sails. "Perhaps we should slow down," the navigator Talibah commented. "We can't see past our noses. We're likely to run up his stern."

"Good," Renenet replied.

☠ ☠ ☠

The crew was excited, anxious for a fight. There was much sparring, knife-throwing, and target shooting, not to mention snarling, snapping, and howling.

Jenny was terrified, but thrilled just the same. A few weeks before, she was scrubbing out pots for a few pence a week, taking it home to a drunken father who called her worthless and sometimes beat her unconscious. Now she was sailing with a crew of pirates—strange, fierce creatures who somehow accepted her just the same. Her hand moved up to her scarred and thickened ear, and the white line that ran from her lower lip to her chin where her father's fist had split her wide open. Her eyes narrowed, and she gripped the handle of her knife. No one would ever do that to her again. Even if she died fighting whatever monstrosity Billy Bones turned out to be, it was better than dying under her father's fists.

☠ ☠ ☠

One night the mists cleared from Renenet's mind, and she dreamed of something other than swirling white. She dreamed of the smell of death. She dreamed of the cry of battle, the crack of bones. She dreamed of a ship ablaze. Was it the *Judgment* or the *Plague*? She could not tell.

Renenet awoke in the darkness, gold eyes wide and staring. Her prophetic dreams almost always came true.

☠ ☠ ☠

It wasn't the *Plague* they saw first. It was her handiwork. Floating wreckage, smoldering chunks of hull, scraps of sail. Bodies—and parts of bodies. No survivors clung to the wood or cried out for help. Blood swirled in the water. The air was weirdly quiet. As the bow of the *Judgment* nudged the detritus aside, the hulking shape of Billy Bones's pirate ship came into view. The mists cleared for a moment, revealing the black flag with three dancing skeletons. The *Plague* was a big vessel, bigger than the *Judgment*. Her hull was stained a rusty red, like dried blood. Her sails were scarlet. On her decks stood scores of men—or something—swathed in hooded robes.

The crew of the *Judgment* stood on deck, alert and at the ready. Jenny hid behind the mast, her knife clenched in her trembling hands. The captain had ordered her to stay on the *Judgment* and out of the way. Well, Renenet hadn't ordered her not to look, had she?

Renenet strode to the bow. "Ahoy! This is Captain Renenet of the pirate ship *Judgment*! I would have a word with you!"

"Don't you know who you're talking to?" came a hissing voice from the deck of the *Plague*. It was a whisper, but the voice was loud, as if the speaker was inches from Renenet's face. The voice buzzed in her ear like a noxious insect.

"Captain Billy Bones, I presume," she said.

One of the hooded figures stepped forward as the ships slowly pulled alongside each other. "And still you dare approach me?"

"Obviously." Renenet's ears twitched with irritation.

"And what is it you want?" The voice had an ugly, mocking undertone. The other figures on the deck had not moved. Their stillness was unnatural. A scent of death—old, unburied death—wafted across to the *Judgment*.

"A map. We have reason to believe you possess a map to the island of Luxor. We are willing to barter—"

Billy Bones laughed, a hideous, rasping sound. "And what do you suppose you have, that would possibly interest us?" He threw off his robe. As one, the other *Plague* crewmen did the same.

They were not undead, flesh-dripping zombies, as Renenet had expected. They were skeletons. Gleaming white bone dressed in velvet and silk rags, armed to the teeth with swords and pistols.

Billy Bones leaned forward, his monstrous grin somehow growing wider. Renenet did not blink. She did not flinch. She merely raised an eyebrow.

Billy Bones pulled back an inch or two. Did his death's-head grin slip a little, or was that a trick of the mists? He was clearly unhappy that Renenet showed no fear of him. *His kind feeds on fear*, the Captain thought.

"Gunpowder," she said. "Cannonballs. Rope."

"Skin," called Dendera from behind the main battery. There were yipping barks of laughter around her.

Billy Bones' hollow eyes blazed red. "Aye, we'll have your skin! And your blood as well! We'll strip your flesh from your half-breed bones, you bitches! You'll soon beg us for death! We'll—"

He was still ranting when Renenet gave the yelping howl that was the order to board. Moments later the pirates of the *Judgment* were in the air, swinging across the gap to the *Plague* with terrifying snarls and barks of rage.

Renenet's boots connected with Billy Bones' chest, and she heard ribs crack. He fell to the deck and scuttled backward, like some huge, ugly spider. She lost him in the mists.

The fighting was on in earnest. The battle for the merchant ship was like a walk on a sun-soaked beach compared to this. The skeleton pirates fought relentlessly. There was no sense in shooting them. Bullets passed through their bodies, perhaps taking a rib or two, but doing no real damage.

Renenet realized that if she and her crew prevailed, there would be no survivors on the *Plague*. The skeletons fought until they were destroyed. She cut one in half, and although its legs went dead, it sat up on its rib cage and swung its cutlass at her, gnashing its teeth. It was not until she struck its head off that the thing stopped moving entirely.

Killing it (if that was the correct word) gave her immense satisfaction. These were foul, unnatural things; soulless, animated by Ra knows what. Their very existence was an offense to Anubis, he who judges souls, lord of the dead. They had no place in this world or the next.

The battle raged. Although beheading the skeletons killed them instantly, it wasn't so simple a task, as they were skilled and ferocious fighters. For long, agonizing minutes, it was hard to tell which side was winning. Swords flashed, pistols fired. The deck was strangely clean of blood—the skeletons had none to give. The crack of bones filled the air as the *Judgment* crew pressed the attack.

Her crew was beautiful and terrible, fangs bared, foam flying from snarling lips. Renenet's heart swelled with pride. More and more skeletons dropped to the deck in heaps of useless bones as their skulls flew from their bodies like gleaming white cannonballs.

Not that the *Judgment's* crew went unscathed. Akila had taken a terrible slash to her lower leg. She quickly bound it up with a scarf and kept fighting, leaving a trail of crimson behind her. Blood flew as Mosi took a bullet in the hip. Eyes narrowed with rage and pain, she split the skull of her attacker neatly down the middle with her cutlass.

Sabah, the young lookout, had been killed, and four brave shipmates with her. Each death scoured Renenet's heart, but there was no time for mourning now. Now was just for the fight.

It was bad. But they were winning. A grin crept over Renenet's muzzle. Soon she'd be holding the map; soon they'd be heading home.

But where the hell was Billy Bones? She hadn't seen him fall. She hadn't seen him at all since they'd boarded the ship.

"Bones, you coward!" Renenet roared. "Come out and face me!" She turned in a circle, scanning the embattled deck for some sign of him.

The mists near the stern parted abruptly. Renenet gasped at what she saw. Billy Bones had a chain in his skeletal left hand, a cutlass in his right. The chain was wrapped tight around her younger sister's neck. Dendera clawed at it with both hands, her eyes bulging, tongue lolling. She dropped to her knees as Bones pulled back his cutlass low, intending to gut her.

"No!" screamed Renenet.

A tiny form leapt from the mists, appearing at Billy Bones's side. Jenny. Now Renenet would have to watch the child die, too.

The girl let out a howl and drew back her long knife. In a perfect imitation of the Luxor pirates' decapitation strike, she swung at Billy Bones with all her strength. Her blow severed his cutlass arm at the elbow. It dropped to the deck with a loud thump.

Renenet threw her cutlass. It whirled through the air, whistling a death song. Bones turned to look, and the blade caught him in the mouth, severing the skull above the jaw.. He collapsed with an undignified rattle.

Jenny was already unwrapping the chain from Dendera's neck when Renenet reached them. Dendera gasped, choked, coughed. Then she took the girl in her arms and hugged her fiercely.

The pirates of the *Judgment* made short work of the rest of the skeletons. Without their leader, the remaining bone-pirates fell quickly. Soon nothing moved aboard the ship but the bloodied dogwomen, panting with exertion, grinning in triumph as they kicked bones overboard.

Renenet found the map in Billy Bones's cabin, in a jeweled box beneath the skeleton pirate's bed. She hugged the map to her breast, fierce tears of joy streaking her fur.

"You found it!" Dendera croaked over her shoulder. Renenet nodded. Dendera sat on the dead pirate's satin-draped bed, poking at the soft covers. "What the hell does a skeleton need a bed like this for? It's not like they can feel anything. It's not like they can get cold. They could sleep in a coffin! Or a rum keg, for that matter! And why do they have to sleep at all? They're dead!"

Renenet smiled and nodded, still gazing at the map. "I'm taking his pillow," said Dendera.

☠   ☠   ☠

Later, when they had thoroughly looted the *Plague* (finding no food, of course, but plenty of gunpowder, cannonballs, and several chests of gold coin and exotic jewelry), Renenet glared at Billy Bones's deserted ship. Just the sight of it offended her.

"Let's burn it!" Dendera hollered. A howl of approval went up from the crew.

"Let's," Renenet replied. Moments later, torches littered the deck of the *Plague*. Cut loose from the *Judgment*, she drifted away into the mist as her sails caught fire. Soon there was nothing left to see but a hellish glow, drifting farther and farther into the mists until it was gone.

☠   ☠   ☠

That evening, after the dead had been wrapped in silk and returned to the womb of the sea, the crew of the *Judgment* ate, drank, and laughed raucously. They'd cried and howled for those fallen, but the time for mourning was through. Now the crew tended to their wounded and divided the spoils. Some gnawed on the bones of their fallen enemies as they lounged about the deck. Not that they tasted good—the bones were old and dry. But the victory made them seem sweet and juicy.

Jenny carried the radius and ulna of Billy Bones's right arm, the one she had severed. She held it up and admired it, still not quite able to believe what she had done.

"What're you gonna do with that?" Dendera laughed. The young gunner was already well into her cups. "You're not gonna chew it, are you?"

Jenny giggled. "No. I thought—I thought maybe I'd carve a whistle from it." For just a moment, her eyes went hard and flinty.

"Good girl." Dendera pounded her on the back. Grinning, Jenny tucked the bones into her belt.

Jenny walked among the *Judgment's* crew, admiring them all, thinking them the most beautiful, fearsome creatures in Creation.

Akila had stitched up the dreadful slash in her leg herself, after dousing it with rum. She was now thoroughly drunk, and feeling no pain. "Damn," said Dendera, looking at the wound. "I'd hoped we'd have to cut it off. It's about time somebody on this ship had a pegleg." Akila roared with laughter.

The bullet in Mosi's hip was more challenging. It had passed through Mosi's thick muscle and lodged against the bone. Talibah, the navigator, had a little medical training. She pulled the ball out of the flesh with a pair of long, bronze tweezers. The first mate gritted her teeth, her eyes rolling, but made not a sound. Jenny watched in wide-eyed horror and fascination, hand over her mouth, as Talibah poured rum into the wound and stitched it up. Renenet placed a hand on her shoulder.

"You see? That could have been you. I should strip your hide for disobeying my order to stay aboard the *Judgment.*"

"Don't you dare!" bellowed Dendera. "She saved my life. If she hadn't had the guts and the heart to join the attack, I'd be a dead woman now."

Jenny looked up at Renenet. "I will accept any punishment you give me," she whispered.

The Captain smiled, just a little. "As much as I hate to admit it, Dendera is right. Sometimes, when circumstances call for it, a pirate must use her own judgment and do what is right. Even if the captain told her not to."

Jenny grinned hugely and threw her arms around the captain. Renenet hugged her tightly for a moment, then peeled the child off of her. "You will make a fine pirate, young Jenny. But our time together is nearing an end. We will set sail for Luxor immediately. We will find you a safe place along the way. I've heard tales of The Sisterhood, a band of female pirates who—"

"Please," said Jenny. "Take me with you."

Renenet scowled. "To Luxor? But why? Don't you want to be with your own kind?"

"Not particularly, Captain."

"But . . . but you'd be the only human there. You'd be alone."

"No she wouldn't! I'll take the little monkey in!" Dendera said, weaving a little as she patted Jenny on the head.

Renenet snorted. "A fine mother figure you'd make! What will you teach the lass, to be a boy-crazy, cannon-blasting, rum-swilling hyena like you?"

"Bite me," said Dendera, and passed out on the deck. Moments later she was snoring.

"Please," said Jenny. "I won't stay forever. I just want to see."

Slowly, Renenet nodded. "All right, child. Now pour some water on that silly beast at your feet before somebody steps on her."

☠   ☠   ☠

That night, Renenet dreamed of Luxor. She dreamed of the great pyramid, gleaming in the sun as the *Judgment* pulled into port. She dreamed of crowds on the docks, cheering, barking and howling with joy. She scanned the faces and saw Geb, his big handsome ears and gentle eyes. He raised a hand to her, smiling.

Renenet smiled in her sleep. Her prophetic dreams almost always came true.

Return of the Black Seraph
by Kelly Swails

Late afternoon sunlight sparkled off the water as a breeze carried the clean, salty smell of the ocean over *The Cloudrunner*. Jacob pulled the fishing net across the deck for the last time that week, and tepid seawater washed the wood clean of muck and fish guts. When he tugged on the cord that opened the net, two fish flopped out.

"Is that all?" Marcus said, scooping up the fish and tossing them into a half-full bin.

Jacob smiled down at his brother-in-law. "Yep, looks to be."

"We aren't very good fishermen."

He shrugged. "Catch enough to feed ourselves with enough left over to make a decent profit. Not much more you can ask for."

"Owning your own ship helps," Marcus said. "If we had to rent ship-time we'd have to find a new line of work."

"I can't argue there," Jacob said as he looked around the boat. It was bigger than most of the fishing boats that called Port Salude home, and it served him well.

"I wonder what it would be like to sail in a real ship." His brother-in-law looked up at him, eager curiosity splayed across the youngster's face.

"Not much chance of that around here," Jacob said. "Nothin' but skimmers and fishers."

"I suppose not. Though, if I joined a band of pirates, I could."

Jacob stared at the younger man. He was seventeen, and had begun fishing with Jacob not long after Jacob had arrived in Port Salude. Marcus had joked about joining up with pirates before, but this time Jacob could tell that his wife's brother was serious.

Jacob reeled in the net. "Pirates are murderers and thieves, Marcus, and you are neither. Swab the deck before we both slip and tumble into the Azure Sea."

"I bet it would be exciting," Marcus said as he pulled a mop from its locker. "Sailing the world, seeing all sorts of places, making all that booty. Not to mention the women! I bet—"

"It's not all rum and roses," Jacob said, a little more sharply than he intended. He softened the edge from his words before he continued. "You'll find plenty of women at ports, but they smell like rotten fish and will make you piss fire for a month. Any woman that will lay with a pirate is a woman you don't want."

Marcus didn't try to hide his smile. "I suppose you'll tell me there's no gold either?"

Jacob stared into his brother-in-law's eyes. "There is plenty of gold and silver and precious stones, but none of it's yours. You can argue you've earned it, but you haven't. Not really. The gold is tainted with the blood and sweat of those who worked and died for it. Then once you have the precious gold in your hands, you find yourself always running from those who want their money back. You're never anywhere long enough to appreciate it. But most of all, you don't have a place to call home."

Marcus shrugged. "Your ship is your home."

Jacob put the net in its place and watched the younger man mop up the last of the water. Marcus moved with an easy grace, his lanky body instinctively countering the dips and swells of the boat on the water. His face held the knowledge of youth: that he knew everything about the world and his place in it. Jacob envied and pitied him.

"You live on the ship, sure, Marcus. But a home is more than that. I've sailed the world on various merchantmen, once setting foot on land only three days in the span of a year, but the first home I had is the one I made with your sister."

"You're a fisherman, what makes you think you know about being a pirate?" Marcus mumbled.

"What was that?" Jacob asked, knowing full well what the young man had said.

"I said it sounds like I'd rather be a fisherman than a pirate."

Jacob let the matter drop. Arguing with the boy would do nothing but make him want to be a pirate even more. Looking to the horizon, the older man said, "It's getting late. Let's take it to shore."

"Aye, Captain."

☠   ☠   ☠

Jacob stood on the quarterdeck of *The Interceptor* and watched as his buccaneer crew heaved the last of their prisoners into water littered with the remnants of the merchant ship *Goldensky*. The wreck's former occupants sank into the Indigo Deeps, as the acrid smell of scorched wood wafted through the ocean breeze. Jacob smiled. His crew drank from casks of stolen wine and danced to the music of a violin as they celebrated their victory. If there was a joy that matched commandeering a year's worth of booty from one ship, he couldn't fathom what it would be.

A grappling hook soared over the rail as another caravel brushed along their port side. Jacob's senses jumped as a single man boarded. No one onboard *The Interceptor* had heard or seen the ship approach; Jacob was sure of it, and that frightened him. All the members of his crew were old sea dogs, and no one had ever come within a league of their position, let alone boarded his ship, without someone raising the alarm. The jubilant cheers of the crew stopped as they looked from Jacob to the visitor and back again.

The figure was huge, almost eight feet tall, and dressed in a dark robe. He cleared a space around him by raising his hands and muttering a few words. Ten sailors fell, dead before they touched the deck. The rest of the crew—men who had stared down cannon barrels and laughed, men who had fought swordfights without breaking a sweat, brave men, *his* men—stared at the vision before them and paled. One soul cried, "It's him! It's him! Gods of Mercy, save us all!"

But the newcomer only had eyes for Jacob.

☠ ☠ ☠

Once on solid ground, Jacob and Marcus sold the day's catch to their usual fishmonger, changed their wet clothes for dry, and headed to the local tavern, The Last Copper. When Jacob opened the door, he was rewarded with the heavy smell of fish chowder, tobacco smoke, and pungent beer. In the far corner, a table of Jacob's friends sat drinking mugs of dark brew and mopping up soup with fresh biscuits.

"Jacob!" Tobias bellowed when he saw him enter. "It's about damned time you showed yourself!"

Jacob sighed and smiled. He didn't frequent the tavern much—in truth, the constant dicing made the angel tattoos on his forearms ache—but sometimes he made an appearance.

Marcus motioned to the barmaid. "Two stouts."

Jacob and Marcus joined the men as the barmaid set down two frothy mugs. Jacob moved to pay, but Marcus beat him to it.

"You don't need to do that," Jacob said.

"I know I don't." Marcus laid the coins on the barmaid's tray.

Jacob was proud that younger man desired to pay his own way. He doubted it would be long before Marcus found a young woman and settled down.

"Did you hear the news?" Tobias said. "Pirates were spotted around the island."

Jacob's stomach fell and his forearms twitched. He strived to sound casual as he said, "I hadn't heard that, no. Whereabouts?"

"I dunno."

"That's unusual, isn't it? Pirates here?" Nicolas, a boy Marcus's age, asked.

Tobias nodded. "Not too many pirates around these parts. Black Seraph kept 'em at bay. But now that he's been quiet, maybe the pirates reckon that they can start taking over the territory again."

"Who's the Black Seraph?" Nicolas said.

"You've never heard of old Blacky?" Tobias asked, incredulous.

"He's not from around here," Marcus said. Nicolas's family had arrived in Port Salude six months prior, and he and Marcus had become fast friends. If they weren't on a boat or asleep, they were together.

"Black Seraph's a pirate hunter," Tobias said. "He sails the seas looking for thieves, and when he finds them. . . ." Tobias drew his thumb across his neck. "No survivors."

"So he's a mercenary of sorts," Nicolas said.

"More like a vigilante. Pirates killed his wife."

"Really?" Nicolas was more interested now.

"Yep. See, Blacky and his young bride had just started a honeymoon cruise when pirates invaded their ship. They beat him unconscious, raped and killed his wife, and burned the ship. Blacky came to, escaped the flaming boat, floated to the nearest island on a half-burned piece of hatch, and was nursed back to health by the locals. Once he was strong enough, he dedicated the rest of his life to finding the bastards."

A hush hung over the table until Jacob broke the tension. "See, Marcus? You don't want to be a pirate. What if the Black Seraph comes after you?"

"The Black Seraph doesn't really exist," Marcus said, laughing. "Or if he does, he's not hunting anymore. That's why pirates are coming around to claim their territory. Right, Tobias?"

"Maybe." Tobias looked troubled at the idea. "'Better eat all your supper or the Black Seraph will get you.' That's what my mother used to tell me and my sister. Scared the spit right out of me, I tell you. What about you, Jacob? Your mom threaten you with the Black Seraph?"

"No," he said quietly as he stood. "I don't mean to be the first to break up the party, but I've got a long day tomorrow." He left the tavern and walked the darkened streets to his home, rubbing his forearms the entire way. Jacob found himself amused at the myth of the Black Seraph and troubled that Marcus didn't seem to believe it.

☠ ☠ ☠

Jacob willed his legs not to shake as he descended the ladder to the deck and approached the visitor. "And who might you be?"

The visitor chuckled as he opened his robe. "I have been sent by the Gods of Wrath," he said. "You are to come with me."

Jacob swallowed a scream as the robe the visitor wore unfolded to become a pair of black wings that nearly spanned the deck. Jacob's men tripped over their fallen comrades as they avoided the inky feathers.

"A dark angel," Jacob whispered, his voice shaky.

"Gods of Mercy, save us all!" a man cried.

"I've been sent for your soul," the angel said as he touched the two men closest to him. A current of night-fire spread through the crowd. The men convulsed as the power of the gods flashed through their bodies. The crew retched and shat as they died.

Jacob's voice quivered. "That wasn't necessary. I would have gone with you willingly."

"Oh, but Jacob," the dark angel chuckled. "When you come back you'd have done the same to them. I have just saved you the trouble." He touched Jacob's forehead.

Jacob felt his heart stop as his bladder loosed its contents and darkness consumed him.

☠ ☠ ☠

137

The morning after visiting The Last Copper, Jacob woke to Rebeka's sniffles from the next room. He stumbled out of bed to find his wife crying in the kitchen.

"What's wrong, love? Surely I wasn't *that* bad last night."

She ignored his attempt at humor as she wiped her face with a towel. "It's Marcus. He's gone."

"Gone? What do you mean gone? Gone where?"

"He and that stupid friend of his have gone to join up with a band of pirates."

Pain prickled Jacob's forearms as Rebeka handed him two crumpled sheets of paper. The first was a hastily scrawled note in Marcus's handwriting that said he and Nicolas had gone to join Captain Atzaul and his band of Avengers. The second was a recruitment flyer that one of the boys had probably ripped from a posting board on the docks.

"SEE THE WORLD! ENJOY RICHES THAT WILL SURPASS YOUR WILDEST DREAMS! IMPRESS THE LADIES! JOIN CAPTAIN ATZAUL'S AVENGERS ON THE GOOD SHIP *REVENGE*," it said in bold letters. Across the bottom was a meeting time and place.

"Please, sit down." Jacob set the papers onto the table. He hoped his wife was too distraught to notice how much his hands shook as he did so.

"What do you mean, 'sit down?' That boy doesn't realize the danger he's in. We can still catch him—"

Jacob touched his wife's shoulder. "The meeting was at midnight. They left hours ago."

"How do we know unless we look?" she asked.

"I know a thing or two about pirates," Jacob said in a soft voice. He avoided looking at his wife by turning his attention to the parchment. "There are a few places this Captain Atzaul might try to recruit after they leave here. It wouldn't hurt for me to go look."

"Yes, we will do that." Rebeka quickly turned to the cupboards and started throwing supplies into a cloth sack. "I'll pack the food. You get our clothes."

Jacob stared at her for a moment as his mind whirled. "Hold it now, Rebeka. The Avengers aren't known for their virtuous attitudes toward women. If anything happened to you, I would never be able to live with myself."

Rebeka set her hands on her hips. "Are you saying I can't take care of myself?"

Jacob had seen her lift fish barrels twice her weight enough times to know that she would give any man a solid fight. Still, something in her eyes told him he could convince her to stay. "Of course not, but use your head. What if Marcus changes his mind and shows up here later tonight? Don't you want to be here when he does?"

Rebeka teared up again as she nodded. "You're right. I don't like it, but I'll stay."

"It's better this way, you'll see." He hugged her before returning to the bedroom to pack a few belongings. When he left, she walked him to the door.

"I hope the wind finds you right," she said.

"It always does. It always brings me back here." He finished the goodbye and kissed her.

She grabbed his shoulders and looked him in the eye. "We are going to see him again, aren't we?"

"Of course." Jacob kissed her forehead as his arms began to throb. He would see Marcus again, sooner rather than later. He doubted his brother-in-law would enjoy the reunion.

☠ ☠ ☠

Jacob awoke to find himself lying on the deck of the *Interceptor*. Not much time had passed since he had blacked out—the position of the moon told him that—but the deck had been cleared of his men, and for that he felt grateful.

The dark angel stood over him. "Notice anything different?"

Jacob looked around. "Deck's clear," he said, forcing the words from his dry throat.

"Not with the ship. With you."

He looked himself over and found he was completely naked. "Blimey," he said. He jumped up and searched the deck with his eyes, but his clothes were nowhere to be seen. A breeze ruffled the angel's wings, but Jacob didn't feel it on his skin. He couldn't feel the wood underfoot or the movement of the ship, either. "Blimey," he said again, this time in a whisper. "I'm dead."

"You are," the angel confirmed. He smiled, and if Jacob had been alive, gooseflesh would have prickled his body. "I'm here to collect on a debt for the Gods of Wrath," the angel continued. "Do you remember making such an arrangement?"

Jacob nodded; his voice failed him. Years ago, during his first summer as a pirate captain, he and his crew had come across another band of pirates looting a merchant ship. Jacob, being young and cocky and overconfident, wanted the swag for himself, and so he challenged the pirate gang. They fought back, and the resulting battle—the pirates fighting each other, the sailors battling both sets of pirates—reached massive proportions. Jacob led his end of the fight as well as he knew how, but before long it became apparent that his youth was no match for the salty dogs he challenged.

When his ship took on more water than could be emptied, and a quarter of his men lay dead, he prayed for the first time in his life to the Gods of Wrath.

"Please," he said. "Get me out of this and my soul is yours." The Gods of Wrath must have seen something they wanted in Jacob, because Jacob's next cannon blast devastated the enemy pirate ship. The sailors surrendered before the smoke cleared. The resulting bounty paled in comparison to the reputation Jacob garnered. Before the next summer, he convinced himself that he had won that battle with nothing but his own prowess.

The dark angel's appearance now told Jacob the Gods of Wrath had not forgotten who had *really* won that battle. "What do they require of me?"

☠ ☠ ☠

Jacob stood on the deck of his fishing boat, alone in the darkness. The Azure Sea slept all around him, the only sounds coming from waves lapping onto the *Cloudrunner's* side. The better part of a week had passed since Marcus had left. Jacob had done his best to ignore the pain in his arms. He knew for certain that he wouldn't be able to rest until he found Marcus and brought him home.

As the sun peeked over the horizon, Jacob came across an island that wasn't on any map. It looked to be deserted—which in itself wasn't unusual—save for the galleon anchored alongshore flying red flags.

Jacob gasped as his forearms burned white-hot. Pushing up his sleeves, he saw that his tattoos had changed from black to white. Breathing deeply to calm himself, he reached for his spyglass. In the burgeoning sunlight, he was able to see a line of men walking along a path to a small mountain at the center of the island. Marcus and his friend Nicolas were among several other young men in the middle of the pack. While they weren't bound in any visible way or held at sword point, they all looked scared.

Jacob judged the distance to the island against the horizon. If he timed it right, he'd reach land just as full darkness hit. Repeating the mantra "Marcus isn't a pirate, he isn't a pirate, he isn't a pirate," eased the ache in his arms.

☠ ☠ ☠

The dark angel before him smiled. "Jacob, you will rid the seas of pirates."

Surprise knocked the fright from Jacob's mind. "Why would the gods want me to do that? Pirates are nothing but beings filled with wrath. Why do the gods want to see the pirates come to harm?"

"It's not my place to question. If I had to guess, I'd say your killing pirates is less about purging the seas of crime and more about torturing you. That your existence is dependant upon seeking and killing men not so different from yourself might amuse our masters."

☠ ☠ ☠

Darkness surrounded Jacob as he crept through the foliage of the small island. No sentinels were posted, which made Jacob's job easier. Captain Atzaul was either lax or confident. Jacob navigated easily in the dark. He followed the pirate's trail—they might be a terror on the water, but they were no woodsmen—and before the moon was overhead he entered the giant mouth of a cave.

Water dripped in the distance as Jacob peered through the darkness. A cacophony of noise erupted from somewhere to his right. He followed a narrow tunnel toward the noise, using the walls as a guide. Spongy moss cushioned his fingers and muck underfoot made each step treacherous. The end of the passage opened into an immense, brightly lit chamber deep within the cave. Across the doorway a waterfall thundered into the space, filling a small river that ran to parts unknown. From his vantage point, he saw a ring of perhaps a hundred pirates circling a group of twenty initiates.

Inside the circle of young men stood a man that could only be Captain Atzaul. He was freakishly tall with black hair slicked back into a ponytail. Jewels dripped from his fingers and ears, and his smooth skin belied his age. He might not be a monster like some of the other pirate captains were rumored to be, but he didn't look quite human, either. He spoke in a deep, melodic voice.

"Drink up, lads, drink up! Profess your allegiance to me by partaking of my body! Become one with me, as each and every member of my crew has before you!"

Jacob's eyes snapped to a large goblet being passed from one boy to the next. He recoiled when he saw it was filled with blood. Only then did he notice the ragged cuts on Captain Atzaul's wrists. Blinding pain ripped through Jacob's arms, making him gasp and fall to his knees. He knew then that mere breathing exercises would not stop the Black Seraph from coming out of retirement.

Jacob couldn't stop the power taking over his body and his senses. As he began to change, he could smell the metallic blood in the chalice and see every detail of the cavern with crystalline clarity. He felt adrenaline and magic pump through his veins, strengthening his muscles and tightening his reflexes.

Some inner sense of Captain Atzaul's stopped the proceedings below. "Who goes there?" he cried as he peered to the tunnel, his hands dropping to the hilts of the paired swords at his hips. Two hundred eyes turned as one, though the kneeling boys continued to drink from the goblet.

"The Black Seraph," Jacob said as he stepped into the cavern. He started the transformation, growing to eight feet tall and sprouting massive black wings from his back. Muscles rippled beneath his flesh, and his eyes turned from brown to an icy gray.

Gasps filled the chamber as one sorry fellow in the front of the crowd fainted.

"Kill him!" Captain Atzaul shouted. The crowd of pirates turned into a raging mob as they charged.

Jacob allowed himself to finish the change. His wings ripped through his clothes, and the knife he wore on his belt became a magnificent black sword. Power thrummed through his body as he pointed the weapon at the nearest man. Night-fire crackled through the air as a half-dozen pirates convulsed and hit the cavern floor, dead.

In Jacob's experience, this usually caused the surviving foes to scream and flee. This time, however, their comrades' deaths only served to ignite the buccaneers' passions. So, one by one, he slew his attackers before they could get within twenty paces of him.

"Why won't you stop?" Jacob asked. But the only response was another pirate falling to Jacob's magical flames.

"They cannot stop," Captain Atzaul replied. "They've all drank my blood, ye see. They'll feed themselves to the sharks if I tell them. Cut off their own balls and eat them, if I tell them. Rape five wenches before slicing their own throats. There is nothing these men won't do for me." His thunderous voice echoed through the chamber.

Jacob looked through the crowd and saw Marcus, still on his knees, waiting his turn with the chalice. His brother-in-law didn't raise his head to look at the Black Seraph. Jacob pointed. "Give me that one."

"Halt!" Captain Atzaul said. Instantly the crowd of pirates—what was left of them—stopped climbing over the smoking, burnt bodies of their crewmates. "So that is all ye require? One boy? That hardly seems worth all this trouble."

Jacob realized the captain was mocking him. "Then give him to me," the Seraph replied. He descended the uneven stairs that led to the cavern floor.

"Why should I?" Atzaul said. "Ye and I both know that ye'll not leave my crew alive. The answer is no."

"Allow me to change your mind." Jacob pointed his sword and flung all of his power into the pirate captain. The energy bounced off, filling the entire chamber. Sparks flew as the air crackled, and pirates in all directions fell to the ground. In the circle, Nicolas died retching. Jacob's heart stopped beating until he saw that Marcus still kneeled, unhurt.

"Your powers won't work on me," Jacob's adversary chuckled. "I have a little protection from the Gods of Wrath."

"Have a parlay with them, do you?"

"I have. Ye will have to kill me with yer own hands."

"That shouldn't be too hard." The Black Seraph pulled a knife from a felled pirate's belt and threw the dagger across the cavern, aiming for the captain's heart. Atzaul dodged it without so much as blinking. Before Jacob heard the knife skitter across the cavern, he charged the pirate.

Atzaul drew two swords from his scabbards and attacked.

Clutching his sword with both hands, Jacob blocked Atzaul's first barrage of blows and tried in vain to stab at the captain's chest. The Seraph's thrusts never breached the captain's clothing; Atzaul pushed aside Jacob's sword as one would brush aside an annoying bumblebee. Jacob rushed the pirate, attacked from the left, and stumbled as Atzaul feigned right. Frustrated, Jacob slashed his sword left, right, then left again, but Atzaul used both his swords to deflect each attempt.

Laughing, the captain said, "Having fun yet, Black Seraph?"

"I was about to ask you that very question," Jacob replied as he opened his wings. He pushed off the cavern floor, rose to the top of the ceiling, and dived, pointing his sword at the captain. Atzaul stood firm and gazed into Jacob's eyes as the captain's pair of swords crashed together.

Jacob gasped. Pain flooded his shoulders, and he fell to the ground. Atzaul twisted his blades. Jacob screamed as his nearly-severed wings fluttered uselessly.

Atzaul pulled the swords free, wiped the blood from the blades, and looked at the Black Seraph as a cat might gaze at a mouse with a broken leg.

"Your reign ends here, Black Seraph."

"That's where you're wrong." Jacob forced the pain to the back of his mind. He reached up and grabbed Captain Atzaul's wrists. Power surged through the Seraph and into the still-weeping cuts on the captain's arms. The pirate's blood smoked and boiled as the vengeance of the Gods of Wrath— Or was it Jacob's vengeance?—filled his body. Captain Atzaul writhed and screamed, his face contorted with agony.

Jacob tightened his grip.

At last, Atzaul's eyes rolled back into his head and he fell to his knees.

Jacob released the dead man and scrambled to his feet. His ribs ached; he had broken two or three when he'd fallen, but the power of the gods healed him quickly. Even his torn and bloody wings didn't feel so bad, now. He reached Marcus before Atzaul's corpse slumped completely to the ground.

Marcus still knelt beside Nicolas's prone body, the chalice of blood spilled at Marcus's knees. A red-headed boy nearby, who looked as though he had just woken, gazed at Jacob. "Where am I?"

"It isn't important," Jacob said. "You're safe now."

The redhead scrambled to his feet. "Are all these men dead?"

"Yes," Jacob said.

"Who did it? You?" The boy looked like he couldn't decide if he wanted to run or vomit.

"Yes," Jacob said. Growing impatient, he hauled Marcus to his feet. "Come on, Marcus. We're going home."

Marcus stood of his own accord, but didn't move. Jacob snapped his fingers in front of his brother-in-law's face, but didn't get a response.

"Marcus. Wake up."

"What's wrong with him?" the boy said.

"Quiet." Jacob slapped Marcus once, twice, three times. The third was hard enough to sting the Seraph's hand, but Marcus still stared off into the middle distance. Jacob looked around at the other initiates still kneeling on the floor. Their eyes held the same blank stares.

Jacob turned to look at Captain Atzaul. Of course. When the boys had drunk his blood, they became his disciples; with him dead, they had no free will of their own. They weren't pirates, not really—Jacob's pain-free arms attested to that. But they weren't really alive, either.

Choking back a sob, Jacob laid Marcus gently on the floor and retrieved his sword. As he pointed it one more time, he filled the room with a gentle stream of energy, folding Marcus and the frightened red-headed boy into the power. Dead men tell no tales, after all.

☠   ☠   ☠

Early morning sunlight spilled across Jacob's front yard as he stared at his front door. Since he'd been gone, the chrysanthemums had blossomed and the tomatoes in Rebeka's garden had ripened, but otherwise home was just as he had left it.

Strange how nothing and everything can change all at once, Jacob thought. He wondered if the Gods of Wrath found it amusing.

When he opened the door, his wife dropped the lump of dough she had been kneading, ran to him, and hugged him so hard it felt like an attack. "You've been gone weeks! Where's Marcus? Did you find him?"

Jacob gently extricated himself and held Rebeka at arm's length. "I couldn't find him. Everywhere I went, it seems I had just missed them. I suspect Captain Atzaul has sailed these seas longer than I have. I just couldn't catch up with him."

The disappointment in Rebeka's eyes nearly wrenched Jacob's heart from his chest. He held her as she cried. When her tears subsided, she leaned backed and noticed his scraggly appearance.

"Here I am carrying on when you've nearly killed yourself searching for my brother. Look at you! A person could think you've not eaten or slept in months."

Jacob forced a grin. "It's nothing that a warm meal can't fix."

She returned his smile. "I think I can manage that."

She pulled pots and pans from the cupboards. After several moments she called, "It's not like Marcus will never be back. Captain Atzaul might come around these parts again this time next year."

Jacob could hear in her voice that she was trying to convince herself as much as him.

"Absolutely." Jacob said. He sat in a driftwood chair, and scrubbed his face with his hands. "Absolutely."

THE CAPTAIN OF THE RED CORAL
by Dean Leggett

The sea mist helped hide my tears. I truly loved Captain Jerald. But his heart belonged to his wife, Heather.

She didn't know him the way I did.

Why, Goddess, does this have to hurt so much?

For the past eight years—one-third of my life—I've lived, learned, and experienced more than I ever thought possible—all in the company of the handsome privateer who welcomed me to his crew when he pulled me from the Azure Sea.

I had given more of myself than I ever thought possible—my loyalty, spirit—given everything for the captain and the ship.

Why did it come to this? Are there answers floating somewhere on this endless expanse of waves?

I closed my eyes and listened to the footsteps of Bosun Reginal. The creaking of his old leather boots always gives him away. I've learned to recognize each sailor without looking. Reginal, the boots, of course. Ole One Ear inhales right before opening a conversation. Captain Jerald's rapier rings would gently rattle as he approached.

"How is he doing, Reginal?" I smoothed my auburn hair. I knew I was attractive, the sailors' eyes always lingering on my curves. But I must have looked a mess this day. Crying for hours had taken a toll on me.

I heard Reginal shift the cutlass at his hip. "The Captain is resting calmly, Kira. The fever has finally broken. His mindless rambling and drooling have also subsided."

"Thank the Goddess," I breathed.

"Maybe the serpent's poison will run its course." Reginal joined me at the rail, and we searched the horizon for any sort of motion beneath the blue green waves.

The sun finally broke and brought the full light of morning to Reginal's face. Reginal is very handsome in his own way, taller than most, with dark locks spilling over his broad shoulders. Not quite seasoned yet, but well on the way; he will make a good first mate one day.

I am sure he would be first mate now, if it weren't for my skills in barter and my eye for seeing the gold in an ordinary cargo. Some, in years past, whispered that I was too weak to be first mate. I had proved them wrong, though, and now was not the time to change that.

"We will find a cure for the Captain." My voice was strong, and I worked to keep my lip from quivering. "All that I could find missing was an amulet, the one I purchased for him at Port Newville a few years back."

"So if gold was not the motive, maybe it was revenge for something he did. Local myths say the serpents are vindictive in nature." Reginal agreed.

"I promise you, Reg, I will set things right."

"Don't you mean 'we,' little lass?"

I slapped him hard across the face. "Don't call me that."

Rubbing his jaw, he smiled. "Well that's the spirit."

He had only tried to snap me out of my gloomy mood.

"Enough of this, Reg. Raise the mainsail. Let's catch the morning wind with all haste. Let the sea's breath guide our way back home."

Reginal returned to the half-deck to give more detailed orders to the men. The crew was hired for skill, not numbers. Jerald felt that a small crew of highly trained sailors would be worth thrice the count in ordinary deckhands.

As Reginal brought us to full sail, I drew my sword and examined the blade. The act wasn't out of need, but provided my mind well-needed centering. My heart felt heavy, and my thoughts churned with anger at the recent events. After a moment, I slid my blade back into its scabbard and headed to my cabin to start another day of tough decisions.

I set the morning schedule for the crew and then returned to Captain Jerald's room. As I pulled the canvas curtain aside, I smelled the strong odor of herbs mixed with sickness. The poison was now visually evident. Even in the dim lamplight I saw the veins showing in his face. My throat tightened as I noticed he was looking at me. A day's growth of stubble had taken hold on his usually clean-shaven face.

"How are you doing?" I shuffled to the side of his bed sling, bent, and brushed the sweaty blond hair out of his eyes.

Our youngest crewmember, Saltmore, was tending him currently. Despite the boy's nervousness, Saltmore's voice remained clear: "The Captain's rambling about '*sweetness*' finally has passed. He's calmed some. I think the she-daemon took his soul, as well as his tongue."

I raised an eyebrow at Saltmore's remark. I had not heard anyone ever refer to the Corilla as 'daemons.'

I motioned for some privacy. Saltmore nodded and left us alone.

I took Jareld's hand. "I promise I will get you home to your wife. She will take good care of you. For now, just rest. You will be in Heather's arms soon." Tears threatened the corners of my eyes. I kissed him gently on the lips, knowing he couldn't protest, and wondering if he truly saw me or was staring at something far beyond this cabin. "I know your heart belongs to Heather, but that doesn't stop my loving you." Tears fell freely now. I tucked the blanket around him, blew out the lamp, and returned to the deck.

The next evening brought the lights of Port Newville into view. We'd made better time than I'd expected. I felt my heart pound as we closed the distance to the harbor.

"Reg, hoist the bow lantern. Prepare to dock!"

Entering Port Newville at night would not be easy. The harbor guards were known to open fire on ships, a precaution against pirates operating in the area. At the very least, there would be a stiff fine to pay.

The Pelican Pier was open, and I was confident that Jerald would soon be ashore. Taylor and a few of the other sailors had already fashioned a litter.

Saltmore was on deck holding a strong lantern to help guide our way. As we scraped paint against a piling, I spotted our first problem—Pier Master James Michelson. The second son of Newville's Duke Benjamin the Third, he demanded that all seadogs call him "Lord James."

"What brings you back so soon, First Mate Kira?" Lord James's tone was as snide as ever. "I would have ordered my men to open fire if I had known it was you." He spat in the water.

"Lord James, it is an honor to have you personally greet us at such a late hour." I forced a smile. "We've had an incident. Captain Jerald has been bitten by a sea snake and needs treatment and rest. It may be some time before he is back on his feet. We will pay for docking for this day and the next, then we will take the ship out and anchor in the harbor until the Captain is ready to sail again." I finished with a small curtsey. With my head lowered, I could see how shiny his boots were. I wondered if one of his hangers-on had licked them clean.

"Well, First Mate Kira, I will take your payment for the docking and for a week under the watch of my guards. As a service to Captain Jerald, the crew will be allowed to come and go as they please to keep the ship ready for sail. But until I see Captain Jerald return, the ship will remain under guard."

I opened my mouth to protest.

"If you have any problems with that, First Mate Kira, take it up with the Duke himself!" Lord James turned smartly and headed toward the port office. It wasn't until he melted into the shadows that I noticed Reginal's hand firmly holding mine in place. He'd feared I would draw my cutlass.

I pulled away and bent to pick up one of the litter poles. Four of the crew assisted as we headed into the harbor's residential area. Even at this late hour, a few people moved about. Most stayed clear of us, fearing our patient contagious or cursed. We found the house fairly quickly. Reginal and I had been there many times before.

I knocked at the door. "Heather, it is Kira and Reginal. Please . . . it is important, Jerald has fallen ill."

I could hear the scraping of the wooden bar, the soft glow of lantern light spilled out of the window, and the door quickly swung open.

Heather darted out. "Jerald?" She held his hand, and tipped her face to mine. "What happened?"

Her tears almost reignited mine as well, and my throat clutched tight.

Luckily, Reginal answered for me. "Jerald was attacked by a serpent. We dropped sail for some fishing off the shallows of Bendol Island. It came late in the night, to his cabin. We found kelp and saltwater near Jerald. He was bitten hard in the shoulder. It had pulled him halfway across the room, maybe wanting to take him into the sea. And it well might have succeeded if Kira hadn't driven it off."

Heather's face relaxed, but only a little.

Reginal continued: "Kira fought it in the hall. It sliced her boot with its tail, ripped an amulet from around Jerald's neck and fled back to the sea. One Ear caught a glimpse of it as it returned to the depths."

"I could have chased it or tended to Jerald," I offered.

"She saw to the Captain," one of the other sailors said. "She might have saved his life."

Heather motioned to move Jerald inside.

"Help Heather get him in some fresh clothes and into bed," I said. "The sooner he is changed and resting, the better. Heather, do you mind if Reginal and I stay here for the night?"

I had my pack with me and set my things by the fire and hung my sword on the peg next to the door. It seemed like just yesterday that I had met Heather . . . but that was more than six years ago.

☠ ☠ ☠

A storm rolled in early and merged the night into the dawn. Reginal and I dressed at first light and checked on Jerald and Heather. Her weeping had kept us up most of the night, but now she lay silently, huddled next to the Captain.

We left quietly, Reginal heading toward the central marketplace, me to the Kaero, the famed library of Port Newville. I wore my thick maroon skirt and new soft leather tunic. My clothing selection looked a touch wrinkled, and my face, I was sure, told a tale of woe. Both were in need of a cleaning, and I hoped the morning storm would help on both accounts.

I wasn't disappointed. It rained just enough to improve my appearance. Then it opened into a deluge just as I reached the Kaero. I huddled close to the doors and out of the rain. I wrung out my hair and wondered how well this step would go. I'd brought enough coin, but places like this were hard to fathom—would they have what I sought? With a heavy sigh, I headed in.

The Kaero was filled with a soft blue-green light. I never liked magical illumination.

"Can I help you?" The woman tried to look older than her years.

Damn soft-landers, pretending their work extracts a toll. Have her climb the main mast in a driving rain that would tear the scales off a grouper! My eyes rolled at her haughty glare. She caught my reaction, and I guessed it would cost me dearly in good coin.

"I need to buy knowledge . . . anything you have on the Corilla, the so called she-daemons of the Southern Isles." I closed my eyes and thought of the crew and the ship, and Jerald. "Our captain was attacked at sea, and he was bitten. I search for a cure, and so anything, anything at all you have on the Corilla will help." I do not recall if I started my plea looking directly into her eyes, but my eyes were locked on hers now.

She took a step back and stared. "Oh sorry, yes. Time would be important. Follow me." She turned and headed up to the upper levels.

Maybe this would not be as painful as I first anticipated. She directed me to a table.

"Wait here. We just purchased a new collection of knowledge last week. It hasn't been fully reviewed, the text is old and a few pages are falling out.

We were able to spell the decay, but we have not had a chance to catalog it all. Normally, such items are not allowed for public review, but I will take an exception due to your circumstances."

My eyes widened when I saw the massive tome she placed in front of me.

"This collection appears to reference many of the creatures in the World-Sea. This—along with many other books—was brought in, apparently found in a treasure stash deep in the Cove of Night." She leaned into me close and looked around her as if someone would hear. "Pirate treasure these books be." She placed a dozen smaller books on the table.

"How much for, say, the whole day of reviewing these? I would also like to make some notes for reference, but not more than a page."

Her eyes narrowed. "Three gold Lentals up front. If you find a cure and learn more about this creature we can return one coin for your time."

Expensive, but I knew I had little choice. These books could hold many answers I've been searching for.

"Done," I responded quickly, not bothering to bargain. I'd brought local coin with me from the ship's treasury. She took three Lentals and left.

I opened my pack and dug around for a leather-wrapped ink vial and quill.

The pages of the big tome were sturdy, but they did not appear to be in any discernable order. The binding lacked the ability to hold them all in place. I spent hours reading—thank the Goddess Jerald had taught me how to read. There was a vast amount of material about creatures in the sea, but only a very few pages on the Corilla. One entry brought chills to my neck. It read: *"Never trust them, they desire men as much as wealth. They lure sailors into their grasp with lusty promises, and only serve out sweet venom with their kiss. Once envenomed, the only cure is drinking of Corilla blood."*

I felt surprise at the simplicity and directness of the cure. I never would have thought of it. Trolling for a Corilla should be no trouble, as I knew where a concentration of them swam. Finishing the last of my notes, I placed the pages I had sorted out back within the binding. I slid the notes into a scroll tube, secured my ink vial, and drew a symbol of good fortune on my arm with the remaining black from the quill. I gathered up my gear; it was time to head back out to sea.

As I hurried down the stairs I realized it was dark out. Had I spent an entire day here?

One library keeper sat near the entrance. I placed the massive tome in his hands and bowed quickly, thanking him and headed out into the night. The air smelled fresh, and I took it deep into my lungs. The clouds were gone, and early stars shone brightly; I would have enjoyed this city under other circumstances. On the path back to Heather's house, a few coppers bought me some dried meat on a stick.

Reginal was using the washbasin by the fire.

"How is he?"

Reginal didn't need to answer. The look on his face told the story.

"Reg?" I pressed him nonetheless.

"He appears to be in a trance, Kira. He responds sporadically to Heather's voice, but mostly he just stares. He may appear better, but I fear he is actually getting much worse. The poison is strong, and I think his time is measured in days, a week, two . . . no more."

I walked quietly into the back bedroom. Heather spooned Jerald what smelled like spiced broth.

"We need to set sail," I told her. "I know what we need to cure him." I waited for a response, but she kept her attention on Jerald. "I could use Reginal's sword arm, but I understand if you need him here. I hope to be clear of the harbor shortly after first light."

Still no response.

"Heather, I'm going back to the ship. We're going to Raven's Bay."

Heather and I never had a close relationship, more of an uneasy truce. She knew better than Jerald that I had love for him.

"Heather. . . ."

She shook her head. "Take Reginal. I'll . . . we'll . . . be fine." She set the bowl down next to the bed and left the room, closing the curtain behind her. I sat next to Jerald, maybe for the last time.

He looked at me and smiled, but I knew he didn't recognize me. I held his hand, then leaned in and gently kissed him on the forehead one last time.

Heather was helping Reginal near the hearth. They both looked up at me when I strapped on my sword again.

"Reginal, we leave at first light. We need to catch one of those . . . serpents—the blood of a newly-dead one is needed for the cure."

Reginal nodded with a grim expression. I collected my gear, gave Heather a nervous hug and returned to the night-soaked streets.

The air was a bit cooler now. The chill felt good; I needed to clear my head. My way to the port office was uneventful. A few drunks and beggars hung about, one touching my cloak. The venomous look I gave him stopped his hand; I was in no mood to suffer outcasts this night. Neither was I in the mood for Lord James. His title might well be 'Lord,' but his actions branded him a thug. Stopping just under the heavy wooden sign creaking in the breeze, I tried to calm myself with a few deep breaths.

The bell jangling above the door caused all four men in the office to turn. Lord James was, of course, among them.

"Well, if it isn't First Mate Kira come looking for some favors." With a nod to the tall brutish man: "Or maybe to *give* some favors?"

"Lord James, I need to arrange for the *Red Coral* to sail. As you well know, Jerald is ill, and I must sail to hunt down a serpent to cure him." I held his eyes with my gaze. "You must take my word and release the *Red Coral* into my care. I will be gone less than a week." I knew Jerald didn't have that long to live.

Lord James stood quickly. "Don't dare talk to me in a demanding tone! You should be on your knees asking such favors."

One of Lord James's companions snickered: "She could be doing other things than talking while on her knees."

It turned my stomach that I had to put up with this banter. "Lord James, please, can we speak in private?" I let my face soften, and cast my eyes downward in my best demur expression.

Lord James gestured at the men. "I will meet you before the hour's out at the Cranky Gull."

"For a celebratory drink," the snickering man added. They cackled and were soon gone from my sight.

Lord James surprised me when he rested his hand on my shoulder. "I am sorry I was harsh with you earlier. Please, sit. Let us discuss the situation."

I swallowed hard and prayed I was up for this.

☠ ☠ ☠

The horizon was showing signs of light as I reached the docks. An extra guard walked the main pier. I was able to make my way to the *Red Coral*, where Reginal waited.

I pulled a freshly sealed scroll from my pack and presented it to the chief guard. "This is from Lord James. The ship has been released to me, and we are setting sail with all haste." I glanced toward Reginal, "Cast off now!"

The guard paused, looking at the seal. I pulled the gangplank on board, taking note that the wind was in our favor. We were underway, and the main sail was catching the dawn's breeze as the port bell sounded. I watched our wake—ribbons of light trailing behind us in the morning sun. I wondered if they would send any military vessels after us.

"I take it that scroll wasn't a release order," Reginal said.

The wind burned my eyes as I shook my head. "No. Things didn't go well at all with Lord James. But I expected that and had a scroll ready. I pocketed his signet ring just in case."

Reginal looked distant. "We'll have a good start on them, Kira. We'll catch the wind around Crescent Isle and turn north-northwest and into the Horseshoe Atoll to start our search for a serpent." He paused. "If that is all right with you, *Captain*."

"Jerald is still our captain. Don't presume that just because he is on shore any ranks have changed." My eyes locked onto his.

Reginal shrugged. "You are in command. You may need to come to terms with that, Kira. Even if he pulls through, he may not be able to sail again. I saw his eyes."

If I was ever to become Captain, I would need Reginal on my side; he truly would make a strong first mate. "Reginal, let's get the crew ready." I pushed back from the rail. "Seadog One Ear! Get over here!"

One Ear was always a sight. It was as if we snagged a corpse one day and dragged it up. "Yes, Mate Kira. How can I serve ye?"

I looked him over, still thinking I might find a barnacle growing somewhere on his worn frame. "Get every member of the crew armed. Spears will work best, and we should have enough of those. Sharpen them up; we need to kill us a Corilla."

"Aye, I'll tell 'em to aim for the throat."

"Use the empty vials we have in the galley to gather the blood. I don't know how much we'll need, One Ear. But we must get blood from one that is newly-dead."

"So I'll aim to get us plenty."

I nodded. "A gold Lental to each sailor who kills a Corilla."

"Right away, Mate Kira!" One Ear started barking orders and took a deck hand below with him.

The day passed quickly. We were making fine time, but it didn't feel fast enough. Some of the crew bickered over the best of the harpoons. It amazed me how efficient the sailors were at killing anything that moved near the surface. By sunset we had collected an assortment of fish and one old boot with a silver buckle.

Somehow, I knew it wouldn't be long before the first Corilla caught wind of our vessel in these waters—it was their territory, after all. And it was time for me to head below and plan our return to port . . . assuming we were successful.

I would grab some shut-eye. It wouldn't be long before they came across at least one. I was exhausted enough to sleep for a week.

☠ ☠ ☠

The bang on the door startled me awake and sent me out of my chair with my sword drawn. I checked myself quickly and responded, "Enter!"

Reginal ducked into the room, grinning merrily. The look on his face told me we had both our quarry and trouble. The items sliding across the desk told me we were turning back toward Port Newville.

"Whom do we owe the Lental to? More than one man? More than one Corilla caught?"

Reginal's expression turned darker as he recounted the story.

"We used our handsomest sailors standing on the bow for bait. They rose for it, three of the serpents. Saltmore harpooned one and wrestled it onto the deck. Before anyone could slay it, though, the she-daemon tore free and ripped Saltmore from neck to navel with its dagger. It turned out to be One Eye that dealt the serpent the killing strike. The other two Corilla got away."

"Are you all right, Reg?" It wasn't often I'd seen him this shaken over the death of a sailor.

He shook his head. "I will be, Kira. Saltmore was young, too young. It was unsettling. *She*, I mean *it* looked so human from the waist up. Damn. It was even wearing a tunic and a ragged skirt, floating there on the surface, and then climbing up the side of our ship! I heard the stories, that they can look as human as they want. But I'd never seen one up close. Her face was so innocent at first. Then her eyes glowed, and the fangs grew. We pulled her to the port side and her legs turned into a serpent's tail—bright red, shiny black, and thin white stripes. After it gutted Saltmore, One Ear pinned it to the deck with a spear through its neck. I collected the blood you wanted. Got a couple of vials."

I could smell its blood on him. I looked for my wine skin. I'd had very little to eat or drink since dining with Jerald a few nights past. Goddess, it seemed like an eternity ago.

"Reg, please do what it takes to get us back to port with all haste."

Nodding, he shut the door behind him.

I needed to eat and review the plan again before we reached the harbor. I would be taken into custody the moment we returned. "Lord James" would make a scene for taking the ship, for forging orders from Michelson, for no doubt other charges, too. He wouldn't make it pleasant, but someday he would get what he deserved.

The seas calmed as we returned to the docks. Against heavy protests from Reginal and the crew, I had them bind my hands behind me. I stood on the bow for the port guards to see as we approached the dock directly. The main pier was clear, and I knew I would be taken into custody immediately. I'd told Lord James what we were after, and we had the serpent hanging from the main sail boom as proof of our mission. Lord James would be looking forward to my "punishment."

The bell sounded, and Reginal lead me amidships as the gangplank was secured. I smiled at the sight of Michelson and his two henchmen. It reminded me of a pompous priest and his two little acolytes; all they needed were candles and some incense.

Reginal cleared his throat. "Lord James, Kira wishes to be held responsible for the unauthorized sailing of a vessel without the captain or the city's permission. She is now under your custody. Please understand that our captain is very ill and requires the antidote we acquired. I humbly request your permission to head at once to his residence."

Lord James appeared impressed, gaze flitting between the dead serpent and the small red coin pouch Reginal offered him. Reginal had a larger pouch hidden under his cloak, the ship's treasury, which I'd told him to take directly to the captain. The city's officials were corrupt, especially Lord James.

"Be on your way," Lord James told Reginal, then added a clipped laugh. "Give my best to Captain Jerald."

The acolytes led me to Lord James's personal holding cells. I doubted I was the first bound woman to be taken there. The light from candles in the office reached down the corridor, letting me see the dirt and cobwebs that lined my temporary quarters.

There was a small cot and a few blankets. I stretched out and closed my eyes. I needed to be well rested for what was to come.

☠ ☠ ☠

"Kira?" Reginal's voice was hushed. I had expected to see Lord James long before seeing Reginal again.

I sat up slowly.

Reginal set my pack just outside the cell, where I could reach it if I needed.

"Did the cure work?" I gripped the bars so tight my hands turned white, fearing this could all be for naught.

"We were too late, Kira," he replied. "The captain passed away two days ago."

I opened my mouth, but he reached a hand in through the bars and touched a finger to my lips.

"Kira, there wasn't anything we could have done." He pulled his hand back. "Heather and I spoke at great length. She wants to sell us the *Red Coral*. She told me Jerald wouldn't have wanted to break up the crew, and said he had talked about granting you the ship once he retired. She wants the current ship's treasury and the maps we found of the Snow Rift. But she signed the ship over to you."

"I can't, Reg, I . . ."

"I know the truth, Kira. Jerald honestly would have wanted you to have the ship. He loved you like a sister. From the day he pulled you out of the sea, he cared."

All I could do was clutch the bars. The cold iron gave support and kept me from falling to my knees.

Reginal leaned in close. "I also have a plan to get you out of here. The crew and I took up a collection. We plan to buy your release from Lord James."

"Don't! The crew shouldn't sacrifice for me. I will serve my time and take my public lashes as I deserve."

As if on queue, Lord James walked up behind Reginal. The lord's sick smile made my stomach churn. "I need to work out the details of Kira's punishment, Reginal, but I will take your suggestion into consideration. Move the ship to the Southern Way docks, and wait for further directions."

Reginal left quickly.

Lord James opened the cell door. "It is a shame. I would have enjoyed dispensing your public lashes, *Captain* Kira. Actually, you are free to go. As planned, you will attend to my room at the Mermaid's Rest. Dress nicely, and you can pay your fine tonight."

I forced a smile and managed to endure the brush of his hand as I headed to speak to Heather in person. "I will just need a few hours to prepare myself James." I had hoped my face didn't betray my loathing, but it was not my face he was looking at as I spoke.

☠ ☠ ☠

Heather was more cordial than I thought she would be this close to Jerald's passing. With tears in her eyes, she gave me the *Red Coral's* deed. I put the scroll case in my pack and gave her a long hug. Then we cried together and shared a few choice memories of Jerald's antics. I promised to visit her often.

But we both knew that was a lie.

I stopped to change at a local bathhouse. How I wished I could return there after paying Lord James what he felt he had coming . . . the touch of the man made my skin crawl. I paid to have a private bath drawn. I loved the feel of warm water against my skin. I leaned over the edge of the tub and pulled an ancient gold coin from my pack. We found a few of them last summer while taking a break on a small, nameless island. The coin was twice as thick and wide as a gold Lental, but cut in a square shape with rounded corners. As I soaked, I washed it clean. I held it up and wondered if this little coin could save me a night of disgust— Lord James wanted it badly enough.

I dried off, put on an old but well-made dress, brushed off my cloak, and placed my other clothes in my pack.

I pulled my hood up as I left the bathhouse and placed the coin in my mouth for safekeeping. It was now time to meet his lordship.

I kept my hood up and head low and set a silver coin on the counter as I walked up toward Lord James's private room. I knocked once and entered.

He was wearing only his drawstring trousers and sitting at a desk. He directed me to sit on the bed.

"You look lovely tonight, Captain Kira."

His eyes walked up and down my body, and I felt as if sewer rats crawled across my skin. I allowed my anger to rise as I gave him a slight grin. He opened the center desk drawer, pulled out the red coin pouch I'd seen earlier, and dumped the contents on the desk.

"I pray you brought the relic I requested."

I nodded and gently took the coin out of my mouth.

"I must say that is a strange hiding place for such a treasure, but I find it very alluring." He shifted in his chair.

I turned the coin in the light, my saliva made it glimmer. "I didn't want to be taken for a maiden of the night and robbed of it." I smiled seductively and handed him the coin. "It is the real thing, the purest of soft Zavalli gold." I allowed my eyes to play across the surface, hoping to keep his attention there.

He bit into the coin to test the metal. With a sick smile, he sucked my saliva off the coin. He slowly pulled the coin out of his mouth. "If your kiss is half as sweet as this coin leads me to believe, we will have quite a night. I know now why Jerald kept you around."

He licked his lips. I got up from the bed, leaned over the desk, and kissed him long and full on the mouth, my teeth pricking his tongue. His head flopped back, and he licked his lips again. "Sweetness, such sweetness..." His eyes closed and a line of drool spilled out of his mouth.

Very few knew we could look as human as we wanted, for as long as we wanted. It helped that I'd learned to walk among men even before I met Jerald. He took my heart the first day I looked into his eyes. Jerald taught me many things in our time together, although I never did learn to share. He should have returned my affections.

I gathered up the coin pouch and the relic, and put both in my pack. Then I pulled the hood over my head and headed out into the night and back to my crew and my newly acquired ship.

HAUNTED ISLE
by Steve Winter

For thirty minutes, Calab watched the ship grow larger on the horizon. Its three sail-studded masts and fluttering pennants stood out clearly. The enemy was less than a mile away.

Hornbill Jake grabbed a handful of Calab's shirt in his tar-grimed hand. "Listen here, Calab m' lad," he said, pulling the boy's attention away from the approaching vessel. " 'Tis a sorry thing for a young one such as you to be caught in this plight, just a week after bein' pluck'd from a plundered prize. But here we be, and you with us, so best be ready to face what comes."

"Will we surrender?" Calab asked.

"There'll be no surrender today," Hornbill replied. "Surrender's for those as expects mercy, and there's nae such a man in this crew.

"But here we sit," he continued, "our keel ground out on this reef by a captain wi' no more sense than a squawkin' parrot. To wind'ard and closin' fast is a Commissioner wi' sixteen guns and ridin' high on empty holds. A'lee is naught but rocky coast that no man aboard ha' seen before. I warrant that cursed coast weren't here when last we crossed this latitude. There it taunts us, ten cables off, and us pinned till the tide lifts us free. So we're in debt to the devil, Calab, and he's comin' to collect his due and proper."

Hornbill spat on *Tikal's* deck and leaned across the gun that he commanded, staring forlornly at the approaching vessel.

Calab, along with Shanks and dark, massive Arl, crewed the gun under Hornbill Jake. The boy had seen it fired only once, when Hornbill and the others showed him the steps for loading and running out the weapon. He'd loaded it for the second time minutes ago in preparation for the coming fight.

Calab stared up at *Tikal's* sails, flapping uselessly in the breeze.

Hornbill tugged Calab's shoulder again, drawing him in close over the gun barrel, along with the other two men. "We've precious little time now," he whispered. "At five hundred yards, she'll swing broadside to us and start to poundin'. We can't maneuver, so we're as good as dead here. But the light's failin'. In half a glass, there'll be enough dark, powder smoke, fallin' riggin', and screamin' all round to hide whatever we do. So when I give the word, grab anythin' that'll float and heave her overboard to land'ard. We'll make for that island, where no Commissioner's ship will follow us over this hull-hookin' reef. Whatever lies there, it's no worse than burnin' with *Tikal* or swingin' from a yardarm at th' end of a tarred rope."

Hornbill's face pressed close up to Calab's so that the boy felt the sweating man's stubble. "Keep your eyes on me, boy, and nowhere else," he commanded. "You'll have more than enough to fill 'em right here."

"Yes sir," Calab answered. But he swung his eyes back toward the other ship when a voice called out, "she's turning!"

157

He saw the puffs of smoke—first one, then another, then six more in rapid succession—before hearing the thuds that followed. To his surprise, he could see black dots of iron flying toward the ship, toward him. They hit the water fifty yards short and kicked up plumes of spray. Calab lost them at that point, all but one. That one skipped up from a wave like a flat rock skipped across a stream. It screamed over the ship, slicing a rope as it passed before plunging beneath another plume of water.

Then the ship shuddered under Calab's feet as cannon roared back. He felt the hull groaning on the reef and heard iron balls whistling through the air. Most of all, he heard Hornbill's shout to stand clear and be ready with a roundshot.

Hornbill lowered the glowing linstock to the cannon's touchhole, and flame thundered from the muzzle. The carriage slammed backward across the scarred deck before wrenching to a stop against taut ropes. Calab scuttled forward with the twelve-pound shot in his hands, but Shank pushed him away from the gun's muzzle. He shoved a sponging pole down the barrel to douse smoldering cinders before Arl rammed in a powder charge. Only then did Shank wave wildly for Calab to roll in the ball.

The ship pitched so violently that Calab nearly dropped the shot. His shoulder slammed hard against the gun's muzzle. Shank held him on his feet, Calab pushed the cannonball into the barrel, and immediately Arl was there with the ramrod, driving it back to the breach.

"Heave!" roared Hornbill. Eight arms hauled on the thick ropes. Wooden rollers groaned in greased blocks until the gun carriage banged against the gunwhale.

As he stepped away, weight fell on Calab's shoulders and dragged him to the deck. Thrashing, he realized that loops of rigging sliced from high on the mast had fallen onto him. He wriggled his way out of the tangled mass, all the while watching Hornbill and Shank lever the gun carriage sideways to bring it in line with the Commissioner's ship.

Again Hornbill set the glowing linstock on the gun's touchhole, and it crashed backward in a burst of flame and concussion that forced Calab's eyes shut. As he opened them, still lying on the deck, the gunwhale exploded inward. Jagged splinters of hull as big as Calab's forearm and sharp as cutlasses whipped and spiraled over his head. Shank fell to the deck screaming in front of Calab, where the boy saw that the toes and front half of Shank's right foot were gone, and a piece of splintered oak was speared through his calf.

Smoke drifted across the deck, stinging Calab's eyes and parching his throat. His ears rang so painfully that, though he saw Shank was screaming, he could barely hear it.

Someone jerked Calab to his feet. It was Hornbill, now motioning for Calab to grab Shank by the arm and drag him away from the gun.

"Get 'im to land'ard, lad!" the gunner shouted. "Get 'im to Arl!"

Across the deck, Arl heaved a barrel overboard and followed it with a grate and a portion of smashed decking. Calab was barely within the man's reach when he, too, was snatched up and hurled into the waves. The boy surfaced in time to see Hornbill and Arl lowering Shank by the arms and then dropping him before following themselves.

Suddenly Hornbill was behind Calab. "Grab somethin', boy, to keep afloat!" The surface of the sea was black in the fading light, but fires burning on *Tikal* cast it into a confusion of orange and yellow flickers. More bodies, alive and dead, splashed around Calab. Hung up on the reef, *Tikal* couldn't sink, but she was doomed. Only the dead and maimed stayed aboard.

Clinging to a broken spar and kicking to drive himself forward, Calab reached the island sometime during the night. Like all the other accumulating detritus from *Tikal*, he was battered and bruised against the rocks by the time he fought his way through them. Beyond the boulders, he found a rising shelf of gravel and bedrock pitted with standing pools. Calab collapsed onto the stony bed. Despite his aching, exhausted limbs, he could not sleep.

For a while, Calab thought he might be the only survivor to make it ashore. *Tikal* was still visible in the darkness as a glowing redness near the waterline. The Commissioner's ship, lanterns blazing, stood off the reef. Calab thought it had hardly moved since the fight. Certainly it made no attempt to pick up survivors or rescue injured from the burning *Tikal*.

As the early morning light grew, Calab saw that he wasn't alone on the island. Others had dragged themselves onto the rocky shelf. Among the splintered wood, sails, ropes, sea chests, and barrels clogging the boulders that lined the island coast floated more bodies. Some were burned, some shattered by cannonballs, some battered and torn by the rocks themselves.

On the shore, men nursed their wounds, cast glances at their wasted ship and its hated vanquisher, and then worked their way into the steep, forested slopes behind them.

Calab picked his way across the stony shore, unsure which way to proceed.

As he neared the tree line, a shout drew his attention. He saw Arl standing near a jumble of boulders perhaps a quarter mile away. Someone lay at his feet. Calab assumed it was Shank.

Carefully, he jogged across the uneven stones to rejoin his gun crewmates.

"It good to see you, Calab lad," rumbled Arl. "We feared mebbe da sharks eat ya or ya be dashed to tatters on dese toothy rocks." He clamped his thick, tattooed arm round Calab's shoulder and gave the boy an uncharacteristic squeeze.

Shank's face was pallid even through the dirt and powder residue. The oak splinter had been removed from his calf and a strip of linen tied round it. Sun-bleached sailcloth bound his foot, but Calab saw from the shape that it was more stump than foot.

Shank raised himself on one elbow and extended his other hand. Dried blood stained it. "Ye wouldn't have water, would you, Calab? I'm hurtin' bad."

Calab shook his head. "There are shallow pools in the rocks back where I came ashore. Maybe we could get water there."

"Be no good," said Arl. "Everyt'ing along here be brackish fro' the tide. We got to move inland 'n' fin' us a spring."

"What of Jake?" Calab asked. "Have you seen him?"

"Hornbill hike t'other way down da shore lookin' for you," Arl replied. "I 'spec he be back soon. Now give us a han' here." He motioned to their wounded comrade.

Together Arl and Calab lifted Shank, though the lifting was done mostly by Arl. At his size, Calab could do little more than help the man balance. Between them, and with many winces and curses from Shank, they hobbled up the stony slope to the edge of the forest. By the time they reached it, Hornbill Jake had rejoined them, though Calab neither saw nor heard his approach.

Jake took Shank's drooping shoulder from Calab. "Move on ahead a pace, boy, an' pick us out a good path."

Calab stepped forward in the underbrush, and then paused. "Where are we going?" he asked.

"We need water an' food," Jake said, "an' a spot where we can rest an' tend to Shank where no Commissioner's men'll find us."

Calab stared at Hornbill without reacting for several moments.

"I know what yer thinkin', lad," the gunner said. "Maybe 'twouldn't be such a bad turn were the Commissioner to take us. Maybe ye'd be returned to suchever family as ye've left. Maybe ye'd get off this ha'nted isle and leave us band o' freebooters behin'.

"Maybe all that'd be, but ha'e we treated ye so foul that ye'd do us so black a turn? Did we not pluck ye from the sea as yer ship sank an' teach ye to crew a gun as a man? Ha'e we not shared, and shared alike, all we had, as we would wi' any true shipmate?"

"I don't want to leave," Calab replied simply. "But I don't know how to find water or shelter. I've never been on a haunted island before. What must I do?"

"Ya folla yer nose, little gunner lad," Arl laughed. "Jest folla yer nose."

They pushed into the forest for hours, steadily climbing. It was not, as Calab had feared, impenetrable jungle. The trees and plants were unfamiliar shapes, but they weren't so different from the woods near his home—his former home, Calab reminded himself. He swung Shank's curved cutlass to slice away a bit of impeding foliage. It wasn't necessary. He could have brushed it aside easily, but he enjoyed swinging the weapon, despite his aching arms. The slightly curved blade was dark gray, not polished like the swords men carried in cities, and it wore a heavy sheen of oil for protection against salty spray. The blade was scarred and pitted from use and age but kept razor sharp.

At his next swing, the underbrush exploded into raucous noise and color. A shrilling whirlwind burst past Calab. The boy dropped Shank's cutlass as he stumbled back and fell, then watched the wild colors disappear into the leafy canopy overhead.

Behind him, Hornbill and Arl laughed. He looked up at them quizzically from the ground.

"'Twere a parrot, lad," Hornbill laughed. "Ha'e ye never seen one afore?"

"No, I haven't," Calab replied.

"They're common round these latitudes, though I didn't know they could be found on ha'nted isles. Perhaps we'll catch one for ye someday, for they make fine pets shipboard."

As he stood, Calab noticed Shank's drooping head and asked, "Is he all right?"

Hornbill shook his head. "He's fadin' fast, lad. If we don't fin' him water and food shortly, I doubt he'll make it."

"Dat leg won' stop bleedin'," added Arl.

Turning back to his task, Calab resolved to double his efforts. He hoisted the cutlass and pushed into the brush, clearing a path for the men, his eyes darting right and left for any sign of water or something edible.

They advanced what Calab believed to be another mile when he halted, his eyes frozen forward.

"What be the matter, Calab?" asked Hornbill.

Calab raised the cutlass and pointed ahead to where an opening in the forest canopy allowed a shaft of brilliant light to penetrate the gloom. In the light stood a trio of wooden Xs. Lashed to each X, spread-eagled and upside down, was a man, his blouse torn open, his stomach slashed crossways. Each man's entrails, lungs, and heart were pulled out across the ribcage to hang down across his chest and bloodstained face.

"Gods alive," whispered Arl. He plucked up the talisman hanging round his neck and pressed it to his lips. "Dis be de work of evil spirits fo' sure."

Hornbill peered into the unaccustomed brightness. "That's Legbone LeBoux on the right," he whispered, "*Tikak's* barber. Many's the time he stitched me t'gether after a fight."

He stepped cautiously into the light and peered more closely at the slain sailors. "Not spirits," he declared. "Not they who did this. Spirits there may be, but this be the work o' jenrats. Ye can tell by the bite marks on their arms and faces."

"Den dey be guided by an eviler hand dan even dey has," protested Arl. "Never has I seen a man hung upside down dat way by no jenrat."

"May be," Hornbill replied thoughtfully. "And they ain't eaten—just bit."

Calab wondered whether the same fate awaited Hornbill, Shank, and Arl. Only after a moment did he realize that he shared the same peril.

Three heads turned as one toward a snap from the left. In an instant, Hornbill's hand flew to his cutlass and Arl's to his heavy knife. Hornbill retreated to the shadows, then no one moved for nearly a minute. Calab heard only the croaking of tree frogs, but he dared not move until Hornbill gave some sign.

One minute stretched to two and two into what seemed a very long time to Calab. Finally Hornbill motioned to Arl, and the two of them hoisted Shank between them. As quietly as possible, they moved to the right at an angle that carried them away from the dead men.

Time was difficult to judge in the forest. Calab trudged ahead of Hornbill and Arl, exhausted from navigating the difficult terrain and the constant care to make no unnecessary sound. Jake told him to cut no underbrush. Calab assumed that was to leave the faintest trail, but it made their progress more difficult.

The gloom beneath the trees was nearly impenetrable when their path met a narrow river. All four collapsed on the bank and plunged their faces into the water. Calab drank till he thought his stomach would split, and then splashed the cool liquid over his sweat-soaked neck and shoulders. He rolled onto his back and let his long hair drag in the stream. His legs shook from fatigue, his hands and face were scratched raw, but at last, his muscles could relax.

Staring upward toward the open space where the trees parted above the river, Calab saw the sky for the first time since leaving the site of the three dead men. Dark orange dusk was shot through with blood-red arteries of cloud. Beneath the canopy where he lay, the darkness was almost complete. Calab crawled a few yards from the bank, closed his eyes, and slept.

☠   ☠   ☠

He was awakened by Arl's hand shaking his shoulder. "Time to move again, wee man," Arl rumbled.

Calab tried to rise, but pain in his limbs stopped him. He rolled onto his stomach and tried again more cautiously, getting onto hands and knees before standing slowly. Arl grinned at him and slapped his shoulder painfully, but then pushed a generous chunk of dripping coconut into Calab's hand. "Hornbill fin' some coc'nut trees 'long da bank. Good food! You eat."

Calab didn't need to be told. When the coconut shell was scraped clean, he used it to scoop up water from the river and again drink his fill.

Food and water revived him. Calab looked around their sleeping spot. Hornbill and Arl had collected more coconuts and lashed them together with twisted grass and reeds. Hornbill offered the bundle to Calab. "This be your load, boy," he said. "Sling 'er over your shoulder and ye'll have nae trouble wi' it."

Shank gave no reaction when the two men hoisted him between them. His eyes were glazed and dull beneath drooping lids. The mangled foot dragged on the ground, its sailcloth wrapping torn and blood-soaked.

"We'll follow the river downstream," Hornbill declared. "Pick up yer sword, Calab lad, and take the lead. If there's a way out of this festerin' forest and off this ha'nted mound, it'll lie near the shore, not 'neath this roof."

It was the first time Jake had referred to the cutlass as Calab's. The boy felt proud, but then glanced at Shank hanging limp between his crewmates. Calab pushed silently past them, adjusted his load, and proceeded along the riverbank.

The going was not as easy as Calab assumed it would be. Where sunlight reached through the canopy, the bank was overgrown too thickly to hack through. He was forced to lead them away from the bank to find clearer paths while keeping constantly mindful never to lose track of the river. Unlike the previous day, however, Calab was grateful to have cool water nearby and the coconuts for a midday meal.

For hours they marched steadily and silently, keeping the river always on the left. Sometime in the afternoon, Calab glimpsed motion at the limit of his vision. He had seen things, or thought he'd seen things, indistinct and fleeting: monkeys or parrots flitting between the trees, he assumed. But this was large, and dark, and holding its position relative to Calab.

"Up ahead, Jake," Calab whispered across his shoulder. "Something moving parallel to us, to the right of our path."

"Are ye sure, Calab lad?" Hornbill asked. "I've spied nary a thing shadowin' us."

Arl leaned in close to Hornbill and whispered, "Da boy be right, Hornbill. I seen it too, 'bout forty paces on. It be big, an' it be alone."

Hornbill motioned downward, and he and Arl lowered Shank to the ground. Both men drew their blades while peering into the shadows ahead. At another silent motion from Hornbill, all three fanned out and worked their way carefully forward.

Calab glanced back to where Shank lay. He wanted to be sure they could find that spot again. His attention was pulled to the front by a stifled cry from Arl. It was an exclamation of surprise, not pain or shock. Arl and Hornbill had moved some distance ahead of Calab, and he raced to catch up.

Ahead of them lay an immense clearing, and filling it was a jumbled city of stone. Vines snaked so thickly up the sides of a central pyramid as to nearly obscure its massive blocks. Around the pyramid's base, trees grew through crumbling roofs, their enfolding roots preventing the walls from toppling.

Hornbill whistled softly and pushed the crumpled, broad-brimmed hat back from his forehead. Arl raised the necklace talisman to his lips and waved a quick magic sign in the air.

Calab stared. The eerie panorama was unlike anything he'd ever seen or imagined. Scowling, Hornbill adjusted his belt and walked cautiously forward. Arl followed with reluctant steps.

Calab trailed in their footsteps. His pace was slower than Jake's, slower even than Arl's. He wasn't aware that he was falling behind. His eyes were everywhere but on Jake and Arl. Despite its desolation, the city had a savage grandeur that clutched Calab's imagination.

Everywhere he saw fantastic details. Lichen-crusted stones bore detailed bas-reliefs of snakes, fish, soaring birds, and horrid monsters. Tumbled pillars were circumscribed with undecipherable runes. Immense stone heads arrayed in ranks stared in unison toward the great pyramid. Everything towered over the boy, reaching higher even than Arl's topknot. A chill ran up Calab's spine. The stone heads were carved into likenesses of things both familiar and macabre. Their near-human features only made them seem more monstrous.

Arl's hushed voice brought Calab back to his friends. "No jenrat hands raised up dese piles," he whispered. "This be devil-work."

"Devils need no roofs nor stairs," Jake answered. "But ye're right that this be nae a jenrat city. If they had a hand in its buildin', it weren't for their own use."

He pointed toward a doorway in a nearby building. The opening was nine feet tall yet only two feet wide. Calab glanced around at other buildings. Despite differences in details, every doorway was built in the same tall, narrow shape.

Arl spun on his heels and peered back the way they'd come. "Did you hear somethin'?" he asked. Calab shook his head. Jake merely crouched and watched in the direction Arl indicated.

They remained that way for several minutes, until Hornbill snorted. "T'ain't nothing there. Ye're spooked is all. This place be dead. We'll be the same 'less we keep movin'."

"These twistin' alleys and chok'd streets are a proper maze," grumbled Hornbill. "We might wander all day in such a labyrinth an' never find a proper exit. Let's drop the devil-talk and find a way through. We must keep on downstream toward the sea."

Calab looked around. Despite the profusion of saplings, vines, and waist-high grasses, he decided they were in a plaza of sorts. The surrounding buildings had a presence about them, an air of undeniable importance. Though the architecture was alien, Calab felt the same sense of authority here that he'd known from the governor's palace at Port Colinhugh.

Hornbill interrupted Calab's musings. "Boy," he commanded, "scale yon pyramid and scout the layout o' this cursed place. We need a path through this maze, and the sooner we're through, the sooner we'll again breathe clean sea air."

Calab dropped his load of coconuts and jogged toward the towering monument a few hundred yards distant. On reaching it, he was startled to see the size of the cut stone blocks that formed it. Each was taller than him.

His jump barely enabled him to catch the edge of the first block. By the time he struggled and dragged himself atop it, the boy knew he could never scale the pyramid that way. Calab circled the pyramid to his left, using the flat ledge atop the first layer of stones as a walkway. Several times he needed to leap crumbling gaps or skirt knotted tree roots and vines.

When he turned the first corner, Calab saw what he'd hoped for: a set of carved stairs ascending the side of the steeply sloping wall. Even the steps were a challenge. Like the doorways, they were sized for someone much taller than a man. Each was a climb for the determined boy. He scrambled upward on hands and knees, step-by-step.

Along the way, Calab studied the carvings lining the low sides of the staircase. At first, he thought the sinewy line paralleling his ascent was no more than a simple, geometric decoration. But he soon realized that it was not abstract. The line represented an enormous snake, and it was locked in a battle with numerous figures that Calab could interpret only as angels.

Topping the pyramid at last, Calab stood on a level platform barely ten feet square. The snake designs that flanked the stairs extended across the flat stones to the center. There they rose into a sculpture of two snakes twining around one another before merging into a single head. Its jeweled eyes stared down into Calab's, and its open mouth revealed curving fangs of what looked like carved ivory. Unlike everything else he'd seen in this city, the snake looked as if it were newly carved. Every scale and muscle was cleanly defined, and no lichens grew on its polished surface.

Curious, Caleb touched one ferocious fang. It felt stingingly hot as he slid his finger across its tip. When a drop of red dripped from the fang to splatter against the stone floor, Calab stared for several moments before realizing that it was his blood. A deep cut in his fingertip bled freely. He'd felt no pain, only the strange heat.

Calab hastily wrapped the bleeding finger with his kerchief and recalled why he'd been sent up the pyramid. From its peak, the entire city stretched out beneath him. Much of it was hidden or overgrown by encroaching forest, but the plan was clear.

He saw that Jake's aggravated observation had been nearly correct. The buildings were arranged symmetrically, but the pattern was mazelike. Calab studied it until he felt confident in remembering a path to the river. Though buildings and trees obscured his view, he'd seen what he believed was a small boat or canoe on the bank.

The climb down was more difficult. The boy struggled to hang on as he lowered himself down each ledge. Only a few steps from the bottom, his strained, torn fingers slipped from the rock. He tumbled backward with a shout. Arms and legs twirling like a whirligig, Calab bounced across the remaining steps before thudding to the soft ground, dazed.

When Calab opened his eyes, Jake and Arl loomed over him. "Are ye all right, boy?" asked Jake. "We heard yer cry and seen ye tumble as a man shot from the rigging. Such a fall could ha' broken your arms and legs altogether."

Calab stirred and sat up. "I'm not hurt," he said. "At least, I don't think I am. Only my finger. . . ." He held up the bandaged finger.

Arl placed his hand on Calab's back. "Ye're pale as an airy ghost, son. Put ya head down and breathe deep. It's da sodden jungle air of dis evil place that bedevils ya."

"I thought I saw a boat near the stream," Calab said. "We can reach it, if I remember the way. It's small, but it may hold the four of us."

"That's my lad," Hornbill said. "A boat'd be a fine thing, just what we need. Ye recover your wits now. Then we'll find this boat o' yours, fetch

Shank, and be on our way downstream." He spat hatefully. "The sooner we're quit o' this place, the sooner I'll rest."

Calab drew in his legs to stand, but froze when he looked past Arl.

The big man extended his arm. "Take dis hand, Calab, and let Arl help ya up ."

A cry of alarm rose in Calab's throat. He screamed an unintelligible sound of terror and warning. Though Arl turned instantly, it was too late.

A thin blade whipped through the air. Its smooth arc carried it through Arl's neck without slowing. Arl's head tipped forward to drop next to Calab's knee. The body crumpled to a heap, fountaining blood from the neck.

Calab stared into the face of the attacker. Though vaguely man-shaped, it was no man. The form, draped all in black, was impossibly tall and thin. A scale-covered hand held the sword that dripped Arl's blood. From beneath the cloak's dark hood gazed the head of a snake. Its vertical pupils gleamed and a forked tongue flicked the air. As Hornbill drew his cutlass and charged toward it, the creature melted into the ground.

Jake jerked Caleb to his feet. "We've got to be gone from here, lad, and harry quick, or the snake folk'll do for us the same as they done to poor Arl. Do ye remember the way to the river? Can ye get us there?"

"I think so," stammered Calab. "I mean, yes. I remember. It's this way."

Calab stepped around Arl's corpse as he led Jake out of the plaza. They moved hesitantly, Calab scanning each intersection before turning to right or left. But the city's symmetry was clear in his mind, so they made no wrong turns.

"The river's around the corner of the next building," Calab told Jake. "The canoe that I saw, if that's what it was, will be to our right."

"Good lad," Hornbill said. "Ye've done well. Now step behind me an' be ready to sprint when I goes.

"An' hold that cutlass high," he added. "If anythin' gets in your way, cut it down if you can, go 'round if you can't."

Jake glanced around the corner and pulled back. "She looks clear. One small buildin' twixt us and the river. I seen the canoe where ya said. Let's hope she has paddles aboard."

Hornbill winked, then he bolted around the corner. Calab dashed after him. He saw the area leading to the river as he remembered it: weed-choked and open except for a single collapsed building.

Calab pushed himself hard to keep up, but he fell behind the fast-moving man. Waist-high grasses dragged on the boy's legs and breeches. He shouted as Jake reached the crumbling wall of the building.

Jake slowed momentarily and looked back over his shoulder. In that moment, a shadow lunged from a wall. Jake shuddered to a stop, transfixed by the red-tinged glint of polished steel. He looked down at the blade, then sideways at the cloaked figure holding it. Slowly that figure rose until it towered above Jake, tall and thin and terrible.

Like an explosion, the sword sliced through Jake's belly, and a fan of blood followed in its wake. Jake's entrails rolled out into the weeds. The gunner dropped to his knees and toppled forward, where he was hidden from Calab's sight.

"If anythin' gets in your way, cut it down if you can, go 'round if you can't."

Those words hung in Calab's ears like the spectral shape of the killer hung in his vision.

Calab ran. He circled behind the collapsed building, as much to avoid Jake's body as the creature. He heard stones shifting on the far side of the wall, and the sound spurred his feet even faster.

The canoe was in sight just forty yards ahead, but something stood between it and Calab. He thought it was a signpost on first sight, but as he approached at a run, there was no mistaking Shank's face. The head was spitted directly in Calab's path.

"If anythin' gets in your way, cut it down if you can, go 'round if you can't."

Calab raised Shank's cutlass above his shoulder. Veering aside only slightly, he swung it with all the strength and anger he could muster as he passed the grisly spike. The heavy blade sliced into the wooden post and sheered through. Shank's head toppled to the ground, but Calab was already past.

In one motion he tossed the sword into the canoe and slammed his shoulder against the raised prow. The vessel ground across the gravelly bank, then dropped free into the water. With a leap Calab was inside, groping for a paddle, and driving the canoe into the current. An inhuman shriek of fury followed him for long moments, and then the city fell behind.

☠ ☠ ☠

The moon reflecting off the water flashed in dizzying patterns. Calab stood unsteadily on the deck of the Commissioner's square-rigged sixteen-gunner. Two men in long scarlet coats and white breeches eyed him warily.

The younger of the officers addressed him. "You say you are from *Tikal?*"

"Yes sir. I was a gunner's mate."

"And before that?"

"A passenger aboard *Silver Princess*, sir," Calab replied, lowering his eyes to the deck.

"Taken by *Tikal* a week out of Port Copinhugh," the young officer said. He raised Calab's chin with his hand. "Keep your eyes forward, boy. Tell us again what followed *Tikal's* destruction."

Calab's eyes burned. "We swam to the island, where we passed that night and the next. All three of my gun mates were slain by a creature in an ancient city in the forest. I escaped by means of the canoe in which you found me adrift."

The officer's eyes flashed in the lantern light. "Don't try my patience, boy. Simple, truthful answers will serve you better than these fanciful, impertinent lies."

Calab glared back.

The older officer, the Commissioner himself, extended his hand between them. He spoke in a level tone. "As you can see, lad, naught but a rocky bar lies beyond the reef, where burns *Tikal's* hulk still. No forest. No city. Only hours ago did we conclude our fight. Any freebooters who escaped to that barren islet will certainly die there of hunger, thirst, and exposure, but none have yet spent a full night. Surely you can understand why your account strikes our ears as fanciful.

"Nonetheless," he continued, "I am inclined to accept what you say."

The young officer turned toward his captain, eyes wide.

"I have seen things as strange as your tale, and stranger, in these latitudes," the Commissioner said. "Besides which, I do not take the son of Magistrate Hollings for a liar."

Both Calab and the young officer started. "Yes, I recognize you," said the Commissioner with a slight smile. "You shall return with us to Port Copinhugh, where your future will be decided. You are back among friends, boy."

Calab looked back to the glowing hull of *Tikal,* licked by dying flames, and his heart sank.

THE ADVENTURE OF KEVA THE FREEMARINER
AND THE NOTORIOUS PIRATE-HUNTERS
by Jason Mical

Lord Stockton looked up from his accounting ledger at the sound of approaching feet. He placed the book's ribbon between its pages, shut it, straightened it, and steepled his long fingers. His assistant Darcy entered his study and stood before him, her hands behind her back.

"Gaspar says we can sail with the evening tide, milord," she said, her blue eyes turned to the floor.

"Excellent, Darcy. I expect that you'll want to come as well?"

The young woman made brief eye contact before dropping her gaze again. "Oh, sir, I wouldn't ask that of you."

Stockton sighed. "I know you wouldn't, Darcy. How long have you worked with me now—two months? Three? You're not the laborer I hired off the streets anymore. You've done well for yourself. You're attentive to your tasks, and you've got a perception about you that's remarkable for someone your age. You learned to read faster than anyone I've known, and you can handle yourself on a ship. It's time to find out how well you do on something other than a delivery run. You have all the makings of a good pirate-hunter, and I mean to see if my investment has paid off."

Although Stockton's face remained a mask of businesslike stone, a smile played across Darcy's delicate lips. "Oh, sir. Milord. Lord Stockton. Yes, of course. I'd love to go. I'll see to our final preparations and pack my things. Thank you, sir!"

Lord Stockton rose, filling the room with his height as much as his carriage. He was a broad-shouldered man, well-muscled and used to life aboard a ship. He hid most of his body under silken breeches and coats lined with lace, and the powder on his face covered most of the sunspots he'd acquired as trophies for his years on the sea. "Don't forget my chest, now. It's in my room. I'll pack the last of my things myself. That will be all," Stockton told her.

Darcy scampered off. Stockton considered the wistful excitement of youth; the girl was barely out of her teens, and eager as a gull to put out to sea. She'd arrived at Port Myrna looking for work at the docks, and he considered himself lucky to have found her before a pressgang—or worse—got hold of her. She'd helped him with the research, of course; she knew about Keva and the danger the pirate posed. And still she was willing to put her hand into the lion's mouth.

But more than that, she was an orphan drifting from meaningless job to meaningless job, no future in sight except for rum and death; it was a life he'd had so many years ago. If he could rise from the stink of the bilge to become a Lord, then so could Darcy. Lord Stockton allowed himself a sallow smile at how much the girl reminded him of himself at that age.

☠ ☠ ☠

That evening, with Port Myrna several leagues behind them, Lord Stockton had the lookout ring for the officers to assemble. Both the first mate, an imposing Derenki named Olavi, and the weapons master, a one-eyed gnome woman called Wag, were sailors he'd hired before. He didn't recognize the bo'sun, a Basilisk whose name Stockton couldn't pronounce, but Darcy said Olavi recommended him. Everyone referred to the lizard-man as "The Whip," which seemed appropriate enough.

Lord Stockton stood before the officers, the buttons on his red captain's jacket shining from a fresh polish, his hands behind his back, and his cutlass dangling from his belt. No one said anything; Darcy stood in the back of the room, her arms crossed, observant. Stockton noted how she picked a position that would let her see the entire room and gauge responses to his speech. Another point in her favor.

"Gentlefolk, welcome aboard the *Lady Grace*. Our adventure promises to be most lucrative. As many of you know, piracy has become an increasing thorn in the side of nations in the Core—and eliminating pirates to safeguard trade is what Stockton Securities specializes in. For those who have not met me, I am Lord Stockton." He made a small flourish and continued.

"Our quarry on this voyage is an up-and-coming freemariner named Keva." The officers murmured in recognition. Good. "She's an elf, and although she's been a small-time operator for years, she's recently become much more brazen in her attacks. Her ship, the *Fortunato*, has taken an estimated eighty thousand pieces of gold worth of cargo, weapons, and cash—and that is from our sponsor alone. Our sponsor has seen fit to offer a large share of their recovered losses as reward—forty thousand to be split, plus whatever we find aboard *Fortunato*. Of course, we are to provide Keva's head as proof the deed is done."

Lord Stockton let the amount of the reward sink in. He saw minds crunching numbers; with officer's portions, that meant most of the people before him would earn more money for a month's work than they usually saw in a year. Stockton saw that Darcy was watching too, not missing a beat. He noticed she was fighting a grin; her share would be more money than she had seen in her entire life.

"Now then, I have spent the past several months researching Keva's activities. I have ten pieces of gold that says I know her better than her own mother." Stockton took a piece of paper from the desk behind him and unrolled it. A small painting of a pretty, if intense, elf stared back, elegant nose and hard eyes peering from a mass of golden hair loosely tied back in a sailor's tail. "This is Keva. Age unknown. Other aliases unknown." He traded for another roll of paper. "This is the *Fortunato*," he said, referring to a charcoal sketch of a long, two-masted schooner. "She's built for speed, and Keva lowered her freeboard so she practically sits at the waterline. She's got a firegunner aboard, so most ships surrender after a short fight.

"We'll do no such thing," Stockton said after a brief pause. "Keva operates primarily between Port Myrna and Ro'tanga, and stays far enough away from Prado that she doesn't attract too much military attention. She does, however, move in a predictable pattern. She knows better than most that the southern thaws bring rare oils and furs from the frozen islands. And somehow, she can't resist attacking the traders that bring such goods. After that, she comes north to take merchant ships before retiring for the autumn and starting the cycle over again.

"This being summer, it is most probable she's in local waters now. A few well-placed hints to properly connected people, and the *Lady Grace* is known in pirating circles as being a merchant prize with an easy pile of gold for the plundering. So our line has been cast. She's out there, and now she'll come to us."

Olavi had been briefed in advance, and Stockton trusted him to answer any questions the crew might be too afraid to address to their captain. After the officers left, Stockton motioned Darcy to his table. "What were your impressions?"

"A good crew, milord. But if it comes to a fight, how can we match a firegunner? That witchcraft will set our whole ship ablaze if we get too close. Or for that matter, how can we fight a ship that rides so low in the water? Our shots will pass right over her hull."

"Excellent. I'm glad you're thinking in those terms. I've had the *Lady Grace* for thirty years, since before I opened Stockton Securities. She's a schooner, like the *Fortunato*. She may not sit as low, but we can make up for that in speed. I've added enough extra sails to run circles around Keva's ship. She's got a firegunner, sure, but that gnome you saw earlier—she's an airformer. The only one of her kind I've ever met with such a talent."

"You mean she can use magic to shield the ship from the *Fortunato*'s fire?"

"That, and she's as good as a cannon when it comes to destroying ships. Better even—she doesn't need to reload. Just give her a bottle of wine, point her in the right direction, and get out of her way."

Darcy nodded, processing this new information. "Were you finished, milord?"

Stockton nodded. "Indeed. I'd like to see you at second watch tomorrow."

"Sir?"

He laid his hand on his sword. "It's time you learned how to use one of these."

☠ ☠ ☠

"Parry. Now riposte. *Riposte!*" Lord Stockton twisted his rapier, and Darcy's clanged to the deck. "Never give me an opening, ever. If you hesitate, you die."

Darcy said nothing. After two weeks at sea, her skin was a golden brown, her hair streaked with yellow. Sweat poured off her face, but she never complained; she simply picked up the rapier assumed an *en garde* stance, and awaited Lord Stockton's next move. He made a lazy, high sweep that she parried easily and counterattacked. Quickly, he stabbed at her unguarded leg and stopped as the point of his blade touched her flesh. She flinched, but still said nothing.

"Always guard. Never let your confidence get the better of you. Defense first, then offense."

"Hey, lighten up on the kid, Captain."

Stockton whirled around to face whomever was being so insubordinate. Wag the gnome stood on a small crate, her hands on her hips.

"That's enough. I'm responsible for her training. Any more out of you, and I'll have you disciplined."

The gnome's eyes remained steely. "You've given her a red rose already, Captain. Perhaps you should save the rest of your favors for another day."

Stockton glanced at Darcy, who said nothing and hadn't moved a muscle throughout this exchange. She did indeed have a bloom of blood on her leg; he certainly hadn't meant to cut her. Damn.

"It's just a scratch. She needs to be tough out here," he told Wag, unsuccessfully trying to swallow his anger at the gnome's interference. "And you're dismissed," he said to Darcy in a more congenial tone, nodding.

Darcy walked towards the cabin, using her leg gingerly. Wag jumped off the crate and hurried to her side, offering her shoulder for support. The height difference made it an almost comical gesture, but rather than turning down the gnome's help, Darcy put her hand on Wag's shoulder and used the gnome as a cane.

Stockton watched them go into the hatch, and called the bo'sun over. "Keep an eye on Wag," he said. "The last thing I need is my secret weapon going soft before the fight. Understand?" The Whip hissed, which Lord Stockton took to mean an affirmative.

☠ ☠ ☠

In the cabins, Darcy eased herself onto her bunk. Her leg hurt like a sting from a dragonbeetle. The wound was deep.

"Are you all right, child?" Wag asked. The one-eyed gnome's scarred face took on a kindly countenance. Wag's salt-crusted black hair, already beginning to bleach from their time at sea, hung in her face as she examined the wound.

"I'll be fine," Darcy said. She looked at Wag. "Thanks for speaking up. Milord means well, but he gets carried away sometimes."

"Carried away, my uncle's mechanical leg! He's hurt you. Do you want me to send for the doctor?"

"No need," Darcy said with a halfhearted smile. She placed her hand on her leg, muttered a few words Wag wouldn't understand, and felt the warmth infusing her flesh. When she moved her hand, the wound had been erased.

"Well now," Wag said, her eyebrows raised. "The old saying is proven true once more. There are all kinds of secrets on a ship."

"And I trust you'll keep mine?" Darcy asked.

"Of course, child. But if you see me doing some of my magic—do me a favor. Get down and stay out of the way. I doubt you'll be able to fix yourself if it comes to a proper fight, despite what Lord Muckitymuck thinks."

"I've fixed much worse than this," was Darcy's response.

☠ ☠ ☠

"Have you gotten over your pride?" Stockton asked Darcy as the second watch began the next day.

"My pride was not injured, Milord," she replied as she drew her rapier. Darcy cracked her neck and loosened her shoulders, and Lord Stockton removed his red overcoat.

"I'm glad to hear it. Now, let's see you properly respond." Their blades met, and indeed Darcy seemed much quicker today. He must not have cut her deeply; she moved on her leg as if nothing had happened. Stockton briefly thought about Wag's overreaction, but soon excised it from his mind as he turned instead to the dance in front of him.

He'd shown her only the basics of swordplay, and despite his embarrassing her at the end of yesterday's lesson, she had picked up on the underlying fundamentals of fighting with remarkable speed. She knew how to use the nine-square grid for her attacking and guarding and could at least hold her own against an average swordsman.

"Sail ho!" the lookout shouted. Stockton called a halt to the lesson, sheathed his cutlass and strode across the deck to the mainmast. "She's a schooner, sitting low. And she's coming up fast," the lookout called from aloft.

Stockton's heart started to race. *Finally*, he thought, *I've got you.* He pulled a spyglass from his trouser pockets, adjusted the prism at the end, and focused on the vessel—a mere speck on the horizon. The image across the prism was clear as day, and there was no mistaking the length and draft of the ship: it was *Fortunato*. "All hands!" he called. "Prey sighted. Get ready!"

The alarm bell clanged three times, and the crew began a flurry of activity. As smooth as clockwork, the battle sails were unfurled, the conventional guns were armed and Wag paced back and forth among the crew, handing out firearms and boarding pikes while taking large swigs from a bottle of foul-smelling wine. Darcy disappeared belowdecks—Stockton wasn't yet ready to risk her in the fight against Keva—and the excitement in the air was almost palpable.

A kind of silence descended across the ship. The wind cut through the sails, snapping them like whips, and the rigging groaned as it rubbed, but the crew performed their tasks quietly. They lined up on the *Lady Grace's* port side, hunkered down, watching *Fortunato's* sails grow larger.

Lord Stockton donned his red coat but remained on deck, walking quickly among the crew. "This is it. There's plenty of gold waiting for sailors who find glory and honor today," he said. "Keva won't give up easily, especially once she sees through our ruse and realizes she's been duped. But that's in our favor, lads and lasses. It means she'll make mistakes. She'll get sloppy. And we'll be there, ready to take our prize from under her. Now, let's give her something to be afraid of!"

Lord Stockton raised his arm and let out a shout, which the crew picked up in kind. The sound was deafening; a hundred people yelling at the same time, all focused on a single objective. Stockton himself felt giddy; long ago, he quit feeling nervous before a fight. He knew he had Keva right where he wanted her, and he was ready to spring his trap.

The *Fortunato* sped toward the *Lady Grace*; the wind was slightly in Keva's favor, and Stockton guessed she would try to use it to make a surgical strike and then give herself distance as she gauged his response. When *Fortunato* closed to about a sixth of a league, Kiva turned slightly to port. A burst of light sprang from *Fortunato's* starboard side. "Brace for impact!" Stockton shouted.

The water between the two ships sizzled and boiled, but *Fortunato* was too far for her firegunner to be effective. The magic stopped a couple hundred yards short of the *Lady Grace*. *Fortunato* was turning to regain the wind, and Stockton saw his chance. "Close!" Stockton bellowed, and the helmsman tacked to starboard to gain more of the wind.

If Keva expected him to fire at long range and reveal his hand, she was sorely mistaken, Stockton thought. "Prepare the guns. Third-shot only." He didn't want the pirate to know exactly how well-armed he was; if she still thought *Lady Grace* was a fat merchantman, let her continue to hold to that illusion. Every third cannon rolled forward. *Fortunato* swung back to close the distance–now only a thousand yards or so—and there was no doubt this time that her firegunner could hit *Lady Grace*.

"She's trying to bluff us down," Stockton said to no one in particular. "She wants us to surrender without a fight. Turn toward and fire!" *Lady Grace* slipped starboard, exposing her broadside. The quaking concussion from the cannonfire rumbled through Stockton's legs. He loved that feeling. He even allowed himself a wolfish grin.

Stockton's smile vanished when his cannon's shots sailed between *Fortunato's* rigging, causing no damage. He'd told the cannoneers to expect the lower draft, but even so, they aimed high. "Wag!" he called. "Tell them to aim lower. And get ready for our full counterattack." The airformer nodded and shouted orders belowdecks, and cannons rumbled as their crews adjusted the aim.

Fortunato meanwhile turned to starboard herself, and her firegunner must have adjusted, because a horrible smell of sulfur filled the air. Before Lord Stockton could open his mouth to warn the crew, flame burst from *Fortunato's* side and the sea boiled. The shot struck *Lady Grace* in her stern, the wind from the firegun tearing rigging and catching sails and rope on fire.

"Where's my airformer?" Stockton screamed. Moments later the air itself started to solidify between the ships. "Fire crews to your stations!" he bellowed, and several crewmen rushed to extinguish the flames.

The ships drew close enough that he could count the sailors on *Fortunato's* decks. *Fortunato* turned again and cut straight for them; whether Keva expected him to surrender, or merely wanted to continue the fight without wasting any more of her firegunner's resources was anyone's guess, but either way it would make Stockton's job easier. Wag appeared next to him, the gnome's face black with spent gunpowder smoke. "Ready to give 'em hell, Captain," she said lustily.

The fire crews worked quickly, and soon *Lady Grace* resumed the closure, her bow pointed at *Fortunato*. Surely Keva must realize that he wasn't going to surrender; Stockton imagined her wondering why he wanted to close for a fight rather than strike his colors or flee. "On my mark," he told Wag.

The distance between *Lady Grace* and *Fortunato* closed. His crew clutched their boarding pikes at the ready, and the enemy crew seemed prepared to initiate the endgame. "Now," Stockton whispered.

The gnome pointed at *Fortunato*, and Stockton steadied himself as the air in front of him turned into a vacuum. It spiraled out from Wag's hand until it reached *Fortunato's* deck, where it cut through sailors and wood like a colossal battering ram. Men screamed as as the magic crushed them like a giant's clenching fist, and *Fortunato's* mainmast cracked and collapsed. Stockton watched in triumph as the sailors aboard the enemy ship scrambled about in panic. He scanned for a sign of Keva, but didn't see her. *That* was disappointing. He wanted her to witness first-hand his destruction of her ship and crew.

"Let's get this over with," Stockton said. He signaled the helmsman, and Olavi readied the sailors to board. *Lady Grace* slipped alongside the now-crippled *Fortunato*. Stockton's men launched grappling hooks at the enemy ship, grabbing her and reeling her in.

A piratical yell echoed across the waves as several dozen sailors stood from their hiding positions alongside *Fortunato's* port rail, bellowing for blood and gold. They made no move to cut the boarding ropes, but instead, as one, began reeling the *Lady Grace* closer.

"Sir?" Olavi asked, his blue eyes searching Stockton's face for an order.

"Prepare to be boarded," Stockton said. No matter; he could just as easily finish this here as on Keva's ship. *Fortunato's* sailors fired hooks of their own, and the space between the ships became a rapidly-closing web of rope and metal. As Keva's crew swarmed over the expanse like spiders, Stockton drew his sword and pointed it at them. "For gold and glory!" he yelled, and his crew took up the cry.

"I'm not getting paid for direct combat," Wag replied. She scurried aft and took up a position by the ship's wheel.

"On my signal, disable that bitch's scow," Stockton yelled at the gnome's retreating form. Wag nodded and waved, indicating her understanding.

Keva may very well have been the only elf aboard her ship, as a veritable menagerie climbed over *Lady Grace's* rails. Basilisk stood next to human and H'leng-ru, and Stockton even counted a couple of dwarves in their midst. An Al-Kabar, his fur decorated with war symbols, appeared in front of Stockton swinging a wicked scythe. Stockton parried, and his counterthrust stabbed into the creature's shoulder. The Al-Kabar howled in pain, and Stockton kicked at him, sending the dog-man over the rail and into the sea.

Stockton risked a look at the rest of the battle; his crew fought hard, but was quickly losing ground. *Damn it, where is Wag?* he thought. A pale-looking human climbed a boarding rope, and Stockton wasted little time in driving his rapier into the sailor's heart. The lad appeared barely old enough to fight. A damn shame, but not Stockton's problem.

Stockton's ears popped and the air briefly rushed out of his lungs as the gnome's magic swept over him. He silently thanked Wag for finally joining the battle. A handful of Keva's sailors popped off the deck as if a giant hand picked them up and flung them into the drink. The remaining enemy sailors paused a moment, allowing his crew to stick swords in a few unprotected guts. Again, Wag pointed, and more sailors flew into the water. Keva's sailors looked nervously at each other, and Stockton knew he had them right where he wanted them. The enemy was on the verge of retreat, and it was time to break their spirit and take their leader's head.

"Attack! *Attack!*" he screamed. He rushed the nearest pirate he could find, cutting into a gaudily-dressed, dark-skinned dwarf. The dwarf fell, dead. Stockton's crew pressed forward, as the enemy's morale unraveled and finally broke. Kiva's pirates swarmed back toward their ship.

"Is it too late to join this party?" a voice behind him asked. Stockton turned; Darcy stood on deck, a cutlass at her side.

"Get back where it's safe!" Stockton hissed. "You could be hurt up here!"

"Hurt, milord? The only time I've been hurt aboard your ship is by your hand. And I fully intend to keep it that way. Lads! Let 'em have a full taste!"

Stockton squeezed his eyes shut and fought the urge to vomit as the realization of his blunder hit him like an iron anchor. *Fortunato's* guns opened fire, tearing *Lady Grace's* hull apart at the waterline. The ship began to list immediately, and the pirates returning to *Fortunato* started cutting the boarding lines.

"Anyone who doesn't want to be harmed can join me on my ship," Darcy announced. She touched her face, and the illusion melting away, revealing her elven features. "Anyone who surrenders peacefully will get a full share of the reward I've been offered for capturing the notorious pirate-hunter 'Lord' Stockton, and ending Stockton Securities' interference with the legitimate plundering of the sea. And I promise you—that reward is more than this powder-faced peacock was going to give you!"

For a moment, no one moved.

Then Wag stepped forward, followed by The Whip and several other sailors. Eventually, the entire crew of the *Lady Grace* stood as one.

Lord Stockton's anger became a white-hot flame. *No. No no no. I spent months tracking this bitch. This is impossible.*

He raised his sword and charged Keva, his vision tunneling from rage. She braced herself and sidestepped. Stockton turned, slashing wildly, not caring that the elf deflected his blows as easily as he had turned aside her attacks less than a day ago. He threw away all sense of form, pummeling her blade until his shoulder ached. Stockton began to slow, and Keva adjusted her stance. Stockton panted from the exertion. Keva shook her head, and kicked him in the stomach, sending him sprawling to the deck.

"I spent months studying you," Keva said as she pointed her rapier at Stockton's prone form. "As soon as I heard you'd been hired to capture me, I knew I'd have to find you first. It wasn't difficult. You're as mechanical as a clock and as subtle as a dragon. I'm just surprised that no one thought to capture you before I did. Fortunately, I found a benefactor willing to pay far more than I could win from years of plundering seal oil and furs. You were right about that. I *have* been moving up in the world."

She gently tapped Stockton with the flat of her blade as a boarding ramp extended from Fortunato. "I suggest we continue this discussion aboard my ship. Your ship may not be with us much longer."

His former crew filed across, past Keva, with Stockton bringing up the rear. "Oh, milord," Keva said. "A piece of advice. *Never* give us an opening."

The pirate laughed, and slapped Stockton's rump with her blade. He fell forward in a heap, his ears burning at the laughter of Keva's crew. Behind them, *Lady Grace* collapsed, her decks splintering and her masts cracking like matchsticks. As she slipped beneath the waves, Lord Stockton watched, humbled, as his pirate-hunting career disappear with her.

SHIPMATES
by Stephen D. Sullivan

"By the Gods of Wrath and Mercy!" Captain Plutark cursed. "Where did that crag come from? Hard to starboard!"

The crew of the *Marauder* hauled on the steering winches, changing the angle of the dreadnaught's metal rudder. The big ship listed onto its starboard side, barely missing the huge, jagged rock stabbing out of the surf.

The captain of the Iron Pirate vessel paced the bridge, his dark eyes scanning the choppy waters of the Southern Azure Sea for more unexpected obstacles. The ocean ahead surged and boiled, sending gouts of mist into the afternoon air. Sunlight peeked through the dark clouds, turning the spray silver and gold.

"To port now! To port!" Plutark called as another crag thrust up out of the ocean. "Curse the gods!"

The crew reversed direction and frantically moved the winches the other way. The *Marauder* began to turn once more, but this time not fast enough. The ship's metal sides scraped against the black stone.

"Teats of Kabree! Work faster, you dogs!" the captain cried. "We'll never catch that Bellarite at this rate!" Even as he spoke, more deadly crags emerged from the savage sea, like stony fingers reaching for the ship. Despite the escalating hazards, the pirate captain remained fixated on the white-sailed merchantman bobbing in the distance.

Standing just below the bridge, the Midknight named Menalo shook his head. "Why not let her go, captain?" he called to Plutark. "Their ship is small and these waters far too dangerous."

Plutark leaned over the bridge rail and scowled at the trio of armored warriors standing against the cabin bulkhead. "A lot you know!" the captain replied. "If you Midknights had as much brains as muscles, you'd realize that you can't judge a Bellarite's worth by her size!"

Menalo smiled, knowing that the crest of his helmet hid his face from the captain.

Cretia, the tall warrior on Menalo's left, grinned as well. "You can't expect Captain Plutark to give up such a prize!" she said, her tone laced with mock disbelief. "Don't you know that all Bellarites are filled to the gunwales with treasure?" Her blue eyes sparkled with anticipation of the catch.

The young knight opposite her clapped his hand on Menalo's shoulder guard. "Well played, Menalo," he whispered. "That iron-headed dog will catch that Bellarite now, no matter the cost. We'll be earning our pay before you know it."

Menalo folded his arms over his broad chest. "That's the plan, Josun," he replied. "Assuming old Plutark doesn't put us on the bottom of the sea first."

"If you didn't want him to take chances, you shouldn't have goaded him," Cretia whispered. She pulled off her helmet and tossed her curly black hair in the wind. "But I'm glad you did. Such strategies will advance you through our ranks—so long as you don't set your aim too high."

Menalo held her eyes with his own. "Don't worry," he told her, "I know my place."

Josun snickered. "At least on *this* trip!"

Menalo wanted to slap the teenager, but he didn't. He'd been working hard to keep Cretia in the dark about his ambitions; now the boy had tossed them out onto the deck for all to see. Despite Josun's quip, Menalo kept his face and body impassive. "I know where my loyalties lie," he reassured his commander.

Cretia nodded slowly. "I'm sure you do." She adjusted her hair, put her midnight-blue helmet back on, and gazed toward the fleeing Bellarite.

Menalo shot Josun a withering glance. The young mercenary paled and he mouthed the word, "Sorry."

Menalo inclined his head slightly. He didn't speak, but his eyes said, *"If you're not sorry now, you soon will be."*

The *Marauder* veered precariously through the ever-changing sea of crags and shoals. On the bridge above the knights, Plutark continued to curse and bark orders. Despite the crew's best efforts, the Bellarite ship continued to draw away.

Josun peered nervously at the churning, ever-changing sea. "Do you think the Bellarites are causing this? Can they be calling up rocks from the deep to scuttle our pursuit?"

Cretia shook her head. "Not unless they've got an Arch Mage aboard. And if they did, they'd be moving a lot faster."

"So, what do you think is happening?" Menalo asked, deliberately giving his superior the opportunity to show off her knowledge.

She studied him, as if to divine his intent. Menalo kept his face as sincere as possible, chuckling silently only when she turned back to the ocean.

"The closer we get to the Obsidian Isles," she said, "the worse the conditions are likely to become. The Bellarites are probably counting on that."

Josun paled. "We're close to the Black Cliffs? Isn't that dangerous?"

"Pirating's dangerous," Menalo replied. "So's being a Midknight."

Cretia grinned poisonously at the youngster. "Surely you knew that when you put on the armor," she said.

Josun swallowed and bobbed his head. "I like fighting," he said. "But magic makes me nervous."

Cretia and Menalo both chuckled and watched the Bellarite, which was still keeping its distance. The sun dipped toward the sea and, on the bridge above them, Plutark seemed to have had enough.

"Open the box and chain the elemental to the mainsail," the captain commanded. "We'll catch that Bellarite if we have to chase her south all the way to the Isles of the Black Cliffs!"

Cretia nodded approvingly. "About time," she muttered.

Josun shot a nervous look at Menalo. The mid-rank knight couldn't tell if the boy was worried about the elemental or about the Black Cliffs and the notorious pirates who called those crags home.

Neither worried Menalo. He'd heard the Pirates of the Black Cliffs were ruthless, of course, and anyone who sailed the southern seas had heard of their terrible leader—Red Jack Sirus. Red Jack couldn't be everywhere, though, and the seas were very wide. Besides, as Menalo had told the boy, being a Midknight meant accepting—or even savoring—certain risks.

Menalo and the other two knights stepped aside as the great metal doors behind them creaked open. A handful of sooty pirates emerged from the *Marauder's* dark interior, hauling a rune-covered metal crate. Four chains ran out of a hole atop the crate's front door and were fastened to the box's sides. The chains glowed slightly.

Josun spat on the deck to ward off the magic.

The Iron Pirates unfastened the chains from the sides of the box. Gripping the shackles tightly, four sailors lashed them onto winches near the main sail. When they finished, a fifth sailor unfastened several large bolts and opened the crate.

A gust of wind from inside the box nearly knocked all three Midknights off their feet. The howling of a hundred damned souls filled the air.

"Heave!" cried one of the pirates working the winches. As one, the crew began hauling on the chains. Slowly, the chained elemental emerged from the box. It was a ghostly, glowing presence, almost invisible in some spots and in others looking like a tatter of translucent sheets formed into the shape of a human being. It smelled like a coming storm. The elemental screamed in agony as the pirates dragged it into place before the mainsail.

Cretia laughed and, on the bridge above, Plutark cackled gleefully. "Make it fast!" he called to his crew. "Lash it with the enchanted chains if it doesn't cooperate! By all the gods, we'll have that merchantman!"

With the elemental chained to the sails, the *Marauder* surged forward, slicing through the waves toward her white-sailed quarry. Fewer crags thrust up through the waves now, and Plutark steered through the prominences skillfully. With each passing moment, the Bellarite ship grew closer.

All three Midknights loosened their black-bladed swords in their sheaths.

"Ready the cannons!" Plutark ordered.

Gun ports swung open on the *Marauder's* sides, stern, and bow. A pair of guns even appeared on the front of the bridge.

"Ready, Captain!" called the first mate, a red-haired woman named Ariana. Menalo caught her eye and winked at her; she winked back. The Midknight tried not to think about the private victory celebration he and his lover would share later; such thoughts might be a fatal distraction during the upcoming battle.

"Wait for my signal!" Plutark called as the *Marauder* sailed ever nearer to its quarry.

Cretia and Josun hurried to the bow of the ship, and Menalo followed. His body tingled with anticipation; he knew his fellow mercenaries felt the same.

A white-robed figure appeared on the aftercastle of the Bellarite ship. She gestured toward the *Marauder* and called out something Menalo couldn't hear above the chop of the waves.

Cretia drew her sword, and the dragon-turtle brooch at her neck flashed blue-green. An arc of yellowish light shot from the mage toward the Iron Pirate vessel. The Marauder shuddered as the Bellarite magic struck its bow. When the spell hit Cretia's sword, the enchantment vanished like mist on a summer morning. Cretia snorted and muttered, "Pitiful."

Menalo drew his bow and fired a black-shafted arrow into the white figure's breast. The mage gasped, fell over the Bellarite's rail, and disappeared into the surging waves. She didn't resurface.

"Nice shot," Josun said.

"Lucky," Cretia put in. Beneath his helmet, Menalo's face reddened.

Plutark guffawed and bellowed, "Fire!" He pointed toward the Bellarite expectantly, but nothing happened.

"Powder won't burn, Captain!" Ariana called.

"Curse the gods!" Plutark roared. "Unbox the salamanders then! I want that Bellarite's sails in tatters!"

"Aye, Captain!"

The Bellarite ship swerved and darted through the waves, making just enough course changes to keep the *Marauder* off her heels.

Menalo fired twice more, trying to land a shaft on the enemy bridge, but his arrows fell short. Cretia smirked at him. Menalo scowled. "I don't see *you* doing any better."

She shrugged. "Why should I waste the energy?"

Suddenly, the *Marauder* shook with the thunder of the Iron Pirate's cannons. Fire, black smoke, and the stench of sulfur filled the air. Josun ducked reflexively. Menalo and Cretia chuckled.

The Bellarite ship shuddered, and its main mast broke into splinters. The merchantman's bright white sails fluttered to her deck like a flock of wounded birds.

A cheer went up from the Iron Pirates.

"Prepare to board!" Plutark called. "No quarter! No prisoners!"

Cretia beamed at her fellow Midknights. "*That's* what I like to hear!"

The Bellarite ship floundered and listed onto her starboard side as she tried desperately to turn away. The *Marauder* pulled in alongside her, and the pirates pelted her with grappling lines. In moments, they lashed the two ships together and threw boarding planks over the side.

"This is what they're paying us for," Cretia told her companions. "Follow me!"

Wielding her black-bladed sword, she rushed across the plank without a moment's hesitation. Menalo did the same. Josun and Plutark's crew followed right behind.

An enemy dagger glanced off Menalo's left shoulder plate as the Midknight leapt to the Bellarite's deck. Menalo turned and found a scrawny boy, barely past his majority, with a knife clutched in one hand. The young sailor appeared frightened; Menalo's dark eyes gleamed. He feinted toward the sailor's face. The boy brought up his dagger to parry. Menalo twisted his sword under the boy's guard and ran him through. The youngster crumpled to the deck, clutching his belly. Menalo stepped over him and killed the sailor rushing to take the boy's place.

The Iron Pirates swarmed over the merchantman, cutting down Bellarites left and right. The tang of blood and salt mingled in the air. The pirates' quarry begged for quarter, but the buccaneers gave none. Cornered and outnumbered, the Bellarites fought with desperate fury.

"This way!" Cretia called to Menalo and Josun. She pointed toward the bridge where the Bellarite captain and first mate were trying to rally their crew.

"Cut off the head and the body will fall," Josun said, repeating an old Midknight saying. The youngster grinned as he and Cretia sliced their way toward the bridge.

Spotting a rope dangling nearby, Menalo decided to try a different approach. He grabbed the line and climbed up to the ship's rail, pushing a Bellarite overboard as he did so.

An agile swing brought him clanking down on the aftercastle, behind the Bellarite defenders. Several whirled to face him. Menalo cut the first sailor down before she could bring her sword up. He parried a thrust from the second, beat the man's rapier aside, and put the tip of his longsword through the second mariner's eye.

The sword got stuck, though, and before Menalo could pull it out, the ship's bosun stabbed at him with a boat hook. The Midknight ducked aside, cursing, and yanked hard on his sword. It came free, but he lost his footing and stumbled back against the outside rail.

The bosun lunged, looking to ram the spear end of the boathook through Menalo's chestplate. Menalo twisted away at the last instant, grabbed the weapon's shaft, and pulled with all his strength. The bosun sailed past the mercenary and smashed into the rail. Menalo grabbed the bosun's belt, heaved, and flipped his opponent over the side. The man crashed into the waves and didn't resurface.

While Menalo had been fighting for his life, someone had set the ship afire—whether by accident or design, the Midknight couldn't tell. Orange flames flared across the ship's decks, and burning pieces of canvas danced through the air like salamanders caught in a gale. The scent of smoke and guts mixed with the tang of sea spray.

Through the blaze, Menalo spotted the ship's captain. He was trying to fend off a band of Iron Pirates and had his back turned to the Midknight. Behind his dark blue visor, Menalo's eyes sparkled. He rushed across the bridge to kill the man.

The captain must have sensed him coming, though, for he whirled just in time to parry Menalo's thrust. The Bellarite turned the mercenary's sword aside and, unexpectedly, smashed a mailed fist into the side of Menalo's face.

The Midknight's helmet kept him from being knocked out, but the force of the blow made his head ring. Menalo staggered back, only barely turning aside a deft thrust from the enemy captain. The mercenary reeled, trying to recover his wits, as the Bellarite slashed at him again and again.

Menalo backed up against the rail, defending himself desperately. He heard the crash of the waves below and smelled the brine through his faceplate. He didn't relish trying to swim in armor; he needed to kill this man—and quickly.

Menalo darted forward, beat back the captain's parry, and sliced for his enemy's neck. The captain anticipated the trick and caught the Midknight's blade before it reached its target. He spun and kicked the mercenary in the knee.

The captain's toe found the gap in Menalo's knee joint, and a shock of pain stabbed through the Midknight's leg. His knee buckled and he fell to the deck. The captain raised his sword for the kill.

Then he gasped and staggered back, blood spurting from his mouth. In the next instant, he fell to the deck, dead.

Menalo lurched to his feet. Standing over him, Cretia pulled her black blade from the captain's body.

"I'm sorry," she said, not meaning it. "Was that supposed to be *your* kill?"

Menalo shook his head. He wasn't about to give her any satisfaction at his discomfort. "There are no bonuses for body count," he said, "nor for the rank of the slain. You can kill whomever you please."

A haughty smile tugged at the corners of Cretia's thin lips. "Always," she replied. The eyes of the dragon-turtle broach at her throat glimmered red in the firelight.

The rest of the Bellarite sailors didn't last long after the death of their captain. As the sun dipped into the western sea, not one of the merchantman's crew remained alive.

Plutark strode about the enemy's deck clapping his hands with glee. "Well done! Well done, one and all," he said. "I daresay you Midknights have earned your pay for this battle." He beamed at Menalo, Cretia, and Josun.

"Don't we always?" Cretia replied.

"Of course," Plutark said. "That's why I hired you to supplement my company. I don't suppose you'd help control the fire while my crew ransacks this scow?"

"Is there a bonus in it?" Josun asked. He'd suffered a number of cuts and bruises during the fight, but the blood covering his dark blue armor belonged mostly to his enemies.

Plutark scowled at the boy and shook his head. "It's always about money with you mercenaries," he said.

"'Mercenary' does mean 'warrior for hire,'" Cretia noted.

"And damn fine warriors, too," Menalo added. "Thanks to us, you haven't lost even one of your pirates in this skirmish."

Plutark rubbed his stubbly chin. "Aye," he said. "I suppose that's true. Make yourselves useful as you see fit, then. But keep out of the way of my crew. I want every last bit of gold off this crate before she sinks."

"We'll be on the *Marauder,*" Cretia replied, "getting ready for the next fight." She turned and walked toward a boarding plank leading back to the Iron Pirate ship. Josun went with her.

Menalo caught Ariana's eye. "I think I'll help out here," he announced. "I barely worked up a sweat during the fight anyway."

Cretia snickered. "Next time, try staying off your backside," she called over her shoulder. "It's easier to work up a sweat while standing."

Menalo steamed. Cretia's position within the ranks of Midknights made it unwise to confront her. Silently, he added another mark to the list of Cretia's offenses against him. Someday, he would hold her to account. Not today, though. He cast a withering stare at his superior's back and then hurried to help Ariana with the looting.

Darkness surrounded the ships by the time the pirates had transferred the merchantman's cargo into the *Marauder's* hold. Waves lapped over the Bellarite's main deck by then, though small pockets of fire still burned on the portions of the ship that remained above water.

Menalo cast a final glance at the scene as he crossed over to the Iron Pirates' vessel. All in all, it seemed like a good day's work, well done.

As Menalo set boot on the *Marauder* once more, Plutark's men cut the last of the lines holding their ship to the sinking Bellarite.

The elemental hung sagging and out of breath beneath the *Marauder's* mainsail, but the ship's mechanical screws quickly pulled the dreadnaught away from the doomed merchantman. The pirate crew cheered as the Bellarite vessel slipped beneath the waves.

Plutark paced the bridge, looking both proud and pleased with himself. Ariana appeared happy, too, which pleased Menalo as well.

Josun pointed toward a reddish glow near where sea met darkened sky. "What's that light on the horizon?"

"Another burning ship?" Ariana suggested.

"It could be," Menalo agreed.

Cretia tucked her helmet under her arm, and peered into the gathering darkness. "It could be, but it's *not.*" She whistled at Plutark and pointed toward the distant light. "Captain. . . ?"

Plutark paled. "Gods of Mercy deliver us all!" he gasped. "Turn her about! Head north as fast as you can! Get the elemental working again. Lash it if you have to!"

"But, Captain," Ariana replied, "it's exhausted already. Pushing it further may kill it."

"Better it than all of us," Plutark shot back. He cast a nearly frantic glance over the crew on deck. "Hop to it, all of you!" he shouted. "Man the oars! Fire up the screws! We need all the speed this rust bucket can give us!"

Immediately, the pirates began scurrying across the decks, carrying out the captain's orders.

Josun looked around, confused. "What is it?" he asked. "What's wrong?"

For a moment, Menalo didn't reply. Watching the distant red glow, his spine had gone cold. "You don't want to know," he finally said.

Josun went even paler than the captain. "It's Red Jack, isn't it?" he said. "The captain thinks that glow is Red Jack Sirus and the *Scarlet Skull!*"

Cretia slapped the boy hard across the face. "Keep your mouth shut!" she snapped. "We're in enough of a fix without you panicking." Then, to Plutark, she called, "Captain, what do you want *us* to do?"

"Prepare to fight," he called back. "And if you've any conscience for it, *pray.*"

Slowly, the *Marauder* turned back the way she'd come. The elemental wailed piteously as the crew lashed it with enchanted chains. The ship's oarsmen fell into a rapid, steady rhythm as the dreadnaught's engines gradually built up power.

Sweat poured down the pirates' faces as they worked, and they peered fearfully to stern. With each passing minute, the great metal ship gained speed. Yet, moment by moment, the red glow drew closer.

Menalo and the other Midknights gathered at the rear of the bridge, watching as the new enemy approached. Cretia nervously fingered the dragon-turtle brooch at her neck.

"Isn't there something we can do?" Josun asked her.

"Not yet," the Midknight leader replied. Her eyes appeared distant, thoughtful.

"But later?" Josun asked. "What can we do later?"

"When the time comes, you'll know what to do," Cretia said. "For now, you could heed Plutark's advice. Praying can't hurt—assuming you've the stomach for it."

Josun didn't look reassured.

Menalo didn't like Cretia's reply, either. In the face of a devastating battle, a Midknight of her station should have had better advice than "pray."

Every sailor in the Blue Kingdoms had heard of Red Jack Sirus, of course. He was the most ruthless pirate in the Southern Azure Sea; even the other leaders of the Black Cliff Pirates feared him. As for unfortunate buccaneers that ventured too near Jack's hunting grounds, buccaneers like the Iron Pirates. . . ? Well, they suffered the same fate as any other prize that entered Red Jack's sight.

Menalo grabbed Ariana's arm as the first mate hurried across the deck to oil the dreadnaught's rear cannons. "What can we do?" he asked her. "Should we join the crew at the oars?"

She stared at him, terror written across her pretty face. "It's no good," she said. "Our oarsmen are well-trained, but Red Jack has demons in his sails. If it's us he's after, we're as good as caught."

"I refuse to accept that," Menalo said. "There must be something we can do."

She pulled away from him. "And I'm already doing it," she said, "or would be if you'd stop yammering at me. We'll fight Jack if we have to, but I pray to the Gods of Mercy that we don't."

Menalo spat and drew his black-bladed sword. "The whole crew can whine and pray if they like," he said. "I have a better solution."

Ariana gazed into his eyes and, for a moment, it looked as though she might say something. Then she shook her head and hurried away to oil the tail guns. Menalo couldn't help but admire her backside as she ran.

The *Marauder* shuddered as it surged through the waves at a frightening clip. The engines groaned, dozens of sweaty pirates strained at the oars, and the chained elemental wailed as loudly as a hurricane. Menalo stood in the stern beside Cretia and Josun. Both the boy and Menalo had their weapons drawn; Cretia did not.

The ranking Midknight watched the pursuing ship carefully, either reckoning the distance or calculating their odds—Menalo couldn't tell which.

The *Scarlet Skull* looked like a phantom weaving across the darkened sea. One moment, Menalo could see the ship clearly, and the next it seemed to be made of mist. Gauze-like crimson sails, which didn't seem to be blowing with the prevailing winds, billowed from the *Skull's* masts. Menalo wondered if Red Jack, too, had an elemental chained to his rigging.

If he did, Menalo couldn't see it. Perhaps Ariana was right; perhaps Jack did have demons in his sails. If so, Menalo saw no sign of them, either. Nor could he determine exactly where the red glow came from. A few red lanterns hung on the *Skull's* decks, but they weren't nearly enough to account for the ship's eerie luminescence.

Menalo shook his head, trying to ward off the feelings of dread creeping over him. *It's just a ship*, he told himself. The few people he saw on deck— and he saw only a few—looked like ordinary pirates. The *Skull's* timbers seemed to be unremarkable, red-painted boards, though exposure to the sea had blackened them a bit. Aside from its crimson sails and the eerie glow, nothing about Red Jack's ship appeared out of the ordinary.

Yet, something about the way the *Scarlet Skull* moved through the waves—the silent, predatory speed with which the enemy ship gained on the *Marauder*—sent chills through Menalo's bones.

"Fire!" Plutark cried, his voice echoing above the howling of the wind and the screams of the ship's elemental.

The *Marauder's* tail guns roared, their harnessed elementals exploding in flashes of fire and smoke. A volley of iron cannonballs streaked across the sea, heading directly for the *Scarlet Skull's* bow.

It was a well-aimed barrage; one of the best Menalo had ever seen. Yet, not one of the balls struck the enemy vessel. The *Skull* shimmered in the darkness, and the cannonballs seemed to pass through its crimson sails, its towering masts, and even the ship's red and black hull.

Deep, mocking laughter echoed across the waves to the *Marauder*.

Josun and Cretia went white as ghosts. "No use trying our bows then," Cretia muttered.

"Gods of Mercy!" Plutark cursed. "Reload! Reload and fire again, damn you!"

The *Marauder's* crew leapt to the task, working furiously in the wind and spray. They flourished their enchanted nets, trying to regather the exploded salamanders. Before they could round the elementals up though, a peal like thunder shook the waves as the *Scarlet Skull* returned fire.

Flashes of red light pierced the darkness as a trio of crimson fireballs leapt from the *Skull's* cannons. Everyone on the *Marauder* seemed frozen as the magical shots sped toward the metal ship.

"Demonfire!" Cretia screamed. "Get down!" She dived for the deck; Menalo and Josun did the same. Plutark ducked, too, as a gout of red fire seared right above his head. The heat of the passing spell frazzled Plutark's hair. He screamed and patted his scorched locks with his hands, but the damage had already been done.

The first fireball landed amidships—barely missing the chained elemental—and exploded into a shower of flaming brands. The pirates on deck screamed and covered their heads. But wherever the magical fire hit, it caught, and soon a dozen burning figures lit the deck like grisly living torches.

The next fireball struck the rear gun ports and exploded into a brilliant crimson blaze. The gunnery mates screamed, but only until the second blast hit and turned them to ashes. The *Marauder* shuddered with the terrible impacts, and an unlucky pirate standing at the forward rail pitched overboard. The demonfire kept burning, turning the rear of the metal ship into an inferno.

Menalo and the other Midknights scrambled to their feet, as did Plutark.

"More speed!" the captain cried desperately. "We need more speed!"

Most of the crew wasn't listening. Mere water would not quench the demonfire. To make matters worse, every flammable thing the victims touched also burst into flame. Two pirates who'd tried to help their friends now burned with the terrible red fire as well.

The remaining pirates jabbed long boathooks at their blazing comrades, frantically trying to push the flaming victims overboard. Only two pirates took up the captain's call for more speed. They retrieved the enchanted chains from where they'd dropped them on the deck and lashed the wind elemental mercilessly.

The creature's screams cut through the air, howling even above the cries of the burning pirates. That helped gust the vessel forward for a moment, but the wailing stopped abruptly as the elemental exhausted itself and vanished into swirling wisps of white vapor. As the elemental died, the *Marauder's* bow heaved down and the ship slowed.

Cretia frowned. "Remember when I said you'd know what to do?" she asked Josun.

"Yes?" the boy replied hopefully.

"Well, if you know," she said, "then now's the time to do it." Clutching the dragon-turtle brooch at her neck, she sprinted to the starboard rail, leapt over, and plunged into the surging waters below.

Josun and Menalo ran to the rail, their mouths gaping.

"S-she *left!*" Josun gasped.

"Without even a goodbye," Menalo put in grimly. In his mind, he added another tick mark to the long list of Cretia's offenses. This time, though, he doubted he would ever get a chance to pay her back.

"Can she do that?" Josun asked. He glanced fearfully from the waves where Cretia had vanished toward the *Scarlet Skull*, now nearly touching the *Marauder's* stern.

"Wake up, boy!" Menalo snapped. "This isn't the Golden Order! We're Midknights! We do what we have to do, and everything else be damned!"

"So, you're going to leave as well?" Josun wailed.

Menalo chuckled ruefully. "If I could," he said, "I wouldn't hesitate. But since I can't, it looks as though you and I will have to fight for our lives together—alongside Plutark and what remains of his crew." He gazed at the pirate captain, standing at the wheel nearby.

The Iron Pirate looked nothing like the steely man who had taken the Bellarite merchantman mere hours ago. Plutark stood slack jawed and hollow eyed. He clung to the *Marauder's* wheel, trying desperately to force the foundering ship to his will. Occasionally, Plutark peered through the fire toward the *Scarlet Skull*, now surging up alongside the metal vessel's starboard flank.

The cries of the Black Cliff Pirates echoed across the deck of the *Marauder*. With the last of their blazing comrades forced into the sea, the remaining Iron Pirates scrambled for their weapons.

Ariana appeared from a hatch at the ship's stern. She was blackened and bloody, but had somehow escaped the fireball that took the rear guns. She stumbled across the deck and into Menalo's arms. She seemed terrified, and the Midknight couldn't blame her.

Josun appeared terrified as well. "What do we do now?" he asked frantically.

"Now we fight!" Menalo replied.

As he said it, the *Scarlet Skull* heaved to the side of the *Marauder*. The metal ship shuddered with the impact, and the Iron Pirates staggered. A hail of grappling lines quickly lashed the two ships together.

In unison, the first wave of Black Cliff pirates swung over to the *Marauder*, like three dozen deadly red spiders descending on stout ropes. As the invaders landed, the demonfire blazing on the *Marauder's* deck extinguished itself.

Though his face didn't show it, Menalo's spirit lifted slightly. It seemed the Black Cliff Pirates didn't want to get burned any more than he did. As the intruders swarmed aboard, he leapt down from the bridge to meet them.

Menalo landed atop the backs of two brigands and bore them to the deck. *They're not ghosts, at least*, he thought as he stabbed his sword through the first one. As that pirate died, the second scrambled to his feet. Menalo thrust his blade through the man's back, and that pirate crumpled as well.

The Midknight barely got out of the way as a second wave of invaders leapt aboard the *Marauder*. Menalo beat back the cutlass of a one-eyed woman as she aimed to take his head off.

He chopped at her, but her sword turned his blade aside. As she parried, another brigand tried to stab Menalo from behind. The Midknight stepped aside, though, and his armor turned the dagger away from his ribs.

Menalo swung his left hand and clouted the knife-wielder in the face. The man's nose shattered with a satisfying crunch, and he staggered back, which gave Menalo just enough time to parry another cut from One-Eye.

Leaving the bridge had been a mistake. At the time, he'd been anxious to get into the fight, but the *Marauder's* main deck was easier for the Black Cliff Pirates to reach; every moment, more and more invaders swarmed aboard.

One-Eye slashed at him again, and again Menalo knocked the sword aside. Broken Nose came in from the opposite side. Menalo spun, grabbed Broken Nose's arm, and heaved him into One-Eye. She shrieked as her fellow's dagger pierced her gut. The move surprised Broken Nose, as well. As he gaped, Menalo lopped his head off.

The Midknight retreated to the bridge stairway. Plutark stood at the top, frantically beating back the swarm of invaders trying to reach him. The Black Cliff Pirates didn't expect an attack from behind, though, and Menalo felled three before they realized what was happening.

The remaining two turned and slashed at the Midknight. Menalo parried both and counterthrust against the one on the right. The Midknight's blade stabbed into the man's shoulder and the pirate fell down the stairs. Menalo kicked him in the face as he crumpled.

The remaining pirate attacked Menalo again, but she'd forgotten about Plutark. As Menalo blocked her swing, the *Marauder's* captain stabbed her in the back. She fell, and Menalo leapt up the stairs.

"Thanks," Plutark said as the Midknight gained the bridge once more.

Menalo dipped his head courteously. Of course, he hadn't attacked the invaders from the rear to help Plutark; he'd done it to gain a strategic advantage for himself. No need to tell the Iron Pirate captain that, though.

While retaking the stairs gained those on the bridge a moment's respite, the main deck of the *Marauder* still teemed with enemy forces. During his months on the ship, Menalo had come to admire the Iron Pirates' ruthlessness and bravery. The savagery of Red Jack's crew, though, easily outstripped the skill of the defenders.

For every Black Cliff Pirate that fell, three of Plutark's crew died; and without the two Midknights fighting, the toll would have been much higher. Though eight invaders lay dead around the wheel, only Josun, Ariana, Plutark, and Menalo remained alive to defend the bridge.

As Plutark turned to attack another set of brigands intent on swarming up the stair, Menalo rushed to help Ariana and Josun fend off another pair of enemies.

Ariana gasped as a cutlass snaked past her guard and traced a long gash down her left shoulder. The woman facing her smiled malevolently, then groaned as Menalo's sword sunk into her back. The brigand staggered forward, taking a final swing at Ariana. Menalo's lover parried just in time, and her foe fell to the deck, dead.

Ariana gazed into Menalo's eyes. "I'm glad you came back," she gasped.

"Me, too," Josun added. He knocked aside a cut from his foe, feinted a stab, and then slashed across the man's chest as the brigand tried to parry. The slice hit home, but the dying man still lunged for Josun. Menalo stepped forward and put a sword through the brigand's eye.

Josun flipped up his visor and beamed at the older Midknight. "Help Plutark defend the stair," Menalo told him.

Josun turned to obey, but stopped and cried, "Look out!"

A loud "CRACK!" split the air. Menalo whirled as Josun stepped in front of him. The boy gasped as the bullet meant for Menalo struck him in the chest, burning a neat hole through his midnight-blue armor.

As Josun collapsed, Menalo spotted the invader who had fired. She stood on the bridge of the *Scarlet Skull*, her pistol smoking. Already, the salamander that fired the brigand's gun had begun to reform. The woman put another ball into the breach of her weapon.

Menalo scooped Josun's sword from the deck as the woman cocked the pistol once more. Using all his might, Menalo hurled the blade across the span separating the ships. The woman pulled the pistol's trigger, but as she did, the black sword found her heart.

She twitched as the gun went off, and her shot sailed harmlessly over Menalo's head. She toppled over the rail and into the deep.

Ariana knelt beside Josun's body. "He-he's dead," she announced. "He gave up his life to save you."

Behind his visor, Menalo scowled. "I didn't ask him to." He pulled Ariana to her feet. "And we'll be just as dead if we don't keep fighting."

Ariana nodded grimly. Just then, an enemy spear buried itself in the belly of Captain Plutark. The Iron Pirate leader crumpled, and the enemy forces stormed up the stair.

"Buy your life dearly!" Menalo cried. He leapt forward and cut down the first two brigands to reach the landing. Another pair mounted the stair behind those, though, and then another.

Ariana raced to Menalo's side, and they met the invaders head on. The Midknight and his lover slashed and parried and hacked and slashed again. They felled three more invaders, but Red Jack's crew kept coming.

The brigands forced Ariana and Menalo toward the stern of the ship, until the two defenders could retreat no further. The demonfire that destroyed the *Marauder's* cannons had died at the same time as the blaze on deck, but the stern rail still felt hot as the Midknight and his lover pressed their backs against it.

The enemy crowded in, eager to kill them, but wary of their prowess. Menalo and Ariana stood side-by-side, their swords describing a deadly arc around them. Any red-garbed pirate who entered that arc died.

Eventually, the invaders stood just at the edge of the circle, stabbing with sword or spear and then dancing back out of the way before the defenders could counterattack.

"Can you swim?" Menalo whispered to Ariana, as they stood with their backs to the rail.

"Not well enough," she replied.

"Me, neither," he said. Silently, he cursed Cretia's cleverness and wished he'd planned an alternate escape the way she had. A spear stabbed at Menalo's gut, but he hacked it aside, breaking the spear's shaft with his sword.

"Bring a gun!" one of the invaders, an emaciated man with a scraggly beard, called to the rear of the pack. "Or some crossbows at the least."

None of the Black Cliff Pirates replied, but movement near the fore of the bridge told Menalo that someone had taken up the suggestion.

Scraggly Beard leered at the trapped defenders. "You've had your run, right enough," he said, "but it's the end now."

"Why don't you just take what you want and go?" Ariana screamed. Sweat and tears streamed down her blood-spattered face.

Scraggly Beard shook his head. "You think it's mere booty we came for?"

"You got nothing we want," a black-haired woman with bone earrings added. "Only Red Jack's crew plunders these waters and lives." The rest of the invaders chuckled at this, as though it were some great jest.

You got nothing we want . . . The thought echoed through Menalo's mind. Perhaps they were wrong. Clearly, there was *one* thing Red Jack couldn't do without.

Menalo looked at Ariana; she gazed back at him with frightened eyes.

Sorry, he thought. Then he stabbed his sword through her ribs and out the other side. Ariana's eyes went wide. She gaped at Menalo, seemingly unable to believe what had just happened. Her mouth opened in a soundless "O" and she slumped to the *Marauder's* deck, dead.

Menalo stood over his lover's body, bloody sword clenched in his right hand. Ariana's eyes stared at him accusingly, but Menalo turned away.

"I want to join your crew!" the Midknight declared, putting every ounce of bravado he could muster into his voice. "I want to become one of you—a Black Cliff Pirate!"

At first, the invaders seemed shocked at his pronouncement. Then, slowly, an incredulous, mocking laughter built among their ranks. Soon, a deeper laugh rose above the rest. The crew fell silent and all eyes turned to a shadowy figure standing on the bridge of the *Scarlet Skull*.

The pirate captain was tall and massive. A blood-red great coat hung from his shoulders, and a wide black belt girded his waist. Black gloves tooled with red designs adorned his hands. Dark pants and scuffed black boots covered his legs and feet. A broad-brimmed crimson hat topped his head. Most of the captain's face remained hidden in shadow, but his eyes blazed red in the darkness.

Menalo knew that this could only be Red Jack Sirus.

"Quite a sacrifice you've made to impress me," Red Jack said. ". . . Or *was* it?"

The pirate's deep voice sent a shiver down Menalo's spine. "It was the best I had to offer," the Midknight replied.

Red Jack chuckled. "Aye," he said. "That it was. And well offered, too. I accept you to my crew, Midknight."

As he said it, a rotten-looking board dropped from the bridge of the *Scarlet Skull* to the bridge of the *Marauder*. The plank hit the deck of the metal ship with a dull clang.

"Come aboard and give me your hand on it," Red Jack commanded.

Menalo crossed over the gangplank without looking back. As he reached the deck of the *Scarlet Skull*, he extended his right hand to Red Jack Sirus.

Red Jack took it and peered into Menalo's eyes. The Midknight suppressed a shudder. Matted black hair tumbled out from beneath Jack's crimson hat. Bleached finger bones dangled from his greasy black beard. Worst of all, the bloody bandages covering Jack's face barely concealed his craggy teeth and rotten skin. He smelled like blood, and puss, and fish guts. *Is he a man, or some kind of sea demon?* Menalo wondered.

Jack clapped his left hand onto the Midknight's right shoulder guard. As he did, fire shot through Menalo's body.

Menalo wanted to scream but couldn't. He stood rigid, images of battle and blood and death cascading through his mind. He saw the world through Jack's eyes, a world of ships waiting to be plundered, women waiting to be taken, and victims waiting to be slaughtered. He felt the captain's unholy desires, and in that moment, Red Jack's lusts became his own.

The pirate captain released him.

Menalo gasped, ripped the metal epaulet from his shoulder, and cast it to the deck. The shoulder ached and throbbed. Burned into it was a blood red brand in the shape of a laughing skull.

Red Jack smiled, and worms crawled out of his mouth. "Not much to give up—was she?"

The Midknight shook his head and rubbed his shoulder. "Not much at all," he replied. Somehow, despite all the fighting and blood and death and betrayal, he felt good—better than he remembered feeling since he set to sea.

"Let's get to work then," Jack said.

The two of them crossed back the over the gangplank to the *Marauder*.

Menalo helped the other Black Cliff Pirates loot the ship while Red Jack shouted orders. Some pirates busied themselves rifling the bodies of the dead, but Menalo couldn't bear to do that. Instead, he led his new shipmates to the *Marauder's* stores and helped ferry the Iron Pirates' booty back to the *Scarlet Skull*.

Well before dawn, they finished stowing the last of the *Marauder's* accumulated swag in the belly of the *Scarlet Skull*. The efficiency of the looting amazed Menalo. What had taken months of battle and hard work for Plutark and the Iron Pirates to earn was captured by Red Jack and his crew in only a few hours.

Plutark should have tried attacking pirate ships, Menalo thought. *It would have saved him a lot of time and effort.* The idea brought with it a memory of Ariana. Menalo smothered the recollection deep inside the blackness of his soul.

As the red orb of the sun peeked up between the dark waves and the iron-gray clouds, the *Scarlet Skull* cut loose and sailed away from its victim. As they pulled out of bowshot range, something exploded deep within the belly of the *Marauder*—some diabolical device left behind by Red Jack's crew.

Metal screamed as the Iron Pirate vessel split in two and quickly sank to the bottom of the sea. With it went Josun, Ariana, Plutark, and the bodies of the rest of the *Marauder's* crew.

Menalo looked away, his mind turning to the future. Plutark's Iron Pirates had been formidable, but Jack's crew had disposed of them easily. What greater prizes might Menalo win now that he was a Black Cliff Pirate?

Clouds, rain, and mist seemed to follow the *Scarlet Skull* wherever she sailed. Menalo didn't mind. The darkness of the weather suited him.

"Dark times for dark deeds," he thought, recalling an old Midknight saying.

They caught and scuttled a merchantman from Tovor at sunset the next day. That battle went even more quickly than the fight aboard the *Marauder*. Menalo only killed two sailors before it was over, and neither man put up a good fight.

"Don't worry," Bone Earring told him with a sly grin, "you'll get the hang of it soon."

"One way or another," a sharp-toothed H'Leng-Ru man agreed. He glanced meaningfully at the moss-covered noose hanging from the *Skull's* top yardarm.

Menalo resisted the urge to kill him.

They dodged through the crags of the Obsidian Isles for most of the next two days and pounced on a Bellarite trader trying to sneak past them on the following night.

Menalo caught the captain on the caravel's bridge and hamstrung her before pushing her over the side. The woman made a satisfying "crunch" as the hulls of the two entangled ships drifted together and crushed her.

But her dying gasp reminded the Midknight of something he didn't want to think about. Before the notion could sink in, he found someone else to kill.

Colorful silk filled the Bellariate's hold nearly to overflowing. Menalo thought it a fine prize, but Red Jack hardly seemed interested. He let the crew do as they pleased with it, and soon cloth tatters festooned both the *Skull* and her crew.

Menalo thought it a waste of loot, but kept silent. Questioning Jack's whims was a quick way to become shark food. The Midknight did, however, approve of the way the newly won silk draped Bone Earring's slender frame. He also approved of the rum that the first mate, a short, gorilla-like fellow, dispensed to augment the silk-inspired festivities.

The combination of pirate girl and strong drink proved irresistible to Menalo. He ignored her squalid hygiene, crushed her to his breast, and kissed her. They coupled fervently behind the forward water barrels as the rest of the crew cavorted amidships. The two of them lay exhausted while the decadent celebration wound down.

Menalo gazed at Bone Earring as she slept, curled in the crook of his muscular arm—but he didn't look for long. Something about the gentle curve of her neck brought back disturbing memories. He soon got up, feeling neither happy nor satisfied, and not even the remainder of the rum could change his mood.

Half a week passed before they found their next target. A swift, tall-masted schooner from East Selene, she eluded them for nearly a day and a half before finally floundering on the shoals of Tambor Quay.

Red Jack's crew waited for low tide before swarming across the sandbars to take the ship. The Selene mariners were ready for them, and drove the pirates back with volleys of crossbow shot. A round of demonfire softened the defenders up, though.

As the Selener ship burned, Menalo and the other pirates swarmed aboard, killing without mercy.

The Midknight cornered the schooner's first mate at the aft of the bridge. The mate swung his cutlass for the pirate's head. Menalo ducked, lunged, and rammed his sword through the man's heart. A gush of warm blood spurted through the cracks in the Midknight's armor and ran down Menalo's arm.

Beside him, Bone Earring chortled. "Bet that felt good," she said.

Menalo nodded, but—actually—it *didn't* feel good. It hardly felt like anything at all. None of the killing seemed satisfying any more. Only the thought of the loot he was accumulating kept the mercenary knight going.

He threw open the ship's rear hatch and peered into the hold below. Small, frightened faces stared up at him out of the darkness.

Bone Earring chuckled evilly. "What kind of fools bring their children to sea with them?" She pulled a rune-decorated crimson globe from a pouch on her belt. Before Menalo could stop her, she dropped it into the hold.

The children screamed as a gout of clinging, red demonfire sprang up among them. Bone Earring threw back her head and laughed.

Menalo pushed her through the hatch and then slammed the lid shut. As Bone Earring's screams died away, he rose to his feet. He looked around the bridge, worried. Had anyone seen him? Killing her had been a stupid, impulsive thing to do!

But no. He'd been lucky. The bridge was clear, and the battle still raged on the rest of the schooner. Menalo kicked the first mate's body over to the hatch and then rushed down to the mid deck to continue fighting.

He killed three more Seleners before the pirates completely overwhelmed the ship's defenders. The mariners' deaths meant nothing to him, though. He walked through the murders with cold, emotionless efficiency. The sooner their prey lay dead, the sooner he could return to the *Skull* and the sooner he could drink.

He would need to drink a lot tonight to wash away his memories—not of betraying Bone Earring, he felt nothing at having slain her. No, it was the faces of the children he needed to forget, their frightened, pleading eyes—betrayed eyes. Eyes like Ariana's.

She was just one girl! he told himself. Yet, the memory of her eyes continued to haunt him.

No one questioned the Midknight's account of Bone Earring's death. The Selene's first mate had tricked her, Menalo said. He'd shoved her down the open hatch. Her demonfire flask had apparently exploded when she hit the deck below. It was a gruesome accident—and one that a portion of the crew seemed to find terribly amusing.

Menalo fought down nausea as Earring's former shipmates—including the terrible Red Jack Sirus—laughed at her demise.

That night, Menalo drank until he couldn't see. While he did, the rest of the crew filled the *Scarlet Skull's* hold with treasure from Selene.

By the time they weighed anchor once more, the *Skull* sat very low in the water.

"Time to make port," Red Jack announced. "We'll trade this rubbish for good gold and then set sail once more." Red Jack, Menalo had learned, disdained all forms of treasure save gold.

The crew cheered the announcement, and even Menalo's spirits lifted a bit.

Though their lookout spotted several vessels close to the horizon, they chased no more ships on their way back to the Obsidian Isles. Menalo felt relieved. Though the lure of sharing in the pirate treasure remained strong, the toll of blood and death weighed heavily on his mind.

He could barely shut his eyes without seeing the faces of his many victims, especially Ariana. Not even heavy drinking drove them away.

A week after they left Tambor Quay, the black cliffs of the Obsidian Isles rose into view. The rocky shores looked forbidding and nearly lifeless to Menalo. As the *Scarlet Skull* drew closer, though, he saw that tattered shanty towns sprawled across many of the jagged peaks.

Red Jack's crew skirted through the shoals and reefs and soon came to a tumble-down village built into a fissure in the side of a cliff.

"Like it?" the H'Leng-Ru, whose name was Kipper, asked.

"Like what?" Menalo replied.

"Port Edward the Eighth," Kipper replied. "The finest town in the Obsidian Isles. I bet you've never seen its like before."

"What happened to the other seven Edwards?" Menalo asked.

Kipper shrugged and showed his sharp teeth. "Named after some kind of king, I think," he said. "Blowed if I know what he was king of, though."

A pretty rotten king from the look of the town, Menalo thought.

Kipper dug his bony elbow into Menalo's ribs, somehow managing to jab the gap in the Midknight's armor. "You'll find yourself a replacement girl here, I'll wager."

Menalo resisted the urge to gut the H'Leng-Ru like a fish.

A squad of gruff longshoremen met the *Scarlet Skull* as she pulled alongside the port's rickety looking wharf. The *Skull's* gorilla-like first mate, who was called Mister Baker, met them on the dock and parleyed. All the while, Red Jack stood on the bridge, watching the proceedings with his burning red eyes.

The longshoremen helped unload the ship's cargo, and, under Mr. Baker's vigilant gaze, carted it into town. The crew hooted and made merry during the unloading, and even Menalo felt some of the darkness slipping from his soul. The scent of the shore and distant cookfires filled his lungs.

It's over, he told himself. *I've done my tour, and now I'm finished. We've landed. I can get out of here and find another ship—another captain.* With luck, he could chart a course back to the Core and link up with his order again. After that, he'd find work more suitable for a mercenary knight.

Once the cargo was unloaded, Menalo mounted the steps to the bridge. He doffed his helmet and bowed to the captain.

"Captain, sir," he said, avoiding Red Jack's baleful stare, "it has been a great pleasure to sail with you, and a good profit to us both, I daresay. Now, though, I need to return to more familiar waters and rejoin my order." He bowed again. "Thank you, sir, and good fortune on your future ventures."

With that, he turned on his heel and walked quickly down the stairs toward the gangplank. The ragged wharf beyond creaked and moaned, but the noise sounded as sweet as a siren's song to Menalo.

As he reached the rail, though, Kipper and Swan, the sailor with the scraggly beard, stepped in front of him, blocking Menalo's way.

"Where do you think you're going?" Swan asked.

"Ashore," Menalo replied. "I'm taking my leave."

Kipper shook his head, and flashed his eyes toward the bridge.

Menalo turned and saw Red Jack Sirus standing directly behind him.

The rotting flesh on Red Jack's face rippled like a bagful of worms as he smiled at Menalo. The captain's eyes gleamed hellishly from beneath the brim of his hat. His voice was as cold as the grave. "No one leaves my crew without permission."

The brand on Menalo's shoulder suddenly blazed as though on fire. Menalo gritted his teeth and struggled not to let the pain show. He doffed his helmet and bowed again. "With your permission, then, Captain," he said through gritted teeth.

Red Jack didn't reply. He merely turned and mounted the steps to the bridge once more.

Menalo turned back, but Swan and Kipper still blocked his way. The H'Leng-Ru grinned, showing his sharp teeth.

"You haven't been given permission," he said.

"He didn't say 'No,'" Menalo countered.

"But he didn't say 'Yes,' either," Kipper replied.

"The captain means what he says—and what he *doesn't* say," Swan put in.

"You mean you'll kill me if I try to leave?" Menalo asked. Despite the burning in his shoulder, his hand strayed toward the hilt of his black-bladed sword.

Kipper and Swan cast their eyes toward the bridge, and both pirates grinned.

"I mean we won't have to," Swan said.

Menalo didn't look back. He didn't need to. He was willing to fight Kipper and Swan, but not the captain of the *Scarlet Skull*. The wharf stood before the Midknight, mere yards away, yet it might as well have been the Far Reaches. In that moment, Menalo knew he would never set foot on it, nor join the rest of the crew in their debauchery at Port George the Eighth.

He cursed and stalked down to his hammock in the crew's quarters. The brand on his shoulder didn't stop burning until he slammed the hatch shut. In the days the ship remained at port, Menalo prowled below deck, muttering curses and wishing he'd studied a few spells along with his swordsmanship.

Three times, he went topside to see if an opportunity might present itself to escape. Each time, though, he found Red Jack Sirus standing on the bridge, watching.

Menalo had never seen the captain fight in any of their skirmishes. Yet, he feared the man—or whatever creature Red Jack might actually be. The wailing, invisible demons stitched into the *Scarlet Skull's* sails were proof enough of the captain's terrible power.

The Midknight silently cursed the day he'd joined the *Skull's* crew. Unwittingly, he had been caught in Red Jack's bloody wake just as surely the ships they plundered.

Even the division of the loot didn't lift Menalo's spirits. The gleam of every gold piece reminded him of the twinkle in Ariana's eyes—eyes long sunk beneath the waves.

Menalo felt relieved when the *Skull* finally weighed anchor and sailed east once more. Wary lest his brand should start burning again, he ventured forth into the sunlight and sea air.

On the third day out, they sighted a fat Bellarite merchantman skirting between two rocky keys. The *Scarlet Skull* gave chase as the Bellarite fled around the larger of the isles.

"She's quick for a cow, but no match for Red Jack," Kipper joked.

Menalo rested his palm atop the pommel of his sword. His body and mind ached for combat; it seemed the only pleasure left to him. He tried not to think of what his love of fighting had cost.

The *Skull* rounded the rocky point of the isle and found the Bellarite dead ahead. The crew cheered, but the cheer quickly died as they spotted the twin Selene warships lying hidden in the cove beyond the point.

"Ambush!" Swan cried.

"Man the guns!" Red Jack bellowed. He raced to take the wheel, but, before he could grab it and bring the ship's uncanny powers to bear, both warships fired.

A savage volley of cannon balls raked across the *Scarlet Skull's* deck. The ship shook violently, tossing pirates around as though they were rag dolls. Menalo barely managed to keep his feet.

One of the cannons must have been seeded with demonfire, for its shot burst into green flame as it struck amidships.

Menalo and Kipper dived away from the terrible blaze, but some of it caught on Swan's sleeve. As the scraggly bearded pirate screamed, the flames spread up his body and consumed him. The burning man ran toward Menalo. Kipper grabbed a boat hook, stabbed it into Swan's chest, and pushed him overboard.

"To your posts!" Mister Baker cried as Red Jack reached the wheel and the enemy ships fired once more.

Again, cannon balls and demonfire strafed the deck of the *Scarlet Skull.* The ship shuddered and pitched to port as Red Jack frantically tried to turn her into the enemy.

The deck next to Menalo exploded into shards of rotten wood, but the Midknight's armor kept him from injury. A shower of splinters ripped into Kipper, though, leaving a long flap of skin hanging above the H'Leng-Ru's right eye.

Green fire burst in the *Skull's* rigging, and the demon-stitched sails wailed and screamed. The Black Cliff Pirates screamed as well. Red Jack and Mister Baker kept shouting orders, but it was impossible to hear them above the din.

Menalo pulled Kipper out of the way as a burning spar fell past.

Mister Baker leapt to the deck, barely missing the green fire burning there. "Man the guns!" he cried. "Get to your posts!"

"Look out!" Kipper hollered.

Menalo whirled as one of the Selene warships crashed into the *Skull's* starboard side. The two ships met with a wrenching shudder and terrible crunching of wood. The impact sent most of the pirates, including Red Jack and Menalo, sprawling to the deck.

As the Midknight got up, the Bellarite boarding party swung aboard.

"Good," Menalo hissed, drawing his black-bladed weapon.

At the head of the invaders came a huge man wearing sleeveless chainmail armor and carrying a wicked-looking spiked mace. Bracers of gold, silver, and ivory adorned his arms, and a matching belt girded his waist. His long blond hair tossed in the fresh sea breeze. He looked every inch a hero.

Menalo leapt forward to meet him.

From nearby, Mister Baker gasped, "Tindalin!"

"And Li Wu!" Kipper cried, pointing to a spearman following behind the big man.

Menalo didn't have time to figure out whether his shipmates were surprised or afraid. The Midknight thrust at Tindalin's chest, but the hero batted the blade aside.

The force of the parry sent a shock through Menalo's shoulder. He barely ducked in time to avoid the follow-up blow from Tindalin's mace.

This one is tricky, Menalo thought.

He backed away from another mace blow, but, as he did, Tindalin kicked his feet out from under him. Menalo sprawled backward onto the deck. He scarcely rolled aside in time as the hero's mace crashed down where he had just been.

Too tricky, Menalo revised. He scrambled to his feet, barely parrying another swing as Tindalin surged ahead. Even parrying, the force of Tindalin's blow knocked Menalo onto his backside once more.

The hero didn't follow through, though. He rushed past the mercenary, into the heart of the pirate crew; clearly the Midknight didn't interest him.

Menalo got up again. He stared at Tindalin's unprotected back as the hero waded into a swarm of disorganized pirates, heading for Red Jack. Behind his visor, the Midknight's eyes narrowed.

That's the last mistake he'll ever make, Menalo thought.

He clenched his black-bladed sword and stepped forward to stab Tindalin in the back. Then, suddenly, a sharp pain erupted in the center of Menalo's chest.

He looked down and saw a bloody spear point sticking out of the middle of his breastplate. Menalo gasped. For a few seconds, he didn't know what to think, what to feel, what to do.

Tindalin tuned and shouted to the spearman who had just run Menalo through.

"Li," Tindalin called. "Stop wasting time!"

With a powerful jerk, Li Wu yanked his spear out of the Midknight's body. Blood spurted into the air—Menalo's blood—making a crimson rainbow in the afternoon sunlight.

"Sorry, Tindalin," Li Wu called. "I'll be right with you."

He hurried to help his friend against the rallying pirates. Menalo slumped to the deck. A great pool of blood quickly formed around his body. The world swirled and faded around him. This was the end.

Oddly, Menalo felt . . . relieved.

Ariana's pretty face danced before his fluttering eyes. This time, she wasn't accusing, she was smiling.

Menalo smiled back. *Gods of Mercy*, he thought, *thank you!*

Then his breath rattled out and he closed his eyes for good.

☠   ☠   ☠

For a long while, everything was black and silent.

Then, gradually, red fog moved in. It pushed back the darkness, suffusing all of creation with an eerie crimson light.

199

Eventually, dark blotches formed in the red mist.

The blotches resolved into shapes, and the shapes into people. People standing all around him—though Menalo couldn't quite make them out.

Where was he?

The mist faded and grew lighter. It was bright now, almost brilliant.

Is this the afterlife? Menalo wondered.

Had he somehow survived the final battle aboard the *Scarlet Skull?*

No. That was impossible.

Surely he was dead. The people were becoming clearer now . . . and wasn't that Bone Earring standing next to him? And beside her, scraggly bearded Swan?

Yes. It was. His old shipmates, whole once more; neither of them burned.

This was the afterlife.

Menalo took a deep breath of the salt air—and then coughed it out in a fit of wracking pain.

Spots danced before his eyes, and his shoulder burned as though on fire. As the spots cleared, the hulking form of Red Jack Sirus stepped into view.

The pirate captain gazed down at the Midknight. Red Jack's eyes blazed and his rotting, bandaged face broke into a terrible grin.

"It's like I told you, Sir Knight," Red Jack hissed, "no one *ever* leaves my crew without permission."

OUR LADY CAPTAIN'S TALE
by Lester Smith

Oh, I was once a baroness—
At age 15 given like a mare
To a man with graying hair and flesh,
Who hoped that I might bear him heirs.

Caged like a bird too young to sing,
I wondered at my barrenness.
Although he plowed me twice that spring,
No fruit grew from his dry caress.

Then he, his pallid passion passed,
His own shortcoming sought to blame
On me! His manhood embarrassed
Would hide by smirching my good name.

So I left to lead a pirate's life,
By quick cutlass and sharp spyglass.
Should we meet the one who calls me wife,
Then let him kiss me—on bare ass!

AUTHOR BIOS & STORY NOTES

J. ROBERT KING

Rob King created his first short story when he was three: "I didn't break the TV. Alan did. Yeah—he put the dog on it. He wanted to see the dog on TV." It was an extremely short story, but the plot (putting a dog on a TV) was interesting, and the main character (Alan) had clear motivation (wanting to see the dog on TV). Even so, this short story was panned by the critics (Mom and Dad), who said it lacked realism and who sent Rob to his room. Since that time, Rob has developed more and more elaborate short stories, such as "The Dread Pirate Fuzzytail," and pretty much perpetually stays in his room on account of the critics.

☠

I got the idea for "The Dread Pirate Fuzzytail" while walking my sons to school. During our walks, they often make up ridiculous stories—many of which feature Peter Francis Geraci and his "Bankruptcy Info Tapes." That particular morning, I tried to come up with a story that would top theirs. With its schizophrenic tone and its twists and turns, I think it succeeds. Of course, if not, I'll be on the phone to Peter Francis Geraci.

PAUL GENESSE

Paul has been crafting fantasy stories since he was four years old and decided to be a writer. He loved his English classes in college, but pursued his other passion by earning a bachelor's degree in nursing science in 1996. He is a registered nurse on a cardiac unit in Salt Lake City, Utah, where he works the night shift keeping the forces of darkness away from his patients.

Paul lives with his incredibly supportive wife Tammy and their collection of frogs. He spends endless hours in his basement writing fantasy novels, short stories, and crafting maps of fantastical realms. His first novel, *The Golden Cord, Book One of the Iron Dragon* series hits the stores in April of 2008.

☠

"The Pirate Witch" combined two of my favorite things: pirates and witches. Who else can steal your gold and put a hex on you at the same time, savvy? If the stars come into proper alignment, I would love to write a full-length novel expanding this story. To see where the treasure and bodies are buried, visit Paul online at: www.paulgenesse.com

DEAN A. LEGGETT

An Air Force veteran, Dean A. Leggett lives in Brown Deer Wisconsin, where he works with a great team of folks for a large Midwestern financial corporation. He enjoys adventuring with his wonderful wife, and playing boardgames with friends.

☠

"The Captain of the Red Coral" was inspired by a painting from LA Williams, one of my favorite artists. I hope you enjoy reading it as much as I enjoyed writing it. If so, I promise to write more.

JASON MICAL

Jason Mical enjoys the dual life of a writing superhero. By day, he works at Edelman Interactive talking to and interacting with online media, and by night he puts his pen to any projects that happen to catch his fancy (or pay a couple of bucks). His work has appeared in numerous magazines and newspapers; Morrigan's *Jeremiah d20 RPG*; WizKids' *Crimson Skies*, *Pirates*, and *HorrorClix* product lines; *Worlds of the Dead* from Eden Studios; the *Beyond the Storm* charity RPG project; and in the upcoming *Fallout d20* from Glutton Creeper Games.

Jason lives in the Pacific Northwest with his wife and two cats, is an avowed caffeine fiend, and watches far too many obscure horror movies for his own good. His first novel awaits editing, and he toils each morning on the second, a lighthearted sci-fi romp about communist invaders from Mars and the end of the world.

☠

Pirates were the original pulp anti-heroes before we had names for either "pulp" or "anti-heroes," and this story is my hat tip to the rapscallions I spent so much time with growing up. In "The Adventures of Keva," I was aiming firmly to create a penny dreadful or story-paper pirate in Keva, and an equally pulpy villain in Lord Stockton. I peppered it with a few genre clichés, but swapped the characters' points of view (with one exception). The smarmy Stockton makes a perfect narrator for the events that unfold, and isn't the villain typically the more interesting character anyway?

JEAN RABE

Jean Rabe is the author of two dozen novels and more than forty short stories. When not writing on an outdated computer—which isn't often—she tugs ferociously on old socks with her two dogs, visits museums, listens to country music, and pretends to garden. She has a growing stack of to-be-read books that she occasionally manages to put a dent in. Jean loves movies "that blow up real good," indulges in fantasy football leagues, plays all sorts of boardgames, injures innocent bushes when she weed-whacks, and loathes shoes. Visit her website at: www.jeanrabe.com.

☠

A Jim Holloway painting inspired my story, "Treasure." I have it hanging above the dresser in the bedroom. A stunning acrylic piece I acquired from the artist when I worked at TSR, Inc., it features a sinking pirate ship and a lovely pirate pulling a makeshift raft loaded with treasure and ale. The lovely pirate is not in the story . . . but her companion is.

LORELEI SHANNON

Lorelei Shannon was born in the Arizona desert and learned to walk holding on to the tail of a coyote. She is now a writer, sculptor, and hearse drivin' rockabilly goth grrrl. She lives in the woods outside Seattle with her beloved husband, two beautiful sons, and an unruly pack of quadrupeds. Visit Lorelei on the web at www.psychenoir.com.

☠

I was thrilled to be given the chance to write a pirate story. I've always been a pirate fan, and now my kids are buccaneer-obsessed as well. In this story I combined three of my favorite themes: Egyptian mythology, butt-kicking women, and dogs. I had more fun than is probably legal writing "Judgment." What else can I say but YAR!

LESTER W. SMITH

Lester Smith has been a baker, a sheet-metal worker, a licensed practical nurse, and an award-winning game designer. Currently, he is an educational writer and technologist for a Houghton Mifflin design house. In that capacity, he has written countless research papers, numerous poems, and plenty of HTML, JavaScript, and PHP. He is also president of the Wisconsin Fellowship of Poets.

☠

Most times my poetry starts from a strong emotion that I've been mulling over, seeking some effective way to express. (Wordsworth may have been dull—give me Shelley, Byron, or Keats instead—but it's hard to argue with his famous definition of poetry.) I don't normally spend a lot of time thinking about pirates, or writing poems about them. So when the invitation came to join this anthology, I wasn't sure where to start. One day at lunch, I asked Sully (Stephen D. Sullivan to the world at large) for some direction.

"We could use more lady pirates in the book," he said.

Fortunately, I collect on my PDA a list of interesting words, especially unusual pairings that sound alike, such as "baroness, barrenness, and embarrass." Sully's comment and that trio launched the quatern, "Our Lady Captain's Tale," with the addition of "on bare ass" (which is basically just "bar-on-ess" swapped around a bit) at the end.

"Local Legend" grew from another lunchtime comment, this time by Jean, who said, "How about a poem from a ship's viewpoint?" I started plotting out a sonnet about a ship that came alive, and pretty soon the voice of an old salt telling a "ghost story" to a new hand took over.

"Treasure" began from another Sully suggestion, to write about a disappearing island. I chose a rondeau for the form. The plan was to write about a pirate's childhood in one stanza, his adventures in the next, and in the last his return to discover only open sea where his home had been. The original repeated line was "As it were nothing but a dream." But I never got back to the island. It turned out that this particular character was more interested in explaining why he left home in the first place, and what he learned from his adventures. Who am I to argue with a pirate?

One last comment: Modern poets don't often get a chance to write old-fashioned words like "smirching," "unfurled," "purview," and "winkled." Nor are they allowed purple phrases like, "pallid passion passed" or "minor manor master." Thank you, Jean and Steve, for the opportunity to play for a while in the waters of eighteenth-century vernacular.

STEPHEN D. SULLIVAN

Stephen D. Sullivan has been a pirate all his life, and a professional writer, illustrator, and editor since 1980. He is the author of more than thirty published novels, none of them stolen. (Though some are based on movies.) His recent projects include *Luck o' the Irish, Fantastic 4,* and *Spider Riders.* Steve's next Blue Kingdoms works are a short story, "The Gift of the Dragons," in an upcoming anthology of his short stories, and the novel *A Reliable Dragon.* Steve has won the Origins Award twice, first for his samurai fantasy novel *The Lion,* and later for his Mage Knight short story *Podo and the Magic Shield*—and he has the booty (trophies) to prove it. His most recent novel, *Dragonlance: Warrior's Heart,* has been nominated for a Scribe Award. With his friend Linda Godfrey, he is the host of Uncanny Radio, a weekly radio show about the supernatural—but not usually about pirates. Listen to it at www.uncannyworld.com. Steve lives in Wisconsin with his wife, two children, and no parrots. More information about Steve and his work can be found at www.stephendsullivan.com.

☠

Stephen D. Sullivan & Jean Rabe

As one of the architects of the Blue Kingdoms universe, I wanted "Shipmates" to tell a story that would touch on many elements of the milieu that Jean and I had created: action, adventure, wild seas, and—of course—pirates. I also wanted to introduce Red Jack Sirus—one of the original Blue Kingdoms buccaneers (and certainly the baddest of the bad). So, I cooked up a tale that included Red Jack, the Iron Pirates—who recently stormed into my subconscious—and a trio of anti-hero mercenary Midknights. As I wrote, the story took a number of interesting twists and turns. Somehow, Tindalin showed up and forced his way in, though I hadn't expected him at all. And I really have no idea where Li Wu, Tindalin's sidekick, came from (he hadn't previously appeared in a story, or even the Blue Kingdom's bible). Together, I think they made a really ripping yarn.

I had a blast writing this tale, and hope I hope that the readers enjoy it, too. Look for more Blue Kingdoms adventures to come—in 2007 & 2008. Check for more info and upcoming projects at www.bluekingdoms.com and www.walkaboutpublishing.com.

KELLY SWAILS

Kelly Swails is a clinical microbiologist by day and a writer by night. This means she spends her days with unsavory microbes and her nights with unsavory characters. When not manipulating body fluids or computer keyboards, she associates with her husband, Ken, and their cats Kahlua, Morgan, and Moonshine. While "Return of the Black Seraph" is her first published story, her work will also appear in the upcoming anthology *Pandora's Closet*, due out August 2007. You can visit Kelly's website at www.kellyswails.com.

☠

Sometimes a story pops into my head almost fully formed. It presents itself—Ta-da!—and I hurry up and write it before I can get in its way. "The Return of the Black Seraph" was *not* one of those stories. When approached for this anthology, I said, "Of course! I love pirates! I can't wait!" And then I was stumped. I turned to my husband, also known as the Idea Man, and he said, "Why not a killer angel?" and I ran with it. I hope you enjoy reading it as much as I enjoyed writing it.

BRANDIE TARVIN

Brandie Tarvin is also the author of "Two For the Price of One" from the *Transformers: Legends* anthology. During the day, she works as a database administrator and lives in Florida with her fiancé and three cats. They all celebrate International "Talk Like a Pirate" Day every year on September 19th.

Plagued by the age-old question "Who would win in a fight, pirates or ninjas?" I found a surprisingly whimsical answer on the waves of the World-Sea. Okay, maybe the question isn't that old, but Wikipedia has an entire page dedicated to the debate. I hope that, in some small way, "Just My Luck" answers that question.

MARC TASSIN

Marc Tassin spent years sailing the seas of everyday life until a few years ago he decided to change course. He set a heading for Writer's Isle and has never looked back. His crew includes his first mate, Tanya, as well as his cabin boy Luc and cabin girl Abby. He also has a fine team of seasoned sailors out of Toledo manning the sails, who have ensured that he always maintains course.

I love the pure joy that comes from an unapologetic tale of high adventure and derring-do. From Robert E. Howard's legendary stories to the heart pounding excitement of Indiana Jones, I have spent many wonder-filled hours playing in these imaginary worlds. With "The Accidental Pirates" I have tried to offer some of that same joy to my readers, and I hope that you walk away from the story slicing the air with an imaginary cutlass.

ROBERT E. VARDEMAN

Robert E. Vardeman is the author of more than fifty fantasy and science fiction novels, as well as numerous westerns under various pen names. Titles include the fantasy *Dark Legacy* and SF novel *Ruins of Power*. Reprint of the Star Frontier trilogy is set for November, 2007, followed by the After the Spell Wars fantasy trilogy in 2008.

Vardeman is a longtime resident of Albuquerque, New Mexico, graduating from the University of New Mexico with a B.S. in physics and a M.S. in materials engineering. He worked for Sandia National Laboratories in the Solid State Physics Research Department before becoming a full time writer.

For more information go to www.cenotaphroad.com.

Writing any short story is a chore for me. "The Coins of Darkun" started with a completely different premise. The ship's spirit-inhabited figurehead was a central character when I started but became a small sidenote when I figured the bad guys had plenty to occupy them with the crew of the

Sea Blade. Playing with the notion of liquid geography and the malleable set of gods and myriad peoples caused even more shifts in what I ended up writing. Jean Rabe said the result was worth a novel—she's right. I discarded a *lot* of ideas and characters that were fun and involving. Here's hoping the Blue Kingdoms is wildly popular and there will be a demand for novels, as well as short stories in the future!

JAMES M. WARD

Jim was born, has lived a pleasantly long time, and has been married a tad over 35 years—thanks to the patience of his wife. He has three unusually charming sons, Breck, James, and Theon. They in turn have given him five startlingly charming grandchildren, Keely, Miriam, Sophia, Preston, and Teagan. In that stretch of time he has managed to write the first science fiction role playing game, *Metamorphosis Alpha*, he worked for TSR and did lots of D&D and AD&D things, and he designed the best selling *Spellfire* and *Dragon Ball Z* CCGs. At the time of this writing, Jim is vastly pleased with his latest design work on the card game *My Precious Present* and the board game *Dragon Lairds*. In a long line of products, his latest two novels from Tor, *Halcyon Blithe, Midshipwizard* and *Dragonfrigate Wizard Halcyon Blithe* are two of his better and prouder creations.

☠

The germ idea for my short story in this anthology came from the *Blithe Fantasy* concept. In that world, some of the warships have the living body of a sea dragon holding the ship on its back. My young captain, Halcyon Blithe is a very magical seventh son of a seventh son. The thought of combining a bit of the wonderful Blue Kingdom's world with a bit of my own was too good to pass up.

KATHLEEN WATNESS

Kathleen Watness was born in 1954 in New York City. After getting a Master's Degree, she spent most of a ten-year stint in the Navy stationed at government research facilities in sunny California. Naturally, since her degree was in marine biology, she ended up settling in the Midwest after her discharge. She lives there to this day and shares a house built about 1920 with a husband, three kids and two cats.

☠

The inspiration for "Cyren's Eyes" came from two sources. The first source is rooted in the nature of the Blue Kingdoms. One of the most mysterious and intriguing aspects of this ocean world is the way lands can appear and then disappear. If a new arrival is away from home when their lands vanish, he or she is stranded. If a mortal can be stranded in the Blue Kingdoms, than why couldn't a god also be stranded? Since magic is fickle, working in some places and not in others, then why couldn't the nature of a god's power—and even the form one takes—also be affected? The deity might even have to relearn how to be a god.

The second source comes from an old saying that states, "Set a thief to catch a thief." Enter the pirates in the story. While Cyren is uncomfortable with the notion of piracy, he's also very practical. So it seems reasonable, at least to him, to use one group of pirates to retrieve what another has stolen. Of course, things don't work quite the way he expects. If they did, where would the story be?

STEVE WINTER

Steve Winter is a writer, web producer, and game designer currently residing in Seattle. He has worked in the role-playing game industry since 1981 and was a newspaper reporter before then.

Well, who doesn't like pirates? When this story opportunity arose, I had too many other projects on my plate to jump in. Other members of my writers' group, however—the Alltierates—did have time. When they circulated their stories through the group for review, those readings made me see that the topic was too much fun to pass up. Fortunately, time is elastic, so I was able to stretch it enough to wrap a loop around a pirate/lost city story. All it took was gobbling quick lunches, constant scribbling in waiting rooms, and a long, cross-country, round-trip flight. When you're steeped in pirates and lost cities, the time seems to rush by.

WALKABOUT PUBLISHING

Great stories by great authors.

Robert E. Vardeman—Marc Tassin—James M. Ward
Lorelei Shannon—Dean Leggett—Kathleen Watness—Paul Genesse
E. Readicker-Henderson—Jason Mical—Kelly Swails—Brandie Tarvin
Stephen D. Sullivan—Jean Rabe—And More!

Blue Kingdoms: Shades & Specters
Blue Kingdoms: Zombies, Werewolves, & Unicorns
Martian Knights & Other Stories
Under the Protection of the Cow Demon
Blue Kingdoms: Buxom Buccaneers
More Blue Kingdoms books coming soon!

Walkabout Publishing
S.D. Studios
P.O. Box 151
Kansasville, WI 53139
www.walkaboutpublishing.com

Official Home of the Blue Kingdoms.